# A MOTHER'S SACRIFICE

Pride, courage and a steadfast devotion to her two small children have kept Elizabeth Fleming strong throughout her years of captivity. And now a handsome stranger has appeared to free the stunning, copper-haired beauty from the ruthless Seneca warrior who holds her prisoner. But her beloved daughter and son must remain behind.

# A WOMAN'S ECSTASY

More Indian than white, Hunt Campbell is a virile vision out of her dreams—a bold adventurer caught between two warring worlds. Hungering for the magnificent frontiersman, Elizabeth surrenders to her awakening passions—savoring a brief ecstasy she must soon abandon in order to rescue her captive young ones. But Hunt knows his heart is unalterably linked to the courageous lady's. And it is his destiny to risk life and honor for her perilous mission . . . and her incomparable love.

## JUDITH E. FRENCH
"A MASTERFUL STORYTELLER"
*Rendezvous*

*Other Avon Romantic Treasures by*
**Judith E. French**

FORTUNE'S BRIDE
FORTUNE'S FLAME
FORTUNE'S MISTRESS
SHAWNEE MOON
THIS FIERCE LOVING

*If You've Enjoyed This Book,*
*Be Sure to Read These Other*
**AVON ROMANTIC TREASURES**

KISSED *by Tanya Anne Crosby*
LADY OF SUMMER *by Emma Merritt*
MY RUNAWAY HEART *by Miriam Minger*
RED SKY WARRIOR *by Genell Dellin*
RUNAWAY TIME *by Deborah Gordon*

*Coming Soon*

JUST ONE KISS *by Samantha James*

# Judith E. French

# Sundancer's Woman

*An Avon Romantic Treasure*

AVON BOOKS ◆ NEW YORK

SUNDANCER'S WOMAN is an original publication of Avon Books. This work has never before appeared in book form. This work is a novel. Any similarity to actual persons or events is purely coincidental.

AVON BOOKS
A division of
The Hearst Corporation
1350 Avenue of the Americas
New York, New York 10019

Copyright © 1996 by Judith E. French
Inside cover author photo by Theis Photography Ltd.
Published by arrangement with the author
Library of Congress Catalog Card Number: 95-94726
ISBN: 0-380-77706-1

First Avon Books Printing: February 1996

AVON TRADEMARK REG. U.S. PAT. OFF. AND IN OTHER COUNTRIES, MARCA REGISTRADA, HECHO EN U.S.A.

Printed in the U.S.A.

RA    10   9   8   7   6   5   4   3   2   1

For Susan Powter and the members of her original "Moving" exercise class. Thank you for giving me back my life.

And special thanks to my friend and editor, Ellen Edwards. Without her help, this book couldn't have been written.

*There is in every true woman's heart, a spark of heavenly fire, which lies dormant in the broad daylight of prosperity; but which kindles up, and beams and blazes in the dark hour of adversity.*

WASHINGTON IRVING

# Prologue

*Albany, New York Colony*
*May 1755*

**I**t was the worst day of her entire life!

Elizabeth Anne Fleming, sister to the bridegroom and oldest daughter of Sir John Fleming of Charles Town, fled from the reception, her cheeks burning with shame. Hot tears stung her eyes and nearly blinded her as she dashed down the brick walk that led through the Van Meers' formal gardens and into an orchard. A low-hanging branch caught her broad-brimmed, beribboned hat; she tore off the hat, flung it aside, and kept running.

Beyond the perfectly spaced rows of apple trees was a split-rail fence encircling a meadow. Elizabeth didn't hesitate. Heedless of her azure silk gown and matching satin slippers, she girded up her petticoats and climbed the fence, then flung herself facedown in the fragrant clover and pounded the ground with clenched fists.

"It's not fair!" Not only was she losing her favorite brother to Sophia Van Meer, a girl Elizabeth considered a featherbrained jade, but she herself had been made a laughingstock in front of the entire wedding

1

reception. The cruel incident played over and over in her mind. Sophia and Pieter's words were louder in her memory than the faint strains of fiddles coming from the manor house.

"Pieter, why don't you ask little Elizabeth to dance?" Sophia had coyly asked her seventeen-year-old cousin, loud enough for Elizabeth and the entire bridal party to hear. "No one else has."

Pieter's scornful reply had pierced Elizabeth to the heart. "That carrot-top child? I'm hardly so desperate for a partner that I'd dance with a speckle- faced colt."

Elizabeth ripped up a handful of fragrant clover and threw it. It was all so unfair. Fourteen was not a child. Some girls were wed at fourteen. Was it her fault if she was still as slender as a boy, or if she'd been born with hateful red hair and freckles? Could she be blamed if her breasts didn't swell out of the neckline of her gown no matter how tightly her maid pulled the laces of her stays? Or that her teeth and eyes seemed too big for her face?

Pieter had been the only one of the Van Meers who'd been nice to her. He was so tall and handsome with his shoulder-length golden hair and Dutch-blue eyes. He'd seemed so sweet. How could he have publicly shamed her?

Elizabeth wiped at her tear-stained face. She'd never be able to face any of them again. Why hadn't she had the good sense to remain in Charles Town with her father and younger sisters, instead of coming here to New York Colony with Mother to take part in Avery's wedding?

She tried to regain her composure. Surely someone would be coming to find her. Her brother, maybe even Pieter, would apologize and beg her to come back to the festivities. "No, thank you," she would intone with restrained dignity. "I have no wish to take part in affairs where a lady may be publicly insulted and—"

The yelp of a dog in pain sliced through her play-acting. Always tenderhearted where animals were concerned, she forgot her own troubles and leaped to her feet. The sound had come from somewhere nearby; she was certain of it. Sophia's little black terrier had run after her when she'd fled the wedding. She wondered if the small creature had been stung by a bee.

"Joop?" she called. "Joop? Where are you?" Spotting a small crumpled heap in the shade of an apple tree, Elizabeth scrambled awkwardly over the rails in her ruined gown and hurried to see what was amiss.

"Joop, you silly pup, what—" Elizabeth cried out and clapped her hand over her mouth. Sophia's terrier lay sprawled on the moss, his eyes glazed and bulging, his lips drawn back over his teeth in a macabre grimace. A black-feathered arrow sprouted from the dog's motionless body.

Joop was dead. She didn't need to touch him to know it. She'd been the one to discover her beloved grandmother dead in her bed two Christmastides ago, and Grandmama's eyes had been open and staring just like little Joop's. Elizabeth swallowed. Who could have done such a terrible thing to a helpless dog? "Oh, Joop," she moaned. She reached out to touch a small, still paw, then drew back her hand.

Suddenly, the orchard that had seemed so bright became a haunt of shadows, and prickles of fear danced along her spine. "Mother," she murmured. "Avery." She'd taken the first running steps toward the swirling music of a country reel when a musket shot rang out.

She lifted her skirts and lengthened her strides, ducking apple branches as she ran. "Mother! Avery!"

Abruptly, the music dissolved into mingled shrieks and roaring flintlocks. Elizabeth stopped short as the bride's father appeared at the edge of the formal garden.

"Mr. Van Meer," she called. "What . . ."

Hendrick Van Meer staggered forward and fell, an ax protruding from his back.

"What's happening?" Elizabeth whispered. Terror made her dizzy. Her tongue seemed stuck to the roof of her mouth. "I don't—"

A near-naked Indian darted around the boxwood hedge and put a foot on Sophia's father's shoulder. The Iroquois' knife blade flashed in the sunlight, and Elizabeth moaned as the savage sliced down and ripped a bloody section of hair from Van Meer's head.

It seemed to Elizabeth that the world had gone mad. The sweet-smelling orchard and gardens had turned to hell. Arrows flew through the air; women screamed as flintlocks boomed. There were Indians everywhere, chopping, shrieking, shooting. Wedding guests and servants ran in every direction; two Indians chased a Dutchman wearing a blood-soaked vest into the maze.

Elizabeth didn't want to think about what would happen to him when they caught him. She didn't want to hear his high-pitched squeal, but she couldn't shut out the awful sights and sounds.

She knew she was a coward, standing frozen when she should be hunting for her mother, but her feet seemed rooted to the ground. Then a riderless horse galloped through the orchard, nearly crushing her under his hooves. At the last second, she leaped out of the way, lost her footing and fell to the ground. Facedown on the trampled grass, she inhaled the acrid scent of gunpowder and crushed green grass.

Bloodcurdling Indian war cries reverberated from

the courtyard. Elizabeth closed her eyes, and covered her ears with her hands. This wasn't real—it couldn't be real. She must be having a nightmare.

Then a moccasined foot kicked hard against her hip.

Elizabeth whimpered as she stared up into the grotesque face of a Seneca warrior. Her cry of terror died in her throat as the brave's war-painted features twisted into a snarl, and he lifted a steel tomahawk over her head. Then she saw only darkness.

# Chapter 1

*Charles Town, South Carolina*
*Summer 1764*

**"N**ine years? You tell me you want me to fetch home a woman who's been a prisoner of the Seneca for nine years?" Hunt Campbell rose to his feet and folded his muscular arms over his chest. "That's a fool's errand," he said softly. "I've been called foolhardy by some, but never stupid. I'm not the man you want for this job."

Sir John Fleming scowled at the tall woodsman dressed in buckskins and high fringed moccasins. "You're hardly my idea of the right person—"

"He's exactly the one," interrupted Robert Bird, the third man in the room. "My employer assures me that Hunt is your only chance. You've already spent years and a small fortune trying to locate Elizabeth. Hunt's more than a scout; he has a foot in both worlds, Indian and white. He has friends among the hostile tribes, and he speaks their languages. If any white man can go into Iroquois territory and retrieve your daughter, he can."

Hunt frowned and glanced around the fancy parlor. Houses like this made him uncomfortable. He felt hemmed in by all the furniture, the ornate mirrors, and the silver tea service. It was a mistake to have come here, and one he wouldn't have made if he hadn't been desperate to earn the reward money Sir John was offering for the return of his daughter. White water and an overturned canoe had cost him every cent he'd earned in trading with the Indians the past two winters, and he was determined not to go hat in hand to his adopted father for help.

Hunt broke the strained silence that had fallen over the room. "I wouldn't have wasted your time if Robert had told me that your Elizabeth was lost for nine years."

Sir John's mouth tightened into a thin line of displeasure. His plump, ruddy face paled to the hue of his powdered wig, and his starched lace stock cut into his thick neck until Hunt wondered how the man could draw enough wind to speak. It was plain Sir John wasn't used to being refused by men he considered his inferiors. "What difference does time make?" he sputtered. "She's alive. She was seen by a Catholic priest three months ago in a Seneca village south of Lake Ontario. For God's sake, Campbell! You may have lived like an Indian, but you are white. How can you walk away from the chance to free Elizabeth? She's hardly more than a child."

Hunt reached for his long rifle, taking care not to mar the polished front of the Irish hunt table it stood against. He rested the stock on the red Turkey carpet between his feet, covered the muzzle with one sinewy hand, and leaned thoughtfully on the flintlock. Choosing the right words to tell the bare truth without hurting John Fleming any more than he'd already been hurt was harder than getting a bead on a charging Comanche horseman. He kept his voice low; these townmen might squawk as loud as blue jays, but he was used to Indian habits. "Your Elizabeth's not a child anymore," he said. "She's a woman grown, with Indian thoughts and Indian ways. If your daughter's alive, that means she's made a life for herself. Best leave her to it."

"Nonsense! What life could she have among savages?" Sir John demanded. "What could equal what I can offer her?" He waved his hand to indicate his grand possessions and by implication, the position he commanded in Charles Town and the colony. "Here, Elizabeth will have rank and privilege, her church, her family. What can she possibly have there?"

The answer might be obvious to Sir John, but Hunt Campbell knew it was likely to be far from obvious or simple, in truth. Suddenly he wanted very much to know what Elizabeth Fleming would choose.

Nearly a thousand miles to the north and west, Elizabeth Fleming settled her split-oak berry basket on the moss and lifted three-year-old Rachel over a fallen log.

"Are there bears here, Mama?" Rachel asked. "I don't like bears."

"I hope there are," Jamie said. "If I see a bear, I'll shoot it with my arrow. I'll kill it and take the skin—"

Rachel giggled at her brother. "You're on'y six." She held up three fingers on one hand and five on the other. "If you see a bear, he'll eat you in one bite."

"He won't! I'll shoot him first." Jamie mimicked drawing an imaginary arrow. "Father will give me an eagle feather for bravery."

Rachel snatched a blueberry from Elizabeth's basket and threw it at Jamie.

"Mama!" he protested.

"Enough, both of you," Elizabeth chided softly.

"It's too pretty a day to argue. Look, there's a bush no one's picked yet. Look at the ripe berries."

Rachel clapped her hands with excitement. "Fat ones! I'm going to eat them all."

"You will not," Elizabeth said. "You'll help me pick."

"Jamie pick too." Black-eyed Rachel always had to have the last word. "Make him, Mama. Make him pick."

"Boys don't pick berries," Jamie said. "Boys hunt. Father said so. Girls pick berries."

His sister shook her head stubbornly. "No!"

"Shh," Elizabeth said. "We'll all pick." She smiled patiently at Jamie's growing pout. "None of that. We'll all pick, and I'll tell you a story about when I was a little girl, far away in Charles Town."

"Tell about the pony, Mama," Jamie urged. "Tell about the pony and I'll help. But if I see a bear, I'm still going to kill it."

"If we see a bear, you'll do exactly what I tell you to," she admonished gently. "Some day you will be a mighty hunter like your father, but your bow is too small to kill a bear yet. You'd only make him angry, and then where would we be?"

"I need a bigger bow," Jamie agreed. "A giant bow."

"Me too," Rachel chimed in. "Me need a bow."

"Girls don't get bows," he said.

"Do, too!" Rachel flung back.

"Enough of that," Elizabeth warned. "I'll tell about the pony, about all the ponies, and about our house and your white grandfather John, if you'll both be very good." She smiled at her sturdy little son. "You're growing up so fast, Jamie. Soon you will be able to hunt with the men. I wish . . ." But she let the words die away. There was no sense in spoiling a wonderful day with her children by wishing for what could never be. Her life in the South Carolina colony was gone. Elizabeth Anne Fleming was as dead as if she'd never lived. And all the happiness she'd ever know was here with Rachel and Jamie in an alien world.

Elizabeth moved her basket to a spot beside the large blueberry bush and began to pick. As she gathered the luscious blue-black fruit, she told the children about the spacious house she'd grown up in, about the carriages and the ships that rode at anchor in Charles Town Harbor. She always spoke in English to them when they were alone, even though their father forbade it and her own command of the language was unsure after so many years. It was another small rebellion against Yellow Drum, one that she'd practiced secretly since Jamie was born.

Rachel dropped onto her belly and wiggled under the bush, and Elizabeth couldn't resist giving the small, brown bottom a playful pat. The little girl giggled and kicked her bare feet.

"The story, Mama," Jamie reminded her. Elizabeth picked up the familiar tale where she'd left off, but her thoughts today were as wayward as her children's.

*How beautiful she is,* Elizabeth thought. *How beautiful they both are. How perfect!* Their backs were straight, their limbs sturdy, and their faces like tiny, bronzed angels. No one would ever mistake them for English children; their eyes were as black as currants, their hair as dark as any full-blooded Indian's, but they were hers—flesh of her flesh and blood of her blood.

Today, both Rachel and Jamie were naked except for tiny doeskin breechcloths that covered their genitals in front and very little behind. Neither wore moccasins; despite the rough terrain, it was safer at their tender ages to go without foot coverings.

"A child with moccasins may wander away in the woods and be lost," a Seneca grandmother had advised Elizabeth. "Without moccasins, stones may bruise their feet and briers may prick them, but they will not go far."

Elizabeth had remembered the advice and followed it faithfully. The thought of losing one or both of her precious babies was too terrible to consider.

Her life as a slave of the Iroquois before her babies were born was not something she liked to think about. The men of the Iroquois Confederacy—the Mohawk, the Oneida, the Onondaga, the Cayuga, the Seneca, and the Tuscarora—rarely beat their wives; the women held high positions of honor in all six tribes. Iroquois women had far more freedom and status than English women. They sat on high councils, decided the fate of prisoners, and started and stopped wars.

But Elizabeth had never benefited from these powers. She wasn't Iroquois; she was an English slave. Treated worse than the lowliest cur dog, she could be beaten, starved, ridiculed, or killed at her master's whim.

Rather, at her mistress's whim, she mentally corrected herself. Seneca wives ruled the house, as did all Iroquois wives. While, technically, she belonged to Yellow Drum, it was his chief wife, Raven, who determined Elizabeth's daily fate.

When Yellow Drum had first brought her to this Seneca village, she'd been unable to speak or understand Iroquoian. No one would communicate with her in English, although many of the Seneca had a good command of the language. Raven had fed her only scraps; she'd given her a flea-bitten dog blanket to sleep on, and she'd kicked and hit her constantly.

In those first months Elizabeth had nearly lost her

mind. All her life, she'd been sheltered and cared for. She'd had servants to make her bed, to dress her, to prepare her meals and to sew her clothing. Here, in the Seneca village, *she* was the servant. She was expected to skin and gut animals, tan hides, carry firewood, cook, and sew. When she'd arrived, she had been totally ignorant of these skills, but she'd learned fast. If she hadn't, she would have died the first winter.

She'd been a lonely, terrified child, clinging to life because giving up had never been part of her nature. And then, when things had seemed the darkest, a miracle had occurred. She had swelled with child. Even before her son was born, Elizabeth had talked and sung to him. She'd carried him under her heart and known that he would bring light into her valley of shadow.

The morning a Seneca wise woman had placed Jamie in her arms had been the sweetest Elizabeth had ever known. He gave her a reason for living, and he brought happiness back to her heart. Rachel had been another blessing, an unexpected joy that restored her lost faith in the Almighty.

"The pony," Jamie reminded her impatiently, breaking into Elizabeth's reverie. "Tell about—"

"The pony!" Rachel shouted.

"All right," Elizabeth agreed. "Let me see. It was a blue pony with yellow spots, wasn't it?"

Jamie giggled. "Black, Mama. A black pony."

Rachel nodded. "Wi'v a white nane and tail."

"Mane," Jamie corrected.

"Oh, yes. She did have a white mane and tail, but . . ." Elizabeth smiled. "I think she was a green pony."

Jamie cast himself onto the moss and rolled over and over, laughing. Rachel squealed with glee, picked up a handful of berries and threw them at her brother. One struck him on the nose. He snatched one up and hurled it back. Rachel ducked behind her mother, and the blueberry hit Elizabeth's chin.

Jamie grimaced. "Ut-oh!"

"Throw berries at me, will you?" Elizabeth teased. She picked two more from the basket and sprang to her feet. Jamie scrambled to get away while Elizabeth squeezed the berries so that juice dripped on to his neck and down his back.

Rachel jumped up and down, clapping her hands.

Elizabeth dropped onto the ground beside Jamie, and he rolled into her arms. She hugged him tightly, then kissed the tip of his nose. "Love you, love you," she whispered.

"Me, too!" Rachel called. "Me, too!"

"Your little sister wants some," Elizabeth murmured mischievously to Jamie. "Shouldn't we give her berries too?"

"Yes! Yes!" he cried.

Elizabeth threw a berry at Rachel. Rachel jumped onto the log and danced along the length of it. "Can't catch me!" she dared. "Can't catch me!"

"Oh, yes, we can," Elizabeth replied, flinging a squashed berry at her daughter.

Rachel bounced off the log and ran toward the basket.

"No! Not the basket," Elizabeth cried. She crawled on hands and knees to grab the basket before her daughter could reach it. Leaping up, she tucked the container of berries into a forked branch high above the children's heads.

Rachel wrapped herself around her mother's knees; Jamie tried to climb up her back. Laughing, Elizabeth dropped onto the log. "I surrender, I surrender," she gasped, as both children slid into her lap. She wound her arms around them and kissed the crowns of their heads. Their thick, dark hair was as soft as raw silk and smelled of mint and blueberries. "I love you," she murmured. "Love you . . . love—"

"Ugly Woman! Ugly Woman, where are you?" called a harsh feminine voice.

"Ut-oh," Rachel said.

"Ut-oh," Jamie echoed. "Mother Raven."

Elizabeth put a finger to her lips. "Shh, don't tell," she whispered.

Jamie shook his head. "We won't."

"Won't," Rachel agreed with a firm nod.

"Ugly Woman!" Raven shouted. "Where are you? I know you came this way!"

The children slid off her lap; Elizabeth stood up and retrieved the basket. She put her finger to her lips again and winked at Jamie. Then the three of them crept away in the opposite direction.

# Chapter 2

*Seneca Country—the American frontier*
*Autumn 1764*

**A** late autumn gale swept down from the arctic tundra, raking the northern wilderness and lashing the cold, black waters of Lake Ontario into a seething frenzy. South of the great lake, ancient trees groaned and bent under the howling fury. Trunks snapped and crashed to the forest floor, sending deer and smaller animals fleeing before the storm.

Gusts shook the oaken gates of the walled Iroquois village, howled through the cracks in the palisade, and ripped at the elm-bark coverings of the Seneca longhouses. Inside, families huddled close around their fires while elders muttered about ghosts and other supernatural creatures that wandered on such nights.

The female slave who had once been Elizabeth Anne Fleming and was now known as Ugly Woman drew another fur robe over her sleeping children and wrapped herself in a blanket.

"I told you to bring in wood before dark," said Yellow Drum's first wife, Raven.

Elizabeth knew it was useless to remind Raven that

15

she had carried in enough fuel to last throughout the night and all of tomorrow.

"She's lazy," Raven told her husband in the shrill whine that never failed to set Elizabeth's teeth on edge. "Lazy and stupid. We'll all freeze in our sleep because of her thoughtlessness."

"She's going for more wood," Yellow Drum replied.

"I'm going," Elizabeth agreed.

"Sell her," Raven urged.

Elizabeth drew in a deep breath and steeled herself for the coming confrontation.

Raven didn't disappoint her. "She is stupid and worthless. Sell her to the Delaware trader. Where else will you get such a price for an ugly fox-haired woman?"

"My daughter speaks sense," said Raven's gray-haired father, Tracks Elk. He drew another deep puff on his clay trade pipe and blew out the smoke slowly. The scent of tobacco mingled with the odors of roasting chestnuts and damp wool.

"Why are you standing here with that stupid look on your face?" Raven demanded. "Go get the wood."

Elizabeth murmured a submissive reply and left the hearth area. Raven's home was the second from the end of a longhouse divided into private areas by thin inner curtains of reeds and deerskins. To reach the two outer entrances on either end of a longhouse, it was necessary for those families who lived in the inner apartments to pass through the adjoining families' living quarters.

Elizabeth passed through her neighbor's home in silence, and they ignored her, as was proper. When six or more families inhabited the same longhouse, rules were established to insure privacy. One of those was to ignore what didn't directly concern you.

Elizabeth untied the exterior door flap and sheltered her face with her hands against the blast of wind. She pulled the blanket tight around her shoulders and leaned into the storm as she crossed the common ground to reach the communal wood storage area.

It was very dark and cold. Luckily, she didn't need to see where she was going; she knew the village streets by heart.

Elizabeth tried not to let Raven's harsh words or those of her mistress's aging father bother her. Raven had threatened to make Yellow Drum sell her many times, and yet she was still here.

"This is my hearth and the longhouse of my family," Raven had railed at Elizabeth over and over in the past. "An Iroquois man listens to his wife in all matters of the home. I do not want you, and I will not have you here, eating my food and ruining the fine skins my husband brings back from the hunt."

"Sell us back to the white settlements," Elizabeth had replied before she'd grown wise enough to hold her tongue.

"Us? There is no *us!*" Raven would fling back at her, usually accompanied by a blow from her fist or a kick. Elizabeth had grown very good at avoiding Raven's physical attacks, but nothing could block the never-ending flood of verbal abuse. "The children are mine by Seneca law. You have no rights to them," Raven always shrieked. "You are nothing! Lower than a toad."

"I gave them life," Elizabeth would insist. "They love me. Even you cannot separate a mother from her children."

"They are Seneca," her mistress would remind her. "Despite their pale skins, they will soon forget you— a deformed female so slow of wit that she cannot even learn to speak the tongue of humans properly."

Yes, Elizabeth mused, as she kept walking into the wind. Yellow Drum's chief wife had threatened to sell her many times, but never to the whites. Yellow Drum had vowed that he would never let her return to her own kind. She knew too much of Seneca ways, he said. She knew where the summer hunting camps and the sacred burial grounds lay. She knew how many warriors Yellow Drum could summon to make war against his neighbors, and she knew how many men carried guns.

"I will kill her before I sell her to the English or the French," he had declared at the council fire last spring. From such a stand, there could be no retreat. An Iroquois war chief's word to his people must be kept, or no one would trust him. He would lose face, and no brave would follow him into battle.

Yellow Drum would not let her go back, but he might sell her to another Indian. Especially now.

Last night, Elizabeth had refused to let her master have sex with her. She had not lain with him since her daughter was born three years ago. Naturally, she had breast-fed Rachel, and it was customary for an Iroquois woman to abstain from pleasures of the mat until her last child was weaned. Elizabeth's milk had dried up in the spring. For months, she'd hidden the fact that she was no longer nursing her daughter. In late summer, Raven had discovered her secret and had demanded that her husband either sell Elizabeth or get her with child again.

Last night, he had tried. She had won that contest, but tonight might be different. Even though Yellow Drum had made it plain that having sex with her was a duty, rather than a pleasure, she knew she'd hurt his pride. Yellow Drum was a stern warrior, but not a cruel one. He had forced her to have sex with him

the first time because Raven had driven him to it.
He'd always performed the act quickly, rolling away
as soon as he'd spilled his seed into her. And the next
few days, he'd always seemed unwilling to look into
her eyes. Still, he could be stubborn and dangerous if
his honor was threatened. He might not want to have
sex with Elizabeth, but if he thought he had to do it
to prove his manhood, he would be difficult to deny
again.

Elizabeth threw up her hands just in time to keep
from walking into the corner of a longhouse. She
knew her way through the village, but the wind made
walking difficult. Her teeth were chattering and her
fingers numb by the time she reached the storage
shed.

Balancing an armload of frozen branches while trying to keep the blanket around her wasn't easy. She
turned to start back, and had taken three steps when
she stopped short. Standing in the faint light of the
opening was the silhouette of a huge shaggy animal.

"Oh!" she cried out, not sure if this apparition was
animal or human.

"Don't be frightened," a deep masculine voice said.
The man parted his robe so that she could see his face.

Elizabeth's heart was pounding. "I don't know
you," she said. Every man in the village was familiar
to her. This could only be the Delaware half-breed
who'd come to trade with the Seneca. Many Blushes
had pointed him out to Elizabeth earlier in the day.
She'd gotten only a glimpse of him across the dance
ground, but he was not a man a woman was likely to
forget.

The stranger's skin was light, his blue-black hair
worn long with a thin braid on either side of his handsome face. His shoulders were wide, broader even
than Yellow Drum's, and his bare arms bulged with

muscle. He had the look of a predatory wolf, and his eyes had followed her.

She hadn't been able to tear her gaze away from him until Many Blushes had tugged at her sleeve. "Yellow Drum is a jealous man," the young woman had reminded her. "It won't do to show a lack of modesty by staring at the trader."

Now, Elizabeth was face-to-face with this man, and she was frightened. "Let me pass," she said.

"Why are you out on such a night?" he asked.

She trembled like a leaf in the wind. "Let me go, I say."

"You don't have to be afraid of me."

"Yellow Drum will come to see what's keeping me." She tried to move around the stranger, but he stepped to block her way. "Please," she said. "I will be beaten."

"Are you his wife?"

She shook her head. "I am unwed. He is my master."

"What do they call you?"

She would not say the hateful words. "My name is none of your affair, Delaware. Let me pass, or I will scream."

"I swear to you, I will not hurt you. I came to see to my horse. He's tied in the abandoned longhouse beyond this building. When I saw you, I wondered who would let a woman—"

"I don't have time to talk to you," she said. "Please, let me go."

He put his hand on her arm, and she flinched. "Let me help you," he said. "I'll carry your wood."

Stunned, she let him take her burden. What manner of madman was this, she wondered, to do a slave's work? "A Seneca warrior does not . . . does not carry firewood," she stammered.

He chuckled, a deep, hearty sound. "It's as well I am not a Seneca warrior."

Words formed in her mind and came tumbling out. "You cannot," she protested. "You will cause a scandal! Men will laugh at you. And . . . and I will be beaten!"

"Then we'd best not let them see us, shall we?" he answered. And before she could do anything to stop him, he turned and strode out of the shelter with her wood.

She hurried to keep up. The wind was behind her now, pushing her along. "You shouldn't do this," she protested. "You don't understand." But he kept walking and she was helpless to do anything but follow.

"You're going the wrong way," she said when he turned left at an intersecting path. "There." She pointed. Again, she heard a deep chuckle.

"Best you show me the way," he rumbled.

There seemed to be no choice but to obey. When they reached the outer doorway of Raven's longhouse, the stranger carefully put the branches back into her arms. "Thank you," she said. She was still shocked. No Seneca man would have thought of helping with a woman's chores, and few females would assist a slave. This Delaware was unlike any brave she'd ever known.

"It will be our secret," he answered.

Still shaken, she hurried through the neighbor's hearth place and into Raven's. She need not have worried. Yellow Drum and Raven were still arguing. No one paid her any mind as she added the new wood to the pile against the far wall.

"Ugly Woman is my property," Yellow Drum proclaimed to his chief wife. "I took her from the English, and I sired a fine son and a daughter on her. I alone will decide when and if I grow weary of her."

"This is my hearth," said Raven. "I say it is time to be rid of her. Winter is coming. Why feed another useless mouth? Take the Delaware's offer. Where will you find another rifle like his?"

"Keep your voice down," Yellow Drum said. "Do you want everyone in the longhouse to hear your nagging?"

"Why should I be silent?" Raven demanded sarcastically. "Last night you went to her mat, and she drove you away. It is common knowledge in the longhouse, probably throughout the village, that you did not scratch your face hunting. Why shouldn't I say what everyone is already joking about?"

Elizabeth crouched in the shadows beside her children and stroked her daughter's hair. Flickering firelight shone on one chubby cheek and made the little girl's soft, dark tresses gleam. "My Rachel," Elizabeth whispered. The Seneca called her Fawn That Drinks at First Light, but in Elizabeth's heart, and when they were alone together, she was always Rachel.

A lump rose in Elizabeth's throat. Rachel and Jamie were her most precious possessions. Nothing and no one would part her from them. She'd rather die. But neither did she wish to bear another child of rape.

"What say you, Many Blushes?" Raven asked Yellow Drum's second wife. The young squaw giggled and murmured something Elizabeth couldn't hear.

Many Blushes was a Cayuga, new to the Seneca village and to her marriage. Yellow Drum had joined with her in early summer. Elizabeth was certain that plump, laughing Many Blushes was the reason Yellow Drum had been willing to stay away from her sleeping mat and Raven's for so long.

"Surely you must have an opinion, Many Blushes?" Raven pressed. "Do you believe that a slave should be allowed to drive her master from her bed?"

"This is not her affair," Yellow Drum said sharply. "Many Blushes is—"

"Is a Seneca wife with rights," Raven interrupted. "Speak, Many Blushes. What say you about your husband's rebellious slave woman?"

Many Blushes made a little sound that might have been agreement or simply air whistling through her perfectly even, small, white teeth. It was a sound that had echoed through the family's private quarters often since Many Blushes had married Yellow Drum, and one that Elizabeth supposed Raven hated as much as she did, but for very different reasons.

"Do not be afraid," Yellow Drum urged. "Tell us what you think about this matter."

"I think all the women at this hearth should do our best to make Yellow Drum happy," Many Blushes cooed. "He is a great man and should be honored in his own home above all."

Elizabeth let out her breath slowly. Many Blushes would be no help. As senior wife, Raven held the power in the family, and Raven hated Elizabeth with all the malevolent enmity of an aging, barren wife toward a younger, fruitful concubine. The only reason she'd put up with Elizabeth this long was that having children increased Raven's status among the Seneca. Now that Yellow Drum had taken a second wife, any children she had would increase Raven's position in the tribe. Elizabeth was no longer necessary to her.

A frigid blast of air gusted through the longhouse as someone opened the door at the far end. Smoke and ashes swirled up in a whirlwind, causing Yellow Drum and the others to cough. Elizabeth heard the exchange of greetings between a newcomer and those at the first hearth. Manners demanded that those who lived in a communal dwelling ignore voices at another firepit, but it was impossible not to know what went on. She twisted around to look at the deerskin drape that divided Raven's hearth space from her cousin's.

A dog growled. Elizabeth heard an unmistakable thud, and then the dog yelped in pain. His claws scratched on the reed floor covering, and he let out a piercing whine as he scrabbled to find refuge in the storage area beneath the sleeping platform.

On the far side of the doorway to Raven's hearth place, a man cleared his throat.

"Enter," Yellow Drum said.

A hand parted the deerskin hangings and the Delaware half-breed's face appeared. Elizabeth's mouth went dry. If he told Yellow Drum that they had spoken—if he mentioned that he'd carried wood for her—she would pay the price.

For an instant his gaze locked with hers. Elizabeth knew the risk she took in meeting his stare so boldly, but his dark eyes were mesmerizing. A shiver ran through her body, and she felt suddenly light-headed. When she had seen him from across the dance ground, she'd been struck by his proud, handsome features and magnificent body. In the woodshed, a few minutes ago, it had been too dark to see him clearly. Now, close up, without his outer garments, she had a full view of his scarred chest, hard-muscled thighs, and long, thewy legs. Unconsciously, she moistened her lips and gripped an upright post to keep from losing her balance.

Then he stepped into the room, straightened, and dismissed her with the barest hint of a smile that made her blood race. Elizabeth drew in a ragged breath. Yellow Drum was a big man, but he had never made their hearth place seem small, as this fierce-eyed Delaware warrior did.

Outside, the gale winds rattled the walls, shrieked

through the seams of the elm-bark roof, and tore at the smoke hole with icy talons. *I should be cold*, she thought. But she wasn't. An inner heat rose to flush her cheeks and scorch her skin, as if she'd been standing too close to the fire.

The stranger spoke, offering a formal greeting to Yellow Drum in a deep, husky Iroquoian with only the slightest accent. The Seneca war chief mumbled a stiff reply and grudgingly motioned his guest closer to the hearth. Without another glance in Elizabeth's direction, the tall half-breed crossed the room and dropped gracefully to the bearskin rug in the place of honor across from Yellow Drum. "It is an evil night," he said. "Winter comes early this year."

Raven's father, Tracks Elk, coughed and leaned forward. "The cry of the wild goose echoes through our village, and the beaver pelts are thicker than normal. We shall see deep snow this year and cold such as few men have known."

The Delaware nodded solemnly. "This man has seen an edge of ice on the streams to the south. The trees bear many nuts. It may be as you tell us, wise sachem."

Elizabeth tried not to laugh. Raven's father was no chief and he was certainly not wise, but it was obvious from the way his spine stiffened and his chin went up that the old man was pleased by the flattery.

"A warrior would have to be a fool to live so many years and learn nothing," Tracks Elk replied.

Raven sniffed loudly, scooped up a bowl of roasted chestnuts, and motioned to Many Blushes. Both women retreated into the shadows. Elizabeth waited for Raven to bring out meat or fish to set before the Delaware, and when she didn't, the hair rose on the back of Elizabeth's neck. She opened her mouth to warn the stranger, then realized what she was about to do and clenched her teeth tightly together.

The first rule among the Iroquois was loyalty to kin; the second was to offer hospitality to any traveler. If Raven didn't give the Delaware food or drink, it was because she wished him ill. Once he had taken refreshment at her hearth it would be impossible for Yellow Drum to harm him.

If Elizabeth tried to alert him to Raven's omission, she would break the first rule and bring disaster on herself. This disturbing stranger was a threat to her and to her children. Whether he lived or died was not her affair.

So why did she feel so guilty?

"This man leaves your village tomorrow," the Delaware said. "You have a fair offer for your slave woman. Is it that you do not wish to part with her?"

"No!" Elizabeth cried.

Yellow Drum's head snapped around, and he glared at her.

She refused to be cowed. "I will not go with you!" she declared to the Delaware.

Raven gave her a rough shove. "Hold your tongue, slave," she ordered. "Ignore her," she said. "She is too stupid to know when to chatter and when to be still."

"As you see, I am lenient with my women," Yellow Drum said, making an obvious effort to control his temper. "I spoil them."

"So it seems," the newcomer observed.

"Buy someone else," Elizabeth said, suddenly fearful that she might be separated from her children. "I stay here."

The half-breed chuckled. "Your household must be an interesting one."

Yellow Drum spat into the fire. "A man of strength such as myself has a strong appetite," he growled.

"Even three women are not enough to satisfy it. Why do you want this worthless slave? Have you no wife of your own?"

The visitor shook his head.

"I do not even know your name," Tracks Elk whined. "Have you a name?"

"He is Sinew," Yellow Drum said. "Sinew of the Wolf Clan."

*Sinew.* The name fitted him perfectly, Elizabeth thought. His hands were lean, his bronzed arms corded with muscle; he moved with the fluid grace of a mountain cat. She couldn't help but notice the two eagle feathers that dangled from a knot at the back of his unbound hair. *Two,* she thought, *two eagle feathers. He is either a lying boaster or a man of valor.*

With deliberate will, she hardened her heart against him. It didn't matter who or what this Sinew was. He was nothing to her, and she'd not let him tear her from her children. If the Iroquois chose to murder him, she would turn away and let him meet his fate.

"So, Sinew," Tracks Elk said slyly. "Why don't you have a wife? Are you too poor a hunter to bring in meat for a household, or are you one who prefers the company of other braves?"

Elizabeth wasn't certain if the Delaware understood the insults or if he simply chose to ignore them. "Some men choose not to marry," he said without rancor. His gaze fixed on the dancing flames that rose from the fire pit. "But as the esteemed elder has said, the winter will be cold. This one will need someone to cure his furs and warm his bed."

Yellow Drum's eyes glittered maliciously in the firelight. "There are many women. Why do you want this one enough to offer such a fine gun and powder for her?"

Their guest chuckled again. "As you say, there are

many women, but not many with hair like autumn leaves. Yellow Drum the Seneca has a great appetite. Sinew the Delaware has a fancy to taste something different—a red-haired woman."

Wanton images of lying beneath this virile stranger while he drove his hard man spear into her body formed in the back of Elizabeth's mind and made her voice quiver. "Sinew will taste the point of my knife first," she said with more courage than she felt. "I am no whore to be passed from hand to hand." Her brazen thoughts shocked her even as she protested loudly. Other women claimed enjoyment from the act of sex; she never had known pleasure. What was wrong with her that she could imagine such an intimate act with a stranger?

"Silence!" Yellow Drum thundered. "It is my will, not yours, that matters. I will keep you, sell you, or cut your throat as it pleases me."

Sinew stood up. "Her manners are less than one would expect, but my offer still stands. One French pistol, one long rifle, powder and shot for each, and twenty beaver pelts."

"Scissors and needles," Raven reminded him. "You also promised a sewing kit."

"And a sewing kit," the Delaware agreed. "But I must have your answer by morning. There is another red-haired woman among the Ojibwa. If you cannot part with this one, I will—"

"Go then, Sinew," Yellow Drum said, rising as well. "And may the wind be at your back and your traps heavy with beaver. This woman I do not wish to sell. At least not tonight."

"So be it," Sinew murmured. He nodded to Raven. Elizabeth trembled with emotion, certain that the Delaware would say something more to her in parting, but he didn't. He turned and left the hearth place without another word or glance in her direction.

"You will let so much slip through your fingers?" Raven demanded angrily. She did not bother to lower her voice. Their neighbors on either side could not help but hear. Even the stranger could not miss her outcry. "You burden me with this woman for yet another winter?"

"Cease your mouth!" her husband snapped back. He pinned Elizabeth with his gaze. "And you! You've shamed me long enough." He pointed to his sleeping robes. "Make yourself ready for me. If you insist on disrupting my life, you will at least give me—"

Elizabeth shook her head. "No." A moment before, she had imagined lying down with the stranger. Yellow Drum she knew all too well, and she would have no part of him, no matter the consequences.

The Seneca's face twisted with disbelief. "What did you say, Ugly Woman?"

"I said *no*," she said stubbornly. She was terrified. Her knees felt as though they were melting to pine gum; her stomach pitched as hard as it had the time she and Jamie had been caught on the lake in a sudden summer thunderstorm and the waves rose as high as her head. Although the thought of going with a stranger was terrible, the certainty of rape was worse. "I will bear you no more children, Yellow Drum. Do what you wish, but I will lie under you no more."

He launched himself at her, but she was quicker. She dodged his charge and put the fire between them. With a howl of rage, he leaped across the hearth at her. His right foot landed safely on rock, but the left struck the edge of the pit, sending sparks flying. Elizabeth did not wait to see what happened. She fled like a wounded doe through the deerskin hanging into the next hearth area.

Ignoring the startled cries of her neighbors, she reached the outer door in three bounds and dashed into the bitterly cold, pitch-black night. Behind her, she heard Yellow Drum's cries of rage mingled with women's shouts of confusion. Then Elizabeth slammed into an immovable object. She bounced back and would have fallen to her knees if strong hands hadn't seized her shoulders.

Too frightened to scream, she threw up her hands and felt the hairy pelt of an animal. Demon or bear, she didn't know what had her, but she was past the point of reason. She struck out at her captor with both fists. All-too-human grunts of pain told her that her blows had found a flesh-and-blood opponent.

Before she could lash out again, she heard Yellow Drum's shout behind her. Someone grabbed a handful of her hair and jerked her back so hard that she felt the bones in her neck pop. In the blink of an eye, she slammed against the frozen earth, and Yellow Drum's foot crushed her chest.

A torch flared. Raven's cruel face materialized in the circle of light. Others crowded close around them. Elizabeth tried to draw a breath, but Yellow Drum leaned down with all his weight, pressing the life out of her. She couldn't see his features in the darkness, but she caught the gleam of a steel blade.

As Yellow Drum's knife plunged down toward her throat, Elizabeth closed her eyes and waited for death to find her. Seconds passed. When she opened them again, she saw Sinew and Yellow Drum in the light of a flaring torch held by Raven. Sinew was wearing a heavy fur robe, and his fingers were tightly clamped around Yellow Drum's right wrist.

"Dead she is worth nothing," the Delaware said. "And if you kill her, you will have the trouble of burying her body in this frozen ground." His voice was low and powerful, heavy with an unspoken threat.

"Take your hand off me," the war chief hissed, "or I will kill you and then the slave and throw both your bodies outside the walls for the wolves."

Sinew shrugged, but he did not release Yellow Drum's arm. "Naturally, you must decide what is best to do with the woman," he said, maintaining a reasonable tone. "But this man has heard it said that the Seneca war chief is wise beyond—"

"Mama! Mama!" Jamie wiggled past Raven and flung himself on top of her. "Many Blushes says you're going to kill her, Father. I won't let you!"

"Raven, take the boy back into the longhouse," Yellow Drum commanded.

"Jamie," Elizabeth groaned. Her son was nearly naked, shaking with cold. "Don't—"

"No!" Her son balled his small fists and pounded Yellow Drum's calf and knee. "Let her go. Let my Mama go! I won't let you hurt her."

"Shh, shh, Otter," Many Blushes soothed, taking the boy's arm. "You must not behave so. You must—"

"Get him out of here," Yellow Drum bellowed.

"Please, Many Blushes," Elizabeth begged. "Don't let him see—"

Jamie shrieked as Many Blushes lifted him kicking and struggling and carried him back toward the house. More and more Seneca poured from the surrounding longhouses. Village dogs barked and snarled. Some braves carried guns. One man placed the muzzle of his rifle against the Delaware's chest. "Shall I kill him for you, Yellow Drum?" he asked. At the back of the crowd, a girl giggled.

"Are you going to make a complete fool of yourself?" Raven demanded.

"No," Yellow Drum said. "I am not." He glanced at Sinew. "Hold him."

Three warriors pulled him away and pinned his arms behind his back. Yellow Drum knelt beside Elizabeth and brought his face close to hers. "You have earned death this night," he said. He seized a handful of her hair and raised his scalping knife.

She closed her eyes once more and waited stoically for the death blow.

# Chapter 3

**E**lizabeth gasped as Yellow Drum yanked her hair. She opened her eyes to see him brandishing a long hank that he'd sliced off inches from her head with his scalping knife.

"See!" he shouted, holding her hair aloft. "I take her scalp and steal her soul."

Elizabeth scrambled to her knees and then leaped up, but before she could get away from him, he struck her across the face. She lost her balance and would have fallen if Raven hadn't caught her. Elizabeth was shaking with cold; her hands and feet were going numb, and she tasted her own blood. The north wind cut through her clothing and tore at her flesh until it seemed even her bones must be frozen. Still, instinct forced her to throw up her arms to try to shelter her face and head.

"She's yours!" Yellow Drum declared to his wife. "Take her and do with her what you will! I don't want her."

Onlookers jeered as Yellow Drum turned his back and stalked toward his longhouse. "What will you do with her, Raven?" one cried.

"Kill her!" howled one squaw.

"I'll take her off your hands," a man jeered.

"Give her to me," called another Seneca brave. "I'll keep her too busy to cause mischief."

Raven put her hands on her hips and looked at the Delaware half-breed. "It's too cold a night for sensible people to stand outside in this wind. Do you still want to pay a decent price for her?"

"I do," Sinew said, shrugging off the warriors who held his arms.

"No!" Elizabeth protested. "No . . . no." Her teeth were chattering so hard that she could barely get out the words. "Raven, please. You . . . you can't—"

"I'll take the horse you rode in here on, as well," Raven added. "No more dickering. Give me all you promised, plus your horse, and you can have her. Yes or no?"

"No," Elizabeth insisted. She couldn't believe this was happening. "Please, no!"

"Yes," Sinew answered.

Yellow Drum stopped and looked back over his shoulder. "Take her and go. Now!" he shouted above the wind. "Before I forget that you came in peace and add your scalp to my string."

"Yellow Drum, don't let her do this," Elizabeth begged. The pain in her face—the cold—were nothing compared to the stark fear she felt at the thought of being taken from her children. "Please," she rasped. She started toward Yellow Drum, but Sinew caught her arm.

"You're mine now," he said harshly. "It's time you learned to take orders." He picked up his fallen robe from the ground and draped it around Elizabeth's shoulders. Then he looked back at Raven. "Does she have warm clothing for travel?" he demanded. "High moccasins for snow? Mittens?"

Elizabeth tried to control her shivering. The robe was heavy and thick. She realized that the dark curly hair on the outside of the skin must have been what she'd felt earlier, when she'd thought she'd run into the claws of a bear. She forced herself to ignore the cold and try to follow what was happening.

"You've bought a slave," Raven said sarcastically, "nothing more." She laughed and others joined in when they saw the trick she'd played on the stranger. "Take her naked or not at all," Yellow Drum's senior wife continued. "Her clothing is mine."

"I've nothing more to offer you," Sinew argued. "Without clothing, she'll die of cold."

"Give me your rifle," Raven said. "I might part with a few—"

"No," Elizabeth protested. "You can't sell me away. I'll do whatever you ask."

The Delaware ignored her. "I have nothing more to trade," he repeated to Raven. "My rifle and my knife are not part of our agreement."

Raven scoffed. "Neither are the Ugly Woman's garments. Take her or not, as you please, Delaware. If you don't want her—"

"I'll give her clothing," a faint voice offered.

Elizabeth was struck speechless as Yellow Drum's newest bride came toward her with a bundle in her arms.

"These are mine and I give them to you, sister," the young woman said. "May they bring you good fortune in your life to come."

Tears gathered in the corners of Elizabeth's eyes. "Thank you," she murmured, still not able to accept the fact that this half-breed stranger would be taking her away from Jamie and Rachel.

She looked into the Delaware's strong face, silently pleading for mercy. He was a stranger, but he'd shown her kindness before. Perhaps he would do so again. "You don't understand," she began. "My son . . . my—"

"We go," he said grimly. His grip on her arm tightened. "Must I bind and gag you?"

"I can't," she stammered. "I can't leave."

Yellow Drum made a crude remark, and Sinew stiffened. "Not another word," he commanded in Iroquoian. "My rifle and hunting bag are in the guests' longhouse. You can change into these things there."

Stunned, frightened, and half frozen, she allowed herself to be led to the dwelling in the center of the village. There she crouched by the fire trying to warm herself as Sinew handed over his trade goods to Raven.

"Hurry," Many Blushes whispered as she pulled Elizabeth behind a storage wall. "Put on my things. Quickly, before Raven forbids it. Put these high moccasins over your own."

"This is your best wrap," Elizabeth protested. "Your otter-skin mittens . . ." In the midst of heartbreak, Elizabeth was deeply touched by the young woman's generosity. The beautiful garments Many Blushes offered were her parents' bridal gifts, meant to be her finest dress for many years to come.

"Yellow Drum will bring me more furs," Many Blushes said.

"My children," Elizabeth whispered. "What will happen to my babies?" Images of Jamie and Rachel's innocent faces flashed across her mind. How could she leave them? Rachel still woke in the night crying out for her mother. What would she do when Elizabeth was no longer there to hold her tightly in her arms, rock her against her breast, and sing the old English nursery songs until she fell asleep again? Who would wipe away her tears? And who would hold Jamie close when thunderstorms rolled overhead and he forgot that he was a Seneca warrior and became a frightened six-year-old?

"I will love your little ones as my own," Many Blushes promised.

"I can't do this," Elizabeth cried.

"You must. Go, before Yellow Drum kills the Delaware and you as well. I heard Raven bid him do it."

"Better if he did kill me." Dying could be no harder than this, she thought.

"No!" Many Blushes cried. "Death is never better. Live, Ugly Woman. The Delaware may be a good man. Go with him. It has to be easier than the life you have here."

Those words echoed in Elizabeth's ears as the village gate slammed shut behind them, and Sinew took her arm. Sheltering her as much as he could with his body, he led her across the wind-scoured meadow and into the depths of the black forest. When they had gone a few hundred yards, he released her and leaned near.

"Stay close behind me," he shouted above the howl of the wind. "If we're separated, you could freeze to death in minutes."

"I can't go with you," she yelled back. "I'll be of no use to you. I don't—"

"There's no time to argue now. Walk, or I'll carry you."

Confusion swirled in her mind as she did as he bid her. She didn't know how long she could walk in this weather or where he was taking her. So far, he'd not misused her, but how could she trust him? Discouraged and sick at heart, she plodded after him.

There was no light in the woods, and he was only a huge, solid shape, wrapped neck to ankles in the odd, curly-haired skin robe. On his head, he wore a close-fitting beaver hood that left nothing exposed but his eyes. She'd spent years learning how to read the eyes of other people. Many times, the ability to guess what another was thinking had saved her from harsh treatment. But tonight, even that ability would do her little good. It was too dark to see his eyes. She had nothing to rely on but instinct. And if she made a mistake in reading this Delaware, it could mean her life.

The earth was hard and cold under her feet. Ice-covered branches scratched her face, and the raw teeth of the gale cut through Many Blushes's thick clothing to chill her body. She had no strength to fight him; it was all she could do to force one foot in front of the other and remain upright.

They walked swiftly for what seemed like hours, changing directions so many times that they might have returned to the center of the Seneca village or wandered onto the surface of the frozen lake for all she knew. Finally, her muscles would no longer obey. She stumbled and fell. The shock jolted her so that she bit through the edge of her torn lip, but she was too weary to care. She lay there, suspended between consciousness and unconsciousness, a curious, dispassionate contentment seeping through her body.

Then pain stabbed through her as the Delaware shook her roughly and shouted into her ear.

"Get up!"

His words were nonsense . . . gibberish.

"Get up! Elizabeth. Elizabeth Fleming. You must get up!"

*Elizabeth? Was he mad? She wasn't Elizabeth. No one had called her Elizabeth in many years. . . .*

"Damn you, Elizabeth! You'll not die on me now."

*English. He was speaking English. The sounds were strange to her ears, but she understood most of what he* said. "You . . . not die." Of course, she wasn't dying. She was just resting here, wasn't she? But why was a Delaware speaking English? If she wasn't so sleepy . . . maybe . . .

The warm contentment was overpowering . . . and the leaves on the ground were so soft. She'd sleep just a little while . . . just a little while . . .

Hunt swore through his teeth, shifted his rifle to the other shoulder, and dropped to his knees beside her. He'd realized that he was driving her beyond the breaking point. She'd lasted longer than he'd had any right to expect under these conditions. Elizabeth Fleming was as tough as any Cheyenne woman, and his heart went out to her display of courage.

It tore at him to drive her on mile after mile when he knew how much she must be suffering. She needed warmth, rest, and food. She really shouldn't sleep now. She'd have a better chance of surviving if she was awake and fighting the cold, but if she had reached the point of total exhaustion, it would require too much of his own energy to try to wake her.

He picked her up. Carrying her the rest of the way would be difficult, but at least he could slip her under his buffalo robe and keep her from freezing. He didn't think the spot where he'd cached his belongings was very far. It would be foolhardy to stop and try to build a fire here in this wind, so it was tote her or leave her to perish of exposure. And he'd invested too much time and effort to find the wench to let her die now.

Mistress Fleming was no slip of a girl, Hunt mused as he cradled her tightly against his chest and climbed a rocky incline in pitch darkness. There was little fat on her, from what he'd seen, but she was tall for a woman and well muscled.

He paused to catch his breath and peered around

at the trees, trying to make out exactly where he was.

He was worried about Elizabeth. Cold like this could kill a man; he'd seen many a good one die in such weather. Elizabeth had proved her grit by keeping on her feet so long. If she hadn't been so strong both physically and emotionally, chances were she wouldn't have survived nine years of captivity. The Iroquois didn't cater to weaklings.

*So why couldn't I have been paid to rescue a child instead of a full-grown woman? She'd sure as hell have been easier to haul.*

White flakes swirled through the air, landing on his eyelashes and brows. It was beginning to snow, and from the smell in the air, Hunt was afraid they were in for a real blizzard. The weather would keep the Seneca off his tail for a few days, but would make it a might unpleasant for them both if he couldn't find the hidey-hole he had picked out.

Gut instinct told him to bear left on the far side of the ridge. He hoped he was right, but it was just too damned black to see more than a few yards ahead. Taking a firmer grip on his burden, he topped the rise and started downhill. Snow was falling faster, turning the leaves underfoot slick and making every step precarious.

Something moved directly ahead of them. Before Hunt could reach his rifle, a deer exploded into motion. Legs scrambling, hindquarters thrashing, the big doe skidded into a stump and sprawled at his feet before regaining her balance and leaping away into the thick cover.

"Glory be." Hunt chuckled as the acrid taste of fear in his mouth slowly dissipated and his frantic heartbeat slowed to near normal. "Who do you suppose was scared worse, me or that white-tail?" he murmured to an unconscious Elizabeth.

The tendons in his knees felt as weak as those of a newborn fawn. For a split second, Hunt pictured himself spread-eagled over a Seneca fire pit being daintily sliced to fish bait—all for the misguided actions of a panicked deer.

"You're getting too old for this stuff," he muttered softly. "Too old and too cautious to call yourself a Cheyenne sun dancer." The irony of that tickled his funny bone and he shook his head in mock despair. "Or even to claim to be a transplanted Irishman," he concluded. When a woodsman couldn't tell the difference between an Iroquois and a doe, it was time he found another occupation.

Another ten minutes of hard walking took him to the bank of an ice-encrusted stream. After that, finding the larger creek and the waterfall was child's play. Keeping from slipping on the rocks was a bit more difficult, but once he'd worked his way behind the first cataract, he found dry footing. He crossed another chancy stretch, and then plunged into the narrow cavern entrance.

The steep decline was littered with chunks of gravel, and Hunt placed each moccasined foot with care. One misstep and he could break an ankle. He didn't want to think about the consequences.

It was downhill all the way, fifteen yards straight, round the boulder left, then take the right split. Surprisingly, it was already getting warmer as he went deeper into the cave. When he reached the underground spring, he shrugged off his buffalo coat and lowered the woman gently to a flat table of rock. Squatting on his heels, Hunt felt around for the fire makings he'd left there two weeks ago.

His fingers brushed against the heap of dry tinder and then the tin box containing flint and steel. In seconds, he had a spark; in three minutes, a tiny flame began to devour the cedar shavings and dry twigs. Hunt used the small fire to light a torch.

Elizabeth began to choke. Her eyelids fluttered, and she groaned.

"Shh," Hunt soothed. "It's all right. You're safe." It was a bald-faced lie. Neither of them was safe, but it had been Hunt's experience that most women—red or white—would rather hear a sugar-coated hope than the plain truth.

It had been his good fortune to know a lot of women, few of them—he had to admit—as strikingly handsome as this redheaded lady he'd come so far to rescue. He lifted the torch high and studied her finely drawn features. Even with the swollen lip and wind-burned face, she was still stunning. If she was a mare, she'd be a thoroughbred, he reckoned, fancy-bred and too expensive for a woodsman like him to do anything more than admire from a distance.

It would be easier to leave her here and carry the torch and the rest of his gear farther back in the cave where he'd pitched camp, then come back for her. But that would mean leaving her in darkness. He couldn't do that; she'd had enough grief in her life and didn't need more from him. If she came to, alone, she'd be scared out of her wits and might wander off or hurt herself before he could return. So instead, he did it the hard way; he propped the torch against the wall, heaved her up and over one shoulder, then picked up his light again.

It was another ten minutes to the spot where the cave opened up to a good-sized room. The temperature at this level was warm enough to bring out a sweat on him. He was dressed for the cold and had been carrying a heavy load for several miles in the teeth of a storm. Once he got the fire going, it was a relief to strip off his buckskin hunting shirt and the wool tunic under it.

He'd laid Elizabeth on a blanket beside the crude hearth, covered her with his tunic and another blanket. He knelt beside her, peeled off her damp leggings and moccasins and began to rub her bare feet briskly.

Her toes were deathly cold, but bore none of the waxen color of frostbite. The fur-lined moccasins had kept her from freezing after he'd begun to carry her. He'd need to get some hot liquid into her body, but not until she was fully conscious.

He worked his way steadily over her feet, massaging each toe in turn, her high insteps and her callused heels. Strange how a foot that must have felt only silk and suede when she was a child could come to walk barefoot over stony cornfields and through brier-strewn woods, he thought, skimming the tops of her feet with light fingertips.

Her ankles were trim, her calves sleek and muscular. Her long shapely legs were those of an athlete. He kneaded her muscles with firm, sure strokes, taking pleasure in the surge of color that flowed under her skin. She was warming up nicely, he thought as he rubbed her knees and lower thighs.

The fact that she smelled like wildflowers hadn't escaped his notice. A man would have to be dead to ignore the texture of her smooth skin or the effect of all that tousled red-gold hair spread across his blanket. And a man would have to be a snake to take advantage of a helpless woman. . . .

Sweat beaded on his lower lip as a log sparked and flared up. It was getting hot in there, Hunt told himself. He shifted his weight to take the pressure off the growing tightness in his groin.

"Elizabeth," he said. "Wake up, Elizabeth." He removed his hands from her bare flesh and pulled her deerskin dress down to her knees. "Elizabeth," he repeated.

There was no reason why she wouldn't come to. Her pulse felt strong enough, and her face was taking on a healthy peach hue. He pulled back the coverings and laid his ear against her chest to listen to her heart.

With a shriek, she came fully awake, rolled away from him, and grabbed a fist-sized rock. "Don't touch me!" she warned in Iroquoian. Bright spots of crimson flushed her cheekbones, making the rest of her face look as pale as mare's milk, and her heavily lashed green eyes dilated in fear.

Hunt raised a flattened palm. "Peace," he said. "I mean you no harm." He couldn't stop looking at her eyes. He'd never seen a woman's eyes that green ... clear and deep ... bottomless. He gazed a mite too long, and nearly missed getting slammed with the rock. It whizzed past his ear and bounced off the wall behind him.

"Damn, woman," he swore. "I . . ." He threw up both hands to protect his head when she reached for another rock. Realizing that his words weren't making sense to her, he switched to Iroquoian. "I'm not your enemy," he said. "And I'm not Indian. My name is Hunt Campbell, and your father sent me to bring you home."

# Chapter 4

**E**lizabeth's eyes narrowed in disbelief. The last thing she remembered, they'd been walking through the woods and she'd been cold . . . so cold. She was still cold; her head hurt, and she couldn't figure out where she was. Nothing made sense—especially this bare-chested stranger who said he wasn't Indian but a white man sent to rescue her.

Her knees felt wobbly and she was shivering so hard that she could hardly speak. The fire called to her. She wanted to creep close to it and soak up the heat, but she was afraid. Her leggings and moccasins were lying in a heap on the floor, and she hadn't taken them off. "Why . . . why did you undress me?" she demanded.

"My name is Hunt Campbell," he repeated, first in the Seneca tongue and then again in English. "I'm a white man. I took off your things because they were wet."

"English?" she asked hesitantly. The sound echoed oddly through the cave. "You're English?" He didn't look English at all. He looked like the devil's own son with great, snapping black eyes backlit with blazing hellfire, and a sensual mouth that could lead a woman to damnation.

A crooked grin spread across his face, and he hesitated an instant too long before he answered in a lazy drawl that made prickles rise on the back of her neck. "Aye, after a fashion. I'm Irish by birth, but I reckon English is close enough. Your father paid me to fetch you home."

Elizabeth lowered the rock but kept close watch on him. If he moved one inch, she'd let him have it square in the center of his forehead. She'd had lots of practice driving crows from the Seneca cornfields. If he thought she was helpless, he'd have to think a second time. "Why . . . what . . ." She struggled to find the right English words. "Where are we?" she demanded, slipping back into Iroquoian. "And why are you half clothed when we're nigh freezing to death?"

His grin broadened until a dimple flashed on one cheek. "You may be cold, but I'm not. We're in a cavern behind No Return Falls. I carried you here after you—"

"I remember," she interrupted. "I . . ." She steadied herself against the wall. She was foggy-headed and trembling with cold. "I fell," she said in English.

"You're safe with me, Mistress Fleming . . . Elizabeth."

"No." She shook her head. "I doubt that." He was as dangerous-looking as any Seneca, tall and formidable, with hard, powerful hands and those eyes that didn't miss a heartbeat. He might be a white man, but he'd bought and paid for her. She couldn't be sure he hadn't purchased her for the reason he'd told Yellow Drum, because he wanted a woman to warm his bed. "No," she repeated in a firmer voice. "I don't know you, and I don't trust you."

He made a quick motion with his right hand that looked as Indian as she'd ever seen. He didn't move like any white man either. True, his nose wasn't as craggy as most Senecas', but his lips were thin and his cheekbones were sharp slabs of granite.

"Your father hired me to rescue you," he said. "He never gave up trying to find you. Two years ago, a French trapper claimed to have seen you with the Mohawk. Colonel Westerly sent two scouts to try and trade for you, but it turned out to be a German girl instead. And nearly four months ago, a Catholic priest saw you in your Seneca village."

Elizabeth watched him suspiciously. The lure of the fire was beguiling. She'd never wanted anything so badly as she wanted to be warm, but she didn't trust him. Worse, she couldn't trust herself. What was it about this man that so unnerved her—that made her pulse quicken and her belly feel as though it was full of butterflies?

She had to be very cautious. She was free of Yellow Drum, but she couldn't allow this mysterious stranger, whatever his real name was, to take advantage of her. "Back away," she said. It was easier to think clearly when he wasn't too close. When he did move back, she inched toward the heat, still holding the rock tightly in her hand.

"I won't hurt you," he said, but his dark eyes kept watching her.

"I don't remember entering a cave." To her surprise, that observation came out in English. The words were flooding back now, filling her head with a jumble of memories, images, and smells.

"I carried you."

She nodded, still confused. "Alone?"

"I could have used some help." He grinned lazily. "You're an armful. Especially uphill."

Her face flushed from an inner heat. "You carried me here." She held her hands over the flames. She wished desperately that she'd had more experience with men. It was hard to know what to say to him.

She forced herself to think of her children. Poor Jamie. She could still hear his frightened cries ringing in her ears . . . still imagine the feel of his small body pressed against hers. Soon it would be dawn. Rachel would waken, and her mother wouldn't be there to bathe her or make her breakfast. What would her children think? Would Raven tell them the truth, or would she say the Ugly Woman had abandoned them?

The stranger broke into her thoughts. "Don't be afraid," he said, lifting an open palm in the universal sign of peace. "I'm going to add more wood to the fire."

She tensed, not relaxing until he'd moved back again. He pointed to the nearest blanket, and she wrapped it around her shoulders. She wanted to sleep, but if she closed her eyes, she'd be vulnerable. If she closed her eyes, she'd see the faces of her children. . . .

"I'll give you my knife if that will make you feel better," he offered.

She held out her hand, certain that he was mocking her. But to her surprise, he drew his skinning knife from the beaded sheath at his waist and, holding it by the blade, handed it across the fire to her.

His fingers were long and very clean. They brushed hers, and she jumped, nearly dropping the weapon into the flames.

"You've been hard used," he said. "I'm sorry for that."

She swallowed the lump in her throat and tried to look tougher than she felt. Was his gentle behavior toward her a trick? she wondered. What kind of man was he to show such tenderness to an ugly woman?

"Aren't you afraid I'll do you harm with this?" she asked.

He shrugged. "No."

Something in his dark eyes made her trust him, just a little. Releasing the rock, she passed the knife to her right hand and glanced down at it. It was a long tongue-shaped blade of tempered steel with an antler handle. The heavy weight lent her courage, and she met his gaze without flinching. "Is my father alive?"

"He was when I last saw him in Charles Town." His mood became somber. "Your father, Elizabeth . . . and your brother Avery."

She blinked in confusion. "Avery? Alive?" A lump constricted her throat. "Avery's dead. He died in—"

"Did you see him die?" he asked gently.

"No, but there was so much blood. I thought—"

"Avery hid under a haystack and escaped the massacre. He's very much alive, and he lives in Charles Town with a wife and four children."

"Sophie Van Meer?"

He shook his head. "I believe this is his second wife. I heard that his young Dutch bride was killed on their wedding day."

Elizabeth stared at him in stunned disbelief. Avery was alive? It was hard to accept. She'd thought of him as dead for all these years. She'd thought them all dead except her. Then a wild hope fluttered deep inside her. "My mother?" she asked in a small voice.

"I'm sorry."

She inclined her head and drew in a ragged breath as the small flicker of hope guttered and went out. "It's all right. I've mourned her for nine winters. Nine years," she corrected herself. "The Seneca killed her."

"No, they didn't. According to your father, she hid as well. She survived the attack and died in Charles Town four years ago, of fever."

"Mama died at home?"

"In her own bed."

"Thank you." It came out first in Iroquoian. She tried again, and this time, she got it right. "Thank you." She covered her mouth with her hand. Her lip was still swollen and throbbing from Yellow Drum's blow, but she ignored the ache. "I can not know ... do not know why my words ..." Impatient with herself, she made a sound of disgust. "For long time, I no ... not speak English. Thank you for tell ... telling me about my mama, and thank you for not leaving me in the forest."

"It's all right, Elizabeth," he answered. "I understand how you feel. We have a lot in common. I was captured by Indians when I was a boy and lived among them until my late teens. I would have forgotten English if it hadn't been for my father's insistence that I teach him to speak it."

"Your father? He was capture ... *captured* with you?"

"My Indian father, Wolf Robe. He's a great man. If I amount to anything in this life, it will be because of him."

She held out her hands to the fire. "So you're really not a half-breed? That was a lie?"

"An exaggeration. Yellow Drum's people don't like white men. It would have been better to say I was a Delaware, but I'm too light-skinned under my clothes to pass as a full-blood. So I claim to be half Indian when it's necessary."

"My father said the half-breed children are an abomination—worse than Indians." She looked down at the flames. "There is a saying in Charles Town. Half Indian, half white, half devil."

"You believe that, Elizabeth?" he asked. She didn't answer." That little boy was your son, wasn't he?"

Pain knifed through Elizabeth. Jamie was safe with his father; Yellow Drum loved him. But the hurt burned into her like a living flame.

"What's his name?" Hunt asked quietly.

"Yellow Drum's first wife, Raven, named him Otter." She blinked back tears. "I call him James, after my grandfather, James Avery Fleming. . . . Jamie." She squared her shoulders. "Jamie is Yellow Drum's son, but I was never Yellow Drum's wife. I was his slave woman. They say that Otter is Raven's son, not mine."

"That's the Seneca way."

"Yes." A log snapped, sending orange and cherry sparks into the air. "It's Seneca custom. It's not my way," she added deliberately in English as she watched his face. She'd gotten very good at judging another person's thoughts; it was what had kept her alive all these years.

"The boy will be all right with them."

*And my baby girl?* she wanted to scream. *What about her? Raven tolerates Jamie, but she hates Rachel. What will happen to my Rachel now that I'm not there to protect her?* But she didn't speak. Keeping her thoughts private was too ingrained in her soul. Weeks and months and years of keeping her own council couldn't be changed in a matter of hours . . . not for a man whom she didn't know or trust.

He broke the silence. "The Iroquois are like the Delaware and the Shawnee in that they believe children belong to God, rather than to their parents. Most Indians treat their young far better than whites do."

She nodded. "Most do." How could she tell him about Raven's threats? *Fawn's clumsy*, Raven would say, calling Rachel by her Seneca name. *You should watch her better, Ugly Woman. She could fall into the river when you're not looking. She could wander off into the forest and be eaten by wolves. Or, Fawn has the proper hair and eye color for a human, but she'll always be ugly. I don't know where we'll find a husband to take her off our hands.*

Raven was careful to utter her threats when Yellow Drum wasn't around, but Rachel heard and she was frightened. The child never let on; she never said anything, but she always crept closer to Elizabeth, and she would never, ever stay alone in the longhouse with Raven.

Yellow Drum loved Jamie, and he claimed Rachel as his daughter, but he had never cared for her in the way he did his son. He would not mistreat her, but neither would he risk Raven's anger to champion her. He was a man who cared for his son more than his girl child; he was a man ruled by his chief wife.

Elizabeth inhaled softly. Yellow Drum had a second wife now. If Many Blushes produced children, Raven wouldn't need Elizabeth's daughter anymore. Rachel would be expendable.

"It's hard to leave your boy behind," Hunt was saying, "but you've got to accept that it's for the best. He will have a good life with the Seneca. It wouldn't be the same if he came with you."

"Because of men like my father who would not accept him?"

"There's a lot of bad blood between Indian and white. A lot of prejudice, most on the white side. And you have to think of your own future, Elizabeth. You can—"

"Find a new man? Marry and forget Jamie exists?" She kept her voice flat . . . emotionless. That was another lesson she'd learned at Raven's hearth. Pretend not to care. So long as a thing wasn't important, Raven wouldn't trouble herself to forbid it. Yellow Drum's chief wife interfered in her slave's affairs only if she thought Elizabeth cared passionately about something . . . or if she could cause her rival unhappiness.

"You won't forget Jamie," Hunt Campbell continued. "I never forgot the sister I lost when our cabin was burned and we were captured. Becca was everything to me—mother, sister, friend. I never saw her again after that day. But I never really lost her." He tapped his chest with a fist. "I keep her here, close to me. You can do the same thing with your boy."

"Was it your choice, to be separated from Becca? Was that her name?"

He smiled. "Rebecca, but I always called her Becca. No, it wasn't my choice. I was ten."

"Leaving you wasn't her choice either, was it?"

"No. The war party that took us split up. She went one way, and I went another."

"You don't blame Rebecca for leaving you?"

He made a sound of derision. "How could I? She had no part of it."

"That's the difference between your sister and me. You're asking me to walk away from my son and—"

"I'm not asking you, Elizabeth. I'm telling you what's best . . . what has to be."

She pursed her lips and stared into the glowing coals. *So easy,* she thought. *It sounds so easy. Go back to Charles Town to the big house on Broad Street. Let Papa clothe me in silks and satin gowns. He'll send me away like Cousin Claire when she was caught in the stable with that young groom. They arranged a hasty marriage for her in Jamaica. Doubtless Papa can find a rich husband for me, far off, in the Caribbean or even England, someplace where no one knows about my ordeal . . . someplace where the myth of my spotless reputation can be maintained.*

"Without Jamie, I can marry well," she said. "My disgrace . . . my mistakes can all be swept under the rug—so long as it is an expensive carpet."

"You can't have Jamie; he might as well be dead to you."

She smiled faintly. "You sound like Raven. 'Your child was stillborn,' she said. 'This one is mine.' She hoped I would die in childbirth. She said I would never bring forth a healthy child with brown eyes and human features." Memories of the two days she'd struggled in labor flashed through her mind. Raven had threatened to smother the coming child if Elizabeth screamed in pain, but she hadn't weakened. She'd bitten through a thick leather mitten, but she'd never cried aloud. And she'd delivered a strong boy child that had become his father's pride and joy.

"I'm not trying to hurt you. You've been hurt enough." Hunt Campbell stood up. "I have to leave you for a few minutes. Some of my gear is back there." He gestured toward the cave passageway. "You rest here while I fetch my stuff. When I come back, I'll fix us something to eat. Are you hungry?"

"Thirsty," she admitted. She needed sleep more than anything, but how could she sleep? This man knew what she was—what she'd done with Yellow Drum. He probably considered her a harlot. Was there a special name for a white woman who slept with an Indian?

"Elizabeth?" he said, interrupting her thoughts. "I'm going now, but I'll be back. You'll be safe here by the fire."

"I didn't want to share Yellow Drum's sleeping mat, you know," she said.

Hunt's face darkened. "You don't have to justify your actions to me," he said. "What's done is—"

"Best we get it out," she said quickly, before she lost her nerve. "He offered to take me as his second wife when Jamie was born, but I refused. He could keep me a slave, but he couldn't make me marry him; it's not the Seneca way."

Her own words sounded foolish. How could she make him understand that not wedding Yellow Drum had been a stubborn act of defiance? It had cost her dearly in suffering. A slave could be beaten or starved, while a wife had rights that must be honored. But she had never forgiven Yellow Drum for forcing her to lie with him, and she would never be a wife to a man she didn't love.

"You did what you had to do to stay alive . . . what any sensible person would do."

"No." She shivered. "No, not any sensible person. There was another captive in the village a long time ago, a French nun. She wouldn't serve as a slave, and they murdered her. I saw a man crush her head with a stone," she whispered.

He took a step toward her, and she shook her head. "Stay away from me," she warned. "I want you to hear it all."

"Talk if it helps you," he answered.

"I was a child when the Seneca captured me. It was a year before I had my first bleeding time. All those months had passed, and I thought . . ." She swallowed against the constriction in her throat. "Raven was a cruel mistress, but I learned how to make myself useful. As long as I worked hard and did what they said, I thought I could stay alive." She broke off, not wanting to go on.

"Say it all, Elizabeth. Get it out and forget."

She crossed her arms over her chest and rocked back and forth. "Raven said she needed a child. She would never be properly regarded among her people if she wasn't a mother. She sent Yellow Drum to my bed. He forced me, and she watched."

Elizabeth couldn't prevent the tears from welling

up. "She named me Ugly Woman. Raven said I had the hair and eyes of an English fox instead of a human. I never thought of myself by that name. Inside, I tried to be Elizabeth. Usually I pretended not to understand when they called me Ugly Woman. They thought I was too stupid to learn Iroquoian properly, but I learned what I had to to stay alive. If that makes me a coward, then I am one."

"I don't blame you for living."

"My father might."

"He won't. He's spent a heap of money trying to get you back."

"*Her* back," she corrected, "trying to get *her* back. He wants fourteen-year-old Elizabeth Anne, the girl who wanted a spoiled Dutch boy to ask her to dance. He doesn't want a Seneca war chief's leman."

"Sir John is an intelligent man. He knows what happens to white girls who live with the Indians. Most take an Indian husband in time. You were with the Seneca for nine years. He would have to expect—"

"Will he expect a dark-skinned grandchild?" She wiped away the tears that kept spilling down her cheeks. "When he finds out about . . . about Jamie, he'll wish I was dead too."

"If he thinks that way, he's a fool."

"I can't go to Charles Town. I can't. . . . I won't forget what I left behind in Yellow Drum's village. You go to Charles Town and tell him you were too late. Tell him Elizabeth Fleming died last summer."

"Tell him you're dead? And what will you be doing in the meantime?"

"Figuring out a way to get my son." *And my daughter*, she swore silently. *I'd rather be a slave—I'd rather be dead—than separated from my children.*

"That's crazy talk."

"Maybe."

"You sleep. We'll talk about it in the morning."

She tapped the flat side of the naked knife blade against her open palm. "I'm going back, and you can't stop me."

He folded his arms over his chest. "I said we'd talk about it tomorrow." The hard, evenly spaced words revealed his effort to control his rising anger.

"It's my life, Hunt Campbell. I'll decide what's right and what's crazy for me."

"You're not thinking straight. You're tired and upset. You're—"

"Stupid? A woman? What is it that makes me unfit to make my own decisions?"

He sighed. "I was paid to bring you back to your daddy in one piece. And, by God, I intend to do it, with or without your consent."

"No matter what I want?"

"No matter what you want," he said brusquely.

"Then sleep with one eye open," she warned. "Because I intend to go back, around you or over you. It's up to you."

"We'll see about that." Turning abruptly, he grabbed up his torch, lit it from the open flame, and stalked down the dark tunnel.

"I mean it," she cried after him. "Yellow Drum couldn't get the best of me, and I surely won't let you. I won't . . ."

Her words echoed through the cavern—*I won't . . . I won't . . . I won't*—until the sound faded, and Elizabeth could hear nothing but the rasp of her own harsh breathing.

# Chapter 5

*R*achel swayed gently as the late afternoon breeze stirred the cradleboard hanging from a tree branch. Elizabeth knelt a few feet away, grinding corn with a stone pestle and humming an old English lullaby. Rachel giggled as she passed a red cardinal feather back and forth between one chubby, starfish hand and another. Elizabeth had greased Rachel's hands so that the feather stuck to her palms, an Indian trick for soothing children that an old Seneca woman had taught her.

"I see you," Elizabeth cried. "I see Rachel." She covered her face with her hands. "Where's Rachel? Where did she go?" She parted her fingers and peeked through at the baby. Instantly, Rachel's snapping black eyes sparkled, and she squealed with delight.

Rachel was small, too young to walk, perhaps eight months. She was bound so tightly in the beaded doeskin cradleboard that she couldn't kick; only her hands were free, and she waved those gaily in the air. Her little face was as round and brown as a nut, and when she giggled dimples appeared on both cheeks.

"Sweet girl," Elizabeth murmured. "Mama's sweet girl."

Suddenly clouds covered the sun, and the breeze began to blow harder. The shadow of a bird fell across the stone *mortar. Elizabeth looked up to see a huge raven swooping down toward the baby. "Go away!" she cried. "Go away!" She tried to leap up to grab the swinging cradleboard, but her legs wouldn't respond.*

*Rachel wailed and rocked violently from side to side. Elizabeth could feel the wind caused by the flap of the bird's wings. "No! Go away!" she screamed. The raven's ivory talons dug into the beautiful cradleboard and the lovely beading began to fall away, bead by bead.*

"No!" Elizabeth opened her eyes with a start and pushed away the blanket. Her heart was racing, her body covered with perspiration.

"Oh," she murmured, still caught up in the awful nightmare. Elizabeth hadn't remembered falling asleep or even lying down by the fire, but she knew she must have. She suppressed a shudder and tried to push away the terror, as memories of where she was replaced those of the dream world.

Clearly, she'd slept. She took a deep breath and tried to clear her mind.

She glanced cautiously around the stone chamber. The room was roughly double the size of Raven's hearth claim in the Seneca longhouse, with smooth walls and a level floor. Overhead, the shadowy ceiling of the cavern loomed; somewhere far off, she heard the rhythmic drip of water.

The wood in the fire pit had burned down to glowing coals, and the odors of bread and cooked fish lingered in the still air. Instinct told her that she wasn't alone. Sure enough, when she sat up, she could see a shaggy form on the far side of the fire. This time she didn't mistake the curly pelt for a bear; there was no heavy carrion scent in the air, and no one who'd ever come close to *ogh-kwa-ri*, the bear, could forget the musky stench. No, this was Hunt Campbell, wrapped in his strange cloak and—she hoped—sleeping soundly.

She swallowed, trying to moisten the inside of her mouth as, slowly, her accelerated heartbeat returned to normal. She'd been afraid to sleep for fear of being molested by this enigmatic woodsman, but he was here and he hadn't hurt her when she was asleep and most vulnerable. Not only that, he'd obviously taken the trouble to cover her with a blanket.

She took another breath. The dream had seemed so real; if she closed her eyes, she could still see the cradleboard swinging. Rachel. A pang of regret pierced her to the quick. *I'll get back to you, sweetheart,* she vowed silently. *I will.*

She glanced over at Hunt and tried to remember what she'd said to him earlier. She must have been suffering from the effects of cold and exhaustion to reveal so much of her private thoughts. It had been a fool's action to trust a man she barely knew, and one she might regret. It would have been better to pretend meek gratitude for his rescue and lull him into believing she would obey his orders without question.

Now she had more immediate needs. Hunger gnawed at her vitals, and she suffered from a raging thirst. She wondered how long she'd slept and how long they'd been in the cave. They were deep inside the earth; she could tell by the constant temperature. It was as quiet as a tomb and much warmer than it had been in the forest.

Dozens of questions rose in her mind. How had Hunt Campbell found this cave? How far had they come from the Seneca village? Was it day or night? She wanted to know all those things and more, but most of all, she wanted to get away from him.

She looked at him again. He hadn't moved. If she

listened carefully, she could hear his slow, deep breathing.

She located her moccasins and pulled them on, one at a time. Then she rose and crept past the fire toward the tunnel entrance. Gravel scraped under one foot; she stopped short, waiting to see if Hunt reacted. When he didn't, she took a few more steps.

Now that she could think, it was obvious what she must do. She had to go back to the village. The awful dream she'd just had could be a warning that Rachel was in danger. The raven in her nightmare stood for Yellow Drum's wife; she didn't need to be a shaman to guess that. Rachel needed her; both her children needed her.

But how could she go back?

Hunt had bought her from Raven. If she returned of her own will, she reasoned, it would be as a free woman. The Seneca might let her stay. She wouldn't rejoin Yellow Drum's household as his slave, but as long as she was in the camp she could see her children. In time, she might find a way to escape with them, or . . .

She might take a Seneca husband. The Iroquois were not all bad people, and more than one man had smiled at her when no one was looking. She couldn't say with honesty that Yellow Drum had gone out of his way to be cruel to her. He'd never tortured or starved her. Many of the Seneca had shown her real kindness, especially since the birth of her son. As a wife, she would have status, and no one could beat her.

Life among the Iroquois was not one she would have chosen, but she would sooner endure a harsh existence in Indian country than desert her children and become the pampered wife of a rich white man. Elizabeth Anne Fleming was dead. She could be Ugly

Woman of the Seneca, but she could never abandon Rachel and Jamie, not for all the riches of all the ships in Charles Town Harbor or all the plantations in the Carolinas. She loved her family, but she loved her babies more, and there would be no place for them in English society. She had learned nothing among the Seneca if she hadn't learned to accept reality.

Elizabeth took another step and peered down the narrow tunnel. She was afraid to take the torch. She would have to find her way by feel once she was beyond range of the fire. Breathing a sigh of relief as darkness closed around her, she hastily donned her outer garment and then moved farther from the dwindling source of light. On her next step, she felt a slight barrier at ankle level, and heard the loud tinkling of hawk's bells.

"Going someplace?" Hunt sprang up and leaped after her.

Elizabeth gave a cry of alarm and started to run. She hadn't gone more than ten feet before she bumped into an overhanging ledge and nearly knocked herself senseless. Before she could regain her equilibrium, he had her.

"Not so fast, Mistress Fleming."

She threw up her arm to ward off the blow she expected to fall at any second. She knew it was useless to fight, but she wouldn't submit to a beating without trying to defend herself. She kicked hard at his kneecap and punched him in the throat with her fist.

Her surprise attack momentarily stunned him. She twisted away, dodged the outcrop of rock, and fled down the black passageway.

"Elizabeth, stop!" he shouted.

She struck her shoulder on a protruding section of wall, stumbled, and slammed into an unyielding barrier. Tears of shame and fear spilled down her cheeks as she scrabbled blindly ahead of her, only to find the way completely blocked by a cascade of boulders.

"Elizabeth." His voice echoed through the tunnel, harsh and angry.

She flinched when his fingers closed around her arm.

"Elizabeth," he repeated. "Listen to me."

She trembled under his touch, waiting for his fist to smash into her face . . . waiting to feel the full force of his rage.

"Come back to the fire," he said. "There's no way out here."

Walking stiffly in front of him, she tried to regain her composure. Smothering disappointment crushed her, making her chest so tight that she could hardly breathe. Words of protest rose in her throat, but she couldn't utter a sound.

"Sit," he ordered, pointing to a spot beside the fire. *Am I a dog to be ordered so?* she screamed silently. Her muscles locked. He could kill her, but she'd not bend her knees for him.

"I said *sit*." He looked into her eyes. "My patience has come to an end, Elizabeth. Sit down, please."

The word *please* hit her with the impact of an icy downpour. Her legs buckled and she would have fallen if he hadn't caught her.

"What kind of man do you think I am?" He turned away and fumbled in his hunting bag, leaving her shaking with an inner chill, one that had nothing to do with cold. Seconds later, he lifted a tin cup to her lips, and she choked at the sharp smell of rum. "Drink," he ordered.

She took a sip. The strong liquor burned down her throat.

"Again."

She tried to turn her head away, but he caught her

chin between his fingers. His grip was firm but surprisingly gentle, and again, she felt that odd sensation
of butterflies in her belly.

"Just another swallow," he urged.

She did as he bid her. The rum stung her broken
lip, but the heat warmed her insides and stopped her
shaking. He downed the remainder of the liquid himself.

"All right," he said. "Now listen to me. Stop acting
like a panicked doe in a forest fire and think. I know
you're not stupid. Are you trying to commit suicide?
It's snowing like hell out there." He motioned with
his chin. "We're having a blizzard. You wouldn't last
fifteen minutes. Do you want to die?"

She shook her head.

"You've got to trust me, woman."

She raised her head and looked into his face. Her
eyes were full of tears and his image wavered, but
she noticed for the first time that he no longer seemed
like the enemy. She sniffed and dashed away the hateful tears with the back of her hand, then stared at him
intently.

He still wore the azure, quill-worked tunic,
stretched over broad, muscular shoulders. His black
hair was pulled tight against his head and tied de-
cently into a queue at the back of his neck with a
beaded leather band, adorned with hanging eagle
feathers. A single silver hoop dangled from one ear,
and a fringed loincloth covered his manparts. His leggings were beautifully sewn of elk skin, his moccasins
stitched with magnificent geometric designs in intri-
cate beadwork that must have taken some skilled
woman weeks to complete.

But even in these clothes, she could see something
different about him, a gentleness that she'd not
guessed at back in Yellow Drum's camp.

"You are a white man," she stammered.

"What have I been trying to tell you?"

She blinked and covered her face with her hands. Every word that came out of her mouth made her sound like a half-wit. His tale of being an Irishman who'd lived among the Indians had seemed too far-fetched to accept, but now . . .

She'd not realized before how young he was—hardly much older than her own twenty-three years. But his eyes . . . his eyes were those of a man who had traveled far and seen much. They were shrewd and full of wisdom. And for all Hunt's pretense of tender concern and gentle manner, his eyes glowed with the watchfulness of a mountain cat, revealing an innate capacity for sudden and deadly violence.

"What did that bastard do to you, woman?" he asked.

She shrugged. "It's done with. No good will come of reliving what can't be changed."

"Keep that foremost in your mind. Put your time with the Seneca behind you. You need rest and food." He rubbed his throat. "But you do swing a mean right hook."

"I'm sorry I hit you," she lied.

"I'm sure." His expression said that he didn't believe she was sorry. "I thought you might try to leave."

"So you strung a trap for me."

A hint of a smile curved his lips. "It worked perfectly, didn't it?"

"You didn't think I might trip and break my neck?"

He chuckled. "It was a length of fishing twine. I knew the string would break before your neck would."

She eyed him warily. She'd obviously gotten in a good lick with her fist. Was it possible he didn't intend to punish her for striking him? "I wasn't running away," she lied. "I . . ." She looked down at the fire, pretending embarrassment. "I needed to pee," she said in Iroquoian.

He scoffed. "And you didn't think you'd just keep going?"

She feigned indignity. "I've been here for hours. Do you think I have no natural—"

"I think you're a clever liar." He took the torch, lit it, and handed it to her. "Follow the tunnel straight to the dead end. I'll give you your privacy for a reasonable time."

"I'm thirsty," she declared.

"You tend to nature. I'll fetch water from the spring. But don't try any tricks. I know only a few of these passageways. If you get lost, you could wander until the torch burns out. Then . . ." He left the rest of the threat unspoken.

*I would die alone in the dark,* she thought with a shudder. It was an unpleasant prospect. "I won't wander off," she assured him. "Just be certain you don't get lost on the way to the spring."

"I'll try not to. On second thought, I'll wait until you get back with the torch. I don't like walking in pitch black either."

She was back in minutes, as she had promised. Again he left her by the fire and set out uphill toward the surface. He paused for an instant to retrieve his line and hawk bells, then retraced his steps through the winding corridor. Soot stains on the walls at eye level, made by countless Indian torches, showed which tunnels to take, but there was no need for Elizabeth to know that. He'd never have found the cave, or known about the many passageways, if it hadn't been for a map a Delaware friend had made for him. Using that knowledge, he'd stopped here and cached precious supplies on the way to the Seneca village.

When he reached the spring, he continued on until he could hear the roar of the falls. The chill grew greater as he continued uphill. Once he could see daylight through the tumbling water, he left his torch and went to the edge of the wet rock. A break in the seething, icy cascade showed a world white with swirling snow. It was impossible to judge the time of day accurately; sometime near noon, he guessed.

Satisfied that no Seneca patrols would be searching for them in this storm, he turned back. At the pool, he filled his waterbag, washed his face, and drank. He'd presumed that getting Elizabeth Fleming free of the Iroquois village would be the hard part of this job. Now he wasn't so sure. She was a hellion, certain to cause him a passel of grief in the next few weeks.

And she could kick like a mule.

He grimaced. Elizabeth had bloodied his nose in the Seneca camp, and she'd been battering him ever since. That behavior would have to end. He'd never been a man to strike a woman, but neither would he be beaten. Unless she learned to show him a fair measure of respect, traveling together would be unpleasant for both of them.

She was fully dressed and crouched beside the fire when he returned to the camp. She looked up as soon as she heard his footfalls on the loose gravel, and for an instant, fear played across her features, and a feeling of protectiveness swept over him. Anger against the Seneca made Hunt sorry he'd been able to buy Elizabeth. He'd never considered himself a violent man, but Yellow Drum had greatly wronged her, and now he was profiting from his evil. It was unfair, and Hunt wished he could have had the satisfaction of giving the Iroquois a taste of his fist.

"Are you hungry?" he asked.

"I need to wash first."

He handed her the waterskin. Hesitantly, she took it from him and walked to a corner of the cave to pour off a little water to rinse her hands. Then she lifted the container and drank deeply.

"Thank you, Hunt," he prompted.

She averted her eyes. "Thank you," she repeated, and flashed him a shy smile.

"You're a fair sight when you smile," he said. She looked down again, in the modest gesture he'd seen Indian girls make a thousand times.

Was that why he was so drawn to her? he wondered. White women always seemed such an enigma to him, but Elizabeth—for all her protests—was strangely familiar.

"It's still snowing," he said as the silence grew between them. He uncovered a grilled fish and two corn cakes. "Here." He offered them to her, then sat in silence while she ate.

She had finished every bite of the fish and had eaten half of the last corn cake when she suddenly stopped and glanced up at him. "Have I eaten your breakfast as well?"

He shook his head. "I had mine earlier." Unconsciously, she'd used the Iroquoian word for *meal* in the middle of an English sentence. Heaven help her if she did that in a Charles Town parlor, he thought. It would cause her no end of trouble.

Compassion for her made him wonder if he'd done her any favors by rescuing her. She was clearly heartbroken by having to leave her boy behind, and he reckoned she'd been a better than average mother among a people who revered children as gifts of the Creator. Women did get over the loss of a child, at least he supposed they did. But she'd have much more than that to face as she tried to readjust to the white world.

He'd been lucky. When he'd made up his mind to leave the woods and learn to live like a white man again, he'd had the good fortune to save Aaron Campbell from a Huron ambush. Not a fortnight later, Aaron's father had repaid that favor a hundred-fold when Hunt had been stricken with mumps. Old Ross Campbell had carried him home more dead than alive and welcomed him into his family. Ross was part Shawnee himself, and the two of them had fit hand in glove from the first minute they'd laid eyes on each other.

Old Ross and his wife had dusted the worst of the wildness off him, taught him how to walk and talk like a white man. They'd insisted that he brush up on the schooling he'd left behind in his sister's cabin, and when Ross discovered Hunt had a knack for figures, he'd taught him the basics of the trading business.

Hunt had been nineteen or so when he came back from the West and landed at Campbell's fort. He stayed with them for three years, first as an adopted son, and later as an employee of Ross's far-flung trading empire. After that, he'd made several ventures into the Ohio country and Kentucky to trade guns and powder to the Indians for furs, and acted as a translator between the Shawnee and the English. He'd traveled down the Mississippi with a Cherokee friend of Aaron Campbell's, and he'd spent a spring in Virginia as a horse trader. He still visited Ross's family when he could, and he'd made a place for himself somewhere between the Indian and the white worlds.

Somehow Hunt doubted it would be that easy for Elizabeth. A woman's reputation was easily damaged, and a white girl who'd lived among the Indians had a lot to live down in the eyes of English society.

She licked the crumbs of cornbread off her lips and wiped her mouth. "Where did you get fish in a snowstorm?"

He grinned and couldn't resist leaning close to wipe a stray crumb off her chin. She flinched, but she didn't run, and again he was struck by her courage.

"What? What are you laughing at?" she demanded. "I know I'm not pretty, but—"

"I wasn't laughing at you," he said.

She drew herself up stiffly. "It looks like it. How did you catch the fish?"

"I caught and gutted them when I left my stuff here. I put them on a ledge behind the waterfall and they froze solid."

"It's a wonder some raccoon didn't find them."

"Lucky for us they didn't," he replied. "Corn cakes and dried meat make for a dull diet."

Her green eyes sparkled in the firelight. "You've got dried meat?"

"I do." He found himself smiling foolishly at her again. "But you're not getting any now. I'm not sure when I'll be able to hunt again."

She sighed with obvious regret. "I'm still hungry."

"I'll put another fish on the rocks to bake."

She nodded, then nudged his buffalo robe with the toe of her moccasin. "What kind of fur is that?"

"Bison. Folks mostly call them buffalo. There are great herds of them west of the Mississip."

"The what?"

"Mississippi River—the big river. The buffalo graze on the grassland beyond. The forests end at the river and the prairie runs on forever. It doesn't stop until you reach the Far Mountains."

"You traded for the hide?"

"I killed the buffalo and paid a Crow Indian woman to tan and sew it for me."

"You've been there . . . to these . . . prairies?"

"Aye. My father, Wolf Robe, took me."

"Your Indian father."

"Yep." Hunt crouched Indian style on the far side of the fire. "He's a good man, Elizabeth. You'd like him."

"I've never known any Cheyenne." She dusted off her hands and turned her back on him. Using her fingers for a comb, she raked the tangles from her fiery red hair and braided it tightly into a single plait.

He wondered what she'd look like with her hair freshly washed and hanging loose in the sun the way the Cheyenne girls wore their hair every morning. Would the sunlight reflect off the strands of auburn the way it did with blue-black hair?

When she moved back to her place by the fire, she didn't look him in the eye. He hoped she was coming to trust him, and he tried to think of something to say that would put her at ease.

"I've never been to Charles Town but the once," he said. "When I met your father."

"You said he's paying a reward for me. Did he give you the money yet?"

"Half. I only took the job because I capsized my canoe and lost my rifle and a winter's pelts. I needed a new stake. I get the rest when you're home in one piece."

She raised her head and met his gaze. "I can't go without my son. Surely, you can understand that?"

"I know you think that. It's a hard thing, leaving your boy."

"Couldn't you take me back? I'd do anything if you would."

"I'm sorry," he said, and meant it. She was caught between flint and steel, and he ached for her. But one of them had to use common sense. Going back into that Seneca village would be suicide. No man could call him a coward, but neither was he a fool. He had a hell of a lot more living to do before he died. "What you're asking, woman, it's not possible."

Her lower lip quivered, but she raised her chin higher and those huge, liquid green eyes glistened with unshed tears. "Then I'd be grateful if you'd go back and get him for me," she said softly.

Hunt shook his head. "I can't. No one could."

She stood up. "Very grateful."

"Elizabeth, you don't understand. Going back there would be—" He broke off in astonishment as she grabbed the hem of her fringed gown and yanked it off over her head. Staring at her, he sucked in his breath.

She wore nothing under the dress but leggings and moccasins. Her breasts were high and firm, not large but perfectly shaped, with flushed pink aureoles and deeper rose nipples. Her waist was as narrow as a girl's, her belly flat above a triangle of bright auburn curls.

"No," he protested. "You don't want to . . ." He trailed off and swallowed. Desire knifed through him.

She let the dress fall to the floor and moistened her lips with the tip of her tongue. "I'd do whatever you ask," she murmured in a whiskey voice that made shivers run up and down his spine. "Anything, Hunt." She looked up at him through thick lashes and held out her arms. "Just rescue my son, and I'll give you whatever you want."

# Chapter 6

**E**lizabeth didn't think she could go through with it. Fear made her sick to her stomach; her skin prickled all over and seemed too tight for her body. She wanted to cry out that it was all a mistake, and cover her nakedness, but she forced her unwilling legs to take a step toward him. Hunt wanted her; she read the lust in his eyes. Indian or white, men were men, and they all wanted the same thing, didn't they?

Why was he hesitating? Why didn't he just throw her down and take her? She could bear the pain, but the waiting was agony.

He stared at her through narrowed eyes, his face as hard as the stone walls that reared around them. Was she too ugly for him? She pushed back the awful thought. Men didn't care. They slept with Basket, didn't they? She was old and used up from too many men, yet braves still came to her hearth place at night. What was it Raven always said? "Under a blanket all women are beautiful. If it were not true, would Yellow Drum get children on such as you?"

Elizabeth tried to smile. "Hunt," she whispered desperately. Tears clouded her vision and made his face blurry. Her insides knotted into a tight ball. She had nothing but herself to offer in exchange for her children. If Hunt rejected her, she would surely die of humiliation.

He didn't move.

The moment stretched into an eternity. She smelled the acrid must of the buffalo robe, heard the low hiss of the fire, saw the faint outlines of pictures scratched into the stone by people long dead and turned to dust.

Shame enveloped her. Her hands curled tight; her nails cut into the palms of her hands. With a deep sob that came up from the bottom of her despair, she let her hands fall slack at her sides. Part of her rejoiced that she wouldn't have to submit to Hunt's rutting, but a deeper part recoiled from the bitter truth that no decent man would ever want her.

"Elizabeth."

Her name came softly to her ears . . . no louder than the fall of a willow leaf. But his call had come too late; her courage had deserted her. She shrank back from the scorn she knew would follow, but before she could turn away, his hands were on her. She gasped as his arms tightened, molding her naked flesh to his body. She closed her eyes and went limp. She willed herself to submit to any indignity so long as it meant a chance to be reunited with her children.

Then his thumb brushed her chin. Gently, he lifted her head, and she smelled his clean, warm breath as he brought his mouth down to graze her lips.

"Oh," she gasped.

He chuckled and touched her lips again. Then, to her utter shock, he lingered there and kissed her with slow, infinite tenderness.

Elizabeth gave a tiny cry as white heat seared her mouth and flashed over her body. Her knees lost their strength, and she swayed against him. His fingers touched her taut breast, and she groaned. Unconsciously, her arms slipped around his neck, and she pulled him closer.

How could anything feel so wonderful? His slow, sensual caress was unlike anything she had ever known or imagined. She had dreamed that a man might kiss her . . . might hold her close to his heart, but she'd never guessed that it could send rippling sensations of sweet music from the top of her head to the soles of her feet.

He murmured her name, then kissed her again.

Her mouth seemed to fit his perfectly. There was no awkwardness . . . no hesitation. Without a single lesson, she knew instinctively to tilt her head just a little . . . to moisten her lips. And his kisses . . . his kisses took her breath away.

He held her, yet she knew that there was no force in his embrace. She could pull away if she wanted to. . . . And she knew she should.

This was all wrong. She'd wanted to seduce him so that he would do her bidding. She'd wanted him to forget his objections and take her back to the village. But she'd not planned on this. She'd not expected to go all giddy and light-headed . . . to be hot and dizzy and shivery all at once.

Hunt traced the line of her lower lip with the tip of his tongue. "You've a mouth made for kissing," he whispered. He sucked gently at her upper lip, and when her mouth parted slightly, he slid his tongue between her teeth.

She turned her face away and he kissed her ear and her hair. "You . . . you shouldn't do that . . ." she began, but she lost her thought as his lips pressed against her cheek and the corners of her mouth.

Her pulse quickened; her heart thudded like a drum.

He found her lips again, and this time when his kiss

deepened, she welcomed him into her mouth. Brazenly, she entwined her tongue with his, savoring the taste and scent of him . . . losing herself in the flood of sensations that threatened to drown her in waves of sensual heat.

His fingertips teased her bare nipple and she felt it harden to a tight bud. Tension coiled in the pit of her stomach, and she moved her hips so that her aching loins pressed against his hard thigh.

"God in heaven," he murmured. "You sweet thing." His breathing was as ragged as her own. He sighed and shifted his weight, trailing damp kisses from the corner of her mouth to the hollow of her throat. Her blood felt like sun-warmed honey.

And then when she thought that nothing Hunt did could astonish her, he committed the unthinkable. He lowered his head, took her nipple between his lips, and suckled like a baby. . . . Except it didn't feel like it had when she'd nursed her children. This . . . this was . . . She moaned as bright ribbons of ecstasy spilled through her veins.

She opened her eyes and let her head roll languidly from side to side. She couldn't believe this was happening. Nothing that Yellow Drum had ever done had made her feel anything but discomfort. He'd planted two children inside her body and she'd not known that a woman could experience such pleasure.

"Elizabeth?" Hunt's voice had taken on a new urgency. "Are you certain you want to do this?"

"Yes . . . yes."

He led her to the buffalo robe and pressed her back against the thick, coarse hair. She looked up at him as he hovered above her. His expression was gentle in the flickering yellow firelight, his eyes heavy-lidded with passion.

"You are so beautiful," he said.

The lie shattered the web of illusion he'd woven around them. How dare he taunt her? she thought. A sob of frustration rose in her breast as the heat fled her body, leaving her shivering in the cool air. Clenching her eyes shut, she twisted out of his embrace and turned on her stomach. "Do it," she said tersely. She clenched her teeth together and prepared herself for what she knew would come.

He swore softly. "What game is this?"

She could not bear to look at him. "Please," she begged. "Just get it over with."

"Son of a bitch." His foot struck a fist-sized rock and sent it spinning.

She heard a slight sound, and then the weight of a wool blanket settled over her bare shoulders.

"Cover yourself," he spat.

She curled into a ball, unable to raise her head . . . unable to face him. He would hit her now, but she didn't care. She didn't even know what she'd done to make him so angry.

"Son of a bitch," Hunt repeated. He turned his back on her and walked away down the tunnel, as furious with himself as he was with her.

He felt sick. He'd had no intention of accepting her bargain. He wasn't going back for her boy, and to let her think he might was dishonest and cruel. That he was capable of such villainy—even under the circumstances—galled him.

"Women," he muttered between his teeth. Elizabeth's father had trusted him to bring his daughter safely home, and he'd nearly broken that bargain as well. He stumbled on, hoping he was going the right way, too stubborn to go back for a light. Eventually, he smelled water and made his way to the edge of the underground pool. There, he dropped to his knees and splashed water on his face.

When she'd stripped off her dress, his first thought had been to refuse her. His second thought had been to run. But his limbs wouldn't obey his brain. He'd been drawn to her exquisite body by a primitive urge so powerful it had been impossible to ignore.

Even after he'd kissed her ... touched her soft skin and felt the warmth of her arms around him, he'd still intended to step back and break off this unholy union. But he'd been caught in the simplest of traps—he'd let his cock do his thinking for him.

She'd been willing. More than willing. He'd never held a woman with more capacity for loving ... or more feigned innocence. He could almost believe that she'd never been kissed before ... never had a man suck her nipples, except that she was the mother of a child. She wasn't a green girl—she was a woman grown, a woman who'd filled a man's needs for years.

Hunt dunked his whole head underwater and came up sputtering. He could still see her body in his mind's eye ... her small upthrust breasts, her smooth belly ... the tan line that rode low on her trim hips. It was evident that she'd followed Iroquois custom and worn nothing but a short shirt in summer.

She'd known what she was doing when she offered him a straightforward bargain, her body for his compliance in rescuing her boy. They'd both been enjoying themselves immensely, until something had gone wrong. What? And why had she acted so strangely and suddenly decided to put a halt to their pleasure?

He was still hot for her, as swollen as a half-grown Cheyenne boy peering into the women's sweat lodge. He ducked his head in the icy water again and tried to make sense of what had just happened.

Elizabeth was a striking woman with a body to fill a man's fantasies, but he'd seen lots of beautiful women, a goodly share of them with bare breasts. Nakedness was no sin among the Indians, and he'd grown to manhood among the Shawnee and Delaware as well as the Cheyenne. Sex was an accepted part of life. Hunt reckoned it to be a much saner philosophy than the one the English professed.

It wasn't like him to be so easily shaken by a woman. His father had taught him better. A warrior who couldn't maintain control over his own actions in the face of duty was considered an inferior man.

He stood up, loosened the rawhide tie at the back of his queue, and squeezed the water from his hair. Freezing rivulets ran down the back of his neck, and he shook himself like a wet dog.

Now that he could think clearly, it was clear to him that Elizabeth had been treated badly. She was either the world's best actress or the emotional innocent he'd thought her to be.

The image of her swollen lip surfaced in his mind, and a black fury possessed him. He wished he had killed Yellow Drum. There was nothing lower than a man who'd beat a woman, unless it was one who'd strip her of every ounce of self-confidence . . . who'd take away her God-given right to realize her own beauty. Murder was too good for the Seneca; he deserved a lifetime of torture.

Hunt's mouth tightened into a hard line. No woman deserved what had been done to Elizabeth. And how much better had he treated her?

He turned back toward the camp with a raw conscience.

"I'm sorry, Elizabeth," he said as he stepped out of the darkness into the dim light of the campfire. She was still lying facedown where he'd left her. He would have guessed she was weeping, but he didn't hear a sound. "I shouldn't . . ." Whatever else he meant to say was lost. She hadn't put her dress back on, and she had the sweetest little bottom it had been his pleasure to see in a long time.

For a second, he was tempted to turn around and go back to the pool and dive in. That urge lasted for two heartbeats. Instead, he retrieved the blanket from the floor where she'd dropped it, knelt beside her, and covered her nakedness.

She twisted around and looked up at him with bleak eyes. She hadn't been crying; there were no tearstains on her face, but it was evident that she was terribly upset.

"Nothing's as bad as that," he soothed, putting a hand on her bare shoulder. "It was my fault."

"No...no," she answered hoarsely. "I just wanted..." She shuddered and closed her eyes. Her long lashes fluttered down like small, feathery birds, and he had to bite his lower lip to keep from kissing them.

She laid her head on his knee. Her hair curled around her face, thick and unruly, its fiery red color so intense that he expected it to scorch his fingers as he stroked it. One of her hands had closed around the edge of the blanket. She clutched it so tightly that her knuckles shone white.

"What's wrong?" he asked. "You're safe with me, I swear it."

"You...you shouldn't..." She sat up, opened her eyes, and looked into his face. "You shouldn't lie to me," she said. Her voice was stretched as taut as a bowstring, and her eyes were as cold as green glass.

She made no effort to cover her bare breasts, and it was difficult for him to keep his mind on comforting her. "Elizabeth," he began.

She took his hand in hers and brought it to her breast. She was shaking, and her vulnerability made his throat tighten with emotion. "I know I'm ugly," she whispered, "but surely—"

"Stop that," he replied. He grabbed hold of her shoulders with both hands and gave her a shake. "Why are you doing this? What do you mean, you're ugly?"

Her face flushed a deep rose and tears glistened in her eyes. "I know what I am," she flung hotly back at him. "But that doesn't mean I can't satisfy you."

He pulled her against his chest and held her. "Listen to me," he said. "No, don't talk, just listen. Your father sent me to bring you back, and that's what I'm doing. I don't think you're ugly. I find you very . . ." He took a deep breath and began again. "Desirable. But this isn't right for either of us. I can't do what you want. I'd like to lie with you. Hell, I'm about to bust out of my breeches just thinking about it, but it's wrong. It's the wrong time, and for the wrong reasons. I can't do it, Elizabeth. And when you think about it, you'll realize why it's wrong."

He felt her tremble in his arms. She gave a faint sob and then whispered, "I had to try."

"I can see that," he said. "I don't hold it against you."

"You don't want a woman like me . . . one who's been used by—"

He pushed her far enough away to look into her eyes. "Get this through your thick head," he said, trying to control his rising anger. "I don't blame you for anything that happened. Who you've slept with or who you haven't doesn't mean a ha'penny to me. I don't pay for my bedmates. I like you; I think you're a courageous woman. I find you damned attractive. But I won't take advantage of you, and I'm not going to be bribed or tricked into getting myself killed trying to snatch your boy from his father."

She stiffened. Her eyes narrowed. "I like you too, Hunter Campbell, but I won't let liking you stand in the way of getting my son back."

"You can't mean to fight me over this."

"I don't belong to Yellow Drum anymore, and I don't belong to my father. You're dealing with me, no one else."

"I want to be your friend."

"Then be my friend. Take me back for my son."

"We're not talking about this anymore, Elizabeth. I don't want to hear another word. My answer is *no*. If I have to tie you up and drag you back to Carolina, I will. Make up your mind. Are we going to do this the easy way or the hard way?"

"Take your hands off me." Her tone was soft, compliant, but her eyes held daggers.

He released her. "Best get your clothes back on," he suggested. "We'll forget this ever happened. Rest, and as soon as this storm passes, we'll—"

"I won't forget about Jamie."

"You intend to make this the hardest money I've ever earned, don't you?"

"Are you a father?"

"Not that I know of."

"If you were, you'd understand. I can't walk away from—"

"No more!" he said.

"What will you do, beat me?"

"I won't beat you, but I may gag you," he threatened.

"Bully."

"Shrew," he snapped.

"I am not," she protested. Snatching up her deerskin dress, she pulled it over her head. "I have a sweet, warm nature."

"Woman, you try a man's soul."

"You're afraid of Yellow Drum. Admit it! You're a coward, afraid of a few Seneca."

"Yellow Drum is a war chief. He didn't get elected to that post by his skill in making maple syrup or weaving baskets. He's a warrior, one of the best. And I'll wager he kills for the thrill of it."

"And you? What are you? A yellow—"

He shook his head. "You think insults will buy you what honey wouldn't? I'm no coward, Elizabeth. I've killed men when I had to. I won my eagle feathers by—"

"I don't believe you won them. I believe that was a lie as much as—"

"Silence, woman. You'll wake the bats with your caterwauling." He sighed heavily and put the fire between them. He'd not let her tirade anger him. He wasn't a coward and he knew it. Neither was he a fool to let taunting cause him to use poor judgment.

"Hunt . . ."

"I don't want to hear it," he said.

"Hunt!" She blanched as white as milk and pointed beyond him, toward the chamber entrance. "Someone's coming."

He glanced in the direction she indicated, then dove for his rifle when he saw the light of a torch bobbing toward them. "Back against that wall," he ordered.

Danger pumped through his veins as he checked the priming of his rifle. Hunt had one shot and one shot only; after that—if it came to a fight—it would be hand to hand.

He was deep in Iroquois territory, and they were trapped here with no way out but that single passageway. If Yellow Drum or any of his warriors had found them, Hunt's best chance, maybe his only chance, would be to shoot first and reduce the odds against them.

Elizabeth flattened herself against the wall and crept closer. From the corner of his eye, he caught the gleam of steel and realized she'd armed herself with his knife.

"Get my shot bag," he whispered. "If I have to fire, I'll throw you my rifle. Can you load it?"

"Yes."

A curious feeling of pride swelled in his chest. She was obviously terrified, but she wasn't dissolving into hysteria like most white women would have done. Elizabeth might be trouble, but she had grit.

The bright ball of torchlight moved closer. Hunt cocked the hammer of his flintlock and tightened his finger on the trigger. A bead of sweat trickled down the nape of his neck. He held his breath, straining to hear footfalls.

"Don't shoot unless you have to," she whispered.

"Who comes?" he called out in Iroquoian, using as hearty a voice as he could muster. An exchange of lead and shot was the last thing he wanted in these close quarters. If gunfire erupted, he doubted either of them would come out of this cave alive. "Are you friend or foe?"

"Greetings to your hearth, brother," rasped a husky reply in the same tongue.

"And to you," Hunt shouted back. "Come forward and be recognized."

"He doesn't sound like a Seneca," Elizabeth whispered.

"Shh," Hunt warned. "Let me do the talking."

A scarred warrior with shaved head and blue-tattooed chin raised his torch high. His clothes were covered with snow; ice clung to his scalplock and crusted his moccasins. His face was blanched with cold. "I am Powder Horn, of the Onondaga," he said. "I seek shelter at your fire from the storm."

# Chapter 7

**H**unt lowered his rifle and motioned to the Indian. "Advance and be welcome, Powder Horn of the Onondaga." He motioned to Elizabeth. "Where are your manners, woman? Here is a cold and hungry man. Share all that we have with him."

Elizabeth exhaled slowly as terror receded from her brain and feeling returned to her limbs. Powder Horn was a stranger. He was Iroquois, but not Seneca. He might not even know that she'd belonged to Yellow Drum or that she'd been sold to a half-breed Delaware.

"Come and eat," she said to the newcomer, trying to keep her tone normal. "Warm your limbs at my hearth." He was suffering from exposure to the storm. His face was blotched with patches of white, and he was shaking with bone-chilling spasms.

Normally, she would have felt more compassion for the man, but she and Hunt were outsiders in Iroquois land where any stranger might be an enemy. She couldn't forget that Raven hadn't fed Hunt at her hearth place. Such a breech of custom could only mean that Yellow Drum's chief wife was plotting something. Raven might have convinced the war chief to follow them and murder Hunt and take her prisoner again. Elizabeth wanted desperately to go back to her children, but not as a captive and not at the cost of Hunt Campbell's life.

"I was hunting a wounded bear," Powder Horn said as he approached the fire and held out his stiff hands to the flame. "My comrades and I split up to try and find his trail, and we were separated at darkness. I've walked all night to reach this place." He pulled two stiff rabbits from his belt and held them out to Elizabeth. "I have no haunch of bear to offer you, but I will share my rabbits."

"And fat rabbits they are," she replied. She tried to catch Hunt's attention and convey her suspicion to him without alarming Powder Horn. The Indian's story stank like four-day-old fish. This was not Onondaga hunting ground, and it was a rare man who would walk for hours on a bad night to reach a cave when he could make a shelter, or find one, before dusk. Still, it would do no good to let the Iroquois know they hadn't swallowed his tall tale.

"Leave the rabbits for tomorrow's meal," Hunt said. "We have plenty tonight." He leaned his rifle against a rock within reach and squatted next to the newcomer.

Powder Horn rubbed his arms and began to pull off his frozen moccasins. "You are not of the Iroquois Confederacy," Powder Horn said as he stuck his cold feet against the warm rocks. He was still shivering, but not as greatly as before. "You sound like a white man, but you do not smell like one."

Hunt laughed. "It is true that I'm not of the Five Fires, but I am human. My mother is of the Grandfather People," Hunt explained casually, "the Delaware. I recently traded with the Seneca war chief Yellow Drum for this red-haired slave woman."

Powder Horn arched a thick eyebrow. "She is not your wife?"

"If she pleases me, I may make her one."

Powder Horn made a clicking sound with his tongue and smiled at Elizabeth. His top front teeth were wide and protruding, the ones below narrow and yellow. *He looks like a beaver*, she thought, returning his false smile with an equally fake one. He should have been called Beaver Tooth.

"A pity a man must travel so far to purchase a slave," the Onondaga observed. "Are there no women to be had in the south?" He lifted a coal to light his pipe, puffed several times, and offered the pipe to Hunt.

He accepted and took several draws on the carved mouthpiece. The pungent odor of tobacco filled the chamber. "There are many women," Hunt replied, "but few want to leave their kin to travel with a half-white man who wishes to winter far from the villages. Females prefer the company of their own kind."

"True," the Indian said, holding his hands out to the fire again. Tattooed designs ringed both his wrists and he was missing the first joint on one seamed finger. He was not as old as Elizabeth had first thought when she'd seen him appear in the torchlight. His body was lean and hard; his ropy muscles were those of a formidable warrior. Only his moon face seemed placid, or would have seemed so if she hadn't noticed the shrewd feral light in his hooded eyes.

Elizabeth dug through Hunt's belongings to find food for the Iroquois. She must keep up the pretense of being a slave until they found out what Powder Horn was really doing here. And she must find some way of letting Hunt know that he couldn't relax his guard, no matter how harmless the Onondaga pretended to be.

"Any sign of the snow letting up?" Hunt asked. The Indian shook his head. Hunt nodded. "I thought it might be bad."

Elizabeth found dried meat and nuts. She laid them on a rock beside the guest and retreated to sit on Hunt's buffalo cloak. Her eyes burned with fatigue, but she was still too frightened to sleep. This Iroquois was too friendly to travelers he'd never seen before. One so trusting didn't survive long on the frontier. Whatever his mission, he meant them no good; of that she was sure.

Minutes passed. Powder Horn wolfed down the dried meat and began to crack nuts with a rock. Hunt talked easily with him, relating the story of a grizzly bear hunt in the far western mountains. The Iroquois nodded and chewed noisily. Elizabeth curled up and pulled a blanket over her. She hadn't intended to close her eyes, but she must have drifted off because Hunt's hand on her shoulder made her start.

"Shh," he murmured.

She tried to sit up as he stretched out on the robe beside her, but he draped an arm over her. "I won't—" she protested, stiffening.

He leaned close and whispered in her ear. "Be still. He asked to borrow you." Hunt pulled her close and covered them both with the same blanket.

She shivered despite his nearness and the weight of the thick wool. She wasn't certain she could trust Hunt, but she knew she couldn't trust the Iroquois. She looked for Powder Horn and saw a huddled form on the far side of the hearth. The fire had burned down to glowing coals.

"I'm not going to hurt you," Hunt murmured. "I told him I don't share my women. Still, I want you close. He may be the kind who doesn't take no for an answer."

Her heart pounded in her chest. It felt strange, lying so close in his arms. She wasn't sure if she liked the sensation or not. She tried to wiggle free and touched something cold and hard. Hunt gripped a tomahawk in his right hand.

"It's all right," he said in English, so low that she could barely make out the words. "You sleep. I'll keep watch." He wrapped himself around her, snuggling against her back.

Elizabeth's breath caught in her throat as her buttocks grazed his groin. His long legs were hard with muscle; his powerful arms encircled her. He lay so close that she could feel the rise and fall of his chest with each breath. She wondered if he would mate with her now. The thought was both enticing and a little frightening.

She didn't fear the act of joining. Instinct told her that Hunt was no Yellow Drum. This long rifle had been gentle with her; he might mount her to quench his sexual hunger, but he wouldn't be cruel. No, her uncertainty came from within her own heart. A strange Onondaga lay almost within arm's reach. She should have been worrying about him leaping up and murdering them both; instead, she was remembering how good Hunt's mouth had tasted when he'd kissed her.

Unfamiliar sensations curled in the pit of her belly. She was acutely aware of the texture of the wool and leather garments that pressed against her skin. Her senses of smell and hearing seemed enhanced to the point of distraction. Hunt's scent enveloped her. Each breath she took made her more a part of him. She could hear the dripping of water from far off, and the mass of earth above her seemed to sigh like a restless animal. She might have been experiencing all these things in a dream, but she had never been more awake in her life.

Elizabeth's chest felt tight, and her blood raced. It was difficult for her to lie still. Minutes before she had been sleeping; now sleep was impossible. Hunt's intimate presence was exquisite torture. If she didn't do something . . . anything to ease this tension, she was certain her heart would burst.

Boldly, casting caution to the winds, she turned toward him, wiggling up until her lips touched his left ear. A lock of his silky hair brushed her cheek, and the clean scent of pine filled her nostrils. "Hunt," she murmured.

"Elizabeth."

Was that a hint of amusement in his whisper? She swallowed. Her mouth was suddenly dry and her breasts felt as full as though they were swelling with milk. She had stopped nursing Rachel months ago and it was impossible for her to be pregnant, so why did she feel so strange?

She tried again to speak, but her mouth was suddenly as parched as if she'd been eating dry cornmeal. Heat washed over her throat and face; she buried her head in the hollow of his neck. His skin smelled clean and intriguing. What would it be like, she wondered, to have this man make love to her?

A groan came from the far side of the fire pit, and Elizabeth heard the Iroquois stir. She tried to turn her head to look in that direction, but suddenly—without warning—Hunt rolled on top of her and kissed her mouth.

She was so shocked that she offered no resistance as the heat of his loins burned through the layers of clothing that separated them. She didn't fight; neither did she return the kiss. She lay rigid in his embrace.

Reason told her that the Onondaga was dangerous

and that she needed to keep her wits about her, but reason had nothing to do with the confusion in her mind or the murmurs of yearning that warmed her body.

Hunt broke off the caress and whispered into her ear. "I'm not going to rape you. I doubt if our friend is really asleep. I want to convince him that we don't suspect him." Bracing himself with one knee and an elbow, he shifted his weight off her. "You're safe with me. You have my word on it."

Elizabeth gave a tiny sigh and turned her face away from the firelight.

Hunt bit back an oath. Being near her was disquieting; having her under him and being unable to do anything about it was enough to drive a man to strong measures. Elizabeth might be innocent, but no woman who'd lived with a man and borne his children could be that innocent. He couldn't shake the feeling that she was playing with him like a bear with a beached trout. For a few seconds, he toyed with the notion of tomahawking the Iroquois and returning to Elizabeth's arms to make love to her with as much tenderness and passion as she deserved.

He had a bad feeling about Powder Horn, and his hunches were rarely wrong. But thinking a man was trouble and murdering him so that you could enjoy a roll in the blankets with a woman were two different things. He'd been brought up with a code of honor that didn't permit such thoughts, let alone actions.

The Iroquois might be exactly what he said he was—a lost hunter. It would be madness to betray the laws of hospitality and take a human life without proof that Powder Horn was an enemy.

Hunt sucked in a deep breath, savoring the scent of Elizabeth's hair and skin. She'd offered herself to him earlier when she wanted to make a bargain with him.

She was old enough to know her own mind, and she was no virgin. By rights, no one could blame him for seducing her now. She'd come to no harm by a full measure of good loving. She needed someone to teach her the joy a man and woman could find together.

Damn, but her skin felt soft to his touch. Her mouth trembled when he kissed her, and her breath was sweet. He'd not wanted another woman this badly in a long time. Not since Spotted Pony.

He tried to think of the Cheyenne girl he'd nearly gotten killed over—the only woman he'd ever asked to marry him. He'd promised her father five horses and a rifle for her, but she'd had a change of heart and married another man. Spotted Pony had been as fresh as a mountain stream and rounded in all the right places. Her face . . . He swallowed. At seventeen, he'd been ready to die for love of Spotted Pony, and now he couldn't remember her face.

He glanced down at Elizabeth. Firelight played across her red-gold hair. He had the strongest urge to lift it off the nape of her neck and brush his lips there. The pressure in his groin increased and he groaned softly. She made a faint sound that sent a flood of emotion washing over him. *If you were mine,* he thought, *I'd never call you Elizabeth. . . . You'd be my Beth.*

She squirmed in his embrace and again he was enveloped in her fresh scent. The jade was taunting him. He knew it. Yet no amount of reason could hold back the intense desire to possess her warm, willing body. He wanted to claim her as his own—to put his mark on her so that all men would know she belonged to him alone.

He was sweating in earnest now. Lust flared into a primitive throb as loud and incessant as the beat of a Seneca water drum. He moved one hand, almost without realizing what he was doing. His fingers slid down her side. When she didn't protest, he dared even more. He pressed his open palm against her warm midriff.

Her breathing quickened, and he kissed the crown of her head, savoring the tickle of her soft hair against his lips. He knew better. He knew he was imposing self-torture on himself when there was no chance of taking the act to culmination, but she felt so damned good in his arms. She hadn't said no, and she wasn't fighting him. He moved his fingertips in slow, lazy circles, not touching her breasts, but moving closer.

He had meant to see how far she'd go—to give her a taste of the fire without getting burned himself— but he'd overestimated his own self-control. He stretched his arm to reach the hem of her dress and slipped his hand under the garment. The bare flesh above her knee was warm and silken.

"Don't," she said, but the stiffness of her muscles had yielded to a gentle molding against his body.

He removed his hand. "Are you certain you mean no?" he whispered. As he leaned down to murmur in her ear, the roar of a flintlock pistol nearly deafened him. The bullet meant for his heart struck the far wall and chips of stone sprayed the chamber. He twisted to face the Iroquois and tried to free his tomahawk from the tangle of blankets.

Shrieking a war cry, Powder Horn charged through the fire pit at them. Elizabeth rolled away, and Hunt leaped up to meet the attack. The Indian's knife flashed, missing Hunt's left forearm by less than an inch. Hunt swung his tomahawk.

Powder Horn sidestepped the blow and grabbed Elizabeth by the hair of her head. Yanking her to her knees, he put his scalping knife against the pulse at her throat. "Move and she dies," he spat.

Hunt froze in the act of throwing his weapon. A second later and his tomahawk would have ended the Iroquois's threats forever.

"Drop it," Powder Horn urged. He pressed Elizabeth's skin with the blade until a single drop of blood welled across the steel surface.

"No," Elizabeth protested. "Don't."

Hunt let the tomahawk fall.

"Better," Powder Horn said. He stepped back, dragging Elizabeth with him until he could reach his rifle. Then he shoved her to the floor and leveled the flintlock at Hunt's belly. "I have need of a woman." He chuckled. "But I have no need of you. I give you a chance at life. Walk out of this cave or stay and die."

"Go," Elizabeth said.

Hunt looked into the Onondaga's harsh face. He stood in the shadows, and it was too dark for Hunt to see his eyes. It didn't matter. Powder Horn had no intention of letting him go. He meant to shoot him.

"Do as he says," Elizabeth pleaded. "I remember now! Those tattoos on his wrists—" She glanced at the Iroquois. "You are an outcast," she accused. "You've killed another of your tribesmen. They've shunned you, haven't they?"

"Quiet, woman," the Indian growled.

"He is outlawed," she cried. "No Iroquois will give him food or shelter."

"I said *be quiet!*" Powder Horn motioned toward Hunt with the rifle barrel. "Leave while you can, half-breed."

"Without weapons?" Hunt asked.

Powder Horn cocked the gun. "Turn and go. Consider the loss of your weapons the penalty for stupidity."

Hunt considered the possibilities. If he went for the rifle, the Iroquois would shoot him. If he tried to leave, he'd get the bullet in his back. "If you wanted the woman that badly, you should have said so. I'm a reasonable man. We could have come to some agreement."

"We have." Powder Horn raised the rifle and sighted down the barrel.

It seemed to Hunt as though his mind was as slow as the lazy curl of smoke drifting up from the scattered coals. "What do you have to gain by killing me?" he asked.

"What do I have to lose?"

"I have a cache of trade goods. I can show you—"

"Liar," Powder Horn said. "Take a last look at your red-haired woman and think how she will groan with pleasure under the thrust of my man spear." Then he squeezed the trigger.

# Chapter 8

◦◦◦◦

**A**s the Onondaga fired his gun, Elizabeth smashed a fist-sized rock into his left kneecap with every ounce of her strength. The rifle spat fire and lead, and she heard Hunt's cry of anguish and knew he'd been hit. But she didn't turn to watch him fall—she was too busy trying to dodge the wooden stock of Powder Horn's gun.

Powder Horn doubled over in pain, but even with an injured knee he swung the rifle butt like a club to try to crush her skull.

*"Onishonk nainnuk!"* she screamed at him in the Iroquoian language as she scooped up a double handful of ash and coals and threw it full in his face.

The Iroquois howled as hot ashes blinded him. Elizabeth scrambled out of reach and grabbed another rock. But before she could throw it, Hunt launched himself onto Powder Horn, and both men crashed to the stone floor in a tangle of flying arms and legs.

Elizabeth gave a cry of joy as tears of relief welled up in her eyes. She'd thought Hunt was dead or wounded so badly that he couldn't rise. For a dead man, he was putting up quite a fight.

Powder Horn was on top of Hunt, but the Indian's nose was streaming blood. Hunt's left fist was pounding the Iroquois's face, while his right hand gripped his opponent's right wrist. Powder Horn had managed to draw his knife and was trying to drive it into Hunt.

Elizabeth ran forward to try to strike Powder Horn in the head with the rock; but before she could reach him, Hunt gave a heave and threw the Iroquois onto his back. Somewhere in the struggle, Powder Horn's knife went flying.

Elizabeth retrieved the Iroquois's rifle, which the two had been lying on. Her first thought was to reload, but everything was happening too fast. In the confusion and semidarkness, she wasn't certain she could find the Indian's shot bag. When she looked back, Powder Horn and Hunt were on their knees. Hunt was bending the Indian back over the rocks of the fire pit. Elizabeth dropped the gun, picked up another stone, and struck Powder Horn a glancing blow off his right temple. The Indian gave a groan and went limp.

"About damn time," Hunt grumbled as he dragged the Indian out of the hearth and brushed the smoking coals off his head. A knot the size of a chicken's egg was swelling on Powder Horn's temple. A thin line of blood trickled down to mingle with the blood on his lower face.

"Is he dead?" Elizabeth asked.

"No such luck." Hunt nudged the unconscious warrior with his foot. "He's still breathing." He glanced at Elizabeth. "What were you doing? Waiting to see if he'd finish me off?"

She added twigs to the coals and blew. As a small flame flared, she looked up into Hunt's face and gasped in horror. His face was even bloodier than Powder Horn's. "You're hurt," she cried.

Hunt squatted and rubbed his face with both hands. "Get me some water."

"Your head. The blood's coming from your head." Suddenly, Elizabeth felt dizzy. She drew in a ragged breath and tried to keep calm. Hunt couldn't be dying. No man could stand and fight if he were mortally wounded, could he? "Where are you hit? Come here, closer to the light, so I can see."

"Damn it, woman, he nearly killed me. What were you doing when I needed help?"

"But I hit him in the knee. I tried . . ." She trailed off, waiting to see if Hunt were truly angry or just grumbling. When he made no move to strike her, she launched into a defense of her actions. "You're the warrior. I'm a helpless woman; you're supposed to protect me."

"Helpless? You're about as helpless as a rattlesnake." He took a few steps toward her, staggered, and fell to one knee. "Elizabeth . . ."

"Oh, my God," she cried. Icy dread swept over her and her heart plunged. "Don't you dare die on me now!" She caught him in her arms and lowered him to the buffalo robe. "Lie still," she crooned. "I didn't know you were hurt so bad. Lie still, and let me help you."

Hunt closed his eyes. "Easy," he cautioned.

Elizabeth was shaking all over. She felt as though an icy hand was squeezing the back of her neck. Hunt's breathing was deep and regular; he felt warm and live in her arms. But if he'd taken the bullet in his head, his wound would be beyond her ability to heal him. "Don't die on me," she pleaded. She couldn't lose him, she couldn't. Her pulse raced as she cradled his head in her lap. Her eyes filled with moisture so that she could barely see. Dashing away the outward signs of her weakness, she felt through his blood-soaked hair with dread. "The blood is coming from more than one place, but there was only one shot. I don't understand how . . ."

Hunt groaned and looked up at her. "Tie up the Iroquois first. So long as he's alive, he's dangerous."

"I want to see how bad you're hurt. I might be able to—"

"Damn it!" he exclaimed, breaking from Iroquoian to English. "Can you never do a thing I ask you? Get some thongs from my pack and tie his hands and feet."

"You should have killed him," she whispered. Her hands were covered in blood. They stung and she didn't know why.

Hunt caught her arm. "Never mind my head. Do something about Powder Horn. I vow, woman, you're as bloodthirsty as a Seneca."

His accusation was so unfair that she cried out in protest. "How can you say that?" she exclaimed. "I hate the sight of blood. It makes me sick."

"Well, don't get sick on me. I feel bad enough already. See to the Iroquois."

"You have one prisoner. What do you want with a second?" She knew Hunt was right. She should tie Powder Horn before he woke up . . . if he woke up. She glanced in his direction. He hadn't moved. Maybe he would die, and they wouldn't have him to deal with. "I just want to see where the bullet is— There!" Her fingers touched something hard and jagged. Blood was seeping out around the object. His hair was matted with gore.

"Ouch!" he protested.

"Be still. Don't be such a— It's not a bullet! It's a rock." She pulled the acorn-sized piece of limestone out of the cut and pinched the scalp together.

"I know it's not a bullet. The ball missed me. I got

hit by some fragments after the bullet hit the cave wall."

"You weren't shot?"

"I wasn't shot."

"Then hold this!" she ordered. "Keep your hand on it, tight." She pressed his palm against the flap of skin. "It's not even that deep."

"Sorry to disappoint you."

"I thought you were shot in the head." The realization left her weak-kneed and giddy. She had to concentrate as she rose and walked unsteadily to his pile of belongings along the wall. It was too dark to see there so she brought his hunting bag and a second pack over to the fire.

"In the fringed bag," he said. "There's a coil of leather. Quick now! Tie Powder Horn's wrists behind his back."

With distaste, she tugged at the heavy Iroquois. He moaned as she rolled him onto his stomach. Working swiftly, she made a loop, slipped it over one hand and drew it tight, then knotted the leather around his other wrist. There was still a length of leather, so she drew up his right ankle and tied that to his wrists. Considering how hard she'd hit him with the rock in the left knee, she didn't think he'd be going far on that leg.

"Hurry up," Hunt urged.

She got to her feet and stood for a moment, staring into the corners of the room. Then she saw what she'd been looking for—Powder Horn's knife. Retrieving it, she tucked it into her waistband and returned to Hunt's side.

"Did you tie it tight?" he demanded.

"If you weren't shot, why did you take so long to jump him?" Elizabeth asked, ignoring Hunt's question. Her stomach still felt queasy, and her hands stung worse than before. Now that she knew Hunt wasn't going to die from the cut on his head, she was in no mood to take any abuse. At worst, he'd need her to sew up the cuts. Her relief was overwhelming, but she still felt that he'd tricked her by letting her think he was mortally wounded. "You took forever to do anything," she said. "Were you waiting for me to kill Powder Horn for you?"

"I probably should have."

"You were pretending to be hurt worse than you were, so I'd feel sorry for you."

"What? Let a chunk of rock hit you in the head and see if it doesn't slow you down for a minute."

"As hardheaded as you are, I wouldn't think a rock could hurt you." She dropped to her knees beside him and looked down at her palms. She needed to wash off the blood. She was going to be sick if she couldn't get it off. She'd always been a baby about blood. Her own blood didn't bother her, just other people's.

"You're one to talk about being hardheaded. You're as contrary as any female I've ever known. Would it make you happier if I had been shot?"

"I have to wash my hands. They're sticky. I have to wash them." She kept her voice low, speaking slowly in Iroquoian.

"There's water there in my waterskin." His tone lost much of its gruffness. "Are you all right, Elizabeth?"

"I have to wash the blood off."

She hadn't realized he'd moved, but suddenly, his arm was around her shoulders and he was holding out the bag. "Put out your hands," he said. He poured some of the liquid over her palms. "Rub them together."

"They hurt." She looked up into his face. "Why do they hurt?"

"Come with me," he ordered. "Can you walk?"

"Of course, I can walk." She didn't know if her legs would hold her, but she wouldn't admit that to him.

"Can you hold a torch?"

She nodded. Why was he asking her such foolish questions? She still felt numb all over except for her hands, and it was hard to think.

"Just do as I say, Elizabeth. I'll take care of you."

Would he? He was so big, so strong, and she wanted so badly to be taken care of. The offer was almost more than she could bear. She was too confused to argue; it was easier to trust him and do as he said.

Almost in a trance, Elizabeth obeyed his orders. She was vaguely aware that he was guiding her down a long series of tunnels. The air became noticeably damper, and she heard the sound of flowing water.

Hunt let go of her arm and took the smoking brand from her hand and jammed the end into a crack in the rock. Just in front of her, she could see a pool of water.

"It's not deep," he said, "but it is cold. We'll wash off all the blood, both of us."

"Yes," she agreed woodenly. "We'll wash it off." She didn't protest but stood as helpless as a child when he tugged her clothing off. She stepped out of her moccasins and into the icy water. It rose to mid-thigh. Gratefully, she sank to a sitting position and began to splash water on her face and neck.

Hunt stripped to his breeches and plunged in beside her. He ducked his head under repeatedly and sputtered and gasped. "Cold enough for you?" he asked.

The water was cold, but she'd become used to bathing in winter since she'd been with Yellow Drum's people. Sometimes they had to break an inch or more of ice to wade in. The cold was unpleasant, but familiar. It cleared her head and made the sick feeling go away.

Hunt touched her shoulder. "I won't hurt you," he said. His voice was deep but very tender. He spoke to her as softly as if she were an injured doe. "It's all right, Elizabeth," he soothed. "I'm just going to unbraid your hair."

Strange. How strange it felt to have a man do such a small intimate thing. Strange . . . but good, very good. She caught her breath, not wanting the moment to end . . . wanting to savor every sweet sensation.

His big, hard fingers were gentle as he untied the rawhide lace and carefully combed out her hair until it fell in waves over her wet shoulders. "Best to rinse it out," he said. "There may be blood . . ."

Docilely, she ducked her head under. Once, twice, she let the clear water wash her clean.

"That's good," he said. His fingers tightened around her hand. He squeezed reassuringly and smiled at her. "Had enough?" he asked.

She nodded, too full of emotion to trust her voice.

He climbed out and offered her his hand.

"This isn't . . . our drinking water . . . I hope," she managed to ask. Her teeth were chattering so that she could hardly get her words out.

"It's not. I'm hardly the fool you take me for," he replied. He was shivering too, and she was glad. He wrapped a wool blanket around her naked shoulders.

Her gaze met his, and her mood lightened. Happiness bubbled up in her chest. They were alive. Alive! So why was she behaving so ridiculously? She began to chuckle.

"What's so funny?" he asked.

"Me." Impulsively, she threw her arms around him and hugged him. "I don't want to fight with you. I thought you were dead. I was so scared. And then when I found out . . ." She broke off in another burst of shivering. "I'm sorry, Hunt. Forgive me. I just—"

He put his arms around her and kissed her.

For long seconds, she floated in the pure pleasure of his kiss. Then a warm trickle of blood down her cheek reminded her that he still had an injury that needed tending. She pulled back. "Your head," she said. "You will die if we don't stop it from bleeding."

He let go of her and put his hand to the gash. "You were scared I was dying?"

She averted her eyes and nodded.

He made a sound of derision. "You probably would have killed Powder Horn if I hadn't come to his rescue. You're a caution with a rock. What was that you called him? A devil?"

She smiled. "Sort of a devil. More of a demon. I think *Onishonk nainnuk* is the blue-faced thing that lives in the woods and eats children." She pulled the blanket tighter around her. Her hands still stung, but not as much as they had. Then she remembered the hot coals and ash she'd thrown into Powder Horn's face. "My hands . . ." she said. "I burned them when I threw the ashes."

"You're burned?" His voice became husky with concern. "Let me see."

"I'm all right. I just . . ." She shook her head. She felt like such a fool getting faint over a little blood. Raven would have made her a laughingstock in front of the other women. Now that she knew it was a simple burn and not Hunt's blood stinging her hands . . . "I can still sew up your cut," she said.

"You can just bandage it. The pool washed it clean."

"Coward. It needs stitches."

"It doesn't need sewing."

"It does. And I'll have to shave your head first. I—"

"The hell you will."

"Don't tell me you're afraid of—"

"Tie the scalp together with sections of hair," he insisted. "It's a Cheyenne trick an old warrior showed me. You do it if you're on the plains where you can't get proper—"

"It won't hurt that much. Jamie fell out of a tree and cut his knee last summer. I put four stitches in it and—"

"I'm not your child. Do as I say. Tie the cuts shut."

For an instant she was lost in the memory of that morning with her son. Jamie had come running to her, his brown eyes dilated with fear. He wasn't weeping, but his mouth was puckered and his breath coming in short, hard gasps. He'd been trying so hard to be brave in front of the older boys he'd been playing with. She'd taken him into the privacy of their hearth place, carefully washed the dirt and blood away, and taken the necessary stitches.

He still didn't cry, not even when she pierced his flesh with a needle. Afterwards, she'd given him a piece of honeycomb dripping with honey and covered the wound with a poultice of Solomons Seal and cattail fluff. She pulled him into her lap and sat holding him tightly, telling him how much she loved him for a long time.

If she shut her eyes, she could still feel the outline of Jamie's body pressed against her, the soft texture of his hair on her face, and the sticky kiss he planted on her cheek.

"Well?" Hunt demanded. "Do you mean to let me bleed to death, after all?"

"What?" The irritation in his voice jerked her from

her thoughts. "Oh. No," she replied quickly. "I'll do as you say."

"I think you wanted to sew it so that you could enjoy every prick of the needle," he grumbled.

"No," she answered softly. "No, I wouldn't." Putting that needle into Jamie's skin was terrible, she thought, but it had had to be done. And so did this.

He wrapped himself in a second blanket, took the torch, and led her back through the maze to the campsite without speaking. When they reached the fire, Hunt pulled a spare linen shirt from his pile of belongings and handed it to her.

"Thank you," she said shyly. Elizabeth turned her back and wiggled into the soft, worn garment. It was clean, but it smelled like Hunt. The white shirt covered her almost to her knees. She rolled back the sleeves and draped the blanket around her shoulders again.

Among the Iroquois, she'd become used to seeing the unclad bodies of other people and she'd regularly exposed her own breasts to public view. She shouldn't have felt self-conscious around Hunt, but for some reason she did. His offering the shirt without being asked was another act of kindness, and she was grateful.

When she looked at the prisoner, she saw that he was fully awake. He glared back at her with hooded eyes full of malice. "What will we do with him?" Elizabeth murmured to Hunt.

"I haven't decided." Hunt added wood to the fire. He motioned to his head. "Let's get this over with."

"Have you needle and thread?" she asked.

"I do, in my hunting bag, but you're not sewing me up."

"It's your head."

"You're damned right it is."

She glanced back at Powder Horn, and again, a strong foreboding came over her. "You should kill him," she said to Hunt. "If you don't—"

"If you want him killed, help yourself."

"I can't do it now. I could have—before—when he was trying to kill me."

"Exactly my point."

She shook her head. "You don't understand. I know the Iroquois. I've lived with them. If you let him live, he'll come after us. He won't stop until we're dead or he is. It's a matter of honor."

Hunt shrugged. "My honor won't let me murder a helpless man."

"You'll be sorry."

"It won't be the first time." He sat cross-legged on the buffalo robe and motioned to his head. "All right."

Stoically, he allowed her to bind up the wounds in his scalp. Carefully, she examined the other two places where fragments of rock had struck the back of his head, but they weren't deep enough to worry about. "I wish I had some powdered root of Solomons Seal," she said. "It would keep this from festering."

"That I don't have, but I'll be fine," he said.

She tied a final knot. "I just wanted to be certain that one stayed shut. That should do it," she said with a sigh of relief. He hadn't complained about the pain and that pleased her. Her hands hadn't been as steady as she'd wished, but being so close to Hunt unnerved her.

"Good," he answered. "Now let me look at your burns."

"They're nothing."

He took her hands in his and turned her palms up. "I've some ointment in a tin container in that bag."

She chuckled. "Is there anything you don't carry in there?"

"No Solomons Seal." He grinned at her. "I spend a lot of time in the woods alone. It pays for a man to be able to look after himself."

"You're not married?" The question slipped out without her realizing she was going to ask. She felt her face flush and wondered when she'd become so brazen.

"No."

"Not ever?"

"No." He dug in the bag until he found the medicine, opened the lid, and began to apply the ointment to her hands with gentle care.

His touch made her go all soft inside. "Most men—" she began breathlessly.

"I'm not the marrying kind, Beth."

Why did that bother her? And why was he calling her Beth? Hunt Campbell and his past meant nothing to her. But she still had to ask. "You've never wanted children?"

"Young ones need a spot to take roots in and a father that stays put."

"You don't like children?"

"Other people's are fine. They aren't my responsibility."

"But—"

"This is leading somewhere, isn't it?" he demanded, lowering his voice so that Powder Horn couldn't hear what he was saying. "I'm not going back for your son. I'm sorry. I know it's hard to accept, but he's better off—you're both better off—if he stays with Yellow Drum."

She jerked her hand back. "You don't know everything. And you don't know what's right for my Jamie." Or my little Rachel, she almost said. "You don't."

He took her arm and she went rigid. "I'm not going to hurt you," he said. Taking a firm hold on her hand, he pulled her firmly into the tunnel. He dragged her along until they were well out of earshot of the prisoner. "Stop acting like you think I'm going to knock your head off," he snapped. "I won't. Now stand here and listen to what I have to say."

"I'm standing," she said.

"But are you listening? I'd say I know a lot more about your son's situation than you do," he replied. "Your experience with the Seneca was a bad one, but the Iroquois are good people. Their ways are different, but that doesn't make them wrong. The English have nearly destroyed a way of life that existed here for time out of time. Call them savages if you like, but there's nothing the Iroquois have done to whites that the Europeans didn't do to them first."

"You condone scalping? Murder of innocent children?"

He shook his head. "Bad things happen in war—to both sides. I've seen Indian babies slaughtered, Indian women raped, villages and crops destroyed by white Christians. My birth sister's husband, Simon Brandt, burned a church full of Indian women and children. He took Indian scalps and sold them to the English. And he wasn't particular whether he took those scalps from hostiles or friendlies."

"I won't argue that there are good Indians, even good Iroquois. I had many friends among the tribe; there were people I came to care about."

"Then you've got to realize that there is a place with the Seneca for your son and no place for him in Charles Town. Stop thinking about what you want, and think of Jamie's good."

Anger flared within her. Why couldn't Hunt understand? A mother's love for her children meant more than life itself. Surely, she could find someplace that would accept Jamie and Rachel for the beautiful human beings they were—even if she had to leave the country and take them to England. First she had to get them away from Raven and Yellow Drum. "Jamie's only a little boy," she argued. "I'm his mother. He needs me."

"An Indian mother will love him just as much."

"Never!" She balled her fists into tight knots. "You have to listen to me. Yellow Drum's chief wife is Raven. You saw her. She's an evil woman. She hates Jamie and—" Elizabeth bit off her next word. She couldn't tell Hunt about Rachel. If he wouldn't go back for one, what would he do for two? "Hunt, please," she said, trying to contain her desperation. "Jamie's not safe with Raven."

"He's Yellow Drum's son, isn't he?"

"Yes, his only son. But he has a new wife. If she has a child—"

"It doesn't matter. Jamie is a fine boy. Any father would be proud of him. A man like Yellow Drum won't let harm come to his son."

"Not his son. Mine."

"He loves him, doesn't he?" Hunt asked.

"Yes, of course, but—"

"Sometimes we have to make sacrifices for those we love," he argued. "You can't protect Jamie from being hated by whites for the color of his skin. Even a child feels hate."

"You're wrong about this," she insisted.

"Maybe, but I won't risk getting both of us killed over it. When you get home to Charles Town, talk to your father. Maybe he can arrange for someone to buy the boy from—"

She scoffed. "Do you think I'm a fool that I'd be-lieve that. It didn't work with me, did it? Yellow Drum would never sell Jamie."

"Or let him go peaceably." He swore softly. "Hate me for this if you have to," he said, "but in time, you'll come to understand that this is what's best for both of you."

"Nothing I can say or do will change your mind?"

"No. I intend to get both of us back to your father's house in one piece—with our hair intact. And mess-ing with a Seneca war chief's only son is the quickest way I can think of to end up dead and without my scalp. We've argued over this too many times. I don't intend to discuss it with you again." He turned on his heel and returned to the fire. Still highly agitated, she followed him.

Hunt took Powder Horn's rifle, found his hunting bag, and began to reload the weapon. Elizabeth set the campsite in order, then she took the rabbits the Onondaga had brought to one side of the chamber and started to clean them for cooking. She worked swiftly, as she always did when she was angry, but the familiar task did nothing to ease her agitation. Fi-nally, she threw down the carcass she was skinning and walked over to Hunt.

"So what we've been through together, that means nothing to you?" she said, unconsciously using Iro-quoian.

He was testing the thongs on a snowshoe. Patiently, he laid down the wooden frame and spoke to her with careful compassion. "It means something, Elizabeth. It means a lot. I care about you, I really do. More than you can realize. But I won't be tempted, bribed, or taunted into getting us killed for a lost cause."

She turned away. "All right."

"All right?"

"You heard me."

"You're giving up?"

"I can't keep fighting you, Hunt. I can't go back for Jamie alone, I realize that. And if you won't, you won't."

"Why don't I believe a word of it?"

It was her turn to shrug. "I'm not stupid. I know when to accept defeat."

"You don't look defeated. Where are the tears?"

She swallowed the lump in her throat. She hated resorting to deceit, but sometimes that was a woman's only weapon. "I'm not a weeping woman," she answered softly. "I don't like your decision. I'll never believe you're being fair to me or to Jamie, but I have to live with it."

"Liar."

"You've won, Hunter. I don't have the strength to fight you anymore," she lied.

"Look at me and tell me that."

She faced him again, her features as emotionless as those of any Iroquois squaw. "You've won," she repeated softly. "And I hope your conscience lets you sleep nights, because mine never will."

"You won't try to escape?"

"No," she whispered.

He stared into her eyes for long seconds. "I hope you mean that. I really do, because we've got a lot of days and nights to spend together. I hope we can spend them as friends."

"Are you my friend?"

"I am."

"And you don't want anything more from me than friendship?" she murmured.

"I'm not a man to be ruled by his cock, Elizabeth. If I could tumble you without harm to either of us, I would. But you're not that kind of a woman. You couldn't be content with a little innocent fun. You'd expect more of me than I can give. You've had enough trouble in your life, and I don't mean to add to it."

Her eyes narrowed. "You think I'm interested in you?"

"I didn't say that," he answered gruffly. "You don't make it easy on a man. I took a job, and I intend to fulfill my side of the bargain without compromising you."

"And if I wanted to be . . ." She made a small sound that could have been amusement. "Compromised?"

"I guess we'll face that when we come to it."

"If we come to it," she answered.

"Keep your hands off me and I'll keep mine off you."

"That's a bargain I'll enjoy keeping!"

# Chapter 9

Hunt and Elizabeth spent another two days in the cave behind the falls waiting for the weather to break. To Hunt's surprise, Elizabeth proved to be good company. She didn't bring up the subject of her son again, and she seemed to hold no grudge against him because of it. He'd always hated whining women, and he admired her for taking defeat with such good grace.

He was amazed at how much he enjoyed hearing her laugh, and she laughed easily. He'd thought her to be a sad woman, but he saw now that the sorrow was only a small part of her complex personality. Not only was she naturally cheerful, but she knew when to keep silent and listen. When she did speak, it was to say something sensible.

"Do you know how to play the peach stone game?" she asked him after the morning meal when he was lying idle on his buffalo skin. "If you are bored with the waiting, I could teach you."

"Do you have peach stones?"

She giggled. "No peach pits, but I could make dice from some of those round pebbles in the passageway. I will mark one side with charcoal from the fire pit."

"Six or nine stones?" he asked.

**114**

"Six." She held out a handful, already marked.

"Certain of yourself, aren't you?" he teased. "What if I'd said no?"

She shrugged. "Then we wouldn't have played, would we?" She put the playing pieces on a strip of hide. "We don't have the proper bowl, but the stones will still flip on the skin. We can keep score—"

"What shall we bet?" he asked.

"Oh, you want to gamble?" Her green eyes widened in surprise.

Her lashes were long and dark and luxurious . . . they were eyes a man could lose himself in if he wasn't careful. *She's not a woman to take lightly*, he reminded himself. Still, he couldn't keep his gaze off her—her vitality burned like a living flame.

"My father disapproves of gambling," she replied primly. "He always said it was a sin."

"We don't have to bet anything if you don't want to," he answered. "Among the Cheyenne, gambling is considered quite acceptable. All respectable women play at games of chance."

She settled down across from him on the buffalo hide. "We can wager if you like," she offered. "My earrings against yours?" She averted her eyes. "Of course, you have only one but it's more valuable than mine. If you don't care to—"

"I thought you didn't gamble."

"Whatever pleases you, Hunt."

He chuckled. "I warn you, I'll take no pity on you because you're a lady. I'll keep your earrings if I win them."

"Of course. You go first."

An hour later, when he'd lost the shirt he'd loaned her, his knife and sheath, and the earring, he began to get suspicious. "For a woman who doesn't gamble, you're very good at it. Are you certain you aren't cheating?"

She looked shocked. "At the peach stone game? Me?" She smiled and a dimple winked on one cheek. "My father said that cheating was a sin. He—"

"I think I've heard enough of your father's wisdom, and I've had enough of this game. Next, you'll have my buffalo skin."

She shook her head. "Don't want it. Too heavy to carry. Besides . . ." She picked at a section of hair. "It looks as though it's getting moth-eaten. The hair's falling out."

"It is not," he protested. "This is a perfectly good hide. It will last me a lifetime."

She looked unconvinced. "If you say so, Hunt. We could bet the skin against your earring."

"Absolutely not." He got to his feet. "I know when to quit." He grimaced. "I should have had you with me after my canoe overturned. We could have gone down to Williamsburg and gotten ourselves a high-stakes card game with the rich tobacco planters. We could have won the money I needed."

Later that afternoon, using a torch for light, he took her far back into one of the low tunnels and showed her the pictures drawn long ago on the walls by some ancient native people. "My father told me that these were here," he explained. "I thought you might like to see them."

"I've never seen anything like these designs among the Seneca," she said, placing her hand over a red-ocher outline of a long-dead warrior's handprint.

"I don't think they were left by the Iroquois. According to the Delaware legends, the Iroquois tribes came here from the south, hundreds of years ago. My guess is that these drawings were made thousands of years ago." He lifted the torch so that the flickering light could illuminate the magnificent sketch of an elk with towering antlers. A mountain lion, perfectly drawn to the outstretched claws and bristling whiskers, sprang toward the elk from an outcrop of rock overhead.

Elizabeth stared in awed silence.

"Seen enough?" he asked finally.

"Let's stay a little longer," she begged. "It's a holy place, isn't it? It feels almost like being in a church."

He nodded. "I've not been in enough churches to know, but yes, it is a holy spot. You can feel the power here." He reached out and took her hand. For the first time, she didn't flinch. "Look," he said, pointing toward a crack in the floor.

"Oh! It's a snake!"

The serpent was drawn in red; it seemed to crawl up out of the earth below. Several hops ahead of the open jaws, a merry brown mouse scampered, tail in the air, tiny, upthrust nose peering ahead for an eternity.

"Oh, look," she cried. "It's wonderful. You can almost hear it squeaking!" She squeezed his hand. "Thank you, Hunt," she said. "Thank you for sharing this with me. I'll never forget it, never."

*And I'll never forget how you look in the torchlight*, he thought, as his heart beat just a little faster. . . . *With that smudge of dirt on your chin, that curling lock of red-gold hair falling over one eye, and my silver earring in your ear.*

For over an hour they crawled into corners and explored the cubbyholes of the cavern. Every inch of the walls had been decorated. Some animal figures were painted in rich hues; others were only sketched with charcoal. But all looked as though they had been created by master artists.

"Do you believe it was done by one man?" Elizabeth asked.

He shook his head. "Generations of men, I'd say."

"Mother had paintings, portraits of our family, and one of Mary Queen of Scots, but I never cared for them. These make me want to cry."

"I didn't bring you here to make you sad," he said.

"I'm not. I'm content, perfectly content."

"Well, neither of us will be content if this torch burns out and leaves us in pitch darkness. We'd best go back and check on our guest. We wouldn't want him to get loose and leave before we do."

"All right," she agreed reluctantly. "Good-bye, little mouse. Keep ahead of that snake."

"I'm sure he'll do that," Hunt said. "If the snake hasn't caught him yet, I doubt he ever will."

Elizabeth chuckled and followed him back up the narrow passage to their camp. Powder Horn lay as they'd left him, legs drawn up, arms bound behind his back, and black eyes wide open, glaring with malevolence.

Finally, when Hunt thought the weather would hold, the two of them set out southwest on snow-shoes. In the end, Hunt decided to leave Powder Horn tied up in the cavern. The Iroquois's knee was swollen, and the Indian was still weak from the whack Elizabeth had given him on the head.

"By the time he works those leather strips loose, we'll be far enough away that we won't have to worry about him," Hunt said.

"Don't count on it," Elizabeth warned. "He's not going to let us go that easily." She felt it in her bones. If Hunt wouldn't listen to her, there'd be hell to pay. She knew it.

"Must you dispute everything I say?"

She kept her voice mild. "Only when you're wrong."

His eyes narrowed. "And you're the judge of that?" he asked with a hint of amusement in his soft drawl.

"I wouldn't be alive if I hadn't learned something about the Iroquois. I say you'll regret it if you leave this man alive."

"Maybe," he conceded, "but life comes dear. I'll not take it without good reason."

"For a man who's lived on the frontier, you have strange ideas."

Hunt chuckled. "For a woman from Charles Town—"

"Charles Town was a long time ago," she replied, cutting him off. "You think this is some sort of game between you and Powder Horn, but it's not. It's serious."

"So's murder, Elizabeth." He nodded toward the cave entrance. "We've miles to make before dark."

"Just so you realize what you're doing."

"I should have thought longer about that before I took your daddy's money."

She sighed with resignation and followed him out under the waterfall and along the slippery, ice-covered boulders to the snow-covered forest. There, they donned the snowshoes and shouldered their packs.

They'd divided up Hunt's goods. He'd carried them into Iroquois land on his horse, the animal that Raven had claimed as part of the price for Elizabeth. Now, in deep snow, there was only so much weight they could carry. Hunt had taken Powder Horn's rifle, powder and shot, and the heavy buffalo robe, as well as his clothes, rifle, and hunting bag. Elizabeth's load consisted of several pounds of pemmican, Powder Horn's knife and tomahawk, and two blankets. She'd argued that she was strong and could take some of his burden, but he would have none of it.

"I mean to travel fast," Hunt said. "Now that the sun's come out and the temperature has risen, the Iroquois will be stirring like bees from a spring hive. The sooner we put the lake country behind us, the better. We're better than nine hundred miles from Charles Town."

"You should have left the buffalo hide if you want to make time."

"We may need it as shelter. Besides, I like my buffalo skin. Where would I get another one this side of the Mississippi?"

"I still say it's moth-eaten."

"It's not moth-eaten!"

Elizabeth concentrated on keeping her bearings and remembering landmarks so that she wouldn't get lost when she returned this way. She'd learned to use snowshoes in the years she'd lived with the Iroquois, and her pack was light. If they hadn't been traveling farther away from her children with each step, she would have enjoyed the vigorous walk with Hunt through the sparkling white forest. She had never felt so alive—so filled with the expectation that anything was possible.

Sunlight turned the evergreens and shrubs into a fairy land of glistening pinecones, ice-tipped boughs, and lacy needles. Now and then the blazing plumage of a cardinal would flash red against the snow-frosted branches of an ancient hardwood, and the rat-ta-ta-ta of giant pileated woodpeckers echoed through the trees and hollows.

Hunter Campbell might have been a white man, but he was a skilled woodsman. He'd been so talkative when they were in the cave that she'd been afraid he'd lack the good sense to be quiet on the trail. She needn't have worried. Hunt was as wary as a cougar. No bird called or branch snapped that he didn't notice and identify. His sense of direction was true. At first, she'd wondered about that when he'd angled south-west instead of straight south.

"If anyone tries to follow us now, our tracks are plain for even a child to see," he explained when she asked. "But if the snow melts, or if we get a few more inches, they won't be able to trail us so easily. I told them I was going north. I know this route, and I think we can reach Delaware hunting grounds in a few days."

His reasoning was sound enough, even if he was taking her where she didn't want to go. They pressed hard all morning and stopped to break ice for drinking water in a rocky stream when the sun was high overhead. Hunt had leaned his rifle against a rock, removed his mittens, then rinsed his hands and cupped them in the crystal-clear flow so that she could drink.

Elizabeth's heartbeat quickened as she knelt to sip from his hands. The water was cold and pure, so sweet that it tasted almost as if it had been mixed with wild honey. Her lips brushed his skin as she drank, and the intimate sensation caused her to tremble.

"Cold?" he asked her.

She looked up into burning eyes as dark and mys-terious as any Indian's. "No, she murmured. "Not cold." He caught her upper arms and helped her to her feet, an awkward movement in snowshoes. Then each took a handful of the dried meat, fat, and berry mixture known as pemmican and chewed while they walked on.

Elizabeth's lips still tingled, and her blood raced. Hunt's lean hands had left invisible brands where his fingers had gripped her through the layers of her

clothing. His enigmatic gaze had unlocked some
sealed box deep within her breast that she'd not
known existed until this moment. She felt as light as
thistledown. The pack on her back had lost its weight,
and she seemed to gain strength with every step.

*He wants me,* she thought. *It doesn't matter that I'm
ugly or that Yellow Drum has used me these past years.
Hunt wants me just the same.* She clasped her mittened
gloves together and tried to subdue the bubbling excitement that made her want to shout for joy.

*He wants me,* she repeated over and over. And then
a delicious thought formed and surfaced in the recesses of her mind. *I want him as well.*

Daily living in an Iroquois communal lodge had
soon eroded away English notions of privacy. She had
heard and seen the full range of human functions,
from belching to copulation. She'd not been able to
block out the night moans of sexual pleasure from
Raven's lips or keep herself from smelling the distinct
odor of desire. Later, when Yellow Drum had deflow-
ered her, she'd felt his hands on her where no man
had ever touched her before. She'd wept as he drove
his erect phallus deep into her body; and in time,
she'd quickened with his seed. She had carried two
children to birth, but she had never known joy in a
man's passion.

She'd thought of it often. What girl wouldn't? The
other women had teased and laughed about the sexual prowesses or lack of it in their lovers, but she had
never felt the excitement or pleasure they clearly did.
She desperately wanted to experience the desire—the
rapture—of mating that others boasted of, but it had
remained a mystery. Until now. . . .

When Hunt had held her in the cave, when he'd
kissed and touched her, she'd felt a stirring of longing. But even that heated fervor was nothing like the

sensations that seethed within her body here in this snow-covered forest.

She could not keep her eyes off him. Each stride he made, each movement, stirred her imagination. His shoulders were broad and muscular beneath his fringed leather hunting coat, but she fantasized about pulling that jacket over his head and running her fingers over his tanned, bare skin. She wanted his hands to grip her unclothed skin, his mouth to kiss and suck her breasts, his hard body to press against her heated loins. . . .

Once a gray fox crossed their path, loping gracefully over the snow and startling her from her sensual reverie. She watched breathlessly until the beautiful animal vanished among the trees. "He didn't seem afraid of us," she said to Hunt.

He smiled at her, a slow, roguish grin that crinkled the corners of his eyes and lit his features from within.

He took as much pleasure from seeing the fox as she did, and she knew it. She was so happy that she wanted to laugh out loud. She'd always loved animals; she'd secretly cared for a bird with a broken wing until it could fly again. And once, she had nursed a rabbit back to health. No one had ever known of her strange feelings except her children. If Raven had ever caught her tending a rabbit, instead of skinning it, she'd have knocked her across the head with a stout stick.

"The fox is smart," Hunt said. "The wild ones know when a predator is hunting and when he isn't. I've seen buffalo and a grizzly bear drinking together from the same waterhole, and songbirds perching in a tree beside a hawk who'd eaten his fill." He shrugged. "We meant the fox no harm and he knew it."

They walked on, and Elizabeth tried to remember

the fox and to picture the buffalo gathering around a pool to drink, but her thoughts betrayed her. Instead, she summoned up the image of Hunt's mischievous grin and the way he cocked his head slightly when he spoke.

*He does want me,* she repeated to herself. *What harm could there be if I let him make love to me?* She was no virgin and no amount of weeping or prayer could change that fact. Who would be hurt if—just once—she let him make a woman of her? The temptation was enough to warm her all over. And as she hurried on, the creaking of the leather ties on her snowshoes seem to echo her question. *Why not? Why not?*

In late afternoon, clouds drifted across the face of the sun and the wind picked up. Two deer, nibbling at young branches, vaulted into the air at Hunt and Elizabeth's approach and leaped away, white tails flashing alarm. "You must have been thinking of roast venison," she teased.

"I was," he admitted, "but I'd not risk a rifle shot. Sound carries a long way in these hills."

Elizabeth's back and legs were beginning to ache again, and her cheeks felt hot and wind-burned despite the bear grease Hunt had given her to rub on them. It was definitely growing colder by the minute. Now and then a few drops of sleet splattered against her face. Her hands were stiff inside her fur mittens. She wanted to ask Hunt where they would find shelter, but her years among the Iroquois had left too great a scar. A slave did not ask questions. She was no longer a slave, but the habit of not asking was too ingrained. Instead, she shifted her pack and kept walking.

Lifting one leg and then the other was hard, so Elizabeth stopped thinking about making love to Hunt and concentrated on her daughter's face. Sweet baby Rachel, so mischievous, so dear to her. . . . Rachel was three now. She'd grown so fast. Her chubby little legs were sturdy enough for her to keep pace with a grown woman for the better part of an hour, and she was smart—really smart for her age. She could tell a robin's egg from a bluebird's, and she knew dozens of nursery rhymes in English.

Where had the years gone? How was it possible that the infant nursing at her breast was now three winters—Elizabeth corrected herself—three *years* old?

Both children resembled their father. Jamie's bones were finer than Yellow Drum's; perhaps his nose would not be as dominant as his father's when he was grown, but his dark brown sloe eyes and high cheekbones were Iroquois. Rachel's skin was a shade lighter, but she, too, carried the beautiful Indian eyes and the sturdy body of her paternal ancestors. Whatever Elizabeth might have hoped before they were born, her son and daughter could never pass as English. It didn't matter; to her, they were beautiful, perfect, the joy of her life.

Moisture clouded her eyes, and she blinked. The thickening in her throat was not so easy to dispel. Her children would believe she had abandoned them. Jamie might have some idea of the truth, but little Rachel would never understand why her mother was no longer there to cook her supper, kiss away her bruises, and tuck her into bed. Rachel would be hysterical. The child would refuse to eat and would cry herself to sleep as she'd done when Elizabeth had spent two nights away from the home village on a fishing trip with Yellow Drum in early fall.

And Jamie? How well she knew her son's reaction. Jamie tried so hard to be a man to please his father. Her son's defense against her absence would be anger. He'd pout and withdraw into himself. Jamie would never weep, but his dreams would be troubled, and he'd watch the lodge entrance for her.

How many days and nights would they mourn her before they began to forget her voice or the smell of her hair? Elizabeth stared at Hunt's back. He was a good man, a sensible man. Why couldn't he see that it was impossible for a mother to leave her child? Why couldn't he understand that all his logical reasons for abandoning Jamie to the Iroquois were nothing compared to the ache that burned in her heart?

"Don't be afraid, darlings," she whispered. "Mama won't forget you. Be brave just a little longer."

Shadows cast by the winter-barren trees grew dark, and the sun began to set beyond the western hills. "Can you go on for a while?" Hunt asked.

She nodded, unwilling to waste the energy to speak. Those who could not keep up when the Iroquois were on the march rested forever. After she'd been captured—on the trip back to Seneca country—she'd seen another prisoner's head crushed by a war club because she couldn't keep up with the warriors. She hadn't known the woman. The Seneca had burned her cabin and slain her grown sons and husband. Elizabeth had seen the killing and smelled the awful scent of burning flesh when they'd fired the log dwelling. Elizabeth shuddered. Hunt thought her bloodthirsty, did he? She had seen enough slaughter to last a lifetime, but she had learned the lessons of survival well. If her will was strong enough, her body would respond. She would never admit that she could not walk, not if her feet froze to chunks of ice or wild beasts gnawed at her vitals.

She smiled. With such determination, could she fail to find a way to support her children once she had them safe? She had taken the strike of a copperhead snake to protect Jamie when he was hardly more than an infant.

It had been early summer, and Jamie had just learned to walk. His wobbly efforts had made her laugh, and he was down more than up, but nothing would make him crawl again. He'd climb up on to anything his fat little hands could reach, sway on his bare feet, and set off at a drunken gallop.

Elizabeth had gone to the river with Raven and two other women, Honey Tree and Summer Rain. Honey Tree had a little girl of four years; Summer Rain had brought a young sister with her. Elizabeth had put Jamie down to dip up water, and he'd toddled off after the two girls.

The sun was warm on Elizabeth's face, and the riverbank smelled of crushed mint. Raven and Summer Rain were gossiping about a coming marriage in the village, and Elizabeth was as happy as she'd been for weeks. Jamie had been cutting a tooth, and it had finally broken through and gleamed like a glistening pearl in his pink mouth.

Then Honey Tree's daughter screamed. Elizabeth dropped the waterskin and whirled around. A waist-high heap of rocks separated her from Jamie, and on top of the stones curled a red-brown snake with a flat head and bright triangular markings. Jamie squealed with delight and extended his hand to grab the poisonous copperhead.

"No!" she screamed. There was no way to reach her son, no time to think. Driven by a mother's desperation, she seized the serpent and hurled it into the river. Jamie wailed in disappointment as the copperhead flew through the air out of reach. She'd been fast enough to save her son, but not quick enough to avoid the copperhead's fangs; they'd driven into her hand like red-hot needles.

She didn't need to look down to know she'd been hit, but that didn't matter. Jamie was what mattered, and she gathered him in her arms and covered his face and head with kisses. He kicked and cried, angry that she'd stolen his new toy; he was still protesting when Honey Tree pried him from her arms.

The women pushed her to the ground. Summer Rain made quick cuts with her knife and sucked out the poison. For two days, Elizabeth lay between life and death, but she'd survived and she'd kept her son from harm. If poisonous snakes or Seneca couldn't defeat her, how could the English?

"We should cross another creek soon," Hunt said, interrupting her thoughts. "After that, we follow it north. A Frenchman has a cabin—"

"A Frenchman?" She was so surprised that she forgot her weariness. "Here? On Iroquois land?"

"His name is Baptiste. They say he was once a Jesuit priest, but he lost his faith and finally his reason in these woods. He's totally mad. Lives out here with only a tame bear for company."

"Why haven't the Iroquois killed him?"

"You shouldn't have to ask that," Hunt said. "I've never known a tribe who didn't think that the afflicted were touched by the Great Spirit."

"You think we can find shelter with this . . . Baptiste?"

"Yes, I do. He and his wife, Clay Basket—"

"He has a wife?"

Hunt glanced back at her and grinned. "I told you he was crazy."

"But a priest . . ." She shook her head in disbelief. "A Catholic priest can never marry."

"It's a woods alliance. Clay Basket is Iroquois—a woman of the Cayuga. She was a widow without children or relatives to hunt for her. Her people cast her out to die in a bad winter. She and Baptiste get on well enough. She's deaf and doesn't mind his ranting. They've lived together for years."

"Mad or not, may he have a good fire."

"Not only a fire," Hunt said, "but a snug cabin with a fireplace. There used to be a Jesuit mission and school there, but the students caught the pox from the black robes and died. Then the Iroquois murdered the other priests in retaliation. I think the loss of the children was what destroyed Baptiste's mind. He'd spent his life trying to bring his religion to the Indians and he loved them."

"You've met him?"

"Yes. On my journey to Yellow Drum's village. My father knew Baptiste."

Elizabeth quickened her step to catch up to him. Her legs were cramping, but she tried to ignore the pain. "Which father? Your Indian father or—"

"I was born over the sea in Ireland. The man who sired me was honorable, but I never knew him. He died when I was an infant. After that, I had no father. My white sister's husband despised me. The only thing I ever got from him was a hard fist or stripes across my back." Hunt's features hardened. "If I speak of my father, I mean only one person, Wolf Robe. My father is Cheyenne, from the western mountains, but he lived among the Shawnee and they called him the Stranger. His wife, my mother, was Delaware. It is from her that I inherit my tribal allegiance to the Delaware and their brothers, the Shawnee."

"But you were born Irish," she argued. "You're white, not Indian at all."

He shook his head, surprised that he had told her what he'd told few people in his life. His past was his own and best kept to himself. She was English, for all she'd lived among the Iroquois, while he was only white on the outside. Whatever he'd been at eight years old, when Wolf Robe carried him off, that part had died like last summer's grass. He was Hunter of the Far Mountains, a warrior of the Delaware and Cheyenne. He'd earned the right to wear two eagle feathers and be welcomed at the council fires of the Shawnee.

The Campbells might have washed the Indian war paint off his face, dressed him in white man's clothing, and taught him his manners, but all that was only skin deep. Once he'd completed this mission and returned Elizabeth to her father, he fully intended to set his sights on the Rocky Mountains and not look back until he reached them.

Elizabeth's right snowshoe sunk into a soft spot and she nearly pitched to one side. Instantly he reached out to catch her arm and steady her.

"Thank you," she said, and flashed a smile at him that made his heart plummet.

"You all right?" he asked gruffly. The wave of protectiveness that engulfed him was nearly overpowering.

She nodded. "Yes."

"Let's push on. The creek can't be far ahead." He tried not to think about the effect touching Elizabeth had on him. He wanted her so badly that his loins ached. It was hard for him to keep his eyes on the trail and his senses alert for danger. His cock had nearly gotten them both killed back in the cave, and he tried never to make the same mistake twice. Elizabeth was depending on him to get her safely through this, and he couldn't let her down.

Damn, but he'd supposed they would make better time than they had. He hoped to reach Baptiste's place before nightfall. The sleet was coming down harder and the wind was in their faces. Elizabeth had done well, but he could see that her strength was failing. "I can take your pack," he offered.

"I'll carry my own pack."

"You're tired."

"And you're not?"

He shrugged. "Not so much that I couldn't take your load." *And carry you as well, if I have to,* he thought. *I've done it before.*

She shook her head. "I'm all right."

He brushed the sleet from his eyes and immediately caught sight of a dark shadow slipping through the trees. As he stared into the gathering twilight, he saw a second form and then a third. "Wolves," he said, pointing. "Don't worry, they're no danger to us."

Elizabeth grimaced. "I hate wolves."

He forced a grin. "Probably after those deer we saw earlier."

"I hope," she replied.

His guess proved true. As they followed the gully downhill to a creek, they came upon a half dozen wolves circling a buck and two does. Two deer had reached the far side of the stream, but the third, a yearling doe, had broken through the ice and was trapped by the wolves.

"Stay close to me!" Hunt ordered, stepping out of his snowshoes. Giving a Cheyenne war cry, he charged the wolf pack. The buck and doe fled up the far bank, and the gray wolves scattered. The remaining deer struggled chest-deep in water, unable to reach safety due to a shattered foreleg.

Hunt dropped his pack and took careful aim with his rifle. One shot ended the injured animal's misery. As the deer slumped to one side and started to slide under the ice, Hunt plunged into the stream to seize the carcass.

The frigid water poured over the tops of his high moccasins and wet him to the waist. He waded over the rocky creekbed and reached out for the doe's hind leg. The current was swift under the ice; it tugged at his ankles and made his footing uncertain. He got a good hold on the deer and began to tug on the dead weight when he heard Elizabeth scream. Releasing the leg, he turned to look at her, slipped, and went down on one knee.

"Hunt!" she cried. "Wolf!"

Dragging his skinning knife from the sheath at his waist, he twisted around to see where she was pointing. Not ten feet away, another wolf—a huge white male—slunk toward him, back hunched high, belly to the snow. The animal's lips were drawn back in a snarl.

"No!" Elizabeth's second scream shattered the dusk as the giant wolf sprang at him with gaping mouth and ivory fangs.

# Chapter 10

The white wolf struck Hunt full in the chest, and they went down in the midst of broken ice and black rushing water. For long seconds, Elizabeth stood frozen with shock as wolf and man struggled. Huge jaws capable of biting through a man's thighbone snapped dangerously close to Hunt's face and throat. Then the wolf's snarls turned to a high-pitched keening as Hunt buried the blade of his knife deep in the animal's chest. Dark blood welled up and spilled over the thick fur, covering Hunt's hands and staining the front of his leather coat. The wolf's hind legs thrashed wildly, and then the fierce light faded from the creature's eyes.

Hunt staggered back and threw off the weight of the animal. Dazed, he looked down at the blood-stained knife he still held clenched in his right hand. His left sleeve was torn, and there were several rips down the front of his hunting shirt.

Elizabeth gave a low cry and started toward him. "Hunt, how bad are you hurt?" The current had pulled the wolf partially under the ice, but it lay limp, no longer moving. "Hunt?" Most of the blood belonged to the wolf, but it didn't seem possible that Hunt could sustain such a savage attack without being bitten.

"Get the rifle," he shouted.

Two wolves had come out of the trees and were moving down toward the stream. "Oh, my God!" Elizabeth shrugged off her pack and ran to the spot where Hunt had dropped his. She tore Powder Horn's rifle free and raised it to her shoulder. The hammer was stiff and hard to cock. Her fingers trembled under the strain.

"Shoot!" Hunt commanded.

She pulled the trigger. The force of the explosion sent her reeling back into the snow with the rifle on top of her. She scrambled up, peering through the semidarkness to see if she'd hit her target.

"Remind me to give you some target practice," Hunt said. He climbed the slippery bank and ran to his belongings. She hurried to his side as he reloaded first his own weapon and then Powder Horn's.

Elizabeth's shoulder felt as though she'd been kicked by a horse. "Did I kill the wolf?" she asked. "I don't see—"

"Not even close." He put an arm around her shoulder, and she looked down to see more blood seeping from his torn sleeve.

"You are hurt," she said. "How bad is—"

"Bad enough. Wolf bites are nasty."

She strained to see in the gathering dusk. "Are there—"

"Your shot went wild, but it scared them off." He handed her both rifles. "Keep them out of the snow," he ordered. Then he waded back into the creek and pulled out first the carcass of the deer and then the dead wolf.

"You said the wolves wouldn't harm us," she reminded him as he began to skin and butcher the deer.

"I was wrong," he admitted. "I'll just take the hindquarters, the liver, and the tenderloin. The pack won't stay away too long, not with the smell of all this blood."

"Leave the venison," she urged him.

"I'm taking enough to feed us for a few days. The wolves can have the rest."

"You're hurt. We don't need the meat. Let's go while we can."

"I fought for this venison, and I'm damned well going to eat some of it." Then his features turned serious, and he uttered something in a language she couldn't understand.

"What are you saying?" she asked.

"It's a prayer for the deer, an apology for taking its life."

"Hunt, it's getting dark. It's snowing; you're soaking wet, and we're surrounded by a wolf pack. It's time to go."

"This is the first time I've ever known a wolf that wasn't starving or sick to attack a man."

"How do you know it wasn't hungry?"

"If he'd landed on top of you, you'd know he wasn't starving. He was in prime condition. It makes no sense."

"Maybe he just didn't want you taking his deer."

"Maybe not," he conceded.

Elizabeth watched the forest nervously as he cut a few choice parts from the deer, rolled the meat in a section of hide, and slung it over his shoulder.

"Let me take the venison and the extra rifle," she offered. "It's too much for you to carry." The sleet had turned to snow and was coming down in earnest. Already the wolf's still form was nearly invisible. "This weather is turning bad. Suppose we're caught without shelter? The wolves—"

"You worry too much," he said. "It doesn't matter about the snow. The mission should be less than a mile upstream. A baby could find it with his eyes shut."

"And if you've miscalculated? If Baptiste's cabin is downstream instead of up?"

He laughed. "You of little faith."

Elizabeth kept close behind him as they set out. She didn't see how he could take his close call so lightly. When the wolf had leaped at Hunt, she'd nearly died of terror—fear not just for her own safety, but for him. If he had died . . .

He stopped and put a hand on her arm. "Don't be afraid," he said. "I'll take care of you."

She shivered. The rising wind and creak of the snowshoes couldn't cover the fierce growls and crunch of bone behind her as the wolf pack devoured the remains of the deer. And she couldn't keep herself from looking back over her shoulder to see if any of the animals were stalking them.

They pushed hard, and as the snow fell harder, Hunt began to whistle. Suddenly he stopped short and pointed. "There," he said. She stared, but saw nothing except swirling white. "It's the remains of the church," he explained. "The Indians burned it. The cabin lies beyond. Watch your step. Baptiste is always building something. You don't want to trip over—" He grunted and swore softly.

"What was it?" she asked.

"A post. God knows what one post is doing here." He stayed her with a touch. "I don't smell any wood-smoke, do you? There should be smoke from Baptiste's chimney. You stay here," he whispered.

"Not on your life. Where you go, I go."

He didn't try to stop her as she followed him across a cleared area, past another ruined building to the door of a small cabin. Hunt removed his snowshoes, and she did the same without being told.

The door was fastened on the outside with a wooden bar. Hunt lifted it, pushed the door open, and stepped inside. "Baptiste?" he called.

The only reply was a low meow. "A cat?" Elizabeth said in surprise. "He has a cat?" She stepped up into the darkened cabin and closed the door against the wind and snow. The meow had become a loud purr. Elizabeth dropped to her knees as the cat rubbed against her. "Nice kitty," she said.

"Stay put until I make a light," Hunt ordered. He crossed the room and Elizabeth heard him fumbling against the stone hearth. Something metal fell and clanked against the floor. "I found a fire kit," he said.

Elizabeth petted the cat and waited until a single spark flashed in the blackness.

"Just a minute," he said. He struck another spark and she saw a glow. Within minutes they had both fire and light.

Elizabeth looked around the tidy room. The floor was hard-packed clay, swept clean. A wooden shutter covered the single window, securely locked and barred from within. Traps and a fishnet hung on one wall; baskets and herbs and dried meat dangled from the rafters. There was a wide plank table, scarred from long use, three straight-back chairs with rush seats and a real four-poster bed. A covered crockery jar stood on the window shelf, and an unfinished pine-needle basket sat on a smaller worktable beside a woman's sewing bag. The table was set for two with blue-and-white porcelain plates and bowls, and two pewter goblets.

She could not resist touching a silver fork. How long had it been since she'd seen a proper table setting? Her lips curved upward in a smile. Her mother would think this cabin fit only for the lowest of her servants; even Ruth, the cook, lived better.

For a few seconds, Elizabeth allowed herself to think of her mother's dining room, set, as it often was, for thirty guests. Samuel, the butler, would stand near the hall door, directing a steady flow of maids in starched white caps and spotless aprons and footmen in red vests and breeches. The floor-to-ceiling windows facing the street would be open to catch the breeze off the water, and fan boys in feathered turbans would stand on either side of the heavily laden table pulling the cords connected to the curtain of sea grass matting overhead.

She could almost hear the clink of wineglasses, the murmur of voices . . . almost smell the delicious odors of fresh-baked biscuits hot from Ruth's kitchen: spicy shrimp, she-crab soup, and roast leg of lamb with mint. If she closed her eyes, she knew she'd be able to see her father at the head of the table, rising to offer a toast. And if she looked directly across from her chair, she would meet her brother Avery's mischievous grin. Avery, who—

"Elizabeth? Aren't you going to warm yourself—"

"Yes," she answered, startled from the hot autumn afternoon in Charles Town to the reality of this isolated cabin locked in the grip of another snowstorm. "Yes, I will." The English came easier to her lips now; she took pleasure in pronouncing the words correctly and hearing her own voice say them aloud. Yellow Drum had forbidden her to speak English. She had defied him by whispering to her children, but she had begun to forget her native tongue. A few more years in captivity and—

"Are you frozen solid, woman?" Hunt asked as he awkwardly pulled his hunting shirt over his head. "Get out of those wet moccasins and—"

"Oh," she cried. "I'm sorry, I forgot. You're hurt."

She shrugged off her heavy outer garments and went to him. "Let me see your arm."

"One bite is deep. The others aren't worth mentioning."

"Let me bind it to stop the bleeding," she offered. She glanced around the cabin, looking for a bit of cloth to use as a bandage.

"Not yet. The more it bleeds, the less likely the wound will sicken."

She shook her head. "Not for someone who lost so much blood back in the cave. I'll wash it thoroughly and . . ." She noticed a spiderweb in the corner, high up on the logs. "My mother's cook, Ruth, always said that spiderwebs will stop bleeding."

Hunt grimaced. "My father, Wolf Robe, used spiderwebs for bleeding too, but not for a puncture wound." He knelt on the edge of the hearth and picked up a burning stick.

Elizabeth blanched. "What are you doing?"

He blew out the flame, gritted his teeth, and pressed the glowing end of the branch into the deepest tooth mark. Elizabeth's stomach turned over as she heard the sizzle of human flesh. Hunt's face turned the color of tallow, and sweat beaded on his forehead.

She turned with a cry, ran to the door, and flung it open. Scooping up a handful of snow, she slammed the door and ran back to Hunt. He was still kneeling upright, but his eyes were glazed and he swayed a little. When he saw her coming with the snow, he nodded and held out his arm. Elizabeth clamped the snow over the burn and held it tight.

Hunt rose unsteadily and walked the few steps to a chair. Still sweating profusely, he pointed to a jug on a sideboard. "Get me that, will you," he asked hoarsely.

She brought the container and poured amber liquid

into a pewter goblet. Hunt lifted the cup and drank the rum in one long swallow. "Thanks," he gasped. "I'm not normally a man for spirits, but some things deserve a toast."

"You're crazy," she said, but she knew he was right. A puncture wound could bring lockjaw or turn gangrenous. Better a little agony now than to die horribly later. She poured a second goblet of rum. "Drink it," she advised. "It will help the pain."

"You're still in those wet moccasins," he said.

Sitting on the rug in front of the fire, she unlaced her high leather moccasins and slipped them off. For a few minutes, she allowed herself the luxury of toasting her bare feet, then she stood and lifted a large copper kettle from the iron crane. "I'll heat some water and start supper," she said.

Hunt tapped the crockery jug. "Will you have a glass? It will warm your insides."

She shook her head. "No, Father says I'm too young for—" She laughed. "I guess I'm not too young anymore, am I?" Shyly, she took the goblet he offered her. The rum burned her throat as it went down, but she forced herself to finish it all. "Thank you."

Hunt pushed the cork back into the opening of the jug. "All things in moderation, my father always said. I believe it to be wise judgment. Indians and Irishmen have a poor tolerance to alcohol."

"As do properly-brought-up girls from Charles Town," she replied. The rum had warmed her belly, but it made her a little giddy as well. She wasn't sure she liked the feeling. "I'll melt snow for—"

"Baptiste has a cistern, there." He pointed to the back of the room. "Beneath that wooden seat. The Jesuits are learned men. They devised all sorts of labor-saving inventions. I'm certain the water is full of spiders, but it should do for bathing and cooking."

"You expect me to cook with water full of bugs?" She made a face. "I'll start with snow, as I said before. That, at least, is clean and free of vermin." She relented a little. "But it takes a lot of snow to make water. I don't suppose it would hurt to heat the cistern water for bathing. A hot bath sounds like heaven."

He offered a wan smile. "It does, doesn't it. But grill a little venison first. My belly feels as empty as a dried gourd."

She nodded. "Mine too." The cat rubbed against her bare ankle and purred hopefully. "And I doubt if puss would turn down a hot meal either," Elizabeth said. "Where do you suppose the priest is?"

"He and his woman may have gone to trade for salt and tea. Baptiste has a passion for good English tea. Or they might be visiting some of her relatives."

"With Baptiste?"

Hunt shrugged. "Why not? He's safe enough. I told you, no Indian will harm a madman. They believe they'd lose their immortal soul if they did."

"Wherever they went, I'm grateful for the use of their cabin. I hope they don't mind."

"They're good people. They won't care. If they were here, they'd be honored to have us as guests."

"So long as we don't bring the wrath of the Iroquois down on them."

"Our scalps are the ones in danger. Baptiste's wife is under his protection. They have nothing to fear but the weather, sickness, and old age."

She looked around her at the stout log walls, the simple furnishings, and the stone fireplace. "Once I would have thought this a hovel; now it looks like a mansion to me."

"Your father is one of the wealthy few; he spends more on a suit of clothing than most settlers own in a year. My sister's cabin was poor compared to this. She said we were born in a manor in Ireland, but I couldn't say for sure. Maybe we were hard-pressed to make a living. Lots of the Irish are starving; that's why so many cross the sea."

"All this talk has done nothing to keep us from starving. You sit, or better yet, lie down. I'll prepare the meal."

Hunt uncorked the bottle and poured himself another two fingers of rum. He took a sip, then held his aching arm out over the stone hearth and slowly poured the remainder of the liquor in his goblet over the burn. It smarted like hell, but that was all right. At least he had an arm to hurt. It worried him that he'd not seen the wolf until the last possible moment. If he'd been killed, Elizabeth would have died as well. And she had suddenly become very, very important to him . . . maybe more important than he wanted to admit to himself. He let her wash his wounds and the single gash along his neck. The rum had gone to his head, and her hands were as gentle as her eyes. He wasn't drunk, but he'd had enough to dull the pain and set him to thinking along dangerous lines where Elizabeth was concerned.

He spoke little as she prepared the venison and a hot mush of cornmeal. Watching Elizabeth was restful. She worked swiftly with a natural grace, and she didn't chatter aimlessly. When she brought the food to the table, he surprised her by lifting the lid of the crockery jar and dipping thick maple syrup and ladling it over her mush.

"It's wonderful," she said, putting a finger in the sweet and licking it off. "Raven and I made maple syrup every spring, but she wouldn't let me eat it."

He smiled at her. "My Delaware Indian mother dribbled hot syrup in the snow to make candy. I never waited for it to cool and usually burned my mouth gobbling it down."

"The Iroquois women do the same. Rachel . . . Jamie," she corrected herself, "loved it. At home, Mother's cook used to make marzipan and taffy at Christmas, but I'm certain it never tasted this good." She chuckled. "I know the sugared rose petals didn't." She took another bite of the sweetened mush, then closed her eyes and sighed. "I'm warm and dry, and the wolves didn't get us. I think I'm in heaven."

"You're easily pleased, Elizabeth. More than most."

Her brilliant eyes fixed him with a penetrating green stare. "Perhaps," she answered softly. "Perhaps not."

The playful mood shattered, they finished their meal in near silence. Elizabeth cleared away the dishes, washed and dried them, and returned them to their places on the table. Then she looked into his face again. "I'd like to bathe in private," she said.

"Do you expect me to stand out in the snow?"

She laughed. "I do not, sir. The poster bed has draperies. If you'd lie down and pull them closed, then—"

He'd been waiting for her to bathe . . . to take down her hair and wash it. He always found something sensual about a woman washing her hair. "Why the sudden modesty?" he asked huskily. "It's not as though we haven't been sharing a camp." *Or that I haven't touched you*, he thought. *And kissed your breasts . . .*

Damn, but the room was growing overwarm. He'd been looking forward to a hot bath himself, but not nearly as much as he'd wanted to watch her bathe.

"I know it sounds foolish," she murmured, "but I haven't had privacy in a long time."

Her voice was as deep and rich as the golden aged rum. He swallowed, trying to dissolve the sudden constriction in his throat. What had they agreed on? He'd keep his hands off her if she'd keep hers off him? It seemed a stupid contract, one that hurt more than it helped.

Her eyes were as green as new mountain grass . . . as green and clear as Rocky Mountain jade, and they were framed by thick, dark lashes that fluttered like the wings of a dove. He'd always been a man to fancy a woman's eyes. Many a plain face held eyes full of fire or the promise of shared laughter and freely given love. Elizabeth's eyes drew him. When he stared into them, he felt every ounce of common sense draining away.

"You should lie down," she said. She touched his cheek, and tremors of yearning splintered through him. He nodded, not trusting his voice. He crossed to the bed and stretched out on it without removing his breeches. She drew the thin draperies closed around him and he lay in semidarkness, smelling the woman scent of her and wishing things were different between them.

He closed his eyes and listened as she dipped out the water into a tin basin and stepped out of her clothing. He heard her faint sigh as she sluiced the warm liquid over her bare skin. He heard the thud and crackle of wood as she stoked the fire, and when he could stand it no longer, he opened his eyes and looked through the worn bed curtain at her silhouette backlit by the roaring hearth.

His mouth was dry as his fingers tightened on the Hudson's Bay blanket. "Sweet Lord," he murmured.

Elizabeth . . . Beth was on her knees, hair unbound and hanging over the basin as she poured water over her tresses. The bright glow of firelight behind her left nothing to his imagination. Her small breasts were high and firm; her nipples formed perfect buds. Her waist was narrow above a flat belly and curving feminine hips. Her bare feet were tucked behind her, her arms lifted over her head.

He pushed back the drapery. "Can I help?" he called. "Scrub your back?"

Startled, she looked at him. For an instant he didn't know if she would turn angry or begin to cry. Instead, she remained motionless, gazing at him. Then, she smiled and extended a hand. "I'd like that ... very much," she answered, and her husky voice made him feel as if he'd just stepped off a precipice into thin air.

Their fingers brushed as he took the dipper from her hand, and a massive jolt of electricity shot through his body.

"Have you had much practice?" she asked him.

He let the water run slowly down her wet back. "Not enough." *God, but she was beautiful.*

She pushed a soapy cloth into his hand. "The center," she urged. "I can't reach the center."

He knelt beside her on the stones and began to rub slow, sensual circles along her spine. She sighed with pleasure, and he lowered his head and kissed the silken nape of her neck. It was damp and smelled like wildflowers.

"Lower."

He swallowed. He dipped the washrag in the basin, then squeezed it over the small of her back. The water ran down and collected in pools between her feet.

"Umm," she murmured.

He dropped the cloth and used his thumbs to massage her shoulders and the back of her neck. She turned to him and he lifted the dripping hair away from her face. "You're all wet," he said.

Her lips trembled and she looked at him with huge green eyes. "Yes, I am." She paused for a heartbeat. "And your breeches are getting wet as well."

"I'll have to do something about that."

"I suppose so," she answered.

"Close your eyes, Beth."

She obeyed him without question, and he shed his breeches so quickly that he snapped a leather tie. "Keep them shut," he reminded her.

She moistened her lips with the tip of her tongue. "Hurry, or I'll catch cold," she warned.

"I'll not let you be cold." The lid of the white crockery jar clattered to the table as he spooned out maple syrup and dribbled it onto a plate. Then he dipped his forefinger and anointed various parts of his own body.

"Hunt?"

He chuckled. "Keep your eyes closed." He carried the plate to the hearth, dipped his finger again and let two drops of syrup fall onto her left nipple.

She gasped. "What are you doing?"

"Dessert," he answered. "You'll like it, I promise."

# Chapter 11

**E**lizabeth trembled as the drops of cold sticky substance dripped onto her nipples. "What is it?" she asked. Her voice sounded strained, as breathless as though she'd run a long way. Hunt moved closer, so close that the heat from his body burned hotter than the flames at her back.

"Don't move," he teased lazily.

She kept her eyes shut—waiting. Another drop landed on her right breast and rolled slowly down into the hollow of her bosom. "What are you doing?" She was tempted to peek, but she didn't. "That's not water. What is it? Syrup? Is it maple syrup?" She couldn't keep from laughing.

"Shhh," he admonished. "I don't want to waste any."

She giggled as he spilled more between her breasts. Rivulets ran down to pool in her navel, then overflowed and ran lower.

"Hold still. This would be easier if you were lying down."

"Hunt, you're crazy." She was still shivering, but not from fear or cold but from anticipation. It was impossible to be afraid of a man who poured maple syrup over you.

"Trust me," he said.

Tentatively, she reached out. Her fingertips brushed his naked skin and closed around his erect phallus.

He groaned. "Woman, what are you—"

She felt him shudder under her touch. Shamelessly, she explored the substantial length of his tumescent manhood, caressing the sensitive tip with feather-light strokes, rubbing the engorged flesh until she felt his hot blood surge with primitive lust. "Oh," she cried. Her delight surfaced in a brazen outcry of wonder. "You want me."

The dipper tumbled from his hand onto the hearth-stones, splattering syrup over her bare feet. His powerful arms enfolded her, and he clutched her so hard against his sinewy chest that she could barely breathe.

"Beth," he commanded. "Look at me."

She opened her eyes. For the barest instant, a frisson of fear stabbed through her as she met the scalding force of raw lust in his gaze.

"If we do this, it has to be because you want it," he said, "not as payment for my stealing your child. Do you understand?"

"Yes."

"I want you, but I won't be bought."

"Yes," she whispered.

With a groan, he crushed his mouth against hers in a scorching kiss that caused the earth to sway under her feet. With that kiss, her terror vanished as though it had never existed, leaving in its wake a gathering storm of fevered desire unlike anything she'd ever known.

Her hands clenched his broad shoulders; her lips opened to receive his thrusting tongue. Her heart pounded wildly as he ground his loins against her. Instinctively, she strained to meet him, savoring the feel of his hard, throbbing manhood against her naked body.

Tears clouded her eyes as she parted her lips to welcome his ever-deepening kisses. *I'll remember this night forever*, she thought. *Forever.* Sweet sensations spilled through her body like fiery ribbons of sunshine. Her knees were so weak she wasn't sure they would hold her up. The fire crackled behind her; the stones were warm under her feet, but the conflagration within her burned with a brilliance that no earthly fire could match.

The taste of his mouth was intoxicating; his virile masculine scent made her mind reel. His callused fingers claimed her as his own, trailing down her face and throat with exquisite tenderness. With sensual strokes, he traced the line of her backbone and cupped her buttocks with lean, strong fingers. He kissed the corners of her lips, her ear and throat, then dropped to his knees and pressed his head between her breasts.

"Hunt, Hunt," she murmured. She cradled him against her, running her fingers through his soft hair, feeling his breath against her naked skin. *For this one night I will feel beautiful*, she thought. *I will feel loved.*

He nuzzled her breast like a baby, and she felt the rough prickle of his day's growth of new beard. All similarity to an infant nursing ceased when his warm tongue touched her swollen nipple. She gasped with surprise at the accompanying sensation deep within her woman's cleft.

"Ah, Beth," he whispered hoarsely. "You taste like maple syrup."

She giggled, then closed her eyes as the ribbons of pleasure tightened and vibrated like the strings of a musical instrument. He drew her nipple between his lips and suckled, making her want to moan with pleasure. She whispered his name again and again as an unfamiliar, bittersweet aching grew in her loins.

He chuckled and cupped her other breast in his big hand. "Mmm," he murmured. "Very nice."

She felt something . . . something she could not fathom or explain . . . drawing near. She caught his hand and pressed it between her legs. "Touch me here," she begged him. The feeling was unbelievable. She wanted more . . . something more. She was wet . . . hot and wet and hungry for the act of love.

She rubbed against him so that his fingers would slide deeper into the core of her yearning. "Please," she whispered. "I want . . . I want . . ."

He thrust two fingers higher, and she clenched her teeth and let her head fall back as he gently caressed a nub of pure sensation she'd not known existed. She tossed her head and whimpered with joy. She felt as though she was caught in a raging current that swept her closer and closer to the brink of a bottomless chasm. Yet she was powerless to stop herself . . . powerless to—

With one swift motion, Hunt stood and swept her up in his arms. "Not yet, sweet," he whispered hoarsely. "Not yet." She slumped back against his chest, her breath coming in deep ragged gulps, her mind dazed as he carried her to the bed and laid her on the heaped blankets.

She looked up at him, and he smiled with such tenderness that her confusion fled. The tumultuous singing in her blood could only be good. Hunt would bring her happiness . . . if only for a few brief hours. "I want you," she whispered, holding out her arms to him.

The gleam in his eyes made her heart leap. "And you'll have me," he promised. "As much of me as you can hold." He chuckled softly. "But first . . . first, you must do something about this sticky syrup all over me."

"Me?" Her eyes widened. "But I'm not the one who—"

"It's your fault," he accused. Mischief mingled with desire in his voice as he lifted her hand and planted a damp kiss on the inside of her wrist, then flicked the sensitive spot with the tip of his tongue. "Hmm," he murmured. "None there." He kissed a slow pathway to her elbow, tasting her skin after each caress; then he repeated the pattern, but this time nipping at her with tender love-bites. And he did not stop at her wrist, but took each finger and traced the length with his lips.

Elizabeth's breath caught in her throat as Hunt drew her thumb into his mouth and sucked lightly. "What are you ..." Her thought was lost as his strong white teeth nibbled the end of her index finger, then drew it between his lips. "You shouldn't," she protested. "Your wound ... you could ..." But he only laughed.

"I like sweets," he said. "Close your eyes and enjoy it. Your turn will come soon enough."

He teased each finger, then focused his attention on her shoulder, moving ever closer to her breast.

Waves of pleasure lapped through her body, one after another, until it was impossible to lie still ... until the deliberate, erotic assault on her senses kindled the fire in her loins again. She caught his head and brought it to her breast. "Suck my nipples," she urged him. "It feels so good when you ..."

"For me too," he murmured, slowly laving the tender nub, then scraping his teeth against her damp skin. "Mmm, I found something sweet," he said as he drew the nipple into his mouth. His hands ranged over her stomach, and lean fingers stroked the soft curls at the apex of her thighs before delving inside the damp folds.

Again she could not hold back the gasp of wonder. How was it possible that she had never experienced such feeling before? Hunt licked first one of her nipples and then the other, all the while continuing to stroke her cleft until she was nearly lost in the giddiness of erotic bliss.

"Shall I kiss you there?" he asked. "Would you like that?"

She heard him, but she couldn't summon a reply. A daring thought had risen in her mind. If his lips on her breasts brought her such joy . . . wouldn't the same action bring him gratification?

Tentatively, she slid her hand down over his superbly muscled chest to stroke his left nipple and found it sticky with syrup. To her delight, the bud of flesh hardened under her touch.

Hunt arched his back and groaned, and she felt a surge of power. "Are you sweet?" she dared. She lifted her head and flicked her tongue across his nipple. His shoulders tightened and he let out a long sigh. "Two can play at this game," she said, drawing him between her lips and suckling.

He exhaled softly. "You learned torture well from the Iroquois," he replied, capturing her hand and pressing it against his ardent erection. "Have you nerve enough to . . ." He whispered the rest in her ear.

A hot flush rose under her skin. "I might," she answered.

"Is that a promise?" His hair tickled her breasts as he trailed hot kisses down her midriff and licked the hollow of her navel. "It's sweeter below," he murmured.

As his mouth explored her, a spasm of velvet rapture suddenly exploded deep within her. "Oh," she cried. "Oh." Ripples radiated from a pulsating center.

Hunt rose on his knees and spread her legs apart. "You're ready for me now, aren't you, Beth? You want me as much as I want you, don't you?"

"Yes—yes."

"Say it," he ordered.

"I want you."

Another spasm rocked her body as his rod pressed against her willing flesh. "What do you want me to do?" he demanded.

"Come into me!" She braced herself for his thrust, but he entered her slowly, tenderly, allowing her time to adjust to the fullness of his straining sex. Then he slid farther inside her, and the intensity of her need pushed everything else away. "Yes, yes," she cried.

He drove deep and hard, whipping her need into a white-hot passion. She met him thrust for thrust, losing herself in the abandon of a union so tempestuous that her cries of rapture echoed through the warm, fire-lit cabin and mingled with those of the beautiful man covering her with his sweat-sheened body.

She tumbled from the abyss, was caught and tumbled again, swirled in the bright colors of ecstasy, sheltered by the power of his arms.

Sometime during the magical night, they slept, then woke in a languid tangle of limbs and sweet, lazy caresses to begin the discovery of love and laughter once more, giving again and yet again.

"Is it always like this with you?" she asked him between kisses.

He was propped up on a roll of blankets, and she lay shamelessly astraddle him with her cheek pressed against his broad chest. Hunt had a lock of her hair wound around his finger, and he was trying to plait the ends into a length of his own hair to make a contrasting pattern of red and black. "Do I like making love, or am I always so vigorous?"

She pushed up, saw by his expression that he was teasing her, and snuggled down in the crook of his shoulder. Raindrops were tapping against the windowpanes. Sometime in the night, the temperature had risen, and the snowfall had become rain. "How is your arm?" she asked him. "Oh, it's bleeding," she said with sudden alarm.

"It's all right," he replied brusquely. "Nothing to fuss over."

"You shouldn't have—"

He laughed. "I was hurting worse than this before we—"

"Not in the arm."

"No." He grinned. "Not in the arm. In another limb."

"You should take more care with those bites. They could turn bad."

"I've had worse."

"You don't want to lose the arm."

"I won't. It hurts, but not so bad as it would if it were poisoned."

"Sometimes I think you're more Indian than white. An Iroquois brave would rather have his arm fall off than admit that he's in pain."

"Hmm."

"I'm not questioning your courage. Back there, in the cave, you could have left me with Powder Horn."

His eyes narrowed. "I don't give up what's mine that easily."

"But I'm not yours, am I?" She kept her tone light. "I am my own person."

"You're mine until I deliver you to your father."

She exhaled softly. "And what would he think

about this"—she motioned to the bed—"do you suppose?"

Hunt frowned. "I don't reckon he'd think too much of it."

"Of you taking advantage of me?"

He sniffed. "Is that the way you see it, Beth?"

"No." She shook her head. "You know better. What happened was as much my fault as yours."

"Good. I thought that way myself."

"I'm not sorry," she added.

"Nor am I."

They lay in silence for several moments, and Elizabeth listened to the rain hitting the roof. She knew she should rise and start preparing the morning meal, but she hated to leave the bed and break the spell that held her in its glorious grip.

He brushed her nose with the tip of the joined braid. "Now that we've decided we're equally guilty, I'll admit I'm hungry enough to eat that wolf we left back on the riverbank."

"Me too."

"I think I'd like a deer steak, a few trout, some corn bread with syrup and—"

"Enough." She laughed. "I'll build up the fire and—"

"Stay right where you are, woman," he ordered. "If I hadn't gotten up in the night to add wood, we'd both probably have frozen to death. But it's none too warm in here. You stay under the blankets. I'll get the breakfast." He rolled her over and patted her bare bottom before covering her up.

As he turned away and retrieved his breeches, Elizabeth couldn't keep her eyes off him. His long legs rippled with muscle; his bare arms and shoulders showed the effects of a lifetime in the wilderness. And his sleek, tight buttocks . . . Heat burned her cheeks.

She sighed deeply and hugged herself with both arms. Hunt was beautiful, and for one night he'd wanted her. The memory would be enough to hold her for a lifetime.

"I've no wish to travel in this weather," he said, pulling on his moccasins and a vest. "Brrr. It's damp in here." He threw another log on the fire and glanced back at her. "I'm going out to take a look around the mission, just to make certain—"

"If anyone came last night, they could have had us as easily as catching ducks in a basket," she said.

He grimaced. "You'll be the death of me yet, woman."

"I hope not."

"Me too." He picked up his rifle, checked the priming, and started for the door.

"Put on your coat," she reminded him. "It's pouring out there."

"Yes, ma'am." He grinned boyishly. "Bossy thing, aren't you? Bad as a Shoshone woman."

Elizabeth giggled at his warm teasing. She waited until the door closed behind him, then rose and dressed quickly. By the time he came back in, she'd washed her hands and face, combed the worst of the tangles from her hair and begun to braid it.

"No," Hunt said. "Leave it free around your face."

"And look a hoyden?" she asked shyly.

"I like it that way."

"All right," she answered. Bubbles of happiness made her reckless. Today, she'd do as he asked. Today, she'd forget who and what she was . . . forget all the rules. Feeling as reckless as a Gypsy wench, she laughed and started on the corn bread.

"I promised you breakfast," he said.

"I'll fix it if you'll carry water from the cistern to heat. I think I'd like another bath today." She looked away and felt herself blush again. The evidence of their lovemaking was still to be washed from her body.

"Gladly, provided that you'll scrub my back this time."

She laughed and finished the corn cakes, then put them on an iron spider to bake near the coals. Taking her cloak, she ventured outside in the rain and slush to tend to her intimate needs. The cabin glowed bright and warm when she returned, and for a few long seconds, she allowed herself to imagine what it might be like to call such a place home . . . to come in to her own kitchen and find Hunt waiting there.

"If the rain lets up tomorrow, we'll go south," he said, and her make-believe dream shattered.

She could not go south without her children. She could not do it to save her immortal soul from hell.

"The water's heating in the kettle," he said. "Maybe we've time for that bath before—"

"We do not," she assured him.

"I was afraid of that."

She checked the corn cakes to make certain they weren't burning, then glanced back at him. "Where will you go when my father pays you?"

"West."

Her heart sank. "To the place where the buffalo are?" She never tired of hearing him talk about the places he'd been and the people he'd known, but she couldn't help a faint hope from rising. She didn't want him to go far away—she wasn't certain she could bear it if she never saw him again.

"I reckon to cross the plains to the high mountains beyond them. My father's there. I told him I'd come back when I'd seen all I wanted to of civilization."

"What's it like?" she asked. "Those high mountains?"

He gave her that slow, devilish smile that always made her heart skip a beat. "You've asked me that a dozen times," he teased.

"Tell me again," she pleaded. She wanted to remember everything he told her, to imprint it so clearly in her mind that she'd never forget.

"I feared I was boring you with my tall tales," he replied.

"Never."

"Well, then . . . The high mountains are like nothing you've ever seen or dreamed of. Those mountains rear out of the plains like the fingers of God. They're big and wild and beautiful. There are peaks where the snow never melts, and valleys that no man—red or white—has ever set foot in."

"It sounds like a lonely place to me," she said.

He chuckled. "Maybe. But I've spent so much time in my own company, I've grown to like it."

"And you never want to settle down?" She tried to keep her tone light, although her heart was hammering. "Take a wife? Raise a family?"

He shrugged. "Do I look like the marrying kind?"

She turned away and busied herself with the breakfast to hide her flush of embarrassment. *How could she be such a fool? To dream that a man like Hunt could want a woman like her?* "I was only making conversation," she stammered. "It wasn't a proposal."

"The closest I ever came to a wedding was the time I was captured by a Blackfoot by the name of Stone Knife. I was only fourteen, and I'd been hunting buffalo with a party of young Cheyenne braves. Stone Knife needed a husband for his pregnant daughter whose lover had fled the territory. Strikes Her Teepee was a sweet little fifteen-year-old who stood a foot taller than me, had a voice like a bull elk, and could have lifted me astride a buffalo calf over her head, single-handed. Luckily, my hunting partners rescued me before I became a husband and a father—probably in the same night."

"Oh!" Elizabeth cried. Smoke started to curl from the iron spider. She grabbed for the handle of the frying pan and burned her fingers.

Hunt pulled the pan away from the fire and dumped the corn cakes onto a plate. One missed and landed on the table, but he quickly added it to the pile. "Are you all right?" he asked. "I told you you should stay in bed and let me do the cooking."

"Maybe I should have," she replied.

He brought snow to ease the sting of the burn and ministered to her as tenderly as any mother could do. Strange, she thought, how his hands—so big and powerful—could be so gentle. "It was careless of me to grab the handle," she said.

"You do need constant watching," he said.

He kept up his good-natured teasing through breakfast, and the bath that followed led to a return to the bed and a renewal of their sweet, hot lovemaking.

"Don't be afraid of having another child," he told her, when they lay exhausted in a heap of blankets. "There's no danger of you quickening with my seed."

"Why?" she asked. It was the wrong time of month for her to get pregnant. She'd learned enough of the Iroquois women's lore to know when she was at risk and when she wasn't, but Hunt had no way of knowing her cycle.

"I'm sterile," he said brusquely. "Soon after I came back from the western mountains I caught mumps from a white trader's children. I came as close to dying as a man can get. I would have died if Campbell hadn't found me and taken me to his home. He sent for a physician and paid for his healing. It was the doctor who told me I'd not father children, and he was right. No woman has ever named me, and they've had every chance."

Hunt's tone was matter-of-fact, but the pain in his eyes was plain to see. "Thank you for telling me," she said.

He shrugged. "Only fair to tell you the rules of the game."

"Most men wouldn't."

"I'm not most men. And I wouldn't risk adding to your troubles by leaving you unwed with a babe to raise alone."

*But I already have two,* she thought. Then he kissed her, and she pushed back the regrets and worry. This was their time, and she'd not spoil it with heartache over what could never be.

"You are wonderful," she murmured.

"I'll take that as a vote of approval."

He kissed her again and teased her nipple with the pad of his thumb until she sighed with pleasure and began to return the favor. One thing led quickly to another, and before she realized, the afternoon vanished and darkness fell. Still the rain beat a tattoo on the shingled roof and wrapped them in a snug cocoon of happiness.

It was sometime after midnight when Hunt finally fell into a deep, contented sleep. And it was only then that Elizabeth crept from his embrace with tears staining her cheeks. "I'll never forget you," she whispered. She silently dressed in the firelight and returned to take a final look at Hunt.

He had thown the blankets back so that his chest and hard-muscled shoulders and arms were bare. His dark hair had fallen over his face, and she could catch only a glimpse of his senual lips and strong nose. "I will miss you," she murmured.

She turned away, then stopped and looked back a final time. "Good-bye, Hunt."

She was weeping so hard that she could barely see as she slipped out of the cabin door and closed it firmly behind her. "I'll head due north," she murmured aloud to give herself courage. "I'll follow the stream north." She couldn't think about Hunt or what he'd given her for a short time. She couldn't think about his pain when he awoke and found her gone. She could think only of her children and that precious lives—their happiness—must come ahead of her own.

# Chapter 12

**F**itful moonlight illuminated the shadowy forest floor. Raw wind tugged at Elizabeth's hood and scoured her exposed cheeks and forehead. The half-melted slush underfoot had crusted over, making her snowshoes useless; they hung over her back along with a rolled blanket, some food, and a fire-making kit. She'd not brought a gun. The flintlocks were heavy and she was a poor shot at best. Her only weapon was the scalping knife thrust into her belt.

When she'd traveled about half a mile through the mud and snow, she removed her moccasins and leggings, girded up her dress, and waded into the ice-crusted creek. The black, rushing water was so frigid that her feet went instantly numb. Elizabeth gasped, then forced herself to take one step after another. Slipping and sliding, she traversed about fifty yards, then could stand the penetrating cold no longer. She climbed out on the far side, dried her feet, and pulled on her moccasins. Then she began to stamp up and down to restore the feeling and flow of blood to her toes before she headed into the deep woods.

She knew Hunt would be furious when he woke and found her gone, but she hoped that when his temper cooled he would realize she'd done what was best for both of them. She was wrong to have suggested he endanger his life again by going back for Jamie. She did not think the Seneca would kill her if she returned of her own free will. Even if they made her a slave once more, there would be no point in murdering her. Hunt was another story. Raven could think of a dozen reasons why he should be put to death, and Yellow Drum would be all too happy to satisfy his evil wife's lust for blood.

Before Elizabeth had come to care for Hunt, she'd been willing to sacrifice him for Jamie and Rachel— but no more. Her children had to come first; they had no one else to stand for them. But Hunt had no part in this. The day and night of loving that they'd shared had given her a happiness she'd never known existed. She'd ask no more of him.

How close she'd come to murmuring promises and words of endearment that would have made her a fool in Hunt's eyes. He'd bedded her in spite of her ugly red hair and freckled complexion. He'd ignored her grotesque green eyes and pale skin and treated her with tenderness. For his kindness she would be eternally grateful. Now she must forget her own wants and needs; she must think only of her babies.

She'd been little older than Jamie when she'd first discovered that she was physically unattractive, and that memory was burned into her mind. She'd come skipping down the wide front stairs of her father's elegant town house to join her parents for Sunday morning church services. She remembered the crinkle of her nursemaid's starched petticoats and the annoying buzz of a green-head fly that circled the bowl of honey water on the hall table.

She'd been bursting with excitement, eager to show off the new cherry-colored velvet gown with satin bows and red silk slippers to match, which had just arrived by ship from her mother's favorite mantua-maker in London. "Papa, see my dress," she'd cried as she dashed into the front parlor.

Her father's frown and pursed lips had stilled her dancing feet, and she'd taken a hesitant step backward as she heard his stern voice say, "I don't know where the child got that vulgar red hair and those awful freckles, certainly not from my side of the family."

"It's God's truth," her pretty mother had replied airily. "Elizabeth is a wood thrush in a flock of blue-birds—plain as Charles Town mud and leggy as a colt, I admit. But none of my relatives had carrot hair and legs like a stork. You can't blame me. Aren't our other children lovely enough to turn heads?"

Elizabeth had stared in disbelief and begun to say something in her own defense when her mother noticed her.

"God's heart, child. Go back up to nurse and change out of that gown. Red velvet will never do for you. You look like a great freckled strawberry."

Tears of shame had spilled down her cheeks, and she'd begun to feel sick to her stomach. Suddenly, her stays were choking the breath out of her, and black spots danced in front of her eyes.

"Stop that caterwauling," her father scolded. "What is she weeping about, Madam? We will be late for services. Have you no control over your daughters?"

As she fled from the room, she crashed into her older brother in the hall. "Strawberry! Strawberry!" he'd taunted her.

Later, when her grandmama had found her hiding on the attic landing, the old lady had dried her tears, offered a twist of licorice and practical advice. "No matter if you're red as an Indian, Lizzy, you will never have the sin of vanity to atone for. It's a pity you're the homely one in the family, but your father will provide enough dowry to find you a husband just the same."

"But I don't want to be an ugly thrush," she protested. "I . . . I want to be . . . a bluebird too."

"Stuff and nonsense. Beauty's only skin deep. You're clever enough for a girl. Curb the devil's temper that goes with that hair and learn to pretend obedience even when you don't feel it inside. Fathers and husbands are all cut of the same cloth. They favor females who listen to every word they say. Your father is no different. He loves you dearly."

"But . . . but he called my hair vulgar."

"And so it is—loud enough for a butcher's brat. You'd not have heard what you weren't meant to if you weren't eavesdropping on adults' conversations. You must learn to accept your hair and stay out of the sun. If you didn't run about the woods and fields with the servants' children like a wild rabbit, you'd not have so many freckles.

"Trust in your father, Lizzy. He'll find you a suitable husband somewhere."

She'd tried not to care if her two younger sisters were pretty and she wasn't, but she'd never grown accustomed to her brother's teasing. If she tried hard enough, she could hear Avery and his friends shouting "Strawberry! Strawberry! Red-topped strawberry!"

It was silly to feel hurt over something that had happened so long ago in another world, she thought. She'd adored her brother. He wasn't always mean to her. Besides, being homely had its advantages. It had taught her to use her brains and develop a hard right punch.

Besides, she thought wryly, if she had been more

attractive, Yellow Drum might have enjoyed bedding her. Then she would have had to put up with his sexual abuse over and over, instead of the few times that Raven could browbeat him into doing it.

Elizabeth slipped and nearly fell, catching herself on a sapling and regaining her balance. Her feet still felt like chunks of ice. She shuddered, remembering the bitterness of the black water. Crossing the creek had been necessary; wading upstream was an Iroquois trick meant to slow down a tracker. Anyone following would look for a trail directly across from where footprints went into a stream. Hunt would have to search both sides of the water, and that would take time. If luck was with her, she would be far away from the mission when the sun rose. With that much head start, he might not be able to catch her.

A wolf howled from beyond the far ridge, the long, eerie cry raising gooseflesh on her arms. The white wolf was dead, a stiffened carcass on the stream bank below the crazy man's cabin, but there were many more wolves in the pack. Would she become their prey tonight?

Hunt said that wolves rarely attacked humans. So the Seneca believed, but rarely was not always. If the white wolf had tried to tear out Hunt's throat, would not others of the band be equally bloodthirsty? She hoped she'd not made a fatal mistake by leaving without a firearm.

It was hard to gauge distance in the dark. Trees loomed ahead and on either side of her. The ground was rocky, cut by deep ravines. In spring, it would have made for hard walking; in early winter, in ice and wet, it was a nightmare. She thanked God for Many Blushes's fur-lined moccasins. The tight seams and layers of bear fat made the high skin shoes nearly waterproof—not enough to wade through a creek, but snug against this slushy snow.

Another low, plaintive baying brought to mind every ghost story that Raven's father had ever uttered around a winter fire. "Unholy creatures roam the forest at night," he'd said. "Faceless things with long, streaming hair, and hideous skeletons that devour human flesh."

It had been Elizabeth's experience that skeletons rarely did the living any harm; but there was that word, *rarely*, again. She chuckled aloud at her own fainthearted foolishness and kept walking.

When she was a child, her mother had read stories of wolves to her. In those tales, the wolves had all been evil, and she knew that wasn't true. Wolves were good parents to their young and faithful to their mates. Once, when she was hunting berries with Raven, they'd come upon a den with three playful cubs. Raven had given the little wolves a wide berth, but she'd not feared them. "Only in famine do wolves turn desperate," the Indian woman had said.

"Hunt tried to steal the deer," Elizabeth reminded herself. "The wolf attacked because it was defending the kill."

Hunt's wounds came to mind. Surely, he could not be hurt too badly if he'd been able to make love to her with such vigor. If his injury was going to mortify, she would have seen redness and infection. She—

Her reverie was broken by a sudden feeling of impending doom. She froze and saw the silhouette of a running man appear along the ridgeline.

Her heart in her throat, she moved with infinite slowness to hide herself behind a tree. When she peered out, she caught sight of the intruder headed straight toward her. She couldn't make out who it was. Frightened, she pressed herself into the bark of the tree, hoping to make herself invisible.

Scudding clouds parted, and for a few seconds, moonlight illuminated the figure—not Hunt but an Indian. Was it? Yes, she was certain. The man loping toward her was Powder Horn.

*Turn, turn,* she thought in desperation. As if by magic, he angled to the left around a fallen log. He passed within a dozen yards of her and continued on in the direction of the creek and the mission. And as he ran by, she saw war paint streaking his cruel face.

*I knew we should have killed him,* she thought fiercely. Hunt had let him live, and now the Iroquois brave had come to seek revenge for the insult they'd dealt him. She hadn't seen a gun, but that didn't mean he wasn't dangerous. If he found Hunt still asleep . . .

She knew she should take the opportunity to flee— to put as much ground between her and Powder Horn as she could, but that would mean leaving Hunt defenseless. Instead, she began to follow the Indian. On this moonlit night, a child could have tracked Powder Horn. The hard part was trailing the warrior without being seen.

This was not the way she and Hunt had come to the mission, Elizabeth reasoned. Powder Horn must have assumed that they would take shelter there. The course he was heading would take him to the creek within a few hundred feet of Baptiste's cabin.

If she could wait until he got far enough ahead, she could follow in relative safety. But if she did that, Powder Horn might cross the stream and surprise Hunt before she could give warning. How she would do that, she didn't know. It would be impossible to get in front of the Iroquois; he was taking a direct route while she'd come a roundabout way.

Heartsick, she continued tracking him, occasionally catching glimpses of him up ahead. As Powder Horn neared the creek, she became frantic. If she'd brought a rifle, she could have shot him—or at least fired a warning shot. Now she had nothing with which to defend herself except Hunt's knife, and she knew she couldn't best an Iroquois warrior in hand-to-hand combat.

Suddenly, she choked back a scream of fright as a gray-white form glided down through the branches. The huge owl seemed more ghost than bird as he flapped on great silent wings and bared taloned claws to snatch a small animal from the shadows. The hapless prey gave one gurgling squeal and then there was only muffled rustling in the snow.

Blood pounding, Elizabeth dashed past the owl and scrambled up on a large ice-encrusted windfall. Ahead of her, she saw Powder Horn wade into the waters of the creek. In minutes, he would be standing over Hunt with murder in his soul. In desperation, she cupped her hands to her mouth and uttered a piercing Seneca war cry.

Powder Horn whirled and splashed back out of the stream. He hesitated for a brief second, then began to run toward her. His lean body stretched out over the snow like that of a hunting wolf, but he made not the slightest sound. Elizabeth scrambled off the log and fled back through the trees the way she'd come.

Branches tore at her face and clothing. Her moccasined feet slipped and slid on the wet leaves and icy underbrush. She didn't look back. She ran with every ounce of strength and will she possessed.

Twice she fell. Both times she regained her footing and continued her wild dash to escape her pursuer. Her lungs ached; her legs felt as though they were made of wood. A sharp pain in her side threatened to double her over in agony, but still she kept running.

. . . Until she could hear the thud of Powder Horn's footfalls behind her . . . until the sound of his heavy breathing nearly drowned out her own. Then she stopped short, spun around, and drew her knife.

He laughed.

When he dove at her with outstretched hands, she slashed the backs of three fingers on his left hand. "Aiyee!" he cried out in surprise. His grin became a grimace, and his eyes narrowed as he yanked a war club from his belt. He raised the weapon high, and for the space of a heartbeat Elizabeth wondered where he'd gotten the club.

"Now you die," he said.

She sidestepped the terrible blow and tried to duck away. Powder Horn caught her sleeve and dragged her around to face him while he lifted the club to dash her brains out on the snow. "Your scalp—" he began. But his words were lost in the roar of a flintlock rifle.

Powder Horn's fingers tightened on her arm, then relaxed. His eyes widened in shock, and the war club fell to the snow. Blood bubbled over his lips as he staggered, clawing at his chest.

Struggling to comprehend what had happened, Elizabeth drew in one ragged breath and then another. She began to back away from the Iroquois.

"Are you all right?"

Hunt's voice. She nodded. It was Hunt's voice. But was she really hearing it, or was it in her mind? A strong arm tightened around her shoulders, and she looked up into Hunt's grim face.

Powder Horn gave a long, gasping groan and dropped to his knees. Blood poured between his fingers, still clutching his chest. He went limp and fell facedown in the trampled snow like a boneless cloth doll. His feet churned weakly, and then he lay still.

"What the hell did you think you were doing?"

Hunt demanded. "You could have been killed!" He let go of her and began to reload his smoking rifle.

She inhaled deeply. The pain in her side had faded, but her heart was still hammering. She looked down at the Iroquois and shuddered. "He . . . he was coming to kill us," she said. "Just like the wolves. He was hunting us."

"Appears that way," Hunt answered. His tone was brusque, his features hard.

"I told you to kill him back at the cave."

"You did that."

"You should have killed him."

"He's dead, isn't he?"

She clenched and unclenched her hands. They were stiff with cold, and she'd dropped her knife. She bent and retrieved it, carefully wiping the blade dry before she tucked it back in her belt.

"What were you doing out here, Elizabeth? You were running away from me, weren't you?"

She straightened her spine and stared at him. He was white-lipped with fury, but she knew he wouldn't hit her. No matter what she did, she'd never have to fear that. She matched him, glare for glare. "I was," she admitted.

"What happened between us—back there in the cabin—it didn't mean a thing to you, did it? Just another roll in the blankets."

The unfairness of that accusation cut her deep. "I risked my life to save you," she flung back. "If I hadn't given that war cry—"

"Sounded like an Iroquois yell to me."

"It was . . . but . . ." She stopped. "You knew it was me. You weren't in the cabin, were you? You were tracking me. You didn't have time to—"

"Hell, no, I wasn't in the cabin. And yes, I was tracking you. I thought I'd let you wander around in the woods until you got cold and wolf-scared. I saw *him* . . ." He kicked at the dead man with the toe of his moccasin. "I couldn't shoot because you were between me and him."

"So you waited until he caught up with me."

He nodded.

"Why then? Why didn't you let him kill me? Your troubles would have been over."

"You know me better than that, Elizabeth. But if you couldn't hold your own with one outlawed Iroquois, how in hell do you expect to take on the whole Seneca nation single-handed?"

"I wouldn't be single-handed if you'd help me," she said. A lump was forming in her throat. Her eyes were dry. She had no tears left. Whatever joy she'd found in Hunt's bed felt as dead as Powder Horn.

"I'm not going to get you back to South Carolina without that boy unless I hog-tie you, am I?" he asked.

She shook her head. "I guess not."

"All right, then," he replied. "I guess you're harder-headed than I am."

She looked at him in confusion. "All right, what?"

"I'll help you steal him back."

"What?" Her knees felt suddenly weak. "What did you say?"

"Are you deaf as well as mule-stubborn? I know when I've met my match." He leaned on his long rifle and grinned at her. "I said, I'll help you kidnap your son."

She shook her head again in disbelief. "Why, Hunt? Why would you—"

He pursed his lips and shrugged. "You made me an offer, back there in the cave. You kept your half of the bargain. I guess it's only fitten that I keep the rest."

# Chapter 13

Later, back at Baptiste's cabin, Elizabeth warmed herself by the fire and tried to rub feeling back into her icy feet. She was still shocked by Hunt's unexpected offer to help her get Jamie back—but something else had shaken her almost as much, and she couldn't stop thinking about the incident that had occurred shortly after Hunt had killed Powder Horn in the forest.

Hunt had drawn his knife and knelt in the snow by the Iroquois's body, preparing to scalp him. Just thinking about it made her sick to her stomach.

"No!" she'd screamed, once she'd realized what he meant to do. "What in God's name are you doing?"

He'd turned cold eyes on her. "God has nothing to do with this. I'm going to lift his hair, same as he would have done to me."

"No," she'd protested. "You can't. That's uncivilized."

Hunt's cruel expression had sent cold chills down her spine. "I never claimed to be civilized." He'd hesitated, knife poised over Powder Horn's scalplock. "Give me one reason why I shouldn't do it."

"If you do, he can't go on to the spirit world. His soul will be forced to wander—"

"Now who's uncivilized?" Hunt had scoffed at her. "What would your Christian father say to that?"

"It doesn't matter what I believe," she argued. "Powder Horn believed it. Can't we just leave him—"

He grinned. "For the wolves, you mean?"

"No. Not that. We could bury him. I just—"

"Quit when you're ahead, Elizabeth. If it bothers you, I won't scalp the son of a bitch, but I'll be damned if I'll dig a hole for him."

They'd left Powder Horn where he lay. Now, with the stout log walls securely around her, she didn't want to think of the lonely moonlit glade or the wolves she feared would come slinking in to devour the Indian's body.

She glanced sideways at Hunt and felt a slight breath of fear spiral up her spine. He was seated at the table drinking another cup of spirits with the cat curled in his lap. He seemed the same easygoing man she'd come to know in the last few days, but she couldn't shake the memory of the underlying savagery he'd shown her. Ground that she'd thought was safe had suddenly opened under her feet.

She had misjudged Hunt badly, and misjudging a man could cost her everything. Beneath his lazy drawl and laughing demeanor crouched a spirit as fierce and deadly as any Seneca. She'd not forget that ever again.

When they'd arrived at the cabin and he'd taken off his outer garments, she'd seen that his face was flushed and red. She'd been afraid he was running a fever, but he'd refused to let her examine his wounds. "I've not forgiven you yet," he said.

"I'm sorry you feel betrayed," she answered, "but I'm not sorry I ran away. If I hadn't tried to escape, we'd both have been sleeping when Powder Horn burst in on us. We'd have been murdered in our beds."

"If . . ." he said sarcastically. "If the hunter hadn't objected, the bear would have had a meal." He stroked the sleeping cat gently, taking care not to ruffle the animal's fur. "I'm not so easily killed as you seem to think, woman. I've managed so far without your help."

"You will do what you said . . . won't you?" she asked, studying his chiseled features, desperate for some way to gauge his thoughts. "You'll help me go for my ch— for Jamie?"

He tilted his head slightly and gave a faint smile. Elizabeth shivered as flames from the glowing hearth reflected in the bottomless black pools of his eyes. "I've said as much, haven't I?"

"Can we leave in the morning? I can't wait—"

He threw her a withering look. "I'll do it, Elizabeth," he muttered, "but I'll do it my way. You want my help, you'll take orders for a change." He pushed the crock away from him and stood up. "I still think this is wrong," he added. "Wrong for you, wrong for the boy."

She rose to her feet and looked toward the bed. "Just tell me what you want me to do."

"Are you sure that's what you want, Elizabeth?" Quick as a striking copperhead he sprang up, seized her by the shoulders, and yanked her hard against him. He looked deep into her eyes and she felt her will weaken.

"I . . . I . . ." she stammered. She trembled in his grip . . . not from fear, but from an emotion as old and as powerful. "Hunt . . ." Her bones turned to water and she felt as though she were about to faint. She clutched at him to keep from falling. And in that instant, her need for him was so great that she would have done anything he asked. "Oh, Hunt," she cried.

"Not this way." His tone was harsh, grating. He released her and stepped back.

She turned her head to hide the tears of shame.

"It's different between us now, isn't it?" he said.

She covered her face with her hands.

He went to the fireplace and leaned against the brick hearth with both hands. "Forgive me, Elizabeth," he said. "I shouldn't drink. I guess I'm more Indian than I thought." He squatted on his heels in front of the fire. "I'll put some more venison on to roast. We'll eat our fill, and then we'll sleep. At dawn, we'll set off for a Shawnee village where I've got friends."

She forced herself to look at him. "You promised to get Jamie," she reminded him. Her voice cracked, like an old woman's.

"I'll get your boy if it's humanly possible," he answered. "I may be foolhardy, but I'm not crazy. If I'm going on a raid, I need a war party."

"Will they help—your friends?" The words echoed in her head as though they came from a long way off. "I thought the Shawnee and the Iroquois were—"

"At peace?" He gave a snort of derision. "Barely. There are old wounds between the tribes, old scores to settle. I'll get the warriors I need. If not, I'll look elsewhere. I can't do this alone."

"I'll be with you. I—"

"You'll be where I say you'll be. I'll have no more of your nonsense. You'll wait for me in the village. You'll be safe enough there. Once I get the boy, I mean to put ground between me and Yellow Drum. He'll come after me with every warrior he can muster. I don't need a woman to slow me down."

*But what about Rachel?* she thought desperately. If Hunt went without her, he wouldn't get her daughter.

And if she told him that there were two children instead of one, he wouldn't go at all.

"Let me come," she pleaded. "I won't slow you down. Jamie will be frightened if I'm not there. He won't—"

He blew out the candle on the table, carefully put the cat on the floor, and stood up. "It's not your decision. It's mine. If he's scared, he'll get over it once he's reunited with you. He's only six; hardly hardly more than a baby. I was eight when I was captured, and I got over being afraid."

"You must have been terrified when it happened—when you and your sister were separated?"

He shrugged. "It's not a day I care to remember. I only knew Becca was alive because my father told me later—once I'd learned enough Cheyenne to ask questions."

"Oh."

"Some memories a man's better off without."

"A woman as well," she agreed. Was it easier to forget? she wondered. Would she have been happier if the day of Avery's wedding was a void in her mind?

"Enough talk, best you get some sleep."

"I'm sorry," she answered. She wasn't sorry; her reply came automatically as it had come so often in the years she'd spent in Yellow Drum's lodge.

"Sorry for what? Curiosity?"

"For a woman as well," she agreed honestly. She struggled to hold herself together, to keep from saying something that would bring her even more shame.

He'd rejected her. No, he'd seemed almost disgusted by her. What a fool she'd been. *Spinning dreams of cobwebs*, Raven would have said. *Weaving hopes of rainbow colors.* She'd wanted Hunt to care for her so badly that she'd imagined it.

He'd taken her up on her offer, sex in trade for Jamie. Hadn't he said it bluntly? "... just a roll in the blankets ..." he'd told her back there in the woods.

She meant nothing more to him and she never would. She drew in a jagged breath. For an ugly red-haired woman, she'd gotten more from Hunt than she had any right to ask for. But she wouldn't settle for Jamie. She had to have Rachel as well. She'd think of something, and she'd pay the price, no matter what it cost.

They traveled hard and fast the next nine days. Elizabeth clung to the hope of Hunt's promise that he would return for Jamie as each step took her farther away from Yellow Drum's village. They left snow and cold behind them as they trekked south and west through trackless hardwood forests, open meadowland, and rough mountain terrain.

Flocks of ducks and geese passed overhead; winter-barren trees were left behind. In their place, Elizabeth saw forests resplendent in autumn leaves of red, brown, and brilliant gold. But although the nights remained cool, daytime temperatures made Elizabeth's winter clothing uncomfortably warm, and the afternoon sun shone hot on her face.

In all that time, they never saw another human, although they did come upon an abandoned Indian village and empty cornfields. On two nights, they heard wolves, and once a herd of deer nearly ran them down as they entered a ravine, but there were no traces of people, white or Indian. As they walked, Hunt and Elizabeth often startled rabbits or porcupines or quail. Such small game provided meat when they needed it, but Hunt preferred to snare rabbits at night. That way he didn't have to chance firing his rifle and possibly alerting an enemy to their whereabouts.

To her surprise, the solitude didn't bother Elizabeth. She found herself caught up in the beauty of the vast stretches of hardwood trees and the tumble of white water along the rocky streams. "This country is bigger than I thought," she said one evening when they'd stopped to make camp.

He chuckled. "Big? You don't know the half of it. We're not even to the Ohio, yet. If you could paddle a canoe from the Big Lakes down to *Can-tuc-kee* or stand on a peak in the Blue Mountains looking east across the great plains—" He broke off. "Hell, woman, words can't describe the size of this land. The Cheyenne say that beyond their mountains lies another salt sea, bigger and deeper than any man's ambition. I always meant to go and take a look-see at that ocean, but I never got there yet. Maybe next year." He pointed to an eagle gliding high overhead. "See that bird? If you could fly like he can, you'd see a heap more than walking. Some Indians think eagles are big medicine. They carry the spirits of men who lived long ago. If I couldn't be a man, I don't suppose it would be bad to be an eagle."

"I think I'd be satisfied just to be a man instead of a woman," she'd replied wryly.

"I'm glad you're not."

"Hmmp."

That night, Hunt built a small campfire, then scattered the coals and covered them with dirt. They made their bed on the heated earth and slept warm, wrapped in the same buffalo robe. Hunt lay beside her, but he hadn't approached her sexually since they'd left the cabin. She wasn't certain if that was what she wanted or not. She didn't know if she could turn him down if he did reach out to her.

"How far must we go to find this village?" Elizabeth demanded of Hunt when they'd walked for hours the next afternoon without exchanging a word. He was not cruel to her; he never raised his voice or touched her in anger. But the man she'd come so close to falling in love with eluded her. This Hunt Campbell was a stranger, as incomprehensible as an Indian. He seemed aloof, lost in his own thoughts, often staring off into the distance as though he saw far mountains she could not envision.

"You must have been terrified when it happened," she said. "When you and your sister were separated . . ."

He shrugged. "I don't know, I suppose I was. It's been a long time. When the Shawnee attacked the cabin, we were too busy to be afraid. Becca fired at them; I reloaded for her. When they torched the house, we escaped down a tunnel. They were waiting for us at the other end."

"You and your sister were separated?"

"Yes. Wolf Robe, the man who became my father, took me in one direction; the rest of the party—with Becca—went the other way. I don't know why. Later, my father said that the woods were full of Huron that day. We were supposed to join up with the Shawnee again, but it was too dangerous. We went on ahead by canoe."

"And you never saw your sister again?"

He shook his head. "No. Later, when I learned to speak enough Cheyenne to make myself understood, I asked Wolf Robe about Becca. He assured me that she was alive. It was her they'd wanted—to trade for an important Shawnee prisoner. Months after that, we heard she'd been exchanged."

"I remember the day I was taken as clearly as yesterday," she said. God knew she'd tried to forget the screaming, the blood, the terror. A thousand times she'd wished the day of Avery's wedding was a void in her mind.

"It's been hard on you, hasn't it?" he asked. "The Cheyenne don't keep slaves."

"I don't understand how you got so far west, and then back east again."

"It's a long story," he said, "too long for tonight."

"I'm sorry," she answered. "I shouldn't pry into your affairs."

"Don't be." He sighed. "It's good to have a woman to talk to, even one as troublesome as you are. The older I get, the more old memories seem to drift back into my mind. Funny, isn't it? How you remember things that happened when you were just a tad?"

On the morning of the tenth day, she woke to a cramping in her belly. And when she went apart from Hunt to tend to nature's needs, she saw that she had begun her monthly bleeding. When she told him, he matter-of-factly sliced a section of bark from a cedar tree and shredded the inner lining to make a soft, absorbent filling for the lengths of cloth he cut from a clean linen shirt.

"I hate to ruin a good garment," she said. "I should have thought—"

He shrugged. "Forget it. You barely left Yellow Drum's village with your life, let alone such stuff. We'll make an easy march today. By tomorrow we'll be at the camp, if the Shawnee haven't moved. You can rest there."

She was secretly pleased that he showed none of the superstitious fears of her woman's menses that the Seneca exhibited. Raven and Many Blushes had always gone apart from Yellow Drum during their periods. No one had ever asked her to, and she'd never been comfortable enough with any of the other women to question why.

"When we get to the Shawnee village, the women will put you in confinement," Hunt said.

Startled, she looked at him. "What?"

"The women's hut, seclusion. Don't the Iroquois send women away during their—"

"It's not something men and women discuss," she replied primly.

"I've just made you a bleeding clout, and you think I shouldn't be talking about it?" He shook his head and sniffed in amusement at her. "White women's shyness or Iroquois women's medicine, which is it, Elizabeth? Are you white or Indian now?"

"A little of both, I'm afraid." He must know the feeling well, she thought. It was something the two of them shared. "Going away to a woman's house— that's something the Seneca never made me do."

He leaned on the muzzle of his rifle. "You're not with the Iroquois anymore. These are free Shawnee. They're old-fashioned, and they like doing things the way they've always done them. You'll be treated with courtesy, but they'll shut you up until you quit bleeding. Then they'll give you a ceremonial bath to purify you before you come in contact with any men."

"I thought you were civilized!" she flung back indignantly. "How can you allow such—"

"This is different. You're part of my family—temporarily—and we're running from the Iroquois. I said these Shawnee were old-fashioned, not stupid. Exceptions can be made under certain conditions. Once we get to the village, old rules prevail."

"I just won't tell them," she sputtered. It was ridiculous. She was no longer under Raven's control. She wouldn't be locked up. She'd had enough of confinement and people telling her what to do.

"If you don't tell them, I'll have to," he said. "Under the circumstances, it would be very bad manners not to. Insulting, even. It would put an end to any hope of gathering a party to get your boy back."

He put out his hand, and she shook it off in exasperation. "What does my . . . my condition have to do with getting Jamie back?"

"You'd have to ask the women exactly what power they think a bleeding female has. All I know is that the men believe you'd spoil their aim, make their bowstrings break, their strength weaken."

"Nonsense."

He laughed. "I'll tell you the Shawnee word for moon. *Nibeeshu.* Just say that to the first woman you meet and point to the appropriate spot. She'll tend to you."

"*Nibeeshu.*"

"That's right."

"To the Iroquois, the moon is *woh-ne-da.*"

"The languages are very different. The Shawnee and the Delaware speak a tongue that is understood by most of the Eastern Woodland people. They say the Cherokee to the south talk something like the Iroquois, but I don't know for certain. The plains tribes all have different languages; we communicate with different people by using hand signs."

"And your Cheyenne? Is their language different from the Shawnee?"

"It is, a little. But mostly it's accent. Some elders claim that there are old ties of blood and kinship to the Delaware and Shawnee. The Cheyenne and their neighbors, the Arapaho to the south and the Blackfoot to the north, speak a similar tongue. Close enough to the Algonquian tongue that I learned it easily as a boy. The camp my father belongs to lives apart from most of the Cheyenne. They are a mighty nation of horsemen, buffalo hunters on the great plains. My father's band follow the buffalo in summer and autumn, but they make their home in the mountains. One of my father's wives is Arapaho."

"He has more than one wife?"

Hunt laughed. "Wolf Robe was always a man who loved women. They say his hair is white but snow on the teepee doesn't mean the fires are banked within. He had a Delaware wife when he first captured me. She's the woman I called my mother. She died, and he decided to return to his own people in the western mountains. I was about eleven, I think."

"You mentioned three wives," she reminded him.

"He did have three wives, once—after we rejoined the Cheyenne—but one woman went home to her father. She was very pretty, but a troublemaker. She nearly soured me on beautiful women."

"Lucky for you," she replied, stung by his remark. "I'm what I am."

He frowned. "I don't know where you got your twisted ideas about your looks, but you're fair enough in my eyes."

"No need for you to try and cover what you think," she said. "I know what I am, speckled and red as an English fox."

"Different, yes," he agreed. "But some might say you have hair like a mountain sunset and eyes as green as the first grass of spring."

"A fool might," she murmured.

"Aye, a fool might." He shouldered his pack and strode off without looking back to see if she was following, and she had to run a little to catch up.

"I'll make you a tea tonight of willow bark," he said. "It will cure your headache."

"I don't have a headache," she lied. "And I don't want your tea."

"So you're just yapping at me without reason?"

"I'm not yapping."

"Snapping, then," he said. "Most women are unpleasant and irritable during their moon time—a good reason for shutting them away, as far as I can see."

"You'll not shut me away," she insisted. "Not you or the whole Shawnee tribe."

"We'll see about that."

"We will, won't we?" she replied. "It's barbaric and I won't be part of it. I tell you, I won't."

Hunt lengthened his strides.

# Chapter 14

Elizabeth stared around her at the interior of the Shawnee wigwam, sank down on the pile of thick furs, and sighed in frustration. Only minutes ago, she'd walked into the Indian village a free woman. Now, she was a prisoner once more. The fact that her cell was a snug one with a warm fire and draft-free walls barely made a difference. Hunt had done exactly what he'd threatened. He'd told the first woman he'd met that Elizabeth was experiencing her moon cycle.

Exasperation made her irritable. Why had Hunt abandoned her to these strangers? He was a white man. Regardless of what he'd said, she expected him to consider her feelings and not to betray her confidence.

After a time, her eyes adjusted to the semidarkness inside the windowless structure. Unlike the Iroquois longhouse, the women's sanctuary consisted of a single circular room made of bark sheets rolled over a sapling frame. On the inside of the wigwam, the walls and domed ceiling were covered with deerskin painted in a myriad of mystical designs and soft colors. Exquisite baskets hung from the roof and folded blankets were heaped beside bark baskets on the sleeping platform that ran along the wall, three quarters of the way around the hut.

The central fire pit was deep and lined with rocks; neat stacks of seasoned wood filled a space near the entrance curtain. The packed-earth floor was covered with layers of woven matting and tanned animal hides. The scents of herbs, dried flowers, and fresh pine boughs mingled with the heavier must of fur. Directly over the doorway dangled a string of shells and bright feathers. When she'd entered the lodge, Elizabeth had heard the delicate tinkle of a wind chime; now she saw that it was these pretty shells that had made the music.

Across the hearth sat two Indian women, one very young, plump girl, hardly more than a child, and a serene, handsome woman of indeterminate age. Elizabeth's first impression of the Shawnee had been that there was little physical difference between the Shawnee people and the Iroquois. The villagers she'd seen were somewhat lighter of skin than the Seneca, not as tall or stocky. Although of more delicate build, the Shawnee seemed to be as well-fed, healthy, and clean as the Iroquois. Naturally, the Shawnee wore clothing of slightly different styling and decoration. These women seemed to substantiate her original conclusions. Both had high cheekbones, even white teeth, smooth complexions—free of any tattoos—and light skin.

So far, no one had given Elizabeth the welcome Hunt had insisted they would receive. The only enthusiasm shown toward the newcomers had come from a huge, shaggy, brown dog that had leaped on Hunt, nearly knocking him off his feet, and then covered Hunt's face with wet kisses. The three young braves acting as camp guards had kept a distance and spoken only to Hunt; the girl who'd led Elizabeth to this rounded structure half buried in the earth on the outskirts of the village had not even spoken to her.

The tall woman sitting cross-legged on the far side of the crackling fire cleared her throat and smiled. Her hair and shoulders were covered by a red wool trade blanket with black stripes. Under that, she wore a doeskin tunic and red wool leggings that tucked into ornately beaded moccasins. When she motioned with her hand for Elizabeth to remove her cloak, Elizabeth noticed a wide copper bracelet on her slender wrist.

Elizabeth shrugged off her outer garments without taking her eyes off this person of obvious rank. "Greetings to this hearth," she said in Iroquoian, determined to make her reluctant hostess speak.

The younger girl's eyes widened, and she began to chatter excitedly in a language Elizabeth didn't understand. The older woman pushed back her blanket and regarded her with a smile. *"Bonjour, mademoiselle. Bienvenue a notre village."*

Elizabeth hesitated as faint memories of her childhood French lessons emerged from the recesses of her mind. *"Je ne parle le français,"* she answered. How many times had her tutor, Madame Cordonnier, rapped her knuckles with a fan for her poor pronunciation? She did understand that the Shawnee woman had said good day and something about being welcome.

"You speak English, perhaps?" the Indian woman ventured in soft, clear tones.

"Yes," Elizabeth replied with relief. "Yes, I do. I'm English."

"Ah." The Indian woman smiled again and touched her lips with clasped hands. "It is good. I do not have the grasp of Seneca. My husband knows enough to get by, but he is not here. My name is Sweet Water. This is not our village. I am a visitor too and was reluctant to do the honors. I did not wish to slight Moccasin Flower . . ." She motioned to her companion. "But in her name and that of our hosts, be welcome in this place."

The younger one looked up shyly and said something in her own tongue. Immediately, Sweet Water translated. "Moccasin Flower asks you to forgive her for her bad manners. She has never seen an English woman, and she thought you might be a ghost. She asks your name."

"I'm Elizabeth. Elizabeth Anne Fleming."

"Lissabannflmmin," Moccasin Flower repeated.

"Elizabeth."

"Lizzabett." Moccasin Flower giggled at her mispronunciation. Leaning close to Sweet Water, she whispered in her ear. As she moved, a furry, rust-colored animal poked its head out of her sleeve. Elizabeth watched in amazement as a chipmunk wiggled out and ran up the girl's clothing to hide in her unbound hair.

Sweet Water smiled again. "Her little friend will not bite. Don't be afraid. Moccasin Flower wants to know if she can touch you."

Elizabeth held out her hand and the girl rubbed the skin on the back of her wrist briskly, then giggled again.

"You are kind," Sweet Water said. "Moccasin Flower has newly come to womanhood. This is only her second moon of bleeding."

"And yet she must be locked away as though she were unclean," Elizabeth replied tartly, then quickly regretted her frankness. She didn't wish to offend this important woman. "Are you Shawnee?" she asked her.

Sweet Water nodded. "I am, but we are Mecate Shawnee. We live south and west of here. My husband came to parley with his friends." Her eyes narrowed. "You think of the women's hut as a jail?"

"Isn't it?" Elizabeth wrinkled her nose. "What's happened to my body—and hers . . ." She motioned toward Moccasin Flower. "It isn't unclean or shameful. It's a natural occurrence."

"Of course," Sweet Water agreed. "Women possess the power of life. It is strong medicine, stronger than anything a man can boast. They do not shut us away; we choose to withdraw. Here we do no work. We tell stories, sleep, eat food others have prepared for us, and rest from the chores of day-to-day living."

"Hunt—the man who came with me—said that the Shawnee men would not want me near them."

"No. That is true. But it is not because you are unclean. It is that they believe—we all believe—that a woman is near to the Creator at such a time. You have so much power that it might spill out and accidentally harm a male who has no protection against you."

"You don't mind being put aside?" Elizabeth asked.

"No, I do not. In truth, as the mother of two young children, I find it restful. While I bide here, other hands will rock my little ones, and careful eyes will watch that they do not come to harm."

"Every month?"

Sweet Water glanced at Moccasin Flower and said something quickly in Algonquian. The girl laughed merrily and replied in her own tongue.

"Moccasin Flower wants to know if the white women do not bleed every month," Sweet Water asked.

"Of course they do, when they're not too old or too young, or with child," Elizabeth said.

Sweet Water translated again for her younger friend. "And they do not go apart from the men?" she asked Elizabeth.

"Naturally not."

"Poor white women," Sweet Water said. "Moccasin Flower feels sorry that her white sisters have no time of rest." She gestured gracefully toward a covered kettle. "But you must be hungry and thirsty from your journey. There are corn cakes and honey in that basket, and stew in the pot. We have fresh water, but if you would like tea, I can brew some."

"Tea would be wonderful," Elizabeth said. "Anything you can give me to eat will do fine. I'm starved. We've been walking nearly two weeks." She paused before adding, "Thank you for your offer. I don't mean to be rude."

"You were a prisoner of the Seneca. You have no need to apologize. You have suffered greatly, have you not?" Sweet Water began to dip steaming stew into a wooden bowl.

"Your English is very good," Elizabeth said. Sweet Water had a faint accent she couldn't place, but her speech was that of a gentlewoman.

"I learned from my mother," the Indian woman explained. "She studied with a priest."

*That explains her excellent grasp of the language,* Elizabeth decided. "I'm glad you learned. It was terrible when I was first captured by the Seneca. I couldn't understand anything they said, and no one bothered to translate."

"My husband tells me that Iroquois is very difficult to learn."

Elizabeth couldn't help noticing the beautiful porcupine quill work and the colorful beading on Sweet Water's deerskin tunic. The garment was nearly white with long fringes along the hem and on each sleeve. Around her neck, she wore a beaded choker adorned with a silver cross. Her long, dark hair was divided in the center and plaited into two heavy braids, each wound with red silk ribbons. In her ears tinkled tiny silver bells.

"You wear a cross," Elizabeth said. "Are you a Christian?"

"I try to be," Sweet Water answered in the same husky voice, "but it is difficult, is it not? Especially the part about loving your enemies."

Elizabeth laughed. "Yes, it is." Then she looked at Sweet Water's face more closely. In the firelight, she could see that the Indian woman's eyes were a clear, sparkling blue.

"You want to ask about the color of my eyes," Sweet Water said, almost as though she could read Elizabeth's mind. "My grandfather had blue eyes. He was Scottish."

"Oh." Elizabeth felt her cheeks grow warm. "Was I that obvious?"

"People ask how it is that a woman of the Mecate Shawnee has sky eyes instead of those of a proper human, and so I tell the truth." She offered the bowl and a horn spoon to Elizabeth. "My youngest child, a daughter, also has sky eyes."

"I didn't mean it as an insult," Elizabeth hurried to say. "My own eyes are green."

"So they are."

"The Seneca made fun of me because of them . . . and my hair."

Sweet Water regarded Elizabeth's hair carefully. She took a stray lock between her fingers, rubbed the strands, and raised them to the light. "Red as an Irish fox," she pronounced.

"Exactly." Elizabeth chuckled. "The Seneca said an English fox."

"I believe they are the same animal. But you could dye your hair with walnut hulls."

Elizabeth laughed. "I guess I could, couldn't I? But

then, I'd always know I didn't have the proper color hair . . ."

"For a human," her new friend supplied.

They laughed together.

Elizabeth tasted the stew and found it delicious. "This is wonderful. You have salt." Salt was a luxury, one that she'd known little of during her captivity.

"It comes from a natural salt lick far down the Ohio," Sweet Water explained. "I admit, I like salt with my stew; I always have."

Elizabeth's eyes narrowed. "You really spend every moon time in this hut and you don't mind? Aren't you ever bored?"

"In the hut in our village, some of us do beadwork or make jewelry. And in good weather, we are free to bathe in the river or walk in the forest—so long as we do not come near any hunter. And yes, I do enjoy it. In a larger village, there are more women to gossip and share songs and memories with. I think the woman who first convinced a man that this custom was correct was very wise."

"You have a strange way of looking at things."

"So my good husband tells me."

"He must be a great hunter, your husband," Elizabeth replied, "an important man of stature."

Sweet Water uttered a sound of amusement. "He tells me that as well, especially the part about the stature. But then every husband believes that the Creator has endowed him with a staff of gigantic proportion, does he not?"

Elizabeth couldn't help but smile. The Shawnee, she decided, shared a sense of ribald humor with the Seneca. "I think you might be right about that," Elizabeth agreed.

\*          \*          \*

In the chief's lodge, a dozen men and women were seated around the central fire, while others stood behind them, and still more—mostly half-grown boys—lingered outside near the entrance flap. Hunt, the youngest man seated cross-legged in a position of honor near the hearth, listened as Counts His Scalps, the guest shaman, spoke at length on the current peace between the Iroquois and the Shawnee. This was the fourth day that the council had been discussing Hunt's request for a raiding party to help him snatch Elizabeth's son from Yellow Drum's village.

"The Seneca are many. The Iroquois Confederacy musters as many warriors as there are leaves on the trees," Counts His Scalps reminded the assembly. "If the Seneca, Yellow Drum, protests the stealing of his son—and what father would not—will Shawnee honor be dashed to earth like a rotten pumpkin?"

Ripples of grumbling flowed around the room. One elderly woman made a loud clicking noise with her tongue. Another old warrior with a face like seamed leather nodded his head vigorously and raised a long clay pipe in his gnarled left hand. Hunt noticed that the man's right hand was missing three fingers, and his left, a thumb. His snow-white hair was worn long, held in place by tiny braids of white leather strung with elk teeth. Three eagle feathers dangled from the old man's tan headband.

"Think long and hard, brothers," Counts His Scalps said. The shaman's head was shaved, except for a scalplock, which was dyed red, stiffened with deer hair, and decorated with tufts of down. His coat was red wool, a British military jacket with gold braid and silver buttons, worn over a blue wool breechclout, leather leggings, and woven garters of blue silk embroidered with red silk dragons. Tiny bird skulls swung from his distended earlobes, and his broad hawk face bore a single slash of yellow paint that bisected his face from the right temple to the tattoo of an owl on the lower left side of his chin. Around his neck he wore a necklace of bear claws, a French officer's silver *gorget*, and a tiny leather medicine bag. Clamped through his nose, he boasted a silver disk cut from a British coin.

Counts His Scalps paused until his audience grew restless, then spoke again with the voice of a practiced orator. "Yes, the Iroquois are many, and we are few. But just as the bear fears the angry wasp, so the Seneca fear the valor of the Shawnee." He drew in a breath and looked around, lingering on each face in the circle. "The question is—do we unsheath that stinging lance? Do we risk war? Have we not promised our brothers, the Iroquois, that we will smoke the peace pipe with them? Do we break our word for a stranger, a white-skinned man who will leave us to face the wrath of the Seneca?"

The veteran with the missing fingers cleared his throat. "What the esteemed medicine man says is true. The Iroquois are many and their anger is not to be provoked lightly."

"So speaks a warrior who left his fingers in the coals of a Mohawk fire," Counts said. "So speaks the wise and brave Little Horse."

The old man puffed on the pipe and passed it to Hunt. "It is true. This man did leave his flesh and bones in the ashes of an Iroquois torture fire. But he brought back from the Mohawk village the scalps of two Mohawks stretched on hoops, so that all may see the Iroquois are not monsters but only men."

"Ho," cried a thin man with gray streaking his dark hair.

"Only men," added a second.

"Ho," echoed a middle-aged woman. "We know this to be true."

Little Horse looked around the circle at the elders and honored warriors. "This man would not have come out of the land of his enemies without the aid of his Delaware cousins," he said. "In particular, one whose name we can no longer speak, one who has crossed the river of souls."

"That is true," agreed the thin man. "Little Horse speaks true. If we could speak that hero's name, it might be Walking Tree."

"Yes, it might," agreed Little Horse. "And this Walking Tree might lie uneasy in his grave, his debt not repaid."

Hunt lowered his gaze and stared into the fire. He'd had his say earlier. It wasn't his place to talk now. The Shawnee were like the Cheyenne and the Arapaho. They took their time in making important decisions and nothing could hurry them. If they wanted to fight, they'd come with him. If they didn't, no amount of pleading would change their minds.

Counts His Scalps glanced around the lodge. "Will anyone else speak for this white-Delaware?"

There was silence. Then, without warning, a tomahawk flew through the air and buried in the hard-packed earth at the shaman's feet. From the shadows rose a seasoned warrior, his chest marked with old scars, his stern face chiseled from granite. "This man would speak."

Hunt heard the sharp intake of Little Horse's breath beside him.

"Speak, noble Fire Talon," the shaman said, reluctantly yielding his place.

Fire Talon remained standing where he was. "This man is a guest in this village, but most of you know me," the warrior said.

"Fire Talon," whispered a woman.

"Chief of the Mecate," stated Little Horse for Hunt's benefit. There were general nods of agreement and whispers from the gathering.

Fire Talon's blue-black hair was gathered loosely in a leather thong and hung down his muscular back nearly to his waist. He was dressed simply in a sleeveless fringed deerskin vest, tan loincloth, and high fringed moccasins. His only adornments were a single copper armband encircling sinewy biceps and the four eagle feathers that dangled from a beaded brooch over his left ear. At his hip hung a beaded knife sheath containing a plain, bone-handled hunting knife.

He didn't dress like a chief, Hunt thought, but anyone looking into that proud face and those fierce eyes would know this Fire Talon was a man to be reckoned with. Hunt decided he liked him even before the Mecate spoke.

"This Delaware man has come to us to ask a favor," Fire Talon said quietly. Hunt noted how all whispers ceased and even the old women leaned forward to catch every word.

"True," agreed Little Horse. "He has come to ask a favor."

"At my mother's knee, this man heard of the wisdom of the Lenape, now called the Delaware," Fire Talon continued. "The grandfather people, Lenni Lenape, the true people. Is this not so?"

"It is so," a fat man said.

"The grandfather people," echoed Little Horse.

"These Delaware have taken Shawnee wives and husbands, have joined with the Shawnee in war, have shared food with us in time of famine. Is this not so?"

"It is so," chimed in Counts His Scalps. "They are our brothers. No one disputes this."

"Each must decide for himself," Fire Talon continued in a reasonable tone. "This man listens and
thinks, To whom does a child belong? To the mother
or the father? Those of you who know me, know that
once, long ago, another child was lost and never
found. This man has a debt unpaid, a promise unful-
filled." He smiled, a wolfish grin, and his dark eyes
gleamed. "This man remembers when no warrior
spoke of the color of a brother's skin . . . when the
bond of blood between Delaware and Shawnee meant
more than fear of Seneca revenge." He reached the
buried tomahawk in two long strides and raised it
over his head. "Fire Talon, chief of the Mecate, follows his Delaware brother to the land of the Seneca."

"Fox goes as well," called a lean warrior who
leaped out of the shadows. "What of the mighty shaman? Does Counts His Scalps want death to find him
in his bed?"

"Counts His Scalps fears no Seneca," shouted a
young man in a scarlet hunting coat.

The shaman stood. "Counts His Scalps goes," he
proclaimed.

"Red Shirt goes, as well," cried the younger brave
who'd defended the shaman's reputation.

"And Black Hoof!"

"Feathered Lance has nothing better to do," said
another man.

Little Horse got to his feet, and the meeting dissolved without further ceremony. Warriors and council members spilled out of the lodge onto the dance
ground, where they were joined by an excited group
of villagers all shouting and talking at once.

Hunt stepped out into the pale sunshine and
stretched. In spite of the unseasonable temperature,
the air had a scent of change about it, and since he'd
last noticed more leaves had taken on the gilded tints

of late autumn. The mournful cry of geese winging south added their voices to the one in his head that warned the spell of Indian summer was fast coming to a close. Bad weather on the trail, especially in enemy territory, wasn't anything a man relished. He hoped they'd be able to get to the boy before the bottom fell out and winter sealed the Iroquois land tight.

Fire Talon broke into Hunt's thoughts with a light touch on his arm. "We must talk," he said. "It would be best if we could recover the boy without starting war. You have more volunteers than you can safely use."

"I agree," Hunt said. "Too many men is worse than too few. You know the warriors better than I do. Would you choose the raiding party?"

Fire Talon eyed him dispassionately. "It is a leader's place to pick who will follow him."

Hunt nodded. "It would honor me if you would be that leader."

Fire Talon's thin lips turned up in an elusive smile. "If you wish."

"A man would be a fool to try and tell a hawk how to fly," Hunt replied.

"You show wisdom for a warrior of so few years," the older warrior said.

"Getting the boy back to his mother is what's important," Hunt said, "not who calls himself war captain."

"Tell the woman to make herself ready to travel."

Hunt's eyes widened in surprise. "She's not going with us. I'm leaving her here, where it's safe."

Fire Talon shook his head. "We go to steal a wolf pup. Who better to lure him from the den than his mother?"

# Chapter 15

**"S**weet Water?"

A male voice just outside the wall of the wigwam startled Elizabeth out of sleep. Heart thudding, she sat up and listened intently to see if she'd really heard a stranger speak only inches from her head or if she'd been dreaming.

"I must speak to Sweet Water." This time the stranger used English.

Elizabeth called softly to her friend. "Sweet Water."

Moccasin Flower had left, and three other women had joined them in the four days she'd spent confined in the lodge. During that time, they'd passed the hours by talking, playing a game that resembled dice with pieces of colored bone, and singing old story-chants that related the history of the tribe. Often, Sweet Water read passages aloud from her Bible to the others. The younger adolescents took turns brushing each others' hair and arranging their tresses in different styles.

Like the Seneca, these Shawnee women had keen senses of humor. Often the jokes they exchanged were bawdy, but their jests were never cruel or malicious.

Elizabeth felt that she'd made a friend in Sweet Water, although neither had revealed much about her personal life. Elizabeth had been uncomfortable relating her story to the Shawnee woman, so she'd merely said that her son was still a captive of the Seneca, omitting the fact that Jamie was Yellow Drum's son as well. She hadn't told her that she and Hunt were more than traveling companions either.

When Sweet Water didn't answer, Elizabeth crept to her side and gently shook her. "Someone is calling for you," she murmured.

"Who is it?" Sweet Water asked.

"This man would speak with his wife," came the urgent whisper from the far side of the wall.

"Go to the entrance flap," Sweet Water replied. She put a finger to her lips. "Shh. We thank you. Now go back to sleep and pretend he was never here," she said to Elizabeth.

Elizabeth returned to her bed and pulled the blanket over her, but she was wide awake. She turned her back to give Sweet Water what privacy she could, but it was impossible not to hear and understand her conversation with her husband.

"There is a thing you must know, heart of my heart," Fire Talon whispered in English.

"Does this matter concern the white woman's child?"

For a moment, Talon didn't answer. Elizabeth caught her breath and waited. She knew it was wrong to listen, but she strained to hear what Talon would say.

"Husband?" Sweet Water murmured.

"*Weeshob-izzi Kimmiwun*," he murmured in the beautiful language of the Shawnee, then said her name in English. *Sweet Water*. "*Ki-te-hi*." *My heart*.

"*Ma-tah!*" No. "You'll not soft-talk me, not this time. I'll not have you risk your life for strangers."

He made a tiny noise that could have been a sigh.

"Once this man promised he would find your brother, but I failed you."

"No, Talon, I won't listen to this," she protested. "Colin is dead. He's been dead for fourteen years."

"Do not speak his name," Fire Talon reminded her. "Ghosts of the dead may be lured back across the river by—"

"By calling their names. I know you believe that, but I don't. I loved my little brother; I raised him from a babe. He was always more my child than a brother, and whether he's dead or alive, I'll always love him. No power on earth can convince me that any ghost of his would ever wish me harm."

"He whose name we do not speak was lost to us," Talon continued softly, "but this child can be rescued. It will not be an easy thing to take him from the Seneca."

"It isn't your fight."

"So. This man goes, and so does Fox and Counts His Scalps."

"Leave heroics to the young men, Talon. Stay with me . . . please."

"Remember your sorrow. Elizabeth has endured years of servitude among the Seneca. It is only right that she should have her son," he said.

"What of your duty to me and my children?" she pleaded. "Falcon is only eleven, your daughter hardly more than a baby. Your family needs your strength. Your tribe needs—"

"This man has given his word. He only wanted to tell you, so that you'd not hear it from others. It is true that he is no longer young, but neither is he ready to sit in the sun and tell stories."

"You're not going for the boy's sake. You're doing it because you miss the danger." Fear rang in her voice. "Admit it! Admit that you and Fox and Counts are bored with peace. You love the adventure—the fighting."

"No, Sky Eyes, this man does not love killing. Does he go for the thrill of danger? Perhaps he does long to pull Iroquois tail feathers one last time." He paused. "You'd not want our son to go along, I suppose."

"Falcon? Absolutely not. Don't you dare try to—"

"You cannot keep him a child forever, wife. He must learn the ways of men."

"He's not a man yet. He's not made his vision quest. You can't have him."

"Very well," Talon rumbled.

"I can't stop you from doing what you will," Sweet Water chided him, "but I won't let you take our son."

"This time he will be entrusted with the protection of his mother," Talon relented reluctantly. "But he will not thank you for your concern. He longs to try his wings, this fierce young warrior of ours."

"Eleven is too young to take the war trail."

"This man was younger when he—"

"I don't care. He cannot go."

"As you remind me, he has yet to complete his vision quest. Our son will escort his mother back to our village, as will Cedar Bark and three others of our tribe. There's no telling how long we will be gone, and it is best if you return to our little daughter." Fire Talon sighed. "Do not send me away with anger in your heart, wife of my spirit. We will be together again soon."

"God willing," she answered.

"This man wants to hold you," he murmured so low that Elizabeth could barely hear him. "But if he touches you, others will learn of it, and the chosen men might fear that their luck had been fouled. A man who believes his luck is sour will soon prove it true."

"I want to hold you, too," Sweet Water replied. Her voice deepened and Elizabeth heard the catch of pain in her tone. "Keep the wind at your back, my husband. And place your moccasins carefully."

He did not reply, and Elizabeth heard the soft footfalls as he walked away. In coming to Sweet Water, the chieftain had strained the rules of a warrior. The Shawnee women had explained that a brave was forbidden to touch a woman in isolation . . . forbidden to make love to his wife before leaving on a raid even if she wasn't having her moon-time bleeding. The Shawnee believed that women's soft hearts and soft bodies weakened warriors. A man must show the world only strength . . . and a woman must wait and weep alone.

If only Hunt could love me like that, Elizabeth thought. She had never been a jealous woman, but tonight, she could not keep the tears from welling up in her eyes. *Why not me?* she wondered. *Why can't I be the one with a husband who cares more for me than laws or custom—who would risk honor and position to come to me?*

"He goes to rescue your son," Sweet Water said. "There's no use pretending you didn't hear. We spoke in English so the others wouldn't understand, but you heard."

"I'm sorry for your worry," Elizabeth replied, "but I thank God he is going."

"Thank him when they have returned safely," Sweet Water answered sharply. "For I'm not a good enough Christian to wish your son safe in your arms if it means the loss of my husband."

\* \* \*

When their time of menses passed, Elizabeth, Sweet Water, and another woman named Jumps High bathed from head to toe in hot, scented water, and then dashed to the river in the shimmering orchid light of early dawn to plunge in for a quick dip. Shivering and sputtering, the three climbed up the bank and ran to a nearby wigwam to dress and enjoy a hot meal cooked for them by Jumps High's mother, a plump partridge of a woman with a round, smiling face.

Several days before, Moccasin Flower had removed Elizabeth's garments from the women's house and loaned her a dress. Here in the snug wigwam, Elizabeth found her original clothing cleaned, mended, and smelling of dried cedar chips. On top of the neat bundle lay a dainty armband and bracelet of beaten copper. Now, Jumps High's mother, Touches Corn, added a warm blanket to the pile.

"Thank you," Elizabeth replied, "but I can't accept your gift. I have nothing to give in return."

A frown crossed Sweet Water's handsome features. "You must take them," she advised. "You are a guest here. To refuse would be to insult these good people."

Elizabeth felt her cheeks go warm. "Yes," she replied quickly. "I should have realized." It would be the same among the Seneca. Guests were treated with the highest honor. Nothing was too good for them. "Thank you for telling me." She turned to the other women and thanked them, knowing her smile and gestures would need no translation.

Elizabeth glanced back at Sweet Water. The older woman had cooled toward her since her husband had come to speak with her. She was not actually rude, but she offered none of the open friendship she'd exhibited earlier, and Elizabeth was truly sorry. She liked Sweet Water, and she understood how the Indian woman must feel at having her husband risk danger for a white woman's child.

"I must see Hunt Campbell," Elizabeth said gently to her in English. "Will that be allowed?"

Jumps High giggled.

Her mother admonished her with a slight *tch* sound.

"Of course," Sweet Water answered. "You are not a prisoner here. Now that your time of withdrawal is over, you may go where you please, so long as you do not wander into the shaman's lodge and touch sacred objects, or handle the weapons of warriors who go to seek your lost son."

"I'm not likely to do either," Elizabeth replied tartly. "I've lived among the Seneca for many years. I know what a woman may and may not touch."

Sweet Water inclined her head. "The Iroquois are wise, even if they are not always our friends. Has it occurred to you that your son might be better off living among them?"

Elizabeth felt her own anger swell in her chest, hot and seething. Was there no one who could see that she had to have her children back? Could no one understand her plight? "Do you have children?" she asked.

"I do."

"Would you leave your child with the Seneca?"

"No," she answered. "I would not." Her clear blue eyes filled with tears as she took Elizabeth's hand and squeezed it. "Forgive me. I blame you for my own fears. You do not make my husband go. He chooses to do this thing. It isn't your fault."

Elizabeth gripped her hand tightly. "They—my son," she corrected quickly. "My son depends on me. He's only six winters. I'm afraid he'll think I've abandoned him. When does the war party leave?"

"I know no more than you do." Sweet Water's forehead crinkled with concern, and she nibbled absently at her lower lip. "I go to seek my husband. I will ask Jumps High to help you locate Hunt Campbell."

"But they haven't left yet?" Elizabeth suddenly was afraid. What if he was already gone? What if he left without her? Even if he managed to get Jamie away, that would leave Rachel at Raven's mercy.

Sweet Water spoke to Jumps High's mother in Algonquian, and the old woman answered. "No," Sweet Water assured her. "The war party did not leave. This afternoon will be a False Face Dance, and after that prayers and dancing for the safe return of the men. Tomorrow they go, at first light."

Elizabeth's heartbeat slowed to near normal. She still had time to talk to Hunt and convince him to take her with him. And if she couldn't, then she must reveal her secret. A shudder passed through her. What if he decided not to go for either child? The thought was too terrible to dwell on.

"Please," she said to Sweet Water. "Please ask Jumps High to take me to Hunt at once. It's urgent that I see him."

It was nearly dusk before Elizabeth saw Hunt. He'd left early in the morning with Fire Talon and some of his friends to hunt deer for the evening feast and celebration. She saw him arrive with the hunting party just as the medicine men were beginning the False Face Dance, but before she could reach the admiring circle of women around the hunters and the three fat deer they'd brought in, Hunt disappeared into the crowd.

Shaking rattles made of turtle shell, the two principal dancers—the village shaman and a visiting holy man known as Counts His Scalps—began to weave in and out of the assembly of gaily clad men, women, and children. The shamans, dressed in full ceremonial regalia and wearing large, carved wooden masks, moved with slow, shuffling steps. Close behind them followed a man, face painted, beating on a small drum.

While the Shawnee dress was different, the occasion seemed similar to many Elizabeth had witnessed among the Seneca. This was obviously a joyous celebration rather than a war dance, because the women were present and taking part. Everywhere, people were smiling. Wide-eyed babies had ceased their crying and stared in wonder at the bright colors. Children wiggled and hopped up and down in excitement; women good-naturedly whispered to them to be still. In sharp contrast to deeply religious Seneca events, no one here seemed to be in awe of the shamans. Even the carved masks the medicine men wore were friendly, rather than fierce.

During this dance, the masked men rubbed the faces and bodies of each person with the turtle shell rattles. As each Shawnee was anointed, he or she joined the shamans in song while the remainder of the tribe sang a repetitious chorus. When everyone, young and old, had been blessed, including Elizabeth, the holy men went from one wigwam to another, touching their rattles over the doorways.

Finally, everyone formed a circle with the two masked shamans in the center. Several men left the group to play on other drums, and the dance ended with prayers and offerings of tobacco thrown into a central fire.

After the dance came feasting. Delicious odors filled the air as Sweet Water called Elizabeth to help the women bring out the food.

"I've been looking for Hunt, but I still can't find him," Elizabeth said.

"He's with my husband in our wigwam," Sweet Water answered. "Fire Talon is a great planner. They are probably working out the details of the raid."

"But I must—" Elizabeth began.

"Don't even think about it. Talon will be furious if you interrupt them. There will be time to speak to Hunt Campbell."

Knowing that angering Sweet Water's husband would not aid her cause, Elizabeth did as she was asked. She helped the women carry out platter after platter of fish, corn cakes, baked squash and pumpkin, nuts, honey, mushrooms, roasted meat, and pots of stew and corn pudding. Young men gathered in twos and threes to practice dance steps while teams of women butchered the three deer and cut them into sections to be roasted over open fires.

Near the center of the village, boys were competing in a contest to see who could throw the most arrows through a rolling hoop. On the far side of the clearing, one of the shamans had taken off his mask and was throwing strings of beads into the air for little girls to catch.

Finally, a gray-haired woman called out that it was time to eat, and everyone gathered around to share the bounty of food. Elizabeth was too nervous to be hungry, but Sweet Water insisted that she have a little venison and a corn cake.

"Eat," she ordered. "It will be a long night, and you will offend the villagers if you do not partake of their food."

After everyone had eaten their fill, another prayer was offered for a good winter by Counts His Scalps. The social dancing was begun on the stomp ground by a group of young matrons and maidens, all wearing fringed blankets over their dresses. Elizabeth slipped away from Sweet Water and Moccasin Flower. At the edge of the crowd, she stopped to watch as the dancers swirled their blankets. Each woman put her hands on her hips and executed a series of graceful steps to a quick, lively drumbeat.

"This is called the Quail Dance," Hunt said, coming up unexpectedly behind Elizabeth. The big dog that had jumped up on him when they'd first entered the Shawnee camp dropped belly down and began thumping a ragged tail at Hunt's feet.

"Oh," she said, startled by Hunt's sudden nearness. "I've been looking for you everywhere," she stammered. Now that he was here, she was nearly at a loss for words. She'd thought of him so often during her captivity in the women's house, and now, inexplicably, she was tongue-tied.

He lifted a dark eyebrow in wry amusement. "You've found me."

Elizabeth shivered. "Traitor. You let them lock me up like some sort of—"

He grinned lazily. "Never break custom if you want to make friends." He folded his arms over his broad chest and gave her a long, intense stare. "You seem none the worse for it," he teased.

"Stop that." She'd spent weeks alone with this man—she'd let him make love to her. There was no earthly reason why she should be nervous around him now, but she felt suddenly light-headed under his amused stare.

"Stop what?" he asked.

"Making Indian eyes at me."

He chuckled. "And what exactly are *Indian* eyes?"

"You close them to slits and peer out at me as though you could see right through me . . ." She fumbled for the right words. "... Or know what I am thinking."

"Maybe I do," he replied with arrogant assurance.

*He's more Indian than white today*, she thought with a sudden shiver of excitement. Hunt wore a fringed buckskin vest over a long, indigo blue, ruffled shirt with full sleeves that stretched taut across his muscular chest. His scarlet wool loincloth hung over leggings to touch the top of high, quill-worked moccasins, but left his sinewy thighs exposed with every step he took. Slashes of red paint adorned each chiseled cheekbone, and his hair hung loose down his back with eagle feathers woven into the black, glossy length.

Had he always been so handsome and she'd not realized it? she wondered. Or had something changed about him here among these Shawnee? Whatever the reason, Hunt was every inch a warrior ... a magnificently masculine devil who would turn the head of any woman with hot blood in her veins. She swallowed and tried to keep her tone normal as she answered him. "Sweet Water told me that you were with her husband, but—"

"I've been making plans with Fire Talon," he said. "He's going to lead the party to try and rescue your son. He was making a final decision on who will go."

"You're not leading the party? I'd assumed—"

"Fire Talon is a seasoned Shawnee war chief. He's led dozens of war parties. He knows these braves and the territory better than I do. It only makes sense that he—"

"Did you tell him that I have to go with you?" she demanded. The dog stood up and pushed between them, then butted his massive head against Hunt's hand as though he wanted to be petted. "Shoo," she said to the animal. "Why is this oversized monster . . ." Suspicion made her glance up at Hunt. "Is this your dog?"

"I think I'm his man. I left him here while I went to fetch you. His name's Badger."

"Badger." She glanced back at the big dog who'd placed himself defensively in front of Hunt. "I have to talk to you," she said, but when she put out her hand to touch Hunt, the dog bristled. She snatched her hand back. "Is he going to bite me?"

Hunt grinned provocatively. "Not unless you bite me first." Taking her arm, he led her away from the dancing to a secluded spot between the wigwams and the river. Badger trotted after them, seemingly oblivious to the throngs of people or the other village dogs. "Down, boy," Hunt told the animal. Badger dropped to the ground and began to lick a bear-sized front paw.

"Hunt, please," Elizabeth said. "Did you tell this Fire Talon that I had to come?"

Hunt shrugged. "I told him you belonged here where it was safe," he answered brusquely.

"But I have to go," she insisted.

"That's what Talon said."

"What?" She was totally confused. "What did you say?"

The dog stiffened and the hair on his neck and shoulders rose like an angry lion's mane.

"Badger," Hunt said. "Down." He met her anxious gaze. "Fire Talon wants you with us. He says it will be easier to get the boy if you're along."

Her knees went weak, and she leaned against him for support. "You mean I can go?"

Hunt drew her into his arms. "Yes, God help us. Yes, you can come."

"Oh . . . oh, Hunt. Thank you." She looked up into his face, and he lowered his head and groaned.

"Hunt," she repeated softly. Liquid heat spilled through her veins, and it seemed the most natural thing in the world to rise on her toes and brush his lips with hers.

"Don't," he rasped. "Don't do this to me unless you mean to let me love you."

She kissed the left corner of his mouth and a rainbow of sweet emotion spiraled through her veins.

"Woman . . ."

She traced the curve of his lower lip with the tip of her tongue. "Man," she teased in Seneca.

"Elizabeth." He drew her name out until the last syllable became inaudible. "Do you know what you're asking for?"

"I know what I want," she answered boldly. Tomorrow they would leave on a perilous journey to rescue her son. They might die before they ever had a chance to be alone again. Tonight she would forget her inhibitions . . . her fears. If he would still have her, she would lie with him and find joy beneath his hot, virile body. "I want you," she whispered.

He stared down at her with eyes as black and fathomless as any Indian's. "You're certain?"

"I'm certain," she replied. But she wasn't certain about anything. She was terrified. With trembling fingers, she stroked his clean-shaven cheek.

"Why?" he asked her.

She kissed him again.

# Chapter 16

❦

"**N**ot here," he said breathlessly. "Come with me."

Heart racing with anticipation, Elizabeth let him pull her toward a large wigwam on the outer edge of the village. The dog trotted after them. When they reached the entrance, Hunt lifted the deerskin curtain, and she ducked inside. The dog followed.

"Down," Hunt ordered. Badger folded his sturdy legs and collapsed onto the floor, barring the doorway with his shaggy bulk.

Elizabeth moved to the far side of the fire and stood there trembling, unable to tear her eyes off Hunt, barely noticing the interior of the wigwam.

He shrugged out of his vest and drew his shirt over his head in one smooth motion. Eyes smoldering, he extended a lean hand to her. She waited, frozen to the spot, unable to speak, her gaze riveted on the rippling muscles of his bare chest and upper arms.

"Beth," he murmured. "How I've missed you."

"And I've missed you," she admitted.

He waited for her to take the first step toward him, and when she did, his fingers closed around her wrist. She drew in a breath, savoring his scent, letting the joy of finally being alone with him permeate her soul.

214

"Sweetheart," he whispered huskily.

Unafraid, she took another step.

Swiftly, he claimed her with a kiss so searing that it scorched her mouth, and when she parted her lips to utter a small sound, he filled her with his hot tongue.

The intimate kiss was her undoing. With a cry of longing, she dissolved in his arms, blending herself— body and soul—with him, letting the force of his passionate assault sweep away all of her doubts and insecurities.

"Beth . . . Beth," he whispered between scalding kisses. "You are so full of love . . . so beautiful."

It was a lie—she knew it was a lie—but she didn't care. Hearing the words she'd waited a lifetime to hear was like bathing burned skin in ice water. The relief was so great that she didn't mind the ache underneath.

Her heart was pounding so hard that she thought it might break . . . and she didn't care. She arched her back and pressed against him, feeling the heat of Hunt's rock-hard manhood, inhaling the primitive scent of his male arousal.

"Yes . . . yes," she murmured, touching his face . . . tangling her fingers in his long, dark hair. Sighing, she trailed her hands over his powerful shoulders. She had to touch and taste him . . . had to drink in his smell. She wanted him as much as he wanted her. She wanted to feel the weight of his body, the length of his tumescent sex branding her as his own.

Whispering coaxing words, he nuzzled the sensitive place behind her ear and nibbled at her skin. She gasped as he trailed damp love-bites to the hollow of her throat, igniting an urgent heat.

Pulsing excitement churned in the pit of her belly. Her breasts strained against her gown; she could feel her nipples aching to be caressed and kissed. Each breath seemed a struggle, yet she couldn't get enough of kissing him . . . of touching and being touched. She molded her body to his, driven by the intense yearning to fulfill the rising storm at her core.

"Beth . . . I need you. I can't wait."

His voice ripped from his throat as raw as the primitive need that drove her to wrap her legs around him, to make no protest as he lifted her and tugged her dress up over her thrusting hips. With a cry of wanton desire, she clutched his back, digging her nails into his flesh, driven by a fevered heat that knew no shame.

"Yes. Yes!"

Her unleashed passion snapped his last restraint. Still standing, he plunged deep inside her, and her hot folds received him in a glorious embrace. With a groan, he shifted her buttocks and thrust again. She writhed against him, welcoming his pounding drive . . . whipping his lust higher and higher until the primeval act filled his entire consciousness.

Her moans of ecstasy came just before his own explosion. He felt his seed spurt into her womb, and for the briefest instant, he felt an intense sorrow that he could never give her a child. Then the thought was lost in the pulsing pleasure that coursed through his body. "Beth . . . Beth," he groaned.

He staggered back under her weight, and laughing together, they found themselves lying half on and half off a pile of furs. He was still inside her as he pulled her close and kissed the tears from the corners of her eyes.

His chest tightened. "Did I hurt you?" he asked her. Hurting her was the last thing in the world he wanted to do.

"No." She buried her face in his chest. "It . . . it was wonderful."

"You're wonderful," he murmured. He kissed the crown of her head, inhaling deeply of the clean woman-scent of her hair. He loved her hair; it reminded him of bright flames. He wondered again how she could ever believe herself unattractive. She was beautiful, and she was his. He wanted to go on holding her like this forever . . . to feel her heart beating next to his . . . to feel the rise and fall of her chest with every breath. He wanted to keep her safe in his arms and protect her from all the harm in the world.

"Hunt?"

"Yes?" He raised her hand and kissed the underside of her wrist.

She squirmed until she could look him in the eye. "Promise me that you won't go back on your word. You will take me with you."

There was so much he wanted to tell her, but the love words lodged in his throat like fish bones. It was easier to grin and joke. "Aren't you uncomfortable in that dress?" he teased.

"No. I am going, aren't I?"

"Yes." Reluctantly, he withdrew and sat up. "Here, let me. . . . Do you mind if . . ." He caught the hem of her twisted dress. "Can't we just . . ."

She laughed, a merry sound that made his throat constrict. He'd not heard her laugh often, but he had the notion that anyone who laughed like that must have had a lot of practice. "We should have done that before," she teased as she pulled the garment off and laid it on the fur beside them. "I'll make a nice sight for whoever lives here if they come home."

He stretched out lazily and motioned her close. She knelt beside him and laid a hand on his chest. He covered her fingers with his own. "Wonderful? Was that all I was?" he asked lightly.

Teasing words were all he could offer. His true feelings would only break her heart. Speaking them out loud would be the biggest mistake he'd ever made.

He wanted to beg her to stay with him, but he knew it wouldn't be fair. She deserved more than the wilderness life he had to offer. Still he couldn't help imagining what it might be like to wake up each morning and look into her face, to go to sleep each night wrapped in each others' arms. Elizabeth understood him like no other woman had ever done. They had both shared two worlds, Indian and white, and she knew what it was like to be torn between them— to be both without fully being either.

*I want to show you the spring thaw in the high mountains,* he thought. *I'd like to take you where the rivers teem with beaver and the deer are tame enough to creep close enough to touch them. I'd love you to see the waves of buffalo thundering over the prairie, herds that take three days and nights to pass.*

Leaving her would be like leaving his right arm. When they parted, he'd never be the same. He'd not find another woman like her.

Her green eyes sparkled in the firelight. "You're right, Hunt," she teased. "You were more than wonderful—you were magnificent."

"Mmmm, better." He pulled her down and kissed her lips. "You have the nicest breasts."

Pink ovals appeared on her cheeks. "I always thought they were too small."

He caressed her nipple with the pad of his thumb, and the rosy bud hardened under his touch. "Perfect," he murmured. "Like the rest of you."

"The Seneca said my eyes weren't human, that only the big cats had—"

He laughed. "They do look a little like a mountain lion's eyes, but they're still beautiful."

"I don't believe you, but I like to hear you say it." She glanced toward the doorway. "Hunt, it's still broad daylight. Don't you think someone might come in?"

He sat up and kissed her love-swollen lips. "No. Hear the drums; the social dancing's started. No one will go back to his wigwam . . . least of all Counts His Scalps."

Dismayed, her eyes widened. "Counts His Scalps? The shaman? This is his wigwam?"

Hunt chuckled. "Yes, and yes. He's a visiting shaman, a very important man, but also a vain one. These are his quarters . . . and mine, while I'm here. But you needn't worry about Counts or anyone else. Badger won't let anyone in."

"You planned this," she accused, but the merry look in her gaze told him that she was pleased. He felt familiar stirrings in his groin. "Admit it," she said.

"I wish I had." He rolled onto his side and slid an arm under her. "You are a difficult woman, Elizabeth Fleming." He cupped her breast gently.

"I'm not." Her expression grew serious. "At least I don't mean to be."

He sighed, lazily tracing the outline of her aureole with his forefinger until her nipple hardened. "I don't suppose you can help it any more than a bee can help carrying pollen from flower to flower."

Her mouth curved into a smile. "You do say the strangest things."

"Woman, you may have a troublesome disposition, but you also have lips made for kissing."

She closed her eyes and offered her lips. He couldn't resist the invitation. From lips, it seemed only natural to taste her sweet breasts. After that . . .

he let his fingers stray to caress other mysteries.

"You are insatiable," she whispered as he stroked the bright thatch of curling hair at the apex of her thighs.

"Am I?" He placed her hand on his reawakening rod, then sighed with pleasure as she began to stroke it with feather-light fingers. "Don't stop," he urged, then he drew her nipple between his lips and suckled.

"Hunt."

He moved his head and nuzzled her other breast, teasing her until she lifted it to his seeking mouth. Again his passion grew until the throbbing in his organ became a torture. But this time, he'd not hurry; this time, he intended to make a memory for them both to dream on.

Slowly, they explored each others' bodies, delighting in the texture of hair . . . the curve of a back. Her bottom was softly rounded, her legs long and shapely, her feet highly arched.

"I thought you loathed me," he whispered between kisses.

"I thought I did too." Her eyes were like brilliant pools of green water, luminous and everchanging.

He swallowed against the constriction in his throat. *If a man was the type to settle down with one woman, Elizabeth might be that woman,* he thought, but when he spoke, it was of what lay before them. "I can't promise you what will happen to us in Seneca territory," he said, "but this I will promise. If I live, I'll find your boy and bring you both safe away from the Seneca. And after that . . ." *After that we might find a way to make a life . . . the three of us.* "After that—"

"I don't want to talk about what might happen afterward," she said firmly. "I don't want to think or talk about anything except now."

"I just wanted to say—"

She pressed two fingertips over his mouth. "No, don't spoil it for me," she begged. She rolled over until she laid atop him and let her fingers tease his nipples while her long, naked legs pressed against his shaft. He could feel the heat of her, and she gazed at him through eyes heavy-lidded with passion.

Her words stung him, but he choked back what he meant to say and concentrated on the sensation of her silken body next to his.

"It was never like this for me," she said. "Never." She inclined her head so that her heavy mane of thick red hair spilled provocatively across his face and chest.

"Or for me," he admitted.

She flashed him a heartfelt smile.

An idea came to him. "How well can you ride a horse?" he asked her.

She giggled softly. "Not very well," she whispered, then began to trace a two-inch-long triangular scar on his chest with one finger. "How did you get this?" she asked. "You have two of them, just alike." She leaned down and flicked his taut skin with her warm, wet tongue, and bolts of fire shot through his veins.

He let his hand slip from the small of her back, down over her rounded hip to tease the triangle of soft red curls above her damp cleft. "A gift of the sun," he said. "Among the Cheyenne, a man cannot claim to be a warrior unless he proves his courage in the great Sun Dance."

"These scars are deep. I don't understand how dancing . . ."

"You don't want to know," he said softly.

"Yes, I do."

He shook his head. "Later, darling, I'll tell you later."

"It must have been very painful."

"The Sun Dance is not about pain—it's about sacrifice, about faith in something greater than yourself." He looked into her eyes. "It changes you forever, the Sun Dance." He took a breath and let it out slowly. "It's part of me, my secret name, bestowed on me by a Cheyenne holy man."

She waited, trembling, trust shining in her eyes. And he told her what he had never told another, what had been secret between him and his creator. "The shaman named me Sundancer."

"But you never use that name."

He kissed her mouth, drinking of her sweetness. "That's part of the power," he murmured. "That it's secret."

She sighed. "But you told me."

He kissed her again. "Yes, I told you," he whispered when they separated again for breath.

"I'll treasure your secret," she promised. She kissed the scars on his chest again.

He stroked her inner leg and she moaned and pressed against him. "Elizabeth," he whispered, and thrust a finger gently inside her. "Shall I kiss the flower?" he asked.

"Shall I kiss the stem?" she dared. Before he could answer, she slid lower and took him between her hands. Slowly, she leaned over him and touched her tongue to the swollen head of his organ. He groaned as she drew him between her lips.

Hunt closed his eyes and let the waves of white-hot sensation wash over him. And when the sea threatened to drown his last thread of self-control, he murmured, "Now, it's your turn."

Without speaking, she rolled onto her back and parted her legs. Her breathing was ragged, her muscles tense as he knelt between her knees and kissed the satiny skin along her inner thigh.

She whimpered and clutched his hair.

He groaned. The pleasure-pain of his throbbing erection was maddening, but he wanted to please her more than he wanted to please himself. He tasted the forbidden fruit . . . found the ripe nubbin of flesh and laved it with his tongue.

"Oh," she whimpered, flinging her head wildly from side to side. "Oh, yes . . . do it . . . do it. Please!"

He was more than ready; it took every ounce of his willpower to keep from climaxing before he plunged into her.

Slowly he slid into her silken sheath. She arched her hips to take every inch of him, and he went in deeper. He watched her . . . wanting to see the rapture on her face . . . imprinting her red-gold image on his mind for all time. And when he finally felt her spasms of erotic pleasure, he drove deep one final time, releasing his own passion with an intensity he had never felt with any other woman.

Later, after they had kissed and cuddled and dozed, they washed with warm water from a kettle beside the hearth. Hunt found a bone comb beside Counts His Scalps's sleeping place, and Elizabeth rearranged her hair. When she was finished, he used the comb to make his own hair decent, then tied it back in a single plait.

"You wear your locks long for a white man," she observed as she straightened the end of his braid.

"Only my skin is white. An Indian warrior takes strength from his hair."

"It seems to me that you switch back and forth from Indian to white when it pleases you. I thought it was forbidden for a warrior to be with a woman before leaving on a raid," she teased. Her cheeks were as pink as ripening strawberries, and her face glowed with an inner light. She looked too beautiful to him to be real.

"It is forbidden." He couldn't stop remembering how it had been between them . . . how freely she'd given everything a woman can give and more.

"You broke the rule."

He smiled at her. "With a vengeance."

"Are you afraid I'll bring you bad luck?"

He shrugged. "Can it get any worse? I've lost every ounce of common sense. Only a fool would try to steal Yellow Drum's son and take a woman along when he made the attempt."

Clouds of emotion swirled in her eyes, and an expression of vulnerability flickered over her face. "Then why are you doing it?"

"You're a burr under my blanket."

Her mood shifted, and the tension evaporated between them as she chuckled. "I've been called much worse."

"With good reason?"

She tied the thongs on her moccasin. "I'm afraid so."

The dog opened his eyes and rose to his feet. His ears pricked up and he made a low sound deep in his throat.

"Someone's coming," Hunt said.

He hated to go out, to break the spell they'd both been caught in. He'd come so close to asking her to be his wife, but she'd stopped him. What he'd said was true—she was a burr under his blanket, but she'd gotten deeper into him than he'd ever dreamed possible. He thought that sleeping with her again might weaken the spell she held over him, but it hadn't happened. He wanted her as badly now as he had before—maybe worse. The truth was that he didn't want her for an afternoon; he wanted her for the rest of his life.

For a brief moment, he allowed his gaze to focus on her vibrant features: her full, sensual lips, the high, well-defined cheekbones, and her mischievous eyes, framed with dark, full lashes. Her nose tilted up just a little; her chin was too stubborn for a woman.

Elizabeth's fair skin was scattered with freckles, and one soft bird's wing of a brow bore a tiny scar. He had seen a Crow woman whose heart-shaped face was flawless, a Blackfoot girl with a better figure, but he'd never known a female who tugged at his heart as Elizabeth Fleming did.

He sighed. Obviously, she wasn't as taken with him as he had been with her. She didn't want to let him speak of commitment.

Badger's whine became a rumble. "Down, boy," Hunt said. "It's all right. We're among friends here."

But he knew better. It wasn't all right. He and Elizabeth would have no more time to be alone and intimate. In the days to come, one or both of them might meet a sudden and violent death, and whatever he wanted to say to her would have to wait.

He still wanted to hold her safe and warm in his arms . . . God, how he wanted that.

A familiar voice called his name in Algonquian from outside the entrance flap. "It's Counts," Hunt said to Elizabeth. "Come in."

The shaman entered the dwelling, glanced at Elizabeth, then back to Hunt, and smiled knowingly. "Fire Talon looks for you," he said.

"We're coming," Hunt replied. "We were just—"

"Yes," Counts agreed. His sloe eyes narrowed. "Women are always trouble," he said. "Necessary, but always trouble."

"This one in particular," Hunt said. He motioned

to Elizabeth. "Fire Talon wants us," he said in English.

She looked at the medicine man. "Will he tell?" she asked Hunt.

"He might. Counts is a complex man."

"Thank you," the shaman murmured in perfect English. "I'm glad to know you think so."

Hunt felt his cheeks grow warm. "You do speak English," he said.

"A wise man would be foolish if he didn't," Counts answered.

Hunt nodded and chuckled, more at his own error in underestimating the shaman than at what Counts had said. "And you are a wise man," he agreed. He still hadn't decided if Counts could be trusted or not. Fire Talon seemed to be his friend, but Fire Talon was another unknown.

Hunt exhaled softly. If he had a choice, he'd sooner put his faith in Talon, he decided, but on this mission, he knew he might not get that chance.

Outside, they found that a large group had gathered around the cleared space. Curious women, elders, and children were all talking excitedly. Fire Talon, dressed simply as always, waited. His oak-hewn features were painted for war, and he was heavily armed with hatchet, rifle, scalping knife, and pistol.

A drumbeat silenced the crowd. "This man calls a war party to go into the land of our old enemy, the Seneca, and bring back a stolen child," Fire Talon called in a deep, commanding voice. He spoke first in his own tongue, then in English.

Elizabeth noticed Sweet Water in the group of women. A blanket covered her hair and most of her face, but her eyes were full of concern and fixed on her husband. A handsome boy of about twelve years stood beside her. The similarity of his features to Fire Talon's made Elizabeth guess that this must be their son.

"These warriors go with us," Fire Talon continued. He began to call out their names, and each man joined him amid cheers and shouts of encouragement from the crowd. After both Counts His Scalps and Hunt had left her side to enter the circle, Elizabeth moved to stand near Moccasin Flower.

"Fox comes," Fire Talon announced.

An elaborately painted brave wearing yellow and blue face paint and a foxtail headdress leaped into the air, hurled his tomahawk at a post, and began a furious war dance to the accompanying accolades of the women and children. Other men from the war party joined in the chant and formed a serpentine line of dancers that wove around the post and central fire pit to the heated throb of drums.

Fire Talon raised a hand. When the warriors ceased their dance and all was still, he shouted a final name. *"Scarlet Dawn."*

No one came forward to answer the summons.

The war chief made a great show of looking around, then announced the name again in Algonquian and once more in English. *"Scarlet Dawn!"*

People began to whisper to their neighbors. "Who is that?"

"This woman has not heard of him."

"Who is he?"

*"Scarlet Dawn!"* Fire Talon called again in English. He strode across the dance ground toward the spot where Elizabeth and Moccasin Flower stood. "You," he said, pointing to Elizabeth. "This warrior comes with us. Step forth, Scarlet Dawn, that you may be recognized."

Elizabeth stared at him in confusion.

"Go," Moccasin Flower whispered. "He means you."

Fire Talon took her hand and led her to the center of the circle. "It is forbidden that a woman follow the war trail. Is it so?"

"Yes," cried an old man.

"It is so," echoed a woman.

"Yet, women have walked that trail," Fire Talon said.

"True," Sweet Water answered. "Women have done this."

"Strikes Her Basket!" shouted an ancient. "My grandmother, Strikes Her Basket, took two Mohawk scalps."

"And Whistle in Twilight," added another elderly council member. "Who has not heard of Whistle in Twilight's deeds?"

Counts His Scalps moved to stand at Elizabeth's side. "It has come to this medicine man in a dream," he proclaimed. "A woman's place is in the cornfield and in the wigwam—yet . . ." He paused dramatically, then spread his arms so that the fringes on his sleeves swept the ground. "Yet, our leader decided that this one—" he indicated Elizabeth—"must go."

Fire Talon laid a hand on Elizabeth's shoulder. "It has come to the mighty shaman Counts His Scalps that there are times when a woman must act as a man."

"And this is such a time," Counts said, picking up his cue. "I proclaim that this is no longer a white woman; this is the Shawnee warrior Scarlet Dawn."

"Whoo!" cried an old man. The villagers began to stamp their feet in approval.

"Scarlet Dawn, take this weapon," Fire Talon said, drawing the pistol from his waist and handing it to Elizabeth. "Don't worry, it's not loaded yet," he whispered to her with a wink. "From this night until the moon has traveled twice on its journey, you are no longer a woman," he said for all to hear. "You are a man, and you are part of the raiding party. Do you agree to this?"

Stunned, Elizabeth looked at Hunt. He nodded. "Yes," she stammered. "Yes, I understand."

"Do you agree?" Fire Talon demanded sternly.

"I agree," she answered.

"So, it is done," he said. His eyes sought out the nearest woman in the crowd. "Take this warrior away," he said. "Dress him in a man's garments and make him ready. We leave for Seneca land at first light."

Hunt touched her lightly, and she stared at him wide-eyed.

"Do as he says," Hunt advised. "You asked for this. I didn't—"

But his words were lost in the quick throb of war drums, the cries of painted warriors, and the stamp of moccasined feet in the dust of the dance ground. Giddy with apprehension, Elizabeth allowed herself to be led away by a strange woman. This was all beyond her understanding. The one thing she did know was that somehow she was finally on her way back to her beloved children.

# Chapter 17

Ten days later, Elizabeth lay facedown on a rise overlooking the shallow river crossing near Yellow Drum's walled village. It was not long after noon; the elusive sun peeking through heavy gray clouds was nearly overhead. Every muscle in her body ached. She knew she should have been glad of the rest after marching for so many days through the forest to Seneca land, but she'd been lying there watching the trail since dawn and her joints were stiff.

She'd been incredulous when the Shawnee war chief, Fire Talon, had declared her a man, but his actions and those of every warrior in their party except Hunt had seemed to accept the notion. She'd been treated no differently than any other brave. If any man felt a woman was out of place, he'd never voiced it by word or gesture.

She'd been assigned no more camp or cooking duty than any of the other Shawnee, and she'd done her share of night guard duty with Hunt as her partner. In the long days of walking and the nights of companionship around the campfire, she'd wished that she could understand the Shawnee language so that she could enjoy their jokes and stories. Hunt had tried to explain as best he could, but some things lost their humor in the translation.

230

As he had warned her back in the Shawnee village, there was no time for them to be alone. The hours of night watch were agony. She stood on one side of the sleeping camp; he crouched on the other. All day long, she secretly watched him, marveling at his tireless strides and his ease among these fierce warriors. Hunt moved through the forest as silently as a shadow, radiating animal grace and quiet power. But as badly as she wanted to be held in his arms, they could not touch or kiss or even whisper together. And as much pleasure as it gave her to gaze on him, the watching was not enough; she wanted him so badly that she could hardly think of anything else.

After weeks of heartrending terror that she might never see Jamie and Rachel again, she was going to rescue them. Every man in the raiding party had risked his life for her children's freedom . . . and she couldn't rid her mind of carnal thoughts of Hunt Campbell.

The sound of his voice made her giddy; being near him caused her to drop objects, stammer, and smile foolishly until her jaws ached. He invaded her sleep and haunted her daydreams. Just thinking about him could make her cheeks hot and her skin so sensitive that she couldn't bear the feel of her buckskin hunting shirt rubbing against her breasts and shoulders. If she wasn't walking so far every day—and eating like a bear—she would have believed she was sick.

Instead, she was faced with only one logical conclusion. She was in love with Hunt . . . madly, head-over-heels, struck-by-lightning in love with a steely-eyed rifleman who cared for nothing but the softness between her thighs and the money her father had promised to pay for her return.

Below, on the trail, something moved. A Seneca woman, accompanied by a dog, walked around a bend toward the water's edge. Elizabeth tensed and tried to identify the woman.

Hunt laid a hand lightly on Elizabeth's back, sending pinpoints of sensation through her body. "Do you know her?" he whispered.

"That's Raven, Yellow Drum's senior wife." Malice toward the Iroquois woman bubbled up in Elizabeth's chest, animosity so intense that she felt sick. Yellow Drum's unwanted rapes had not done as much damage to her spirit as Raven's constant physical and mental abuse. Her cheeks grew hot as she remembered the dog dung Raven had thrown at her on the morning of Jamie's naming day ceremony. For years Elizabeth had lived under the older woman's vicious rule. It took every ounce of willpower not to draw the pistol from her belt and shoot Raven stone dead.

Elizabeth was no longer afraid of the weapon Fire Talon had given her back at the Shawnee village. Hunt had spent many hours on the trail teaching her to load and aim the flintlock. She had practiced over and over with an empty gun, until finally, Hunt had let her fire it. She'd killed a sitting rabbit at thirty feet with one shot through the head.

"That's good enough to kill a man," Fire Talon had said in approval. "Never load unless you mean to shoot, and never shoot unless you mean to kill. Can you do this, Scarlet Dawn?"

"If I must," she'd answered.

*If I must.* Now, crouched here on this rise, her own words returned to haunt her. Raven was unarmed and unaware. Shooting her would be murder. Elizabeth knew she could never take a life—even Raven's—so wantonly. But it gave her pleasure to know that she had the power to do it if she wanted to. And the fact that she chose not to fire helped to heal the old wound in her heart.

*I give you back your life, Raven.* Elizabeth smiled and took a deep breath. Raven couldn't hurt her anymore. She would never forget the injustice of what had been done to her, but neither would she hold on to the pain.

Letting go of the rancor was a relief. "I forgive you, you black-hearted witch," she murmured.

"What?" Hunt asked.

"Nothing."

Raven continued to walk toward the river. A group of three women appeared carrying baskets. One had a nursing child in her arms. Behind them came two braves.

"The day is mild," Elizabeth whispered. "They've come to wash clothing."

All yesterday the Shawnee had scouted around the village. Hunters had come and gone; and once, two French traders had approached the Seneca camp. They'd seen several boys, none of them Jamie—and Elizabeth still hadn't summoned enough nerve to tell Hunt or Fire Talon that she had two children.

Elizabeth kept her gaze on the trail, hoping to catch sight of Rachel or Jamie. She pressed her face to the damp leaves so that Hunt wouldn't see the tears glistening in her eyes. She was reasonably sure that Yellow Drum's son would be well cared for, but suppose Raven had done something terrible to Rachel? What if she was ill or even dead?

Jagged dread knifed through her. If she'd been sporting with Hunt while her little daughter suffered . . . If Rachel was dead and she didn't even know it, the guilt would be too awful to bear.

A dog barked in the valley. Hunt whispered to Badger, "Quiet." The big animal crouched low to the ground, his brown eyes sad and liquid.

Elizabeth held her breath and waited. Abruptly,

two boys ran around the bend, the first too tall to be Jamie. The smaller child ran to keep up. Both children carried bows; quivers were slung over their backs.

The youngest shouted, "Wait, wait for me."

"That's Jamie," Elizabeth whispered urgently. "That's my son."

"Which one?" Hunt asked.

"The little one with the otter-skin hood." A lump formed in her throat. *Jamie, oh, Jamie,* she thought. Every fiber of her being urged her to call out his name—to run and gather him into her arms ... to shower him with kisses.

"Don't move," Hunt warned. Inching his way down the slope, he motioned to the warrior, Fox, a few hundred feet away.

She didn't move. Fire Talon's plan was to grab Jamie today only if they could snatch him without witnesses. If they could rescue him without killing anyone or being seen, war between the Shawnee and the Seneca could be averted. For now, it was important that every member of the Shawnee party see Jamie.

A stout Seneca woman stopped and waited for the children. She was too far away for Elizabeth to make out what the squaw was telling them, but both boys took arrows from their quivers and began to walk slowly in the direction she pointed. The dog barked again as a rabbit tore from its hiding place.

Instantly, the chase was on. Boys, dog, and rabbit ran pell-mell toward the ridge where Elizabeth and the Shawnee war party were hiding. Hunt wriggled up beside Elizabeth and clamped a hand over her mouth. "Not a sound," he ordered.

The first time Yellow Drum had used her body, he'd held his hand over her mouth to keep her from crying out. She shuddered as those bitter memories flooded her mind, and she fought a desire to bite Hunt's hand. She clenched her teeth, willing to endure this indignity if it helped to get her son back. Still, she vowed to burn Hunt's ears for not trusting her.

The rabbit dashed closer. Jamie let fly an arrow that missed the zigzagging animal by six feet. The bigger boy shot, but his shaft also went wide. Elizabeth's heart pounded. Much closer and the dog would catch the scent of the raiding party. If the boys came over the hill, Hunt could catch Jamie, but what would happen to Rachel?

"Down," Hunt hissed at Badger.

*Turn!* Elizabeth screamed silently to the rabbit. *Go the other way!* She wanted Jamie, but not if it meant the men, the women, and the other children with him would be murdered to keep from spreading the alarm. And not if it meant leaving Rachel forever to Raven's mercy.

The gray-brown rabbit leaped high in the air and doubled back almost into the dog's jaws. For seconds, dog and rabbit tangled and fur flew. Then the rabbit shot off toward the river with both boys and the dog in full cry behind it.

Elizabeth exhaled with a gasp. Hunt removed his hand. "Sorry," he murmured. "I didn't mean to hurt you."

She snapped her head around. "Don't ever do that again."

"I didn't want you to call out to the boy."

She drew back, insulted.

"I didn't want you to get that woman killed or risk—"

"Would you have put your hand over Fox's mouth? Counts His Scalps?"

He scoffed. "Of course not. They're Shawnee. They wouldn't give us away."

"And you think I would?" she whispered.

"You're a woman."

"That's my son down there." His accusation was so unfair. "I'd die before I'd give us away. I'd let bees sting me to death. I'd let your moth-eaten dog chew me to bits. I'd—"

"Badger is not moth-eaten."

"And I'm not a weak woman."

"Don't take on so." His expression turned grim. "I was looking out for your good and the boy's."

"If you ever do that again, you'll regret it," she warned him.

His face hardened. "Don't shoot bears you can't skin."

"I don't need to skin a bear, only you."

A crow call signaled them to retreat from their observation point. Elizabeth crept slowly backward down the hill, then sprinted to the cover of the woods. There, Fox and Fire Talon waited.

"We saw him," the war chief said in English to Elizabeth. "The little one." She nodded, and he smiled at her. "You did well, Scarlet Dawn." His dark eyes twinkled. ". . . For a warrior with Seneca training." He motioned to Hunt, then spoke to him in the Shawnee language.

"He thinks we're in luck," Hunt translated stiffly. "He believes that most of the Seneca men are away from the village. If we have to take Jamie by force, we may be able to do it without bloodshed."

"I hope so," she said. "I have friends among the Seneca. Most of them are good people. I don't want to see any of them die."

"Neither do I," Fire Talon agreed. "Simply taking Yellow Drum's son would be a coup worthy to be

sung about around the campfires of the Shawnee for
years to come."

Elizabeth had reason to doubt the war chief's sanity
two nights later when she, Fire Talon, and Hunt crept
inside the walls of the Seneca village under cover of
darkness.

Unseasonably warm weather continued to shadow
the raiding party. This was the time of the crescent
moon, and even that pale light was hidden by layers
of thick clouds and all-encompassing mist. Counts His
Scalps had prepared a black oil for the three to rub
on their bodies, assuring them that it would make
them invisible inside the enemy camp. Elizabeth
doubted that the slippery ointment would make her
vanish; it did make her smell of dog and something
she couldn't put a name to.

Counts His Scalps, Fox, and the remainder of the
Shawnee warriors would wait near the camp entrance
to silence the guards. Elizabeth would lead Hunt and
Talon to Raven's longhouse, where the children
should be sleeping. Hunt had argued that there was
no need for Elizabeth to go into the village; Fire Talon
had overruled his objections.

"When the cub awakes, he will see his mother and
not give alarm," Talon had pronounced.

"I've seen the boy," Hunt countered. "I could—"

"The choice isn't yours. This man is war captain,"
Talon reminded him. "Scarlet Dawn goes."

Elizabeth shivered. There were a thousand things
that could go wrong. Fire Talon's scouts had assured
her that most of the warriors were gone, but even one
could throw a spear or shoot a bullet that could kill
one of her children. She was terrified, more so because
the secret she'd kept so long would soon be out. She
knew she should tell Hunt and the Shawnee, but she

was still afraid they'd not endanger themselves further for a girl child.

The dull, resounding boom of a water drum echoed through the village. Sounds of chanting and hand-clapping drifted between the longhouses. The Seneca shaman was performing a healing ceremony tonight. The high beat of a hand drum and the wail of a bird-bone whistle had told her so. Counts His Scalps had concurred. Other than the guards on the walls, the majority—if not all—of the adults in the camp would be present to help with the cure. It might be possible to slip into the longhouse and take her children without any Seneca being wiser until morning.

Hunt pressed close to the inner wall. Elizabeth did the same. Their faces and clothing had been streaked with charcoal so that they would blend into the night. They carried no weapons other than knives. Elizabeth gazed up toward the catwalk that ran along the top of the wall. Her heart rose in her throat as a shadow detached from a darker shadow. Instantly, she heard the cluck of a hen turkey.

Hunt's hand closed over her wrist. "That's Fox," he whispered. "He and Flint Knife have taken the Senecas' places."

"How?" she asked.

"Shh," Talon warned. He touched her shoulder lightly, urging her on.

The familiar camp smells settled around her as she led the way toward Raven's longhouse. Tobacco, corn shocks, drying fish, and damp furs mingled with the scents of tame turkeys shuffling in their cages. Then Elizabeth heard a faint whine, and a dog poked his cold nose into her hand and licked her fingers.

She nearly cried out in surprise. She couldn't see the animal in the darkness, but this dog couldn't be Badger; he'd been left outside the walls. Why wasn't this dog barking or growling at Hunt and Talon? When the animal continued to lick her hand and began to rub against her leg, she decided that the mystery must have something to do with Counts's invisible oil.

An eerie strain of music curled through the streets between the shadowy longhouses ... the shaman's medicine chant. Elizabeth wondered if he was wearing a false face, one of the wooden masks that featured so prominently in Seneca religious ceremony.

Going the long way around to Raven's hearth meant walking past more houses. Surely someone would discover them, Elizabeth thought. Her heart was hammering so loudly that she was certain it could wake the dead. But no dog barked, and no Seneca voice challenged them.

Finally, she crossed a familiar hump of earth and touched the bark covering of Raven's home. Cautiously, she led Hunt and Talon around the end of the structure and slowly pushed aside the heavy door covering. Sweat beading on her forehead, too frightened to breathe, she peeked inside. Only the family dog raised his head to look at her, then closed his eyes and went back to sleep. She stepped over the doorsill. Hunt and Talon followed close on her heels.

The fire on the first hearth had burned low. Elizabeth circled the pit and put her hand on the deerskin that led to Raven's hearth place. What if her children weren't there? What if Raven or Many Blushes was?

A small hiss of air escaped between her teeth as she saw Jamie's sturdy form sprawled on the sleeping platform. She strained to see if Rachel was there, but it was too dark. Whispering a silent prayer, Elizabeth moved across the floor to her son's side. She bent close to his face and tried to keep from weeping as she heard his regular intake of breath and smelled his warm, familiar scent.

Hunt motioned to her to pick him up, but she turned away, looking intently for Rachel. Someone uttered a sleepy sound and a blanket stirred along the back wall. That was Many Blushes's sleeping spot. Rachel wouldn't be there.

Heedless of the danger, Elizabeth went to where her daughter had always slept and jerked back the covers. The bed was empty. Empty! She felt as though a chasm had gaped open under her feet, and she fought to keep back a groan of despair.

Hunt's touch jerked her back from the brink. She took a gulp of air and shook off his hand. She forced her muscles to move as she edged toward Many Blushes's bed.

"No," Hunt whispered.

Elizabeth took hold of the wool blanket. As she lifted it, a tiny starfish hand dangled over the side of the sleeping platform. *Rachel*, she cried silently. Her daughter whimpered and opened her mouth, seeking her thumb. Elizabeth seized the chubby hand and tucked the finger between her rosy lips. Rachel sighed and murmured contentedly.

"What are you doing?" Hunt hissed. "Take the boy and—"

Elizabeth lifted the blanket higher. An adult arm lay across the child's middle. As she tried to pull Rachel away, Many Blushes raised her head and opened her eyes.

Elizabeth's desperate gaze met hers, and instant recognition registered in the Seneca woman's dark eyes. "Please," Elizabeth begged. Many Blushes closed her eyes and turned her face to the wall.

Picking Rachel up, Elizabeth thrust her into Hunt's arms. "She goes too," she said.

Hunt went rigid. "What?"

"You heard me," she replied. "She goes too."

"What are you—"

"Please," Elizabeth whispered. "She's my daughter."

"And the boy?" he demanded between clenched teeth.

"Both of them. They're both mine."

"Hurry," Talon called.

Elizabeth grabbed a blanket and wrapped it around Rachel. From the space beneath Elizabeth's old sleeping space, she pulled the deerskin bag that held their spare clothing. Jamie's cloak lay on the floor by the door; Rachel's moccasins and outer wrap had been carelessly tossed on a pile of furs. She jammed Rachel's things into the bag and slung it over her shoulder. Only then did she go to her son and whisper in his ear.

"Shh, it's Mama. Jamie?"

His eyelids flickered. A lazy smile crossed his lips. Elizabeth noticed that one front tooth was missing. "Mama?" he murmured in Iroquoian.

"Mama," she repeated in English. "Be quiet. Don't make a sound." She held out her arms.

"Why are you—"

"Shh," she warned. "We're playing a warrior's game, Jamie. Are you old enough to play?"

He nodded. Sitting up, he dropped his legs over the platform. Quickly, she slid his moccasins on and tied them tightly around his calves. Then she handed him his cape.

"Is Father here? Did he—" the boy whispered.

"Shh, you'll make our team lose the game," she replied, crouching low. "Jump on my back, and hold on, no matter what." She glanced at Fire Talon. He nodded and started out of the longhouse.

Hunt paused long enough to question. "Why? Why didn't you trust me enough to tell me the truth?"

She looked him straight in the eye. "If I had, would you have come for them?"

# Chapter 18

*E*lizabeth was running in deep snow through a moonless night. Icy branches clawed at her face and clothing; her heart hammered in her chest. She staggered under the weight of both children—Rachel in her arms, Jamie clinging to her back—but she couldn't stop running and she couldn't run fast enough to escape Yellow Drum.

She could hear the crunch of snow and the snap of underbrush behind her. The Seneca's muscular thighs and legs seemed tireless; he gained on her with every stride. Elizabeth waited, dreading the war cry she knew would soon issue from his cruel lips. It didn't come, but somehow, his silent pursuit was even more terrifying.

Little Rachel began to sob, and Elizabeth clutched her against her breast. Each breath of frigid night air tore into Elizabeth's chest, and with each step her limbs grew more wooden and her strength melted away.

"Father! Father!" Jamie protested. He kicked and beat at her with both fists. "Don't let her take me away!" he screamed. "I want my father!"

Elizabeth stumbled to her knees in a piled drift. Somehow, she'd lost her mittens, and the snow was so cold it burned her bare hands. As she struggled to rise, her fingers touched the matted fur of an animal. Stifling a scream, she raised her head and gazed into the red, glowing eyes of a snarling wolf.

*"Give them to me," Yellow Drum thundered. "They're mine. Would you rather see them eaten alive?"*

*She twisted around to see him bound toward her. His face was streaked with paint—half black, half yellow. Around his head, he swung a bloodstained war club.*

*"Give me what's mine," he demanded. "Give me my son."*

*Elizabeth tried to dodge past the wolf, but the savage beast sprang at her. His fierce growl made Jamie cry out. Elizabeth looked down at her little daughter, but Rachel was gone. She'd fallen from her arms into the trampled snow.*

*"Rachel! Rachel!" Elizabeth called frantically. Raw fear coiled in the pit of her stomach. She could hear Rachel whimpering, but she couldn't find her. "Rachel!"*

"Elizabeth." A strong hand shook her. "Elizabeth."

Bewildered, she forced her eyes open and looked up at the shadow kneeling beside her. "What . . . ?" Her jaws ached as though she'd been clenching her teeth. "Hunt? Where—"

"Shh, you fell asleep. You must have been dreaming." His hand gripped her shoulder. It was too dark to see his face, but his voice was as hard as the frozen ground under her.

"The children?"

"Asleep. You cried out."

"I'm sorry."

He cupped her chin tenderly with his lean, callused hand. "It's all right. You were asleep."

Her heart was still racing; her mouth tasted of old metal. The remnants of the nightmare dug at her insides with bared claws. "Did I make too much noise?" She scrambled up. "Where are they?"

He caught her wrist and brought her hand up to touch Rachel's hair. Realization came flooding back. The snow . . . the wolf . . . even Yellow Drum had been a dream. Hunt had Rachel strapped to his back, still wrapped snugly in the blanket.

"She's still asleep?" Tears welled up in Elizabeth's eyes and she dashed them away. Rachel was always a sound sleeper. Once, she'd slept through a dogfight between two village curs only inches from her cradleboard.

"Not a peep out of her."

Elizabeth had to touch her, had to let her fingers slide through her baby's silky hair and lightly stroke a chubby cheek. Warm breath stirred across her hand. "She's all right." It had been a bad dream . . . just a dream, she assured herself. She hadn't dropped Rachel in the snow. Yellow Drum hadn't caught them . . . not yet.

"Of course, she's all right. Did you think I'd drop her?"

She wondered if Hunt was still angry with her. She could understand that. It was his right. She'd put his life in danger—put all their lives in danger—by not telling him the truth. But she'd do the same again even if it meant going to hell for it. "I trust you," she replied softly.

"You don't trust me." His words were terse, his tone different than she'd ever heard from him before . . . not angry so much as full of regret.

She sighed for what might have been. "Jamie?" she asked. "Is he—"

"Asleep as well. Talon has him."

Talon? When had the war chief taken Jamie? she wondered. She'd carried her son a long way before she'd relinquished him into Fox's powerful arms. Fox must have passed him to Fire Talon, she decided.

After they'd gotten the children from the longhouse, she, Hunt, and Talon had retraced their cautious steps out of the village without being seen. In the meadow, Counts His Scalps and the remaining Shawnee braves had joined them. With the armed warriors protecting their backs, they'd retreated across the open ground and reached the comparative safety of the woods.

The raiding party had been several hundred yards into the forest before a cry of alarm echoed from the village. Within seconds, Seneca drums beat a tattoo of danger, and war whoops sounded from the walls of the stockade. Fire Talon had quickened his strides, and the Shawnee had begun to run in earnest.

"Where are we going?" Jamie had demanded angrily. "Who are these men? They aren't Seneca. Who are they?"

She hadn't tried to answer his questions. She'd held him in her arms and run until she thought her heart would burst from the strain. Then, finally, when she was dropping behind despite every ounce of will, the brave known as Fox had held out his arms, and reluctantly, she'd given her precious son into his keeping.

After what seemed hours they'd stopped to drink, then run again. Talon had signaled a halt to rest when they reached the crest of a hill. It was then that Elizabeth crouched and leaned her head against a tree trunk. Obviously, she'd dozed off and had a bad dream.

Memory of that horror still made the skin prickle on her arms. The wolf had seemed so real. "I need to touch my son," she said softly. She needed to put her hands on him, to assure herself that he was really all right.

"He is here," Fire Talon said in English. He caught her hand and brought it to her son's shoulder. "The boy is strong and brave."

"You didn't hurt him?" she asked.

"Is this man one to harm a child?" Fire Talon rumbled in his deep voice. "In Iroquoian, this man warned that he must be quiet for the safety of his mother and his sister. Your son made no sound after that. In time, he slept."

She gathered her courage to ask another question that had been troubling her. "Are they coming after us? What of the Seneca guards? The ones who watched from the walls? Are they dead?" She didn't want to think of them dead; she knew too many people in the village.

"The guards are tied and gagged," Talon assured her, "but very much alive." He grinned, and she caught a glimpse of white teeth in the darkness. "We took their scalplocks but no skin with them—not even a drop of blood."

"It will make a great story," Fox boasted. "The women will sing of us."

The shaman, Counts, chuckled dryly. "If you dance before too many women, your wife, Shell Bead Girl, will have *your* scalp."

"She is too jealous," Fox said. "Have I ever given her reason to distrust me?"

"She knows you well," Talon replied. "So long as she is vigilant, you will not stray into another cornfield."

"I only said the women would sing for us." Fox's hurt tone was obviously feigned for the amusement of his friends. "I never said I wanted their admiration. One wife is enough for any reasonable man."

"Since when is Fox considered reasonable?" Red Shirt teased.

"I'm reasonable," Fox countered. "Didn't I suggest that we leave the Seneca alive?"

"You did," Count agreed, "after Talon ordered it. But it was I who thought to leave the Huron moccasin print on the ground outside the village walls."

"In the Shawnee village, Counts formed the plan," Red Shirt added. "Who else but a wise shaman would leave a Huron footprint and a strip of Huron beadwork on a brier at the edge of the forest?"

"Some would not think it honorable to blame the Huron for Shawnee mischief," Talon said quietly.

Counts His Scalps spat on the ground. "That for Huron honor," he said harshly. "The Hurons roasted my father over a torture fire. Whatever evil I can do them I will do, so long as I live."

Talon chuckled. "This man has no great love for the Hurons either. And it is true that the Hurons started the last war between Iroquois and Shawnee. Perhaps the Seneca will not even find the footprint or the beads."

"They will find it," Counts assured him. "And the time spent chasing Hurons will allow us to reach Shawnee land in safety."

Talon signaled that they should move on. Elizabeth took her place behind Hunt. "I don't understand," she whispered. "Why aren't the Seneca coming after us?"

"They will, in time," Hunt replied. "Counts left signs that will confuse them. It should give us a good lead."

A shiver passed through Elizabeth. Hunt wasn't shouting at her; his displeasure ran deeper than anger. Guilt plagued her; she'd done what she had to for her children, but Hunt might never forgive her. She didn't know if she could mend the breach between them or not, but tonight was no time to try.

Talon's pace was grueling. She concentrated on keeping her footing in the dark; she couldn't chance a fall that might be serious and could delay the Shawnee. They must get as far from Yellow Drum's village as possible because when he returned, he would come after them. She was as sure of that as she was that the sun would rise in the east in the morning.

Yellow Drum would come for his children. And she had no intention of letting them go . . . not so long as she drew breath.

Hunt strode along the semidark trail with Elizabeth and the Shawnee raiding party. On his back, he carried a sleeping Rachel, but the little girl was so light that he barely remembered she was there.

Dawn came later than he'd expected it to this morning, spilling hues of lavender and rose over the wooded hilltops. The air was crisp and cold, heavy with the biting scents of fur and pine. So far they'd been lucky; they'd done what they'd come to do without losing a life or taking one. But their luck couldn't last forever; Hunt could smell snow in the air. Winter was late in coming. When it hit, they'd feel the full force of North Wind's fury. He could think of better situations than being caught in Iroquois territory in a blizzard.

These were child-sized mountains compared to the great towering heaps of stone and earth beyond the great plains. Winter would hold the Cheyenne world in a white embrace. The cold would be fierce enough to snap the trunks of lodge pole pines, and the buffalo skin teepees would glow with the flickering light of fires as the People gathered to wait out the long months of the starving time.

He wondered if his father had kept well. Wolf Robe was strong, but even a man in his prime could be brought low by a charging buffalo bull or a grizzly. He'd not look for Hunt during the winter, but when spring turned the prairie into a knee-high carpet of wildflowers and the buffalo cows dropped their calves, the leathery old warrior would scan the horizon for sight of his returning son.

Wolf Robe, the warrior his brothers the Shawnee and Delaware called the Stranger, was a courageous and complex man. A vision quest and a blood feud with his brother had brought him east into the country of the rising sun, where he'd taken a Delaware wife and adopted a lonely white boy as his son. Years later, twice widowed, he'd returned to the mountains of his birth with Hunt at his side. The sibling whom Wolf Robe had fled to keep from killing was dead, and the Cheyenne welcomed him back with open hearts.

Hunt could have had a good life with the Cheyenne. He'd learned their language and their customs; he'd even been invited to join the elite warrior society of Dog Soldiers. But the white part of him that he'd thought dead for so many years returned to plague his dreams. A curiosity as persistent as a scourge of chiggers under his skin tormented him until he decided to return to his own beginnings and learn more of the white race that had spawned him.

Sometimes, in the deepest pitch of night, he let his mind drift back to the cabin he'd shared with his white sister, Becca. Her face was as clear to him as Wolf Robe's. Becca had been the closest thing to a birth mother he'd ever known. A kindly Delaware woman, and later a Cheyenne, had sewn and cooked for him, and listened to his boyhood boasts and troubles. But none had been as dear as Becca.

She was lost to him, returned to the whites in the town of New York. The Campbells had made inquiries after Hunt had become part of their family, but one red-haired woman in a sea of Dutch and English was impossible to trace. Her husband, Simon Brandt, was presumed dead, lost in one of his wilderness campaigns against the Shawnee. Becca, if she was still alive, could have married and taken a new last name, or she could have returned to Ireland.

The Campbells had been surprised that Hunt held no ill will against Wolf Robe for his original capture. If he ever had, it had been lost long ago in the patience of his Indian father's loving care. Simon Brandt had kicked and beat him with his fists. Marks from Brandt's quirt had left permanent scars on Hunt's back, but Wolf Robe had soothed those hurts with bear grease and rocked a lonely boy to sleep.

The day of his capture was as lost to him as Becca. He remembered running—not away from the cabin, but toward it. He remembered smelling smoke ... and oddly enough, musty earth. And he remembered cobwebs in the tunnel they'd crawled out of to escape the burning cabin. The last whole image he had of his sister was the fear on her face as Wolf Robe carried him away in one direction while her captor pulled her in another.

Wolf Robe had told him that she had been taken as a hostage for the safe release of a Shawnee medicine man. Later, they learned that Becca had been returned to the whites in a peace gesture. Wolf Robe had assured Hunt that his sister was safe and alive, and Wolf Robe never lied to him.

Hunt felt the little girl on his back squirm and heard her sigh. She was waking up. He stepped off the trail and signaled to Elizabeth to take her. The child had slept through the night without a peep; it wouldn't do to have her take fright and begin to cry now. A wailing babe could be heard a long way through these woods.

Fox saw them stop and clicked to Fire Talon. He glanced back and nodded. The braves fanned out to watch the forest around them for any sign of the enemy while Elizabeth untied her daughter and took her in her arms. Rachel opened her eyes sleepily and gave him a dazzling smile—her mother's smile, complete with dimple on the left cheek.

Hunt's heart plummeted. He was still mad as hell at Elizabeth, but he didn't kid himself. He was still crazy for her. And in the pit of his gut, he knew why she'd done what she'd done. Rationally, Elizabeth was right. He wouldn't have gone for the children if he'd guessed there were two of them. She'd outfoxed him and made him look the fool in front of the Shawnee.

He'd never been a man to let desire for a woman cloud his thinking, but this time was different. He couldn't stop watching her . . . couldn't stop thinking about what it had been like making love to her. And all his anger couldn't quench the fever for her that raged within him.

Being close to her on the trail, sleeping near her, and standing watch with her were all enough to drive a man beyond control. The men's clothing she wore— the skintight leggings and fringed breechcloth—left little of her feminine curves to his imagination. Even the hunting shirt strained across her small, upthrust breasts. The thoughts of cupping those soft breasts in his hands again . . . of kissing and sucking them . . . haunted him.

He wanted her. . . . Wanted her so bad that he'd even thought of taking her and her son with him. Jamie could have fit in with his plans to go west. Hunt would never sire a son because of the illness that had left him sterile, but he could have been a father to Elizabeth's boy. A real father didn't have to be the man who planted the seed in a woman; Wolf Robe had taught him that. Jamie's Seneca blood made no difference to him; if an Irish immigrant could become a Cheyenne Sun Dancer, so could an Iroquois.

He'd lied to Elizabeth when he'd said he didn't like children. As a young buck, he hadn't thought much of them one way or another, but now that he was older, he'd wondered what it might be like to teach a son to track and find his way in the woods, to catch trout with his bare hands, and to paddle a canoe in white water.

Most women wanted kids of their own, and he could never father them. But Elizabeth had had a son, and once Hunt had committed himself to getting the boy back for her, he'd allowed himself to dream of what the three of them might have together.

Now there were not one but two kids, and the second was a girl child, hardly more than a weanling. Elizabeth would never risk a little girl on the prairie ... would never consider turning her back on the white settlements to live with the Cheyenne.

Elizabeth was a good mother. She'd put her kids ahead of him, ahead of herself, and that was right, but it ended any thoughts he might have had about offering Elizabeth something permanent. Trouble was, it did nothing to ease the pain in his loins or the hurt in his chest. He hadn't been certain if he felt real love for her, but now, considering how the wound in his heart felt, he knew he did.

First Becca, then Spotted Pony, and now Beth. He had a hell of a record where women were concerned. Some men were born to be loners. He was one and the sooner he got used to it, the better off he'd be.

The little girl was hugging Elizabeth and giggling. Damn but she was a pretty little thing, cute as a bear cub and a darn sight more trouble. He knew next to nothing about girl children. He had no Indian sisters, and girls were kept separate from boys. They played separate games, wore different clothing, even had their own secrets and medicine dances.

Elizabeth was staring at him with doe eyes, expecting him to say something to her. He wanted to give her some of the hurt he was feeling, but he couldn't do it. "She's worth it," he said instead. "If Rachel were mine, I'd have done whatever it took to get her loose from Yellow Drum."

Rachel pointed at him and whispered something in Elizabeth's ear. "She wants to know your name," Elizabeth said.

"Does she speak English?" he asked.

"Some, and she understands fine."

"Hunt," he told the child. "Hunter of the Far Mountains." He repeated the words in Shawnee. "Hunt Campbell."

The shy smile lit up her dark eyes. "Hunt," Rachel said in a clear, sweet tone. Then she stuck her tongue out at him.

Elizabeth laughed. "Rachel, that's not—"

Impulsively, Hunt stuck his tongue out in retaliation, then joined Rachel's giggle with a chuckle of his own. When Elizabeth began to scold him, he put his thumbs in his ears, stuck out his tongue at the child again, and wiggled his fingers. The little girl crowed with delight and tried to imitate his nonsense.

"Enough of that," Elizabeth told them both.

Fox clicked his tongue again. The bushes rustled, and Fire Talon stepped back onto the deer trail. He made hand signs cautioning quiet, then dropped to one knee and set the boy on his feet.

Elizabeth held out her arms to her son. "Jamie," she whispered. She put a finger to her lips. "It's all right," she assured him in Seneca. "We're among friends."

The boy's eyes gleamed with unshed tears. His face was taut, his movements tense. He went to his mother as she bid him, but he didn't soften at her touch. "Who are these men?" he demanded in his father's tongue.

"Speak English," she said.

"You!" He pointed at Hunt. "You stole my mother. Now you steal my sister." Quick as a flash, he drew the knife from the sheath at Elizabeth's waist.

Her face turned ashen. "No!" she shouted.

"You steal my mother. Now you die!" Uttering a Seneca war cry, Jamie ducked away from her embrace and lunged directly at Hunt with the knife poised to draw blood.

# Chapter 19

**H**unt sidestepped the boy's blow and clamped a hand over his wrist. Jamie twisted in his grasp, refusing to drop the knife. Hunt's dog leaped forward, growling.

"Jamie, no!" Elizabeth cried. She tried to grab hold of the child, but Hunt swept him up off the ground and pried the weapon from his clenched fingers. Frightened, little Rachel backed up until she was pressed against a tree trunk and could go no farther. Then she put her hands over her face and crouched down.

"Badger, down!" Hunt ordered. "Down." Hackles raised, stiff-legged, the animal obeyed, but his eyes stayed on his master.

"Let me go! Let me go!" Jamie kicked at Hunt's midsection with a small moccasined foot and drove a balled fist into the big man's chin. Hunt's tooth caught the underside of his lower lip and sliced through skin and flesh, drawing blood.

"Jamie. Stop it," Elizabeth insisted as she put an arm around her son's waist. "Let me have him," she said to Hunt. "I'm sorry—he didn't mean it. He's just a child."

"He's all yours." Hunt stepped back and wiped the

trickle of blood off his chin as the boy turned his fury on her.

"You went away!" Jamie shouted. "You went away with him! You left me!"

"No, no," she soothed, trying to pin his arms and cradle him against her. "Shh, shh, it's all right, darling. It's all right."

Panting, his eyes dilated with anger and frustration, the boy stopped fighting and glared at her. Tears welled up and ran down his cheeks. "I hate you," he said in Seneca. "I hate you."

It was all Elizabeth could do to keep from weeping herself. She'd known that Jamie loved his father and that he'd be upset when they kidnapped him from the Seneca, but she'd never dreamed he'd turn on her. "I love you," she whispered. "I love you."

"No. You don't! You went with him! You left us!"

"Stop," Talon said. The chief squatted down beside Elizabeth and put a hand on Jamie's shoulder. "He is not a small girl child," he said in Seneca. "This is a warrior. Treat him as such, Mother."

Fear prickled the back of Elizabeth's neck. "I'll keep him quiet," she promised Fire Talon. "I won't let him—"

"This is a matter for men," Talon said. He glanced at Hunt. "You take James. He is a brave boy. He does not wish to be shamed by a clinging mother."

Fox laughed. "Like another boy we once knew, eh?"

Talon stared into Jamie's eyes. "You are Seneca, true, but you also carry the blood of your mother."

"I'm not afraid of you, Shawnee dog!" Jamie spat. "Torture me. Burn me at the stake. I am Seneca. I will not—"

"The Seneca and the Shawnee are not at war," Talon admonished gently. "Do not talk of torture among friendly nations. This is a matter for your mother and father to decide. For now, walk with my friend, Hunter of the Far Mountains. He is an honorable man."

Elizabeth looked from Talon to Hunt. "You won't hurt him?"

Hunt threw her a disbelieving look, then picked up the knife and handed it to the boy. "Give this back to your mother, Jamie."

"She's not my mother. Raven is my mother. *This* mama is nothing but a slave."

"Is not!" Rachel flew at him with both fists flying.

"Is too."

"Is not!" Rachel ducked under Elizabeth's arm and kicked Jamie. "Not my mother. I don't like that old Raven. She's mean."

Elizabeth put herself between her feuding children. "Stop it, both of you," she declared. "No hitting."

"I kick him," Rachel said in Seneca. "I kick him good."

"There's no good kicking," Elizabeth said. "I won't have this."

"You're invisible," Jamie shouted at Rachel in Iroquoian. "I make you invisible. I can't see you. I can't hear you."

"No, I'm not!" Rachel retorted. "I'm not!" She tried to find a way around Elizabeth, ready to kick her brother again. "Squirrel penis!"

"Rachel!" Elizabeth felt her cheeks grow hot. The men's laughter only made her embarrassment greater. "What a terrible thing to say."

"He is," Rachel chanted. "He is!" She pointed a small finger. "Squirrel penis!"

"Am not!" Jamie shouted.

"That's very rude," Elizabeth said. "I'm ashamed, Rachel. Big girls don't say such things."

"Raven does," Jamie informed her. "Raven says my father has a squirrel—"

"Enough." Hunt picked up Jamie and lifted him to eye level. "A Seneca warrior does not repeat women's gossip, and a brave does not argue with small girls."

"I hate you, too," Jamie proclaimed, drawing back a fist. "I bloodied your lip and now—"

"Now you will be a man," Hunt said. "You will honor your mother and your sister. You will—"

"She's just a slave."

Jamie's words made Elizabeth's stomach knot. If Jamie turned against her, she wasn't certain she could go on.

"Nonsense," Hunt answered. "You know better than that. You were angry that your mother left you, but if you think back to that night, you know she did not want to go." He spoke softly to the boy and set his feet on the ground. "Do you remember? Your father hit your mother and sent her away. She did not want to go away, but she had to. Now, she's come back for you."

"I'd never leave you if I could help it," Elizabeth said.

Hunt shook his head. "I know how it hurts when someone you love goes away," he said to Jamie. "I wasn't much bigger than you are when my sister and I were captured by the Shawnee. I never saw her after that day, and I was angry with her. I thought she didn't love me anymore."

Jamie's chin quivered. Elizabeth moved to take him in her arms, but Hunt shook his head.

"Did your sister die?" Jamie asked in heavily accented English.

"No, she wasn't dead," Hunt said.

"She got lost?" Jamie's mouth tightened, and for a

moment, Elizabeth saw a miniature Yellow Drum standing before her.

"She was a captive," Hunt explained.

Jamie scuffled the leaves with the toe of his quill-worked moccasin. "Are you still mad at her?" he asked.

"No, I'm not. It wasn't her fault."

Jamie averted his eyes. "I need to think about this," he said, switching back to Seneca. Folding his arms, he turned his back on Hunt.

"Raven did say it," Rachel chimed in. " 'Squirrel penis,' she said." Rachel covered her mouth with her fingers and giggled. "Aunt Many Blushes thought it was funny."

"I don't think it's funny," Elizabeth assured her. "It's rude, and neither Seneca girls nor English girls should be rude."

Rachel chewed her bottom lip and put her hands behind her back. "You is my mother," she said in a rush of words.

Elizabeth's eyes clouded with tears. "Yes, darling, I am your mother," she agreed. "And Jamie's mother."

"Good." Black eyes snapped with mischief as Rachel glanced at her brother. "He not a squirrel penis," she said. "He a squirrel bottom."

The rasping caw of a crow made the men tense and scan the forest for any sign of movement. A few seconds passed. Even the children noticed and were still. Then another crow called, a scolding cry that Elizabeth recognized as one that signaled danger. Instantly, Talon motioned for the group to take cover.

Elizabeth gathered Rachel in her arms and reached for Jamie's hand. He shrugged her away and, scowling, followed Hunt into the underbrush. Elizabeth and Rachel walked into the woods and crouched down behind a fallen tree. Hunt waved her farther back into the hemlocks near the spot where he and Jamie were hiding. Badger bellied down beside his master.

For a long time, Elizabeth heard nothing unusual, then the forest grew unnaturally silent. After several minutes during which she heard only a rustle of dry leaves and the creak of branches in the wind, a murmur of human voices became evident. At first, the sounds were too far away to make out, but gradually footfalls and even laughter drifted up the trail.

Elizabeth covered Rachel's mouth with her hand, but there was no need. The child had been well schooled. She nestled next to Elizabeth as tightly as a quail chick under a hen's wing. Elizabeth held her breath as the scalplock of a Mohawk warrior bobbed into view through the branches.

Two Frenchmen in blue military uniforms tread close on the Indian's heels. One of the soldiers boasted loudly about the amount of liquor he'd drunk at a trading post, and the Mohawk in the lead was ridiculing him in Iroquoian. The hair on the back of Elizabeth's neck rose as nine more hard-faced Mohawk warriors filed past; they wore no war paint, but all were heavily armed with late-model French muskets. Two of the men carried the carcass of a deer slung on a pole between them.

Elizabeth wondered if Fire Talon would attack the unsuspecting Mohawk, but the Shawnee didn't move. The Iroquois and Frenchmen continued on down the hill and along the edge of a gully until the rustle of leaves and good-natured chatter became fainter and fainter. She sighed with relief and smiled down at Rachel. The child returned the smile and winked. "Good girl," Elizabeth mouthed silently as she glanced at Hunt. He held a finger to his lips.

Elizabeth waited motionless. Time passed and her legs began to cramp. Rachel wiggled a foot, and Elizabeth stilled her with a touch.

Abruptly, a twig snapped, and the form of a tall Mohawk scout materialized on the far side of the game trail. He was only visible for an instant; then he was gone. She looked at Hunt, wondering if she'd really seen the last Iroquois or if the scout had been a figment of her imagination.

Hunt nodded, but he didn't move. The boy was so still in his arms he might have been carved of cedar. Only his huge, liquid-brown eyes showed the anger that seethed within his small chest. "Make no sound," Hunt had warned the child before the first group of Mohawk passed. "If you cry out, you put a bullet through your mother's heart." Jamie hadn't betrayed them, but his resentment burned with a white-hot flame.

"Your father would be proud of you," he whispered to the boy. Still they waited. Perhaps a quarter of an hour passed, and then the birds began to chirp and scratch again. A squirrel peered from his hole in a rotting oak and chattered down at the human invaders.

Hunt concentrated on the forest around him, listening intently, watching every stirring leaf and branch. His rifle lay, primed and ready, beside him . . . the weapon he'd prayed he'd not have occasion to fire.

From where he knelt, he could see Elizabeth perfectly, and the sight of her sheltering her little girl with her body brought a lump to his throat. God help her, Elizabeth deserved better than she'd gotten. She needed a strong protector, someone who would keep her from ever being hurt again.

Alone—even without a fat dowry—she'd not go six weeks without having some man offer for her hand in marriage. But how many of the elegant Carolina gentlemen would want her with two half-Seneca children? Hunt couldn't help but grin at the thought of one of Charles Town's finest trying to tame this small firebrand here beside him. Any stepfather trying to use harsh methods with the boy would likely be scalped in his bed—by Elizabeth, if not by her son. She'd not stand for anyone mistreating her children.

Painful memories whirled through his consciousness. Like an aching tooth, it was hard to ignore them, even though he knew they were best forgotten. For an instant, he caught a glimpse of Becca's laughing face . . . and then, something that made a cold shiver run through him. He saw himself crawling on hands and knees through a dirt tunnel . . . the hole Simon Brandt had dug as a secret way out of their cabin.

He shook his head. He could almost taste the sandy dirt . . . almost . . . No, he *could* smell the musty earth scent of the tunnel . . . feel the brush of cobwebs against his face.

He concentrated on Elizabeth, not wanting to remember the day of his capture. It was the boy, he decided. Jamie had made him think of that last day he'd seen his sister. There was no good reason to trouble himself with those memories.

Then an image of Becca struggling with a Shawnee flashed across his mind. He could see only the man's back, but he had the oddest feeling that the Indian brave was familiar, almost—

Jamie's quick intake of breath jerked Hunt back to reality. Not twenty yards away, another Mohawk brave stepped out into a small clearing and paused to tie a knot on his belt. *Don't make a sound*, Hunt begged the boy wordlessly. One move, one rustle of leaves, and he'd have to shoot the Mohawk. The echo of a rifle firing would bring the main party down on them with a vengeance.

The Mohawk tugged at his loincloth, relieved himself against a tree, and walked on without ever glancing in their direction.

It was a good half hour before they dared to assemble on the trail again. "Did you see that last scout?" Hunt asked Talon. "I thought he was going to take a leak on my foot."

"I saw him," the war captain replied. He put his hand on Jamie's shoulder. "You did well," he said to the boy.

Badger whined and thrust his black nose into the palm of Jamie's hand. Absently, the child patted the dog.

*Badger likes him,* Hunt thought, *and he's a good judge of character.* The animal had an independent streak, but Hunt reckoned he was as smart as the average man and a hell of a lot braver than most. Usually, Badger was well behaved, but now and then he'd take it into his head to chase a rabbit or run off for a day or two on his own adventures. When he made up his mind to go roaming, neither rope nor command would make him stay.

Badger thumped his ragged tail against Hunt's leg and wiggled all over as the boy scratched behind his ears. Jamie bent and laid his face against the animal's head. "He looks like he's part wolf," he ventured.

"He could be part grizzly for all I know," Hunt replied. "His mother belonged to my white foster father. She was an Irish wolfhound and mastiff cross. Nobody knew who the daddy was, and she wouldn't say."

Jamie's dark sloe eyes narrowed to slits as he flashed a scowl and folded his arms over his sturdy chest. "Dogs can't talk," he said in passable English.

"I'm not a baby to . . ." He struggled for the words, then dropped into the familiar Seneca. "To believe such nonsense."

"No, you're not a baby," Hunt agreed. And he wasn't. He was tall and husky for six. A man would have to stretch to see any of his mother in him, Hunt reckoned, but the lad was handsome enough, with strong, even features and a proud Seneca nose. His black hair was cropped off at chin level and a lynx claw earring adorned his left ear. Around his neck hung a small leather medicine bag, and his fur-trimmed vest was decorated with magic symbols.

Hunt sighed. Elizabeth would have a time teaching this lad to be a white man. It might be as hopeless as his foster father Campbell's efforts were with him. Indian ways had a habit of sticking with a boy.

"I like dogs," Jamie said grudgingly.

"Me too," Hunt replied, "especially this one."

Jamie nodded and something like a smile played over his lips as he patted Badger's broad head.

*The boy has good blood in him,* Hunt mused, *both Seneca and white.* But in his experience boys were a lot like dogs. Love and patience went farther in training them than harsh treatment. How Jamie was treated while he was growing up would make a huge difference in the kind of man he became. Hunt felt a deep pang of regret that he wouldn't be around to help Elizabeth bring him up right.

"Nice doggy," Rachel said, coming over and putting out her hand.

Elizabeth glanced at Hunt. "He won't hurt her, will he?"

Hunt shook his head, caught the little girl around the waist, and set her on the animal's back. She squealed with laughter and grabbed hold of his long fur with both hands. Badger looked embarrassed but clearly pleased with all the attention. "He likes kids," Hunt said.

"Unlike his master," Elizabeth commented.

"I like kids well enough," he said. "Other people's kids." The old familiar phrase was out before he realized what he was saying. He knew it wasn't true, and he wanted to take it back, but making an issue of the words would be awkward. Instead, he smiled at Rachel and lifted her high over his head.

Elizabeth had dressed the child warmly for the march. She wore a fringed dress in place of Jamie's hunting shirt, and leggings of brown doeskin. Rachel's vest was of otter skin with the fur side in; over that she had a warm cloak with a hood, and on her feet, dainty embroidered moccasins. Her dark hair was neatly braided into two plaits and held back off her face with a beaded headband. Silver rings dangled from the child's ears.

"There you go, back to your mother," he said, putting her in Elizabeth's arms. Rachel's skin was the shade of warm honey, only slightly darker than Elizabeth's fair complexion. No one observing the two could doubt that they were mother and daughter. Rachel was an adorable child; when she grew up, she'd be a real beauty. Hunt felt a pang of reluctance that he wouldn't be there to see her.

Elizabeth hugged Rachel against her breast. "Can you see why I couldn't leave her?" she asked softly.

He nodded. "I only hope you can make your family see it the same way." He glanced toward Jamie. "He won't make it easy on you."

"No."

He covered her hand with his. "I wish it could be different between us," he said. "I wish I could give you the life and the home you deserve."

"I'll care for my own children," Elizabeth replied

tersely. "I only asked that you help me rescue them, nothing more."

"I'm not a man for settlements and English laws," he said quietly. "I've lived the free life too long to fit in harness."

Her green eyes snapped. "Have I asked you for—"

"No, you haven't." Damn, but she was making this difficult for him. She tugged at his heart like no woman had ever done . . . but the mountain winds and open places of the western high country called to his soul with a haunting refrain. "You'll find someone right for you," he added lamely. "Someone who—"

"My personal affairs are my own. Don't worry yourself on our account," she replied in a tone that could have sliced granite.

Talon chuckled, and Hunt clenched his teeth and quickened his pace to move in front of her. Damn the woman; she'd give him the belly gripes with all this prickly behavior. Not worry over her . . . how could he not? He swore under his breath. Maybe Counts His Scalps had the right idea. Females were nothing but trouble, and a man would do well to live without them.

They walked for another two hours before reaching the banks of a river. They followed it south until dusk, then Fox made a lucky discovery.

"Here," he called, pushing away evergreens to reveal a birchbark canoe and paddles hidden beneath an ancient hemlock.

Counts His Scalps found a second boat a few yards away. After a brief conversation with Fire Talon, the shaman and another man pushed the canoe into the water. Jamie slid down the bank and scrambled into the prow of the canoe.

"Wait. He should be with me," Elizabeth called.

"I will watch him," Fox said.

Hunt helped Elizabeth and Rachel into the boat with Fire Talon and two other Shawnee braves. Badger followed Hunt, climbing into the canoe and padding to a spot near the center and lying down.

The canoes were large, meant for three or more paddlers. Hunt, Fire Talon, and Feathered Lance—a stocky young man with a copper nose ring—each took a paddle. Black Hoof took a place near the bow and checked the priming on his rifle.

"Isn't it dangerous, traveling by river in Iroquois country?" Elizabeth whispered to Hunt as they moved out into the current.

"Night is falling. We'll make much better time this way," he replied, glancing at the other canoe. Her son was wrapped in a blanket; he looked small and alone amid the shaman and the other warriors. "Jamie can swim, can't he?"

"His Seneca name is Otter because he swims so well," she said.

"Good." Hunt didn't say aloud what he guessed they both realized well enough. Even a boy who could swim like his namesake would be in deep trouble if he fell into the river tonight. The air was cold and the dark water swift and frigid. Thin sheets of ice formed along the banks and broke away to bob alongside the boats.

"We should have kept him with us," she murmured.

Hunt thought so too, but he hadn't wanted to alienate Counts His Scalps or Fox by demanding that the boy be moved. It wasn't that he didn't trust them; he didn't trust Jamie. He knew how reckless he himself had been as a child.

He sighed, recalling an incident with a crippled buffalo cow. He'd been nearly fifteen, too old to be considered a boy, too young to be counted a man. Another youth had bet him that he couldn't vault over the cow's back. He had ... and nearly been gored to death doing it.

He drove the paddle down, matching his rhythm to that of Talon and Feathered Lance. The canoe shot forward, edging ahead of the other boat. He could barely see the shore in the gathering twilight. Soon, they would be free from the worry of being spotted by hostile Iroquois.

After they had paddled about five miles, Talon asked Elizabeth to open the food packs and pass out dried meat. They ate the trail rations without pausing, scooping up water to quench their thirst.

The river widened. It was so dark that the shaman's canoe could no longer be seen. Hunt heard the sound the boat made as it cut the water and the faint splash of lifting and falling paddles. Elizabeth's shoulders slumped as her breathing grew heavier. Slowly, she relaxed and her head sunk over the child's.

The eerie cry of a loon echoed across the water. Hunt let his thoughts drift. He wished he and Elizabeth were back in the crazy priest's cabin, or better yet, that they were sharing a tepee on the far side of the great plains. In his mind's eye he pictured Elizabeth stripping off her clothing and coming naked and proud to his buffalo robe.

He imagined himself pulling her into his arms and tasting her warm, rosy mouth and firm breasts. Tremors of excitement hummed through his veins as he thought of filling her with his love and hearing her abandoned cries of pleasure. Then the flicker of a campfire on the side of a hill a few hundred yards from the nearest bank yanked him back to reality.

And when he heard the splash, he knew the boy had seen the fire as well and jumped over the side of the canoe.

# Chapter 20

**F**ox's low cry of alarm rolled across the water through the thick layers of fog. Badger's head snapped up, and he whined anxiously.

"Get him!" Hunt commanded. "Get Jamie."

Badger lunged over the side of the canoe. The big dog's weight and the ensuing splash sent a wave of water into the boat; only the quick reflexes and skill of Talon and Feathered Lance kept the birchbark boat from tipping over. Hunt tossed his paddle to Black Hoof, yanked off his powder horn and hunting bag, then ripped off his shirt and moccasins. He hit the icy water seconds after Badger.

Surfacing, Hunt swam toward shore. It was too dark to see more than a few yards ahead of him.

"There!" Counts shouted, pointing.

Elizabeth's voice cracked with emotion. "Jamie!"

Hunt's limbs grew numb, and his body seemed weighed down by the cold. Each thought was an effort as he forced himself to take stroke after stroke. Raising his head out of the water, he tried to catch sight of the boy, but all he could see was the gray curtain of mist that hung low over the river. The sounds of Badger's excited barking were as distorted by the fog as Hunt's own reasoning.

"Downstream!" Elizabeth shouted.

Canoe paddles splashed to his left. "Watch out for that rock!" Fox cried. The spectral shape of the nearest canoe slowed, then angled left and shot toward the center of the river.

Hunt's knee struck something solid. A granite outcrop rose out of the depths directly in front of him. Pushing off with his feet, he called out to the boy in Seneca. "Where are you?"

"Here!" Jamie's frightened voice drifted to him. "Help me! I can't—" The child's words were cut off abruptly.

"Badger!" Hunt yelled. "Get him!" Hunt bumped into another rock, scraping his left shoulder. Shaking with cold, he pulled himself up on the unyielding stone knob. "Jamie! I can't see you."

Farther out in the river, Shawnee voices called to the boy. Hunt wiped the water away from his eyes. Why hadn't they picked the boy up? he wondered. The canoes could move much faster than he could swim. Then the reality of the granite slab beneath him sunk in. The rocks. The Shawnee couldn't come closer for fear of ripping the birchbark canoes apart on the rocks.

Suddenly, the flare of a torch from shore about thirty yards away caught his attention. "Who are you?" cried a voice in Iroquoian.

"Friends," Hunt answered in the same tongue.

"Identify yourself!" a harsher speaker demanded.

Hunt supplied the first name that popped into his near-frozen brain. "Yellow Drum of the Seneca!"

"Who calls?"

"I told you! I am Yellow Drum of the Seneca!" The immediate roar of a musket told him that he'd given the wrong answer. A lead ball whined over his head as he plunged back into the river.

Instantly, the forest behind him thundered with a volley of explosions. The Shawnee returned gunfire. A hammer blow struck Hunt's right thigh, and he went under. He tumbled over and over; his hand touched a stone-strewn bottom. His lungs burned, and he was seized by a nearly overwhelming fatigue. Fighting the desire to lie still and rest, Hunt struggled upward toward the surface of the river and the shower of lead striking around him like deadly hailstones.

Pain lanced through his right upper arm. When he clamped his other hand over the spot, he felt warmth. *I've been hit*, he thought. Badger's yip pierced Hunt's stupor. He gulped air, then dove under and swam toward the animal's cry of distress.

This time when Hunt came up, his hand brushed a kicking hind leg. Clinging to the dog's ruff were two small hands. Badger was clearly tiring; his mouth was barely above water.

"Help me," Jamie gasped weakly.

Hunt reached out for him. "Give me your hand."

The boy let go of the dog and slipped under. Hunt tried to dive after him, but the dog grabbed a mouthful of Hunt's hair and hung on.

"No!" Hunt cried. He slammed the flat of his hand against Badger's nose, and the animal let go. Another musket ball buzzed in Hunt's ear. Badger yelped. Hunt knew the dog was hurt, but he couldn't wait to see how badly. He let himself sink, reaching out with both hands for the boy.

He swam in total darkness, eyes open, straining to see some small shadow. His fingers touched something living and his heart leaped, but when his fingers tangled in the long fur, he knew that it was the dog and not the boy. Still, he wasted precious breath, shoving the weight upward.

He broke water, saw Badger floundering a few yards away, and sucked in another mouthful of air to try for Jamie again.

"Hunter!" cried a familiar voice. A canoe sliced through the fog, and Talon leaned forward, offering a paddle. Black Hoof raised his long rifle and fired toward shore. "Come!" Talon shouted. "Take the paddle!"

Hunt's gaze raked the canoe. *Where was Elizabeth?* Feathered Lance stood and took careful aim. Fire and shot spewed from the Shawnee's musket. *Where was Elizabeth?*

"They're coming after us in canoes!" Black Hoof warned.

Elizabeth's head appeared above the rim of the boat. "Where's Jamie?" she cried. "That's Yellow Drum! Get Jamie!"

"Get down!" Talon ordered as he shoved her back to the bottom of the canoe.

Cold and exhaustion drained Hunt's strength. His right leg was nearly useless. He didn't know how long he could survive in the water, but he couldn't face Elizabeth without her son. He dove again, fighting the river—praying to find the child.

Again, he had to admit defeat. When he surfaced, Badger was there, whining and pawing at his head. He tried to shake off the dog, but when he threw out his hand, it came in contact with bare skin. "Jamie?" He blinked, unable to believe his eyes. "Jamie?" he cried again. Badger whined, but didn't ease his grip on the child's arm. "Here!" Hunt shouted. "I have him!" He threw an arm around Jamie's waist and pushed his head out of the water.

Seconds later, Talon lifted the unconscious boy from his hands. Feathered Lance got off a quick shot at the Seneca canoe that was quickly overtaking them.

Another bullet passed over Hunt's head. "Go!" he urged them. "Go!"

Talon dropped Jamie into the boat, picked up his paddle, and thrust deep into the water. Hunt let his body sink under the canoe and drift with the current.

It was all right, Hunt decided. He'd found the boy. He could rest . . . just a little while. The cold wasn't bad anymore . . . he could hardly feel it . . . he could hardly feel anything.

. . . Until Badger's sharp teeth sank into the flesh of Hunt's injured leg, and long claws dug at his belly and back. Instinct bade him fight back. Blood pounded in his head as he forced his way up to seize the rim of a sinking canoe. Around him, men jumped into the dark water. *Shouting. Shouting not in Shawnee, but Seneca.*

"Die!" a warrior shouted.

Something struck Hunt's head. He lost his grip on the wet birchbark just before the boat flipped over. The heavy barrel of a musket glanced off his shoulder as it sank to the bottom of the river. Frantically, Hunt scrabbled for a fingerhold and found a single cedar paddle. Then the night, the fog, and his wounds blended to a single throbbing ache and finally to an all-encompassing nothingness.

Elizabeth held her children tightly against her as Fire Talon, Black Hoof, and Feathered Lance continued to follow the first canoe downriver. Jamie was trembling uncontrollably, but he'd stopped choking and spitting up water, and his strong breathing told her he'd not die tonight.

They had to get him to shore and build a fire to make him warm, but there was no chance of that so long as the Seneca still posed a danger. She'd stripped off Jamie's wet clothes and wrapped him in her cloak, but the river's cold had done its work. Only fire could heat his body enough to keep him from taking a fever or the lung sickness.

The shock of hearing Yellow Drum's voice had shaken her to the core. There had been no way her son could have known that it was his father's fire he'd seen when he'd jumped over the side of the canoe. If Jamie had made the swim to shore, Yellow Drum would have him now, and no power on earth could have gotten him back again.

She would not . . . could not think of Hunt Campbell. It was impossible to imagine him dead . . . inconceivable that he could survive the river and the wrath of Yellow Drum and his fellow Seneca.

Hunt had risked his life for Jamie, hadn't he? No God could be so cruel as to take the only man she'd ever loved in exchange for her son.

Yet, she reasoned, the Iroquois had halted their pursuit. "Why aren't they chasing us?" she asked Talon.

"Black Drum's shot put a hole in one of the canoes. They started to sink. The others stopped to help."

"Will they follow us?" she asked.

"They will follow."

"We must go back for Hunt." The words were out before she'd considered what she was saying. A lump rose in her throat. If they returned, Yellow Drum would have her children and she would be a slave again—if he let her live. "We . . ." She tried to keep her voice from cracking. "We can't leave him."

"Hunter of the Far Mountains is dead," Fire Talon said gently.

"No," she argued fiercely. "I won't believe that." She shook her head. "He was in the river a long time before he found Jamie. If he didn't drown then . . ." She could say no more.

Talon made a sound of compassion. "Hunter of the

Far Mountains was a brave warrior. If *Inu-msi-ila-fe-wanu*, the Great Spirit who is a grandmother, is merciful, she has let the water take him rather than let him become a prisoner of the Seneca."

"Would they stop chasing us if they had a prisoner?"

He shrugged. "Who can tell what the Iroquois may do? They are as illogical as the white men."

"Then he could be alive," she persisted. "Alive and being tortured. How can you abandon him and call yourselves men?"

"Women are as cruel as green-head flies," Talon said. "They take pleasure in tormenting a man in his tender parts."

"You said I was not a woman," she reminded him.

"That is true. This man said you were the warrior Scarlet Dawn, and you must be. If you were not, you would not be a part of this raiding party. But you still think as a woman," he observed wryly.

"Is that always a bad thing?"

He frowned. "Not always. Women often have wisdom that men lack. It comes from always thinking."

"Exactly," she replied. "We must get Jamie warm. If you land the canoe, I can make a fire and get him dry. You can take the others and go back and rescue Hunt."

"And the dog as well, I suppose," he said wryly.

"Hunt would do it for you." Her son whimpered, and Elizabeth rocked him against her. "If I can't stop Jamie's shivering, he'll sicken and die. Please, Fire Talon."

"You are a stubborn woman, never satisfied. First, you must have your children," he said. "Now that you have them, you want Hunter of the Far Mountains and his dog."

"I don't have to have the dog," she murmured.

"Ha!" He glanced back at Black Hoof. "Hear that?" he asked in Algonquian. "Her meek words say she does not want the dog, but later, what will she say to our women? Will she say we were too cowardly to save the courageous animal? Will our wives call us old men?"

Elizabeth held her tongue, but nothing could still the singing in her blood when Talon signaled the other canoe toward the towering forest on the far shore of the river.

Hunt lay crumpled on a small stretch of sand and rocks, hardly wider than a man is tall. His head and upper torso were above the lapping water line, the lower half of his body still submerged.

Pain flared through his body, but he accepted it. Acceptance of physical pain was a lesson he'd learned during the ordeal of the Cheyenne Sun Dance when thongs were thrust through the skin and muscle of a man's chest and tied, and the initiate must dance and pray until the leather ropes ripped out in a torrent of bright blood. Flesh could be broken and torn; a man's spirit could soar above the earth and touch the light of the Creator.

The world was dark and wet. Hunt remembered another black, wet night, on the endless prairie. He'd been hunting buffalo with bow and arrow, and he'd been separated from his Arapaho and Cheyenne friends by the torrent of shaggy animals. He was riding full out, ready to send an arrow into the heart of a young bull, when his pony missed a step. He heard the crack of the pinto's foreleg like a gunshot. He had the sensation of falling . . . and then nothing more until thunder and lightning had rolled across the sky. Rain hitting his face had awakened him. A cloudburst of water had poured from the heavens until the dry prairie earth became a multitude of brown rushing rivers.

Hunt opened his eyes. Something was scraping the skin of his face. Something large and hairy loomed over him in the wet, cold darkness. A buffalo? He was too tired to care. He let himself sink down in the black void once more. But the buffalo would not let him rest; it continued to lick his face with a rough tongue.

Hunt pushed back the Stygian night and drew in a breath of air. Immediately, he began to choke. Rolling onto his belly, he puked up his guts. When he'd emptied his stomach, he groaned and reached out to grab hold of Badger's hair.

The dog whined anxiously and pawed at Hunt's face.

*Where the hell was he?* Hunt tried to think. His head felt as though a tree had fallen on it. When he put his hand up, he found a swollen gash and caked blood.

Sitting up required an effort greater than he would have imagined. Flashes of memory filtered through his throbbing headache. A canoe . . . he remembered a canoe tipping over on top of him.

His teeth were chattering. He was lying half in the water, soaked through and shaking with cold. If he didn't move, he'd die, and then it wouldn't matter whose canoe had turned over or what river this was. But when he tried to stand, he pitched forward onto his face.

His right leg felt as though it was on fire. Gingerly, he felt for a reason and found it. His finger slipped through a hole in his thigh and hit something hard. His head might be full of river mud, but he could sure as hell tell when he'd been shot. And the damn lead ball was still buried in his leg.

Instinct made him want to rip it out of his flesh, but he forced back the urge. He'd seen a wounded Cheyenne Dog Soldier dance a victory chant and feast on buffalo tongue for most of a night. Sees-Dust-At-Morning . . . his friend . . . Sees Dust. For seconds, the Cheyenne's hawk-faced image surfaced in his mind, and he remembered Sees Dust's hearty laughter. When the medicine man had dug out the Blackfoot arrowhead, Sees Dust had bled to death within minutes.

A loud crack sent Sees Dust's face tumbling back into the past. For an instant, Hunt was confused. Was that the sound of his pony's leg breaking? A second shot echoed across the river, either musket or rifle fire.

He faintly recalled an overturned canoe. Now, someone was shooting. He shook his aching head to try to make sense of what was happening. Obviously, he had nearly drowned, and somebody had taken a definite disliking to him. The question was, who was looking for him—friends or enemies? And how could he tell them apart if he couldn't remember who or where he was?

Badger continued to paw at him. The dog . . . *his dog* . . . seemed to have a pretty good idea of what was going on. At this point, any opinion seemed more rational than his own. Using the dog for support, he gritted his teeth and stood up.

Fragments of human voices drifted to him on the wind. A torch bobbed, and when Hunt wiped the blood out of his eyes, he could make out a canoe with Indians in it. They seemed to be paddling toward him.

"Friends or enemies?" he asked the dog. His words creaked like a rusty hinge.

The dog took a step toward the woods.

Hunt glanced at the dog. "I was afraid you'd say that," he rasped.

The bank wasn't steep; for that he was grateful. He crawled up it on his hands and knees, leaving a trail of blood behind him. He was stark naked; he'd lost his loincloth in the river, but he figured that might have been what saved him. If he'd had any clothes on, they'd have frozen stiff and him with them.

He clawed his way upright against a sapling, took hold of the dog's back, and took a step, then another. After a few yards, he managed a stumbling trot toward the south. Each jolt of his feet hitting the ground rattled his brain and sent splinters of white pain through his wounded leg, but he was putting distance between him and the men on the river.

At dawn, he was still on his feet.

The sun came up in the east as far as he could remember. His headache had become a roaring wave, and he was no longer cold. He was hot, and he was beginning to hallucinate.

He kept seeing a white woman's face . . . a woman with red hair and green eyes. It wasn't his sister, Becca. Becca had red hair, but she wasn't the woman he kept conjuring up in his head. Becca used to sing him to sleep every night . . . something about a cherry tree. He began to hum as he walked and the words came tumbling back.

> . . . Sweet Mary and Joseph
> Walked through an orchard green,
> There were cherries and berries,
> As thick as might be seen . . .

> And up spoke Virgin Mary,
> So meek and so mild,
> Joseph, gather me some cherries,
> For I am with child . . .

He remembered the cabin where he'd lived with Becca and her husband, Simon. He didn't like Simon much, didn't care for the son of a bitch at all. He remembered Shawnee burning the house and taking him and his sister prisoner. He'd never seen her after that day. Simon was dead, but he supposed Becca was alive somewhere in the white settlements, probably remarried with a new family. He wondered if she ever thought of him.

He supposed he ought to do something about making a fire, but he was so hot, he wasn't sure he needed one. He wasn't hungry either, but he was thirsty. Why a body would want more water after he'd nearly drowned was beyond him. The river wasn't far on his right; he'd kept close to it, thinking that sooner or later, his head would clear. Water could tell you where you were, if you knew where you'd started from and where you were headed.

Without warning, his bad leg gave way, and he fell hard against the ground. He called out to Badger, but the dog didn't come to help him. Instead the animal ran ahead into the trees.

"Come back," Hunt whispered. His voice was nearly gone. "Badger."

The bushes parted and an Indian stepped into the clearing. Hunt tried to speak, but the earth swayed beneath him and then opened with a groan and swallowed him up.

# Chapter 21

**H**unt lay in a cocoon of warm darkness. Lately, he had been plagued by nightmares. Only glimpses of the bad dreams remained, but he could remember floating or being carried horizontally above the ground so that he saw the trees and sky pass over him. He remembered intense heat and thirst, the torture of something digging into his leg, and strangest of all, the odd sensation of having food spooned into his mouth as though he were a helpless babe. He lay very still, afraid that if he stirred, the agony or the throbbing in his head would return.

Instead, he heard familiar sounds from his past: a child's laughter, barking dogs, and a flute. The musical notes rose and fell. He wasn't familiar with the tune, but the poignant love song stirred emotion in his soul. He wondered if he had died and crossed the River of Souls to the heavenly hunting grounds beyond the bounds of earth. Surely, only spiritual beings could play so sweetly.

Something damp brushed his right eyelid, then his lips. The tickling sensation brought him higher toward consciousness. Before he could drift into deep sleep again, he heard a merry titter, and a drop of cold liquid rolled down his forehead and into the folds of his left eye.

"Is you 'sleep?" Small fingers pinched Hunt's eyelashes and pried his right eye open. A tiny girl child stared into his face. "You not 'sleep!" she declared with a giggle. "You 'wake."

"Go away," Hunt groaned.

The wet object dripped over his lips and chin. "What—" he demanded. He opened his eyes and tried to sit up, but a wave of dizziness laid him low again. "Ohh," he moaned. The dome of a skin-lined wigwam slowly spun round and round over his head. He sighed heavily and closed his eyes again.

"No," the sprite cried. "No 'sleep. Sleep *two many*." She giggled again. Minute fingers marched spiderlike over his nose. "Wake high. Nooo." More giggles. "Wake up."

When he looked again, he saw what appeared to be a wet turkey feather dancing over his forehead. "Get that thing away from me," he said. He brought his hands up to cover his face. His joints moved stiffly, and one arm ached, but his body seemed whole from the waist up.

The dancing feather tickled the backs of his hands. "Stop that," he growled, grabbing the feather and yanking it away from his small tormentor. "What are you, an evil woods' dwarf?"

The child's lower lip quivered and two tears rolled down her cheeks.

"Don't cry," Hunt said. "Here." He shoved the offending feather at her. She drew in a long sobbing breath, let out a banshee shriek, and fled. He pushed a blanket back and forced himself to sit up. The room tilted, then slid properly into place.

Hunt raised the blanket and checked to see that he still had two legs and his prized possessions. One leg was bandaged above the knee, but he had the required number of feet and toes. His male parts were intact and uninjured. He also discovered that he had an urge to empty his bladder. With a groan, he swung both legs over the edge of the sleeping platform.

The large wigwam was snug and well stocked with food and blankets. Fur rugs covered the floor; firewood was stacked neatly by the entrance curtain. His own rifle and powder horn hung on deer antlers above the doorway. Nothing was out of place but a single feather, a wooden cup, and a child's corncob doll, all discarded on the rug near Hunt's feet.

Absently, he rubbed his chin and was startled to find a full beard. Hadn't he shaved just yesterday? He blinked and tried to reason out the passage of time, while the scent of grilling fish and browning bread tantalized him. He remembered going into the river after Elizabeth's boy, and . . . He took a deep breath and tried to make sense of the situation. He must have been hit worse than he'd thought. He looked around the room again to reassure himself that this was a Shawnee wigwam, not an Iroquois longhouse.

Yes . . . he reasoned. The little girl he'd frightened . . . she was Elizabeth's child. He'd gotten the boy out of the river but—

The entrance flap to the wigwam moved, and a blast of wind cut short his reverie. "Hunt!" Elizabeth's anxious face appeared in the doorway. "You're awake."

He started to rise.

"No, you don't," she ordered, coming to him and laying a gentle hand on his forehead. "Flat on your back. This is the first day you've been without a fever."

"I've got to go outside and—"

"You're going nowhere," she replied brusquely. "What did you say to Rachel? You frightened her half to death."

"She attacked me."

Her concern turned to relief and amusement. "Nonsense. She's just a child. How could she attack you?"

"Your child," he replied. "Capable of anything."

Elizabeth's fingers strayed to his hair. "You're really going to be all right, aren't you?"

"Let me up." He started to rise, and she pushed him back with surprising strength.

"You're going nowhere."

"I've got to pee."

"You can pee in a jar just like you've been doing for weeks."

He felt his face grow warm. "In a jar?"

"You wet your bed, too," Jamie said, bounding into the room. More frigid air blasted from outside. Badger squeezed through the doorway and shook himself vigorously, sending spatters of moisture and mud flying across the room.

Elizabeth turned toward her son. "Close the door. That wind will blow out the fire."

With a yelp of joy, the dog flung himself on Hunt. "Badger," Hunt said, rubbing the animal's head and ears. "Good dog." The animal wiggled and thumped his back leg, then began methodically to lick every inch of Hunt's bare skin. "Easy, easy," he said to the dog, but a lump rose in his throat as he looked into the big shining eyes and patted his side.

"Have careful," Jamie said in awkward English. "Badger hurt with bullet. Better now."

"Badger was hit?" Hunt's fingers found a hairless spot on the dog's shoulder. The jagged furrow was pink and tender but healing. "Good boy," Hunt said. Just below the scar, a beaded strip of leather was woven into Badger's hair. Dangling from it was a tuft of feathers. "What's this?"

"Jamie thought Badger deserved an eagle feather

for his bravery, but he keeps eating them," Elizabeth explained.

"Give him owl feathers," Jamie supplied. "No eat. Still have brave." The boy shrugged off his cloak and dropped it on the sleeping platform. The fur slid to the floor, and Elizabeth pointed at it. Jamie started to protest.

"I don't want to hear it," she said. "Put your cloak where it belongs." Then she turned her attention back to Hunt. "You want the pee jar?"

"I don't want the damned jar," he said, feeling instantly foolish. He still suffered from the effects of the herd of buffalo that had undoubtedly stampeded over his head, but he had no intention of relieving himself in front of Elizabeth and her son. "I want my moccasins and a shirt so that I can go outside and—"

"You fright my sister," Jamie accused.

"Exactly what did you do to her?" Elizabeth demanded, fussing with Hunt's blanket. "She's only a child. You could show a little patience."

"She was torturing me with that damned feather." Jamie giggled.

Elizabeth picked up Rachel's doll. "Are you sure your mind's clear?" she asked Hunt. "You've had a high fever ever since Counts His Scalps removed the lead ball from your leg. He had to do a healing ceremony twice and—"

"Elizabeth, can we talk about this later?" His voice sounded peevish to his own ears, but damn it, he felt weak as a newborn rabbit and he had to go.

"You wet the bed," the boy reminded him in Seneca.

"Speak English or Shawnee," Elizabeth said.

"I am Seneca," Jamie replied. "I will—"

Elizabeth turned on her son. She didn't raise her voice, but her tone became firm. "A Seneca man shows respect at his mother's hearth, and you will speak English or Shawnee until you learn it properly. Once you've improved your vocabulary, you can use sign language for all I care."

Jamie flushed and looked at the floor.

"She's right," Hunt agreed. "All real men, be they English, Shawnee, or Cheyenne, show respect for their mothers."

"*Hahhah, Onna,*" Jamie answered in subdued Shawnee. *Yes, Mother.* He thrust out a small chest and proudly displayed his English. "Brave Seneca warrior show respect for mother. . . ." He flashed Hunt a mischievous grin much like Elizabeth's. "And you—poor hurted captive."

Elizabeth reached out and touched Hunt's cheek again. "Hunt is a guest here, not a captive, Jamie."

"Not captive," the boy echoed. His lower lip protruded in a pout. "If my father have him—"

"Your father does not have him, we do." She glanced at Jamie. "And I believe you have something to say to Hunter of the Far Mountains."

Jamie pursed his lips and frowned. Staring at the floor, he rubbed one moccasined toe in a small circle. "This man has thank of you, for save life of river."

"For saving your life, not the river's," Elizabeth corrected him gently. "Now, take Badger, put your cloak back on, and go to Sweet Water's to get your sister. Oh, take your sister's outer wrap as well." She fixed Hunt with a disapproving glance. "You frightened Rachel so that she ran out of here without her fur."

"*Onna,*" Jamie protested. "Me just—"

"*Me* just go and get your sister. She spends more time at Sweet Water's than she does at home." She turned back to Hunt. "Sweet Water is the wife of Chief Fire Talon. They have a little girl, Star Girl, younger than Rachel, but still old enough for her to play with. The children are inseparable."

"Star Girl baby," Jamie said. "Fire Talon's son, called Falcon, my friend."

"Yes, he is your friend," Elizabeth agreed. "Falcon is eleven," she explained to Hunt. "Jamie thinks the sun rises and sets on his every word."

"Falcon friend," Jamie insisted. Elizabeth pointed to the door. When the boy started for the entranceway, Badger got up and ambled after him.

"What's this?" Hunt grumbled. "Has he stolen my dog as well?"

Jamie laughed. "Come, Badger. Come."

"Among the Seneca, one who saves a life becomes responsible for it," Elizabeth said. Her green eyes shimmered with reflected firelight as she turned her warm smile on him. "You risked your life to save Jamie's. He—and I—owe you a debt we'll never be able to repay."

Hunt shook his head. "There's no need to talk of debts between us. Badger's more to thank than me. Jamie swam like a fish, and Badger was there for him to hang on to when the cold got to him."

"You make brave," the boy admitted reluctantly. "You shot, still swim. I no can swim more. Cold water. Badger save, Hunter save, too. You brave for Shawnee. Seneca braver, but you brave, me guest."

"You *guess*," Elizabeth corrected.

Hunter looked into the boy's eyes. "Jumping out in the river was a foolhardy thing to do," he said. "You're brave, Jamie. You just have to learn to think before you act."

The boy chewed on his bottom lip. "Me see fire of camp," he said. "Think Seneca be there." He grinned. "Me right. Am Seneca fire. Am Father." Jamie tapped his chest with his fist.

"What does he mean?" Hunt asked Elizabeth.

She looked amused. "It means that when you shouted that you were Yellow Drum, that wasn't the best answer."

"My father shoot," Jamie boasted. "Come in canoe get me back."

Hunt rubbed his forehead. "Yellow Drum?"

Jamie giggled. "You shout you Yellow Drum. My father Yellow Drum. He mad, shoot at you."

"Shot at me? Shot me, I'd guess. But someone's been taking care of me," Hunt said carefully, as though walking on bird eggs. This talk of responsibility made him giddy. He stumbled for the right words and found himself breathless.

He couldn't keep his gaze off Elizabeth. She looked like a vision in a simple doeskin shift and fringed leggings. Gone were the men's clothes; in their place were the beautiful, beaded garments of a Shawnee woman. No, he decided, it wasn't the tunic that made her look so lovely; it was the happiness that radiated from her face.

He liked seeing her here before a fire in this intimate family setting. He even liked hearing her fuss at the boy for throwing his clothes on the floor; it reminded him of his sister and the feeling of family.

"Next time you meet Seneca, you no say you Yellow Drum," Jamie advised. "Maybe Father no shoot you."

"Out." Elizabeth pointed to the door. The boy and his tail-wagging animal left the wigwam. Elizabeth secured the heavy fur covering.

"No need to do that," Hunt said. "I need to go out."

She picked up a clay container and tried to hand it to him. "You're too weak to walk, Hunt," she said. "It's cold out. Be reasonable. I'll turn my back if you're modest."

His cheeks burned. "You've been doing . . . *that* for me?"

"Someone had to." She laid her hand on his arm. "You nearly died. You'd been shot twice, hit in the head—even if the bullet just grazed your thick skull, and you nearly drowned. You were hardly in any—"

"How long ago?"

"Three . . . no, almost four weeks ago."

"Where are we?"

"Fire Talon's village. He didn't want to take you back where we assembled the raiding party. He didn't want to risk bringing the Iroquois wrath down on them. We're somewhere near the Ohio. You've been out of your mind with fever."

"I remember being in the river and a boat over-turning—not much after that."

"The Shawnee sunk one of the Seneca canoes. We had to leave you in the water, but I made them go back and look for you. They found you wandering in the woods near the river."

"You made them?"

She smiled. "I convinced them that it was the honorable thing to do, after you'd shown such courage." Her fingers tightened on his arm. "You did save Jamie," she said softly. "I'll never forget it. Never."

Hunt grimaced. "I can't believe I was so stupid as to tell Yellow Drum that I was—"

She laughed. "How could you know? How could any of us know he would be there hunting deer and bear? They could have been hunting anywhere within a hundred miles."

"And he didn't follow?"

"I don't think he realized Jamie was there. He only guessed that strangers were on the river. If he'd known about the children, the devil himself wouldn't have kept him from pursuing us."

"The Seneca don't believe in the devil," he reminded her.

"Whirlwind, then. He's half human, half spirit, and mean as the devil." The corners of her lips tilted up in a teasing smile. "You look like a supernatural being yourself with all that black hair on your face."

"You might have shaved me while you were doing all that nursing."

She smoothed away an unruly lock of hair, and her eyes twinkled. "I've never shaved a man. I wouldn't know how to begin. Yellow Drum used to pluck his chin hairs with a clamshell. I could do that if you like."

Hunt scratched the right side of his beard. "I don't think so. I'll shave it myself, if you can find a knife with a decent blade."

"I think I can. You lost yours in the river." She chuckled again.

"I'm glad you find my condition so amusing."

"It's just that . . ." She took a breath and tried to talk without dissolving into laughter. "It's just that I was so afraid you'd die that I never took time to really think about how different you looked with a beard." A slight giggle slipped out. "The Seneca make masks of corn husks and animal hair. They represent spirits known as Husk Faces. They can do powerful magic. Which one are you, do you think?"

Hunt shifted uncomfortably. "Make Water. My clothes and moccasins, woman. I'm going outside."

Meekly, she brought a clean hunting shirt, a belt, a loincloth, and leggings. "Do you need help?"

He scowled at her. "I've been dressing myself since I was out of leading strings."

She waited, averting her eyes, while he struggled

into his shirt and belt, then wrapped the red woolen loincloth over his genitals. When Elizabeth dropped to her knees to help him with his moccasins, he jerked them away.

"I said, I can do this myself." As he began to slide the first one on, his toes and sole came in contact with something wet and slimy. "What the hell?" he demanded, dumping the moccasin upside down. A large clump of cooked squash plopped onto the rug. "What? You're using my moccasins to store—"

Elizabeth covered her mouth with her fingers and giggled. "Rachel. I'm sorry." She giggled again. "Rachel hates squash. I should have known she hasn't been eating it." She took the other moccasin from him and turned it upside down. Fish bones, a lump of well-chewed wintergreen, and a rabbit leg tumbled out.

"Rachel," he echoed.

"I'm afraid so."

Hunt pushed himself upright. Again, dizziness attacked him, but he choked it back. She moved to support him, and he slid an arm around her. "I'm not used to leaning on a woman."

"I can see that." She made a small sound that might have been amusement. "It really would be better if—" She broke off as she heard a sound from the entranceway. "Come in," she called when a hand appeared at the curtain. "Wait, it's tied shut." She looked up into Hunt's face.

"Go ahead. I can stand." He thought he could stand. His knees felt like wet cornmeal; his legs s̲ ̲ ̲d to belong to someone else. And his stomach ̲ ̲ struggling to turn itself inside out.

Elizabeth pulled back the entrance flap and gestured a slim Shawnee woman wrapped in a blanket into the wigwam. "I hope Rachel was no trouble."

"Not at all. Jamie said that Hunt was better. I've brought a pot of deer soup. Talon always says that my deer soup would snatch a man back from death." She turned toward Hunt and pushed back the blanket that covered her hair. "Welcome to—" she began.

Hunt stared at her in disbelief as gooseflesh raised on his arms. He collapsed back onto the sleeping platform as all strength drained away. That voice, those eyes, could belong to only one woman on earth. "Becca?" he rasped. "Becca?"

# Chapter 22

E lizabeth looked at Hunt and shook her head. "You're wrong. The fever's troubling you. This isn't your lost sister—this is Fire Talon's wife, Sweet Water."

Sweet Water made a small, strangled sound and took a step toward him. "No . . ." she whispered. "My Colin is dead."

"Dead, hell!" Hunt insisted. "I don't know what's happened to your hair, but I'd bet my immortal soul that you're Rebecca Gordon Brandt, born in Ireland and lost on the frontier when I was eight years old."

Sweet Water's eyes widened and she swayed slightly. "Mother of God," she murmured, extending a hand toward Hunt. "Colin? Can it be?"

"You had red hair," he answered hoarsely. "Red as an English fox."

"And so it still would be," she said, "did I not dye it with black walnut hulls." Sweet Water moved closer to him. "With that great black beard it's hard to tell, but your eyes . . . Your eyes could be Colin's."

"You're both crazy," Elizabeth insisted, taking the Shawnee woman's arm. "His name is Hunt Campbell."

He rubbed a hand across his eyes. "Becca," he said.

"You remember that day. You'd sent me to the creek for water. I didn't come back, and you came to look for me."

"Anyone could know that," Elizabeth argued. "Indians could have told you."

"What did they call the man who captured you?" Sweet Water demanded.

"My father was Wolf Robe of the Cheyenne," Hunt said, "but the Shawnee called him the Stranger."

Sweet Water flung herself on him and began to kiss his face and hair. "Colin! Colin!" she cried. "They said you were dead."

He put his arms around her and held her as she wept tears of joy. "Becca," he murmured. "Becca, don't . . ."

Elizabeth stood transfixed, watching them, still unable to believe what she'd heard. "His name is Hunt Campbell," she repeated. "Hunt, not Colin."

"My father, Wolf Robe, gave me an Indian name," he explained when his sister had ceased to kiss him and contented herself with sitting beside him and clutching his hand. "Colin Gordon had nothing to do with the man I became. He died the day that cabin burned. I can't remember my Irish father. When I was taken in by Ross Campbell, it seemed only natural that I should adopt his surname."

Sweet Water glanced at Elizabeth. "He speaks truth. Among the Shawnee, a name is something private. My people often take English names."

"But you've taken a Shawnee name . . . a Shawnee husband," Elizabeth replied.

"My father told me that you'd been traded back to the whites," Hunt said. "That's why I didn't look for you among the Shawnee villages."

"I hid my Christian name and my hair," Sweet Water answered. She brought his hand to her lips and kissed the backs of his knuckles. "I grew to love Fire Talon—the warrior who captured me."

"You wed your captor?" Elizabeth asked.

The older woman chuckled. "We've often argued over who captured who, but I do love him, and he loves me. If you only knew how many years we searched for you. Then Fire Talon heard that a white boy died of the pox in the village where the Stranger's Delaware wife lived. We assumed—"

"There was another white boy there. His name was John. We went ice-fishing together." He looked thoughtful. "It must have been John who died."

Elizabeth balled her hands into fists at her sides. "You two—sister and brother. It's impossible."

"Not impossible," Sweet Water said, wiping tears off her cheeks. "My husband's heart will leap with happiness. If you only knew how many nights he went to sleep with ears burning from my chiding over you."

"I still don't understand why you pretend to be Indian," Elizabeth said.

The Shawnee woman turned a radiant smile on her. "I am Indian. It is no pretense. My husband's people are my people. As it says in the Book of Ruth, 'Entreat me not to leave thee or to return from following after thee; for whither thou goest, I will go; and where thou lodgest, I will lodge; thy people shall be my people, and thy God my God.' "

"But you remain a Christian," Elizabeth protested. "You wear a cross, and I've seen you read your Bible."

Sweet Water nodded. "His God is still my God; there is only one. We may call him by different names, but there can be only one Creator."

Still confused, Elizabeth persisted. "Why dye your hair?"

"Practical reasons," Sweet Water said. "I dye my hair dark to keep the English from knowing that I was born Irish. Many white-skinned captives have been forced to return to the English settlements against their will; families have been divided. It seemed better to blend into the tribe than to be a source of trouble to the Shawnee."

Elizabeth exhaled softly. "I asked you about your blue eyes, and you lied to me."

Sweet Water chuckled. "I didn't lie. I said that my grandfather was Scottish. That was the truth. I may have been born in Ireland, but the Gordons hail from Scotland." She looked back at Hunt and squeezed his hand again. "I've waited so long for this," she said softly. "You're an answer to my prayers, Colin."

"Not Colin," he protested. "Hunt."

"Hunt, then. I don't care what you call yourself, little brother," she replied.

Elizabeth dipped a cup of the broth Sweet Water had brought. "Would you like some soup?" she offered.

Hunt grimaced. "What I would like is to go out and relieve myself."

With much fussing and draping of furs around him, they helped him out of the wigwam. Fox was nearby, and Sweet Water motioned him over. Both women returned to the shelter of the house while Fox took Hunt into the forest.

"I have so many questions to ask," Sweet Water said as they warmed their hands at the fire. "Where has he been all these years? What has he done?"

"When he returns, I'll leave you alone," Elizabeth offered. "I know you have much to talk about." She was still worried about Hunt's recovery. His wounds were healing without infection, but he'd lost weight and his face showed the strain of his injuries.

Sweet Water touched Elizabeth's wrist lightly. "What are you to my brother?"

Elizabeth felt a rush of blood to her cheeks. "My father paid him to bring me back to Charles Town," she replied stiffly. "He's been a good friend."

"More than a friend."

Elizabeth's pulse quickened, and she busied herself with adding wood to the fire. "We were..." She stammered, trying to find the words to keep from making herself look like a fool before this beautiful, composed woman. "Hunt didn't want to rescue my son. I tried to persuade him in the only way I had." She covered her mouth with her hand. "I'll go to the children," she said in a burst of words. "Make sure Hunt doesn't tire himself. He's still very weak." Throwing a fur cloak over her shoulders, she moved toward the entrance.

"I have children, Elizabeth," Sweet Water said. "Colin—Hunt was like a son to me. Nothing you could do to save your children would make you less in my eyes."

"Nothing?" Elizabeth straightened her shoulders. "If you ask me if I used your brother, I did. But you needn't worry that I will expect more. My father is ..." The words choked in her throat. Sweet Water had been kind to her, and Elizabeth didn't want that friendship to turn to pity. In desperation, she tried to salvage a vestige of pride. "My father is a wealthy man. He will provide for me when I get home. No doubt, he'll arrange a suitable marriage." Gooseflesh broke out on her arms as she thought of the empty existence that stretched before her without Hunt.

"And my brother?" Sweet Water's blue eyes shone with concern. "What of him?"

"Hunt will be well paid for his trouble," Elizabeth answered. The cold dismissal of those words burned in the pit of Elizabeth's belly as she hurried through the cold wind toward Sweet Water's wigwam.

Hunt's sister knew that Elizabeth had been a slave to a Seneca—that she had put her own life before honor. And Sweet Water also had guessed that Elizabeth had shared Hunt's blanket. What must she think of the woman who'd put her own selfish needs before anyone else's safety?

Shame washed over Elizabeth. She'd lied to her friend, not precisely, perhaps, but in intent. She'd made it seem as if she'd bribed Hunt with her body, and that she thought she was above his class.

While it was certainly true that her father was a titled gentleman and that he would use his wealth to find her a husband, she believed she would find little joy in the arrangement. Charles Town girls who brought dishonor on their families were often married off to planters in the Caribbean. She might make a proper marriage, but the man would be one of her father's choosing.

The stain of her capture and enslavement by Indians would always remain with her. Ladies would watch her from behind their fans and whisper gossip about her past. She imagined herself and her children an unwelcome necessity in some isolated island manor house—the ugly bride of a man who had agreed to give her his name in exchange for the dowry she brought him.

Hunt and Fox came out of the trees. Hunt called to her, but she kept walking.

"Elizabeth," Hunt repeated.

"Time enough for chasing her," Fox said. "You belong in your bed."

Hunt nodded. Even the short distance he'd walked had drained his strength. With Fox's help, he entered the wigwam and made his way to his sleeping platform. Dizzy and trembling with exhaustion, he sat down. "What are you doing?" he demanded as his sister began to untie the laces of his moccasins.

"Hush. Lie down, I can do this." She tugged off the first moccasin. "What's this sticky stuff on your feet?"

"Stop fussing over me," Hunt grumbled. "Rachel stuffed her unwanted dinner in my moccasins."

"Wonderful," Sweet Water said. She pulled a blanket up to his waist and examined the bandage on his arm. "Lie still, you've started this bleeding again."

"It's all right."

"You aren't recovered yet," she said, laying a hand on his forehead. "I think you may have a fever."

"I don't have a fever. It's hot in here," he protested.

Fox chuckled. "She is a bossy woman."

"She's always been bossy," Hunt agreed.

"This is my brother, once known as Colin Gordon," Sweet Water explained to the Shawnee brave.

Fox exhaled softly. "The boy we—"

"Captured at Simon Brandt's cabin," Sweet Water finished. "Fox was with the raiding party that day," she said to Hunt. She glanced back at the brave. "I can't wait to tell Talon."

"Hiiye," Fox murmured. "But it will not be so much a surprise as you think. Talon told me that this man might be your long lost brother."

"He told you?" Sweet Water cried. "And he said nothing to me?"

Fox chuckled. "You know Talon. He is a cautious man. If Hunter died in Seneca hunting ground, he would be dead—would he not? If he lived, there would be time to ask questions once we returned."

"And you kept it from me—both of you?" Her eyes narrowed. "Out of this house, Fox. Go and tell *my husband* that he was right. And also tell him that he'd best find his supper at your wigwam tonight, for there will be none for him in his own house."

After Fox left, Sweet Water turned back to Hunt. "Do you want that soup now?"

"A little." In truth, Hunt was weary enough to sleep without eating. His legs had barely held him, and the walk to the woods had brought sweat beading on his forehead in spite of the wind and low temperature.

"Prop your head up a little," she ordered, lifting a spoonful of the venison soup to his lips.

"I can feed myself."

"Shh," she soothed. "Open your mouth." When he did, she popped the spoon between his lips.

"Now, little brother, where have you been? And what does this woman really mean to you?"

It was his turn to laugh. "Stick a spoon in my mouth and then expect me to answer difficult questions. All women are alike."

She wiped away a dribble of broth. "You were always trouble, Colin, always."

"Hunt."

She sighed. "I'm sorry, but this will take some getting used to."

"I agree. I've always thought of you as Becca."

"Maybe she and Colin belong together in the past."

"Maybe," he agreed, then changed the subject. "You picked a good man for a second husband."

She smiled. "He picked me."

"Talon's one of the bravest men I've ever known," Hunt said between mouthfuls.

"And the kindest. Oh, you're an uncle," she cried. "You have a nephew, eleven. My Falcon is already a good hunter. And Star Girl is—"

"Rachel's friend," he supplied. "I've heard that much."

"I can't believe Talon didn't tell me that he suspected who you were," she said. "I was in the same
village with you and never noticed you. I was angry
that you were taking my husband to war. I avoided
you." She looked down at him. "I'll kill Talon for not
saying anything."

"Does it matter?" he asked her.

"No, not now." She cupped his hand between hers.
"Do you know how many times I've been in and out
of this house? I helped to tend your wounds, but I
never guessed who you were."

"What of Simon Brandt?"

Her mood became pensive. "Long dead."

Hunt was shocked at the relief he felt. His sister's
first husband had given him little but rough blows
and hard words.

"An evil man and best forgotten," she whispered.

Hunt's eyelids felt heavy. The heat of the soup
pooled in his belly, and Becca's voice lulled him into
a peace he'd not known for a long time.

"What is Elizabeth Fleming to you?" his sister
asked.

He didn't answer.

"She says her father's a wealthy man."

He was so tired that it was easier to pretend sleep.

"Don't make the mistake of thinking this can last,"
Becca said. "She needed you to get her children. Now
that she has them, she'll return to who she is."

Elizabeth's image formed in the recesses of his
mind. He reached for her and she eluded him in the
mist.

"She's different than we are," Becca said. "A
woman of her class could never accept living among
the people as I have. She would not be happy married
to a woodsman. She's been accustomed to satin
dresses and velvet slippers in her father's house. She

told me that he will arrange a suitable marriage for her . . . with a rich plantation owner, no doubt."

"She's lived among the Seneca."

"As a captive—a slave. Given the choice, she will gladly return to her position as an English gentle-woman. I am happy as Talon's wife, but I lived on the frontier for many years before I knew him. Elizabeth was born to quality. She isn't like me, little brother. You and I have always known adversity. It wouldn't be fair to take advantage of her when she's just been rescued from slavery and hasn't had the time to think about what she wants of life."

"I think I . . ." The word *love* formed but he couldn't say it. His feelings were too raw to share with the sister he hadn't seen in so many years. And what if Becca was right? What if Elizabeth would be better off among her own kind?

"You care for her," Becca said softly.

"Yes," he admitted. His sister had spoken of fears that had troubled him ever since he'd begun to realize how much Elizabeth meant to him. He wanted Elizabeth, but not if it ruined her life and caused her un-happiness.

Becca sighed and rubbed his forehead. "You must let her go, little brother. You'll only hurt yourself—and her—by trying to change what must be."

"Elizabeth." His lips formed her name, but he was already drifting into a deep sleep.

"There's no place for you in her rich Charles Town future," Sweet Water said, "and no place for two half-Indian children."

To Elizabeth's delight, Hunt's recovery was swift and uneventful. In a week, he was regularly walking to the men's lodge to join Fire Talon, Counts His Scalps, and the other men in smoking, gossiping, and discussing politics. In two weeks, he was cleaning his rifle and talking about joining a hunting party.

Rachel had accepted him as a natural part of the household. Jamie was still reserved, but Elizabeth noticed that the boy was never far from Hunt, and he listened intently to Hunt's every word.

For herself, she could not help but wish the winter would hold them here in the Shawnee town forever. She and Hunt had not resumed their lovemaking, and she wanted to—terribly. But even more, she wanted to go on waking up every morning and seeing his sleepy face. She wanted to cook for him and stitch his moccasins . . . to see her small daughter tucked into the crook of Hunt's arm as he told her a story. She wanted to grow old with him and watch the sunsets together when his black hair had turned to silver.

Elizabeth and Hunt spoke only once of spring. Once was enough. He told her that when the weather broke and it was safe to travel with the children, he'd take her back to Charles Town.

"I don't want to go," she answered, deliberately keeping her tone even.

"I promised your father. I took his money, Elizabeth. It's only fair I bring his daughter home."

"He won't want us," she argued. "He won't want Jamie and Rachel, and he won't want me once he sees that I'm not the child he lost."

Hunt sighed heavily and looked into her eyes. "It's a thing to think of, what you will say about the children. My sister and her husband have asked to care for them."

Anger drove all thought of calm from her mind. Did he think she'd come this far to surrender now? "I won't give up Jamie and Rachel!"

"I told my sister you'd say that, but you'd best think about it. They'd be happier with the Shawnee."

"No! That's preposterous," she flung back. "I won't listen to such—"

"Listen to me," he insisted. "Just listen, and think about what I'm saying. Talon is convinced war is coming between England and the colonies. Charles Town's on the coast. Whatever happens, they'll be in the thick of it."

"Oh, it's all right to send me back into a war, just not—"

"You aren't listening," he said, taking her arms and holding her so that she faced him squarely. "No one's going to force you to do anything you don't want to."

"Liar." It was so unfair. When he touched her, it was almost impossible to keep from trembling—to keep her heart from racing. "You're forcing me to go back to my father," she reminded him.

"That's different." His face twisted, and she read the pain in his eyes. "I gave my word, Elizabeth. If a man's word is worthless, what does it say about him?"

"You and your damn honor!" *What about my honor?* she cried silently. "I wouldn't leave my children with the Seneca. Not with their own father. Why should I leave them here with strangers?" Her eyes burned with unshed tears. Couldn't he see? Didn't he know what she really wanted?

"Sweet Water loves them. And Talon would be a good father. He'd teach Jamie what he must know to survive. Jamie's half Seneca; he'll never make a proper white man. I didn't, and I was born white. Here, with the Shawnee, they'd be someone. Back on the coast . . . you know what people will call them. Half-breed. Red-skinned savages."

She tried to pull away, but he held her firmly. "I'll protect them," she argued. "No one will call them redskins twice, I can promise you that."

"You'll not be able to stop the filthy names. Becca loved me, but her own husband called me a bastard." He pulled her into his arms and stroked her hair. "Just think on it," he suggested. "Talon's planning on moving his tribe west and north to the big lakes. He has friends among the Menominee. That's too far west for the war. Jamie and Rachel can grow up there in peace."

"I won't give them up," she insisted. Her heart was beating so hard that he must feel it. How could he hold her like this and not know how she loved him? "Not for your sister," she managed, "not for anyone."

"What about for their own good?" he asked huskily.

"They belong with me, and they'll stay with me."

"Becca . . . Sweet Water said you'd say that. She also said that if you ever change your mind, her offer stands."

"That's good of her. I'm grateful that she cares enough to ask for them," she told him.

She was grateful, at least she thought she was. But the friendship between her and Sweet Water wasn't the same as it had been before they'd known that Hunt was Sweet Water's brother. The Indian woman's first loyalty lay with Hunt, not Elizabeth, and what woman would want a soiled wife for her brother? The children still played together and slept in each other's wigwams, but some of the warmth had gone out of her relationship with Sweet Water.

Elizabeth still wanted Hunt, and she sensed that his sister opposed their being together. Hunt hadn't said anything more about returning to his mountains on the far side of the great prairie, but he didn't have to. She knew he intended to go, and she realized that there was no place in his future for an ugly woman with two small children.

Which left her with nothing but the few months until springtime. . . .

She meant to make the most of that time, and no false pride would keep her from taking whatever scraps of love she could get from Hunt. She knew he blamed her for not telling him that she had two children, not one. She also knew that he still desired her body—the heat of his gaze told her so. Her only problem was to decide how to bridge the chasm between them.

She wanted to share his bed and his kisses. She wanted to sleep in the safety of his powerful arms and feel again the passion only he could ignite. And if she could pretend for a little while that she belonged to him, it would give her something to dream on for the rest of her life.

# Chapter 23

**T**en days later, Elizabeth stood on a snow-covered hillside at the edge of the Shawnee village filling her gourd container with spring water. The late afternoon sun was bright on her face, and trees sheltered her from the wind. Another five inches of snow had fallen last night on top of the six already on the ground, but she was dressed warmly against the cold in soft wool and furs.

She enjoyed the snowfall as much as Rachel and Jamie did. She'd never seen snow and she'd seen little ice until she'd been captured by the Seneca, but she found the brisk temperatures much easier to endure than the humid heat of Charles Town.

Behind her, she heard shrieks of childish laughter, and she turned to see a half dozen little boys chasing an older youth and pelting him with snowballs. Nearby, three girls were taking turns leaping into a snowbank and making imprints of their bodies in the snow. Another child slid across a frozen section of creek under the watchful eyes of her doting grandmother.

"Mama! Mama! Look at me!" Rachel waved and shouted excitedly to her in Shawnee. "See me! See me!"

"I see you," Elizabeth called back. Rachel and her friend Star Girl—both snugly wrapped in a bearskin—were riding on a sled pulled by Fire Talon's son, Falcon.

He stopped and waved at her as well.

"Go! Go!" cried a red-cheeked Rachel.

Falcon settled the leather dog harness across his chest and began to trudge ahead. Both girls cheered as the sled bumped over a rough section of frozen ice.

"Faster! Faster!" Star Girl yelled.

Obediently, Falcon began to jog, turning left toward the far side of the camp where Jamie was trying out his new bow with an audience of admiring friends.

While he was still confined to the wigwam, Hunt had fashioned Jamie a Cheyenne bow of horn and a dozen boy-sized arrows. Today, Hunt had spent the last hour teaching Jamie how to improve his aim.

Elizabeth had sewn a Shawnee-style hunting shirt for her son; wearing it, he was nearly indistinguishable from the other boys in the village. She crossed her fingers, hoping that Jamie would be on his best behavior today. Hunt was surprisingly attentive to him, no matter how badly Jamie acted toward him.

She sighed. For a man who said he had little use for children, he spent a great deal of time with hers, much more than their father had ever done.

Yellow Drum adored Jamie and never ceased boasting about him to other men, but the Seneca had only tolerated bold, little Rachel. Her impish ways and quick tongue had never captivated him the way they did Hunt. Since Raven had shown open jealousy when Yellow Drum played with the children, he rarely did so. Occasionally, he'd taken Jamie hunting with him, but Rachel had always been left at home with the women.

Hunt, on the other hand, had shown both Jamie and

Rachel how to fish through the ice and how to scale and clean the fish they caught. He taught them to imitate various birdcalls and to identify animal tracks in the snow. He always had time to listen to their endless chatter, and he'd been understanding when Rachel spilled his horn of precious black powder in the sand. He'd also prevented Elizabeth from scolding her when she tried to cut a doll dress from his buckskin drum cover and ruined it.

He never complained when Rachel woke them all in the night complaining that she was thirsty or needed another trip outside to relieve herself; and he hadn't lost his temper when Rachel knocked his knife sheath into the fire and scorched it.

Hunt took the trouble to teach them all new words in Shawnee every day, following the lessons with wonderful songs and silly jokes. Already, Jamie was translating some Algonquian phrases for her, and Rachel was chattering away as though she'd always lived with the Shawnee.

Evenings around the campfire in their wigwam seemed too short for Elizabeth. It was such a luxury to be mistress of her own lodge after living so long under another woman's thumb. Hunt and the Shawnee treated her as an equal, a woman of worth, and she savored the long, peaceful nights of talk and laughter. Often Fire Talon and Fox would bring their wives to the wigwam for a visit. Sweet Water remained kind, despite the concern in her eyes; and Fox's wife, Shell Bead Girl, was a delight, always cheerful and patient with Elizabeth's poor Shawnee.

After eating—if there were no guests or they had not been invited to another wigwam—she, Hunt, Jamie, and Rachel would roast nuts and pop corn while Hunt spun tales of the western plains and mountains. Jamie's eyes widened at the stories of buffalo and prairie fires and huge bears with silver ruffs that walked upright like men.

Sometimes, Hunt would draw animal tracks on birchbark with pieces of charcoal, and the children would try to name the creature they belonged to. Rachel's favorite game was listening to Hunt imitate birdcalls. The player who correctly named the bird won an acorn, and the child with the most acorns could ask for any story or game he or she wanted before bedtime.

The only thing lacking, Elizabeth thought wistfully, was that Hunt had made no move to draw her into his blankets once the children were sleeping. Usually, he would leave the wigwam and not return until she had retired for the night. He was as good-natured with her as he was with the children, but she longed for more than Hunt's friendship. She wanted the passion he'd shown before.

*I'm not ready for it to end,* she thought as she watched the spring water spill over the top of the gourd pitcher. *I want him to take me in his arms and hold me so close that I can feel his warm breath on my face and hear the thud of his heart.*

Her reverie was broken by the high, haunting notes of a flute. Startled, she looked up. The music was coming from a clump of cedar trees about twenty yards from the spring. Lingering notes drifted through the air and fell around her like silvery snowflakes. Emotion welled up inside her, bringing a lump to her throat and tears to her eyes. "Beautiful . . ." she murmured.

Then, abruptly, the tune took on a different air. The ringing notes became a melody of teasing laughter— raindrops striking the petals of spring blossoms. Her heart lightened, and she couldn't keep from smiling. Curious, she propped her water container against a rock and took a few steps toward the unseen musician.

The flute was silent.

"Don't stop," she called.

A ripple of teasing notes spilled over the snow.

"Let me see you," she said.

The flute gave a saucy reply.

Elizabeth laughed. "Show yourself, Flute, or I'm coming to catch you."

She was challenged by the taunting melody that answered. Her gourd tipped over, spilling the water, but she left it and waded through the pristine snow toward the cedars.

Clear, sweet sounds flowed from the left, but when she turned that way, she heard an immediate musical response from the right. Surprised, Elizabeth stopped and looked first one way and then the other. What she had heard was impossible. "Who is it?" she demanded. Someone had been playing a flute outside her wigwam at night, but that musician hadn't shown the skill of this trickster. Whoever made this music was a master flutist.

She started toward the right where the flowing branches of an ancient hemlock hung to brush the snow. A tripping ascension of notes from the left confused her, but she scrambled up the slight incline and pushed away the boughs to confront a shaggy brown wall. She opened her mouth to cry out, and Hunt threw open his buffalo robe and drew her into his arms.

"You?" she sputtered, before he silenced her protests with a kiss. When his lips touched hers, it seemed to her that all the glory of the flute's sweet song flowed into her soul. She swayed against him, savoring his firm jawline with the palm of her left hand and slipping her right arm around his neck so that she could tangle her fingers in his hair.

She supposed that her feet were still on the ground, but she felt as though she were floating in air. Her heart pounded, her mouth molded to his. His kiss was gentle, yet sensual; it drew her doubts and fears from the recesses of her soul and cast them into the crystal-clear air.

"Elizabeth," he murmured hoarsely. And when he kissed her again, she felt the banked fires within her spring to life and blaze up with joy.

"Hunt . . . Hunt," she whispered. "God, how I've missed you."

"I still don't see what I get from this," a man's voice said.

Trembling, Elizabeth pulled free of Hunt's embrace and turned to see a grinning Fire Talon watching them. A flute dangled from a cord at his waist. For an instant, she felt as though she didn't quite fit into her own body. Her lips still felt the imprint of Hunt's lips. Her soul still soared above the trees with the enchanted music.

"Am I interrupting something?" the Shawnee teased.

"Yes," Hunt said.

"N-no," Elizabeth stammered at the same time. She drew in a breath and felt body and spirit settle into place. Her eyes focused on Fire Talon's flute. "That's one," she cried, "but where . . ." She felt Hunt's waist and chest, searching for another instrument. "I don't understand. I heard . . . There had to be two flutes."

"There were." Hunt joined in the laughter. From his sleeve he pulled an eagle bone flute decorated with feathers.

"Which one of you played first?" she asked. "Who's the real musician?"

"Me," both men said in unison.

Feminine laughter came from behind Elizabeth, and she turned to see two village women. One caught her hand. "Sweet Water would not like to see you court a second wife," the youngest matron teased.

"The Pigeon Dance is tonight," the second woman, Quiet Eyes, said.

"Yes, you must wait," her friend agreed. She tugged on Elizabeth's hand. "You do not know our ways, and these men would take advantage of your ignorance. They play games with you."

Elizabeth glanced back at Hunt, wishing they were still alone . . . wishing he was still kissing her. If what he'd done was taking advantage of her, he was free to try again whenever he wished.

He smiled at her, a slow, lazy smile that tore at her heart. "Go along with them," he said. "They'll give you no peace if you don't." He winked. "But I am good, aren't I?" He held up his flute.

"Yes," she agreed. "You are good." And she meant more than the music.

"Tonight," he promised.

*Tonight*, she echoed silently.

Later, after dusk had fallen and the first stars had appeared in the velvet-black sky, Elizabeth nervously took her place at one end of the dance ground with the Shawnee women. Rachel and Jamie had been tucked into bed with other small children in the care of someone's grandmother. "Do not worry," Shell Bead Girl had told her. "Your children will be safe. The Pigeon Dance is no place for little ones."

"But is it any place for me?" Elizabeth wondered aloud, and her friend laughed.

Shell Bead Girl had loaned her a magnificent doe-skin dress with twelve-inch fringes and a cascade of tiny silver beads across the bodice. Shell bracelets

adorned her wrists, and a white doeskin choker decorated with feathers and porcupine quill-work laced
tightly around her neck. Sweet Water had brushed
out Elizabeth's hair, plaiting a thin braid to hang on
either side of her face and letting the rest flow loose
down her back. Shell Bead Girl wove azure ribbons
of velvet and silver drop-beads into the braids;
around Elizabeth's neck, she hung a silver amulet.

"Stay away from Fox," Shell Bead Girl admonished.
"You are so beautiful that you would tempt him."

Elizabeth felt her cheeks grow hot. "Thank you for
saying so," she stammered, "but I know that I'm not
beautiful. I—"

"Nonsense," Sweet Water chided her. "My brother
does nothing but brag about you." She smiled and
touched Elizabeth's cheek. "You are different than
Shell Bead Girl, but that doesn't take away from your
loveliness. Would God have made flowers in so many
different colors and shapes if he did not love them all
equally?"

"Have you not heard the courting flute outside
your wigwam?" asked another woman, a bold matron
Elizabeth knew as Copper Kettle. "My husband's
cousin has been playing his flute for you, but you
never come out and smile at him. You've broken his
heart."

"Your husband's cousin?" Elizabeth was puzzled.
"Hunt plays the flute . . . and Fire Talon, but—"

"Talon helped Hunt play the joke on you," Sweet
Water explained.

"All the men play when they want to catch the eye
of a woman," Copper Kettle said. "Some worse than
others." She giggled. "Surely, you've seen the young
braves looking at you. You could have your pick of
husbands."

"That's true," spoke up Flying Wren. "Little Horse

told my father that he would offer two muskets for you if he knew what clan you belonged to."

A ripple of laughter ran through the group. "Little Horse has seen more than seventy winters," Sweet Water told Elizabeth.

"But he has six sons by three wives," Copper Kettle said. "He thinks your boy has promise."

"It's not the child he's after," Shell Bead Girl teased. "It's another young wife to keep his old bones warm."

"Yes, if Hunter of the Far Mountains doesn't wed you soon, he'll lose you to another," chimed in a stout matron. "You should pick someone to act as your family."

Shell Bead Girl touched the amulet that hung around Elizabeth's neck. "This is our family totem. We will be her family." She took Elizabeth's hand and squeezed it. "I lost a sister in childhood. My grandmother would be glad to adopt you into the Bear Clan. Then we would be sisters."

"And Grandmother would have two French muskets," Copper Kettle observed.

"Elizabeth has her own family," Sweet Water said. "My brother will take her back to the Great Salt Sea to the white settlement of Charles Town. She will wed a white man."

"We'll see about that," Shell Bead Girl said. "I think—"

The sound of a drum silenced their chatter. Quickly, the women moved into line. Another squaw—tall and graceful, despite her graying hair and advanced years—handed out red wool blankets.

"I don't know why I'm doing this," Elizabeth whispered to Shell Bead Girl. "I'm going to make a fool of myself. And . . . and I still can't believe that men think I'm attractive. The Seneca said that my green eyes weren't even human."

"What do the Seneca know?" She shrugged. "We have had blue-eyed women among us, why not green?" Shell Bead Girl gave Elizabeth a long, careful inspection. "Your breasts are small and your nose as well, but those things do not make you plain. No," she said firmly. "You are striking. It doesn't do for a woman to underestimate her qualities. I was once considered a rare beauty. My fame spread far, and a man came from the west to marry me. But that is in the past, and my dark hair has streaks of gray. I am no longer a young woman. You are. Use what you have to your advantage."

"Shh," Copper Kettle whispered. "We are ready to start the dance."

"Do as we do," Shell Bead Girl instructed Elizabeth. "I showed you the step. Open your arms and spread your blanket on the turns like a pigeon." She giggled. "Just don't choose a man you don't wish to sleep with."

Shell Bead Girl used the word for *sleep* that also carried a sexual connotation, and Elizabeth's eyes widened in surprise.

"Most will choose their own husbands," Shell Bead Girl confided, "but some may not. The suspense is part of the fun."

"And if a woman picks a man other than her own?" Elizabeth asked.

Shell Bead Girl shrugged. "It means that their marriage is dissolved. For honor's sake, he can't take revenge or even complain. He must smile and pretend he doesn't care." She leaned close. "I've threatened Fox every year. This time, I may choose another." A mischievous smile played over her lips. "I haven't decided yet. If I do, you're free to pick him. His feelings would be crushed if no one wanted him."

"You say that every Pigeon Dance," Copper Kettle

declared. "You've not deserted your handsome Fox yet."

"But you keep hoping," Shell Bead Girl replied.

Copper Kettle laughed. "If you don't want him, one of us—a younger woman—might as well grab him before—"

"You see what I mean," Shell Girl said to Elizabeth. "You've no need to feel sorry for Fox . . ." She paused. "Or for Hunter. Crow Tracker is the tall warrior with the yellow deer-tail crest. He is a good man whose wife died in childbed. He was always kind to her; her lodge was never without meat. If you wanted to stay here and you didn't want to take Hunter of the Far Mountains, Crow Tracker would be a wise choice."

"She speaks truth," Copper Kettle put in. "Crow Tracker's lance is long and sure."

"Copper Kettle is an expert on the endowments of men," Sweet Water said.

"Copper Kettle can describe a great many of our warriors' prized shafts," Shell Bead Girl added.

"Even Fox's," Copper Kettle agreed. "He is—"

Shell Bead Girl gave Copper a little push into line. "Lucky that he tired of you before we married," she finished tartly.

"Enough of such talk," chided the dance mistress, Claps Her Hands. "There are respectable women present."

The women all giggled.

"We just wanted Elizabeth to know that she has her choice of men," Shell Bead Girl replied.

"Don't let them tease you, Elizabeth," Sweet Water advised in careful English. "It is a dance, nothing more. You can take part without picking a man. Most women dance for the fun of it."

"And some do so to cause a scandal," Copper Kettle said.

"Who are you to talk of scandals?" Shell Bead Girl teased. "Copper Kettle has used up three husbands, and two she snagged during a Pigeon Dance."

"What can I say?" Copper Kettle asked. "I am a woman of great appetite. I love venison, but I don't always wish to feast on deer meat. Men are much the same as food; variety is best."

"Do not judge the Shawnee women by Copper," Sweet Water said. "Most of us remain happily faithful to the same man for a lifetime."

"Faithful you may be," Copper Kettle answered in her own tongue, "but happy? That is a question each woman must answer for herself. We are fortunately free Shawnee women who may follow our own paths, not white women bound by custom to stay with bad husbands for the sake of their souls."

Elizabeth's face must have registered her lack of comprehension. Sweet Water murmured the English translation in her ear, adding, "If you choose to remain with us, you would be welcome, of course. My concern has been for my brother and for you. I only ask that you do not make light of his feelings. He cares for you deeply, and I do not wish to see him hurt again."

"I have no wish to hurt him," Elizabeth whispered.

"Then you and I have no quarrel."

Claps Her Hands shook a turtle shell rattle, and a water drum boomed a reply from the stomp ground. Other drums, large and small, took up the rhythm; and the line of blanket-covered women began a slow, stately movement around the perimeter of the dance area.

Elizabeth concentrated on the steps, swaying when the others did, letting her draped arms simulate the graceful wings of a flying bird. Only gradually did she become aware that the audience lining the cleared space was all male.

Warriors, young and old, stood as motionless as carved statues, all garbed in pagan splendor. Furs, feathers, beads, and silver adorned their magnificent garments. And in the blaze of firelight and the pale ivory flickering of moonlight through the clouds, each man seemed larger than life, and each possessed a wild beauty that Elizabeth had never realized before.

The drumbeats quickened their cadence; rattles and flutes joined in the song. The dancers' steps took on a new pattern as the women tightened their circle, then opened it to receive a single male figure wearing nothing but a small blue loincloth, blue moccasins, and a blue blanket around his shoulders. His hair was all but hidden under a cap of white feathers, and his face was painted with white and blue dots and slashes, but still, Elizabeth recognized Fox.

He swept into the circle with thrusting chest and proud, tossing head. The women dancers began to clap as Fox whirled and stomped, ending his spirited opening by coming to a sudden and complete stop before extending both arms to his wife. Shell Bead Girl turned her face away, forcing Fox to repeat his plea. A second time she refused him, but the third time, she relented and joined him. The circle of women flowed outward until each dancer stood three feet from her nearest partners' hands. Then Shell Bead Girl and Fox danced together, imitating the courting ritual of the pigeon.

The repeating rhythm of the drums was mesmerizing; the smell of burning wood and tobacco, of wool and feathers, of bear grease and herbs made Elizabeth giddy. She forgot about her apprehension and let her body follow the dance while her mind fixed on the man she'd seen when they first entered the stomp ground. Hunt . . . Hunt standing rigidly in the shadows.

His gaze never left her. She felt the force of its power burning into her skin. She read his desire . . . his yearning.

Yet, he could not come to her. He could not make the move. She had to choose, and she could take another.

Once, when she was eight, she and her brother had crept downstairs after her parents had entertained. Her brother had retrieved wineglasses from the table, and they had sipped and sipped until Elizabeth had become foolishly drunk. She felt like that now, without even a drop of spirits. All reason, all caution had left her. She knew only that she wanted Hunt.

And she could have him, if only for a few short weeks. She could take him, Indian fashion, as her husband. No one would blame her, and the arrangement would be finished when he took her home to her father.

Abruptly, she realized that Fox had left the center and returned to the line of men. Shell Bead Girl now led the women. The flute music rose and fell, as each man in turn lifted his own instrument and joined in the call for the women to choose a mate.

Like fluttering leaves, the line of women glided around the dance ground. In and out they wove, and one by one, they began to drop out of the serpentine chain and stretch out their arms to the man of their choice. Sweet Water was one of the first to signal her love for her husband. He lifted the blanket from her shoulders, wrapped it around them both, and led her away into the darkness. Then Copper Kettle chose a man. Elizabeth couldn't tell if it was Crow Walker or not, but she didn't care. She had eyes for only one warrior.

When she summoned up all her courage to fall out of line, she heard Fox call out. "Here, little bird, come to me."

Startled, she looked into his face, but saw that he was only teasing her. He ran forward to snatch Shell Bead Girl from the dancers, but was driven back by the laughter of the women. Elizabeth stopped a few feet away from Hunt.

He waited, his face hidden in shadows.

Her heart swelled within her. Would he refuse her? Shame her in front of all these people? She took a single step toward him.

He lifted his flute to his lips, and once again the exquisite beauty of the sweet, high notes brought tears to her eyes. He had no need to speak, and the music made her brave.

She moved closer and held out her hands, palms up, to him. And as the thunder of her own heart drowned out the drums she walked willingly into the unknown in the circle of Hunt's strong arms.

# Chapter 24

〜∞〜

"**Y**ou know what you've done?" Hunt whispered as he led her to their wigwam. "For this night, we are husband and wife in the eyes of the Shawnee." His lean fingers lingered at her throat before he tipped her head up to meet his long, slow kiss.

"Do you mind?" Logically, she knew she must have walked with him from the dance ground, but she could remember nothing except the man-scent that was Hunt's alone, the sound of his voice, and the texture of his skin pressed against hers.

"I was afraid you'd choose another." He kissed her again, and the sweet sensation washed away old hurts and wove a ribbon of light between them. His strong hands moved over her, touching . . . stroking . . . fanning the heat of her yearning.

She parted her lips, welcoming the deepening of his intimate caress, losing her fears in the warmth of his velvet tongue. One kiss followed another, piling on top of each other until there were no individual kisses, only a long, shared glory of pleasure. And each kiss led her deeper and deeper into a dream world of sensual longing.

"I want to see you . . . all of you," he murmured. And she felt no shame as he tugged her gown off over

323

her head and she stood naked before him.

"Now you, Sundancer," she dared. A sob rose in her throat as she beheld his beauty, the corded sinews of his bronzed forearms, his tight, flat belly, the hard muscles of his thighs. She offered a trembling hand, and he covered it with his. "I want to feel your heart beating," she whispered.

He moaned as she traced the curves of his broad chest with her palm and let her fingertips linger over the ritual scars that knotted his flesh. "Elizabeth." He drew out her name so softly that it might have been a breath of spring wind.

Compassion for the anguish he must have felt when he'd received those wounds rippled through her, and she leaned close and kissed the scarred flesh. A tremor shook him and his arms tightened like steel bonds around her. She pressed her cheek against his chest and felt the tickle of a scattering of dark, curling hair.

The deep, steady throb of his heart was reassuring. *So strong*, she thought. His strength sprang from the earth like an oak tree. With a sigh, she turned her head and traced the outline of his aureoles with the tip of her tongue. His nipples hardened and she felt a surge of desire. Wantonly, she drew a nubbin between her lips and sucked gently.

He groaned. "I have other scars," he murmured.

"Show me where."

He lifted an arm to let her lave the ragged mark below his elbow. "And here," he said, pointing to a place on his left side that showed the discoloration of a long-healed burn.

"Poor thing," she teased. His skin tasted clean and slightly salty.

"There's a bad one, here." He placed his hands on

her shoulders and pushed her down so that she could kiss the blemish on his thigh.

"And . . ." he began.

"I don't see anything wrong with this."

"Look closer," he urged.

"Oh, yes." She joined in his deception. "I do see something that needs kissing." Mischievously, she stroked the length of his shaft with her fingertips. "This is a terrible wound," she murmured. "See how swollen the flesh is."

"Terrible," he agreed.

Chuckling, she administered light, teasing kisses to his throbbing organ. He gasped with pleasure, clutching at her shoulders as she followed the caresses with a more intimate exploration that left him gasping for breath.

"Enough of your torture," he cried, breaking free and sweeping her up in his arms. "The Cheyenne have a way of dealing with troublesome wives."

She laughed up at him until he silenced her with his mouth and dropped her onto the heaped furs of his sleeping platform.

"Before I'm finished with you, I'll have you begging for mercy," he promised her.

"I won't be tied up," she warned him. "Anything but that." She had no interest in games that reminded her of captivity, but she knew instinctively that she was safe with Hunt. He'd never do anything to hurt her.

"Close your eyes," he said.

Obediently, she obeyed him.

"You cannot open them," he ordered. "If you open them, you prove yourself a weak and foolish woman."

"They are sealed shut," she assured him. She felt his body shift and waited expectantly. To her pleasant surprise, the first thing she felt was the pressure of his lips on hers.

His kiss was tender and thorough, hardly torture, she thought. "The Cheyenne have a different view of torture than the Seneca," she whispered.

"I'm getting to that part."

She giggled as something soft brushed her eyelids. "What's that?" she demanded, reaching up to touch the feather in his hands.

"You're cheating," he accused. "You must lie still and not talk."

"Who made up these rules?"

"Submit or admit you are the loser," he said.

She lay back and sighed impatiently. The warmth of the fire and the soft sensual texture of the furs beneath her were soothing, but she didn't want to sleep. She wanted his love. She wanted him to— "Oh," she murmured.

The feather stroked her bare nipple and she gasped, feeling her flesh tighten into an erect bud. "No talking," he warned, before placing his warm, damp lips over her sensitive skin.

"That feels good," she whispered.

He repeated the process, first the feather caresses, then his lips and tongue. She shivered as a wonderful ripple of pleasure brought her fully alert. "Shh," he said. The feather grazed the hollow of her throat.

She waited breathlessly for his touch. Inch by inch, he began to tease her body, bringing forth responses that she'd not known were possible. By the time his tongue brushed the swell of her belly, a light sheen of moisture had broken out on her skin, and she could no longer lie still.

"Hunter," she whispered.

"Shh, we're getting to the good part."

She moaned and tossed her head restlessly. "Hunter." She felt dampness in the cleft between her legs. And the wigwam was no longer comfortable; it had become hot . . . too hot to bear.

The feather tickled the curling triangle of hair above her apex of her thighs, and she clutched at his shoulders. She arched her back, raising her hips to meet him. His warm breath teased her most intimate spot, and she cried out as she felt the heat of his tongue.

"No more," she begged, opening her eyes. "Please. I want—"

He raised his head and looked into her face, his dark eyes heavy-lidded with passion. "But I haven't gotten to the bear claw necklace yet," he murmured.

"Hunter."

With a laugh, he moved his knee to kneel astride her. He lowered his head and lingered over her upthrust breast, then met her eager mouth with his. For an instant, she looked deep into his eyes and read the love within. Then physical need made Elizabeth shameless; she wrapped her arms and legs around him and pulled him down to cover her with his strong, naked body.

He slid into her, and she sucked in a quick, sharp breath. "Ohh," she cried. He filled her with his shaft, then withdrew and plunged into her depths again. She clung to him and called his name, blending her need with his. With each thrust, her desire grew stronger. Together they fused a glory of wordless song and ageless music. And when the radiance burst within her in a thousand fiery cascades of light, she continued to move with him until she felt his spasms of culmination.

Afterward, he held her to his breast and kissed her face and hair and fingertips. Then, wrapped in a blanket of softest otter-skin, they whispered love words late into the night.

Twice more before the dawning, his phallus stiffened with desire and he made love to her again. Each time was new and different; each time was a memory that she could cherish.

"You are like no woman I've ever met," he whispered to her.

"You always say that," she teased. She sat with her legs curled under her while he brushed her hair.

"It's true," he insisted, lifting a lock and rubbing the length across his lips.

"You said I was trouble."

"And you are," he agreed.

She lifted a gourd of water to her lips and drank. "We've not slept," she reminded him. "Soon it will be light, and the children will be hungry."

"Someone will feed them."

"I don't know that."

"I do."

"What kind of mother would I be if—"

"Your children will be fine. To the Shawnee, a child is the Creator's greatest blessing. They will be loved and spoiled and stuffed with the best food Grandmother Swift Runner can prepare."

"Are you certain?"

He smiled at her. "I'm certain. After the Pigeon Dance, the tribe rises late. I thought to take you with me to the sweat lodge. After we've taken the steam, we could roll in the snow."

She tilted her head and glanced up at him. "You're mad, utterly mad. Do you know that?"

He chuckled. "You can't judge until you've tried it."

"I've not tried the bear claws yet, and I'm sure—"

"You've not?" He growled and dropped to the floor beside her. "I forgot to teach you—"

"No more!" She threw up her hands in mock surrender. "I'll not be able to walk if we—"

His eyes widened. "I've not hurt you?"

It was her turn to laugh. "No, you've not hurt me."

"Then, why not—"

"Hunter!" A male voice called from outside the door flap. "Hunter, you must rise and come."

He leaped to his feet and reached for his rifle, hanging over the entranceway. "What is it, Talon? Are we under attack?"

"Not yet," the chief replied tersely.

Elizabeth grabbed for a blanket to cover her nakedness. "What's wrong?" she cried.

Fire Talon appeared in the doorway. "A delegation of Seneca, led by Yellow Drum," he said. "They've come to negotiate the return of Elizabeth's children."

Hunt ignored the two dozen stoic Iroquois warriors who stood guard outside the council house. He passed by without a glance, ducking his head to enter the large log-and-bark structure. A fire burned in the central hearth, but the stern faces of the Seneca sitting around it were nearly hidden in shadow.

Counts His Scalps stood in the shaman's place, splendid in a wolf-head cap and puma-skin cloak. His face had been divided into four equal sections with yellow paint. The quarter that included his right eye and temple was painted blue; the area that covered his left jaw bore a pattern of bright yellow thumbprints. A silver peace metal with a silhouette of His Majesty, King James I, hung from his neck, along with a necklace of bear claws and a small medicine bag.

As Hunt watched, Counts raised a long-stemmed pipe to the four winds, then drew a puff, holding the smoke for seconds before slowly exhaling. Fire Talon, Fox, and Little Horse sat across the fire from the Iroquois delegation. Hunt took a seat beside Fox and waited while the peace pipe was passed among the men.

Yellow Drum scowled at Fire Talon. It was clear to Hunt by the chief's answering glare that the tension between Seneca and Shawnee was volatile.

"I did not come to smoke," Yellow Drum said in badly accented Algonquian. He waved away the pipe. "Give me my son or pay in Shawnee blood."

"Shawnee blood is dear to us," Talon replied in Iroquoian, "but not so easily obtained as you may think."

Yellow Drum leaped up and pointed at Hunt. "This half-breed is responsible. He took my woman and my children."

"This is a council of peace," Counts reminded the Seneca. "There is no need to raise your voice."

"Aye," Little Horse agreed. "A soft voice rolls over the water. Anger's voice is lost." He smiled at Yellow Drum. "Sit, noble Seneca. We will hear your plea."

"Keep the woman. She is useless," Yellow Drum said. "Keep her female cub as well. Give me my son, or I will burn these lodges around your heads."

Hunt's temper flared. It took every ounce of will he possessed to hold his tongue. The arrogance of this Seneca was an insult . . . the thought that he had possessed Elizabeth against her will made his blood seethe with fury. He clenched his hands into fists, but he didn't speak. Not yet, he told himself.

Counts His Scalps threw a pinch of powder into the fire and it flashed up with blue sparks. A scent of bear invaded the council house. Each man smelled the musty odor; Hunt saw the reaction on every face. Common sense told him that there was no grizzly, but the prickling of hairs along his spine told him differently.

"You are of the mighty Confederacy," Counts said

to Yellow Drum. "Who does not know of the wisdom of the Iroquois . . . of their valor in battle? And who does not remember the stench of corpses fallen when brother fights brother."

"You are a warrior as this man is a warrior," Fire Talon said. "You are not a sachem—a wise man. Your way is the way of the ax."

"Enough talk. Give me my son, or you will feel the steel of that ax," Yellow Drum threatened.

Little Horse turned his attention to the gray-haired Seneca warrior sitting beside Yellow Drum. "Tin Hoop," he rasped. "I see you."

"Little Horse," replied the gnarled Iroquois. "I see you."

Little Horse chuckled. "We traded blows, this man and I, long ago."

The Seneca veteran held up a hand with two missing fingers. "Proof of my dance with Little Horse." His laughter was the sound of dried cornhusks rustling in the wind. "A man's honor is gauged by the strength of his enemies."

"None will forget the name of Tin Hoop," Counts echoed. "Not his courage or his wisdom."

"If the Seneca had wished blood, they would not come to parlay," Fire Talon said.

Hunt heard Elizabeth's voice at the entrance. He glanced in her direction and saw a young Shawnee brave bar the way.

"I must go in," she cried.

"Fire Talon has forbidden it," the brave answered.

"Of what do we speak?" Little Horse asked. "The woman or the children? The boy child or the girl . . . or . . ." He looked questioningly at Tin Hoop.

His old opponent took the offered pipe and drew a puff. The scent of ceremonial tobacco drifted up to blend with the stench of the invisible bear. "Yellow

Drum? What say you?" the Seneca asked. "Did we not come for both children?"

Hunt kept his teeth locked together. If he spoke a single word, he could not keep his anger in check. He would challenge Yellow Drum to a fight to the death. Blood pounded in his veins; his mind clouded with a film of red haze. He was not a man to hate other men, but he hated Yellow Drum. His fingers ached to tighten around the Seneca's throat until his eyes bulged out.

"Let them have the woman. I used her long and well and I tire of her," Yellow Drum said. "Let any man take her who does not mind a green-eyed witch."

"And the girl child?" Little Horse leaned forward. "Is she to be a gift to the Shawnee as well?"

"A rifle," Yellow Drum said. "I'll sell her for a rifle."

Hunt lunged to his feet and hurled his flintlock at the Seneca. Yellow Drum caught it, but not before the hammer struck his lip and split the skin. A thin trickle of blood ran down his chin, but he ignored it.

"The price has been asked and paid," Counts His Scalps proclaimed. "Does any man here deny it?" He tossed another pinch of the black substance into the coals. Again the air filled with the smell of a bear.

"Who claims the woman?" Tin Hoop asked.

Hunt would have shouted *I claim her* but Fox's hand tightened on his arm. He swallowed his words and spoke quietly. "Elizabeth is a free woman. She belongs to no man."

"That leaves us with the boy," Little Horse said.

"I am his father," Yellow Drum spat. "His father. For him, there will be no negotiations. Give him to me."

"What say you, old foe?" Little Horse asked Tin

Hoop. "Did this not happen in our grandfather's time? Did not a Shawnee woman take a Seneca husband?"

"Whispers of Autumn was his name. He captured the pregnant Shawnee woman, Seed Planter." Tin Hoop nodded. "I remember this well."

"Seed Planter had a daughter," Little Horse said. "Not by Whispers of Autumn, but by her Shawnee husband. Seed Planter came to love Whispers of Autumn, and her daughter called him father."

"Seed Planter's clan demanded the return of the child," Tin Hoop continued. "Because of this, war raged between Seneca and Shawnee."

"And that war was ended," Counts reminded the men, "when a price was paid to Seed Planter's clan."

"So," Fire Talon said. He glanced at Hunt. "So, this is not a new problem between our peoples."

"You Iroquois were ever a people of law," Little Horse said. "A Shawnee child became Seneca, and we smoked the pipe of peace. Can this not be again? Can a Seneca boy become Shawnee?"

"Not with my son," Yellow Drum insisted.

"Law is law," Hunt said quietly. "Among the people of the plains, there is warfare, but also reason. It seems to me that you must accept a reasonable price for your son."

"My son is not for sale," Yellow Drum thundered.

Tin Hoop glanced at his three fellow Seneca, none of whom had spoken at the council fire. "What say you?" he asked.

"A law once decided is not easily set aside," said the first Seneca to his left.

"So be it," said the second.

The third man looked at Yellow Drum, then back at Fire Talon. "You would risk war with us for the child of a white woman?"

Fire Talon shrugged. "All men must die. It is the way of the Creator."

Tin Hoop spread his hands, palms up. "What price was paid before for the Seneca child?"

"Two dozen guns," Yellow Drum said. "Two dozen guns, forty beaver pelts, and ten strings of wampum."

Counts scoffed. "Ridiculous."

Yellow Drum smiled. "You have our price, Shawnee. Pay or fight."

"We will pay you," Fire Talon said.

Hunt glanced at him. "I don't have that kind of money or trade goods. Perhaps Elizabeth's father might—"

"My tribe will pay," Fire Talon said. "Enough blood has flowed between Seneca and Shawnee. We will pay for your promise that no hand shall be raised against this man . . ." He indicated Hunt. "Or lifted against the woman known as Elizabeth, or her children."

Tin Hoop nodded. "The matter is settled."

Hunt tried not to show his relief as Tin Hoop took the pipe and smoked, then passed the ceremonial object to Yellow Drum. He took a quick puff and gave the pipe to Counts His Scalps. Slowly, each man signified his approval of the decision by a nod and a careful draw on the pipe. When his turn came, Hunt followed the custom. He did not look into Yellow Drum's face again, and when the council members rose, he hurried outside to tell Elizabeth of the sacrifice the Shawnee had made to free her from the Seneca threat.

"It is a high price," he explained when he found her in Sweet Water's wigwam. "It will strip the village of wealth. I'm not sure I can ever repay so much."

"My father can," she insisted.

"It's not money the Shawnee need," Hunt said. "They must have rifles. Without them, they will be unable to find food or protect themselves from their enemies."

"We'll get them the rifles," she promised.

He glanced around. "Where are the children?"

"Sweet Water and Shell Bead Girl took them into the forest. I thought it best if they didn't see their father."

"And if the Shawnee had decided to hand them over?"

"I wouldn't have let them. I'd have run away with them."

"In the middle of the woods—in winter?"

She smiled through her tears of joy. "I've done it before, haven't I?"

"Yes," he agreed, pulling her against him. "You've done it before."

# Chapter 25

〜◦⟩◦⟨◦〜

*May 1765*

**E**lizabeth paused at the edge of the vacant cornfield and looked around at the sprigs of green-
ery sprouting everywhere. Spring had exploded
across the Ohio River Country. The songbirds had returned with the soft winds from the south, and the
trees reverberated with the sounds of fluttering wings
and melodious chirping. Winter with its ever-present
threat of hunger seemed as far in Elizabeth's past as
the memories of slavery in Yellow Drum's longhouse.

She lifted a small bouquet of violets to her nose and
inhaled deeply of the sweet fragrance. Hunt had left
them for her as a surprise; she'd found them near her
cheek when she'd awakened that morning. He'd left
the village before dawn to search for deer. She closed
her eyes and brushed the velvety petals against her
lips, trying to hold the happiness close.

Tomorrow, she and Hunt and the children would
set off for Charles Town, another world. It would
mean the end of this interlude of joy that she'd experienced here with the Shawnee. It would be the end
of her love affair with Hunt Campbell and a return to
the white life she no longer wished for.

They should have departed in March, but Hunt had suffered an accident. He'd fallen through the ice and reinjured the bullet wound in his leg. Several weeks had passed before he'd regained his strength, and by then, the village had been making preparations for the great move that would take them forever from these tranquil valleys and sun-kissed meadows.

"The whites continue to make war on each other," Fire Talon had said at a village assembly. "French against the English King's soldiers, Colonial against French, English against Colonial. Always, the Indian is caught between them. Always, Indian blood spills. It is time for us to move farther west, away from these squabbles."

Hunt explained to her that Fire Talon was taking the tribe to join with some of their Delaware cousins and settle a rich hunting ground near the land of the Menominee, beyond Lake Michigan. "This Ohio Country was promised to the Indian by the English Crown, but those treaties prove as worthless as the rest. More and more immigrants pour across the sea, and there's no land for them but Indian land."

"The winters in Menominee country are cold, and the growing season shorter," Sweet Water added. "But I want Falcon and Star Girl to have a normal childhood without fear of being massacred by militia in their beds. We can learn new ways; there is wonderful fishing, and even wild rice that we may gather."

"It will mean saying good-bye to many friends," Shell Bead Girl had murmured. "Only our camp and a few others will go. Many will stay to fight for this land."

Fire Talon moved close to his wife and took her hand in a rare public show of affection. "For many years, I have been a man of war. Now, I want only peace. I wish to build a new home for my wife." He flashed a smile at her. "Perhaps a house of logs such as she once had before I burned it. I will relinquish my title of war chief and try to learn wisdom in my later years."

Fox had urged Hunter to come with them, to open a trading post and to act as go-between with the French and English as the Shawnee learned new customs.

Hunt hadn't answered one way or another, and Elizabeth hadn't pressed him. She knew that he longed to return to his father in the far mountains, but she also knew that he meant to use her father's reward to repay part of the debt they owed the Shawnee.

In the time since Yellow Drum and the Seneca had come and left the village, she and Hunt had not spoken of the future. They had lived each day, each hour, each minute. She had shut away her fears and gloried in the nights of lovemaking and the days of laughter and companionship.

Last night had been particularly poignant. Her cheeks grew warm as she remembered how they had crept from the wigwam, leaving Badger to guard the sleeping children. Hunt had carried his buffalo robe to a spot on the riverbank just beyond the village.

There, they had taken off their clothes and shared a passion that seemed to grow with each joining. Later, she had lain in his arms and watched the stars overhead. The forest had been so beautiful—the heavens so magnificent—that she was at a loss for words. She had only held him and listened to the steady beat of his heart and thought how lucky she was.

He had taken a lock of her hair and braided it with his. "This will make us one," he'd said. "More than any lines in a book or preacher's words. Wherever you go, part of you will always belong to me."

"Most women never know such a love," she had murmured.

The caw of a crow brought her back to the present, and she gazed across the field that would know no planting this year. Sweet Water and Shell Bead Girl would raise their crops far to the north, and she'd not be with them to dance the harvest home.

"But I'll keep Hunt's strength," she vowed. He had sworn that they would always be linked. Whenever sunset came, she would look west and think of him riding a painted horse in his far-off mountains.

"Mama! Mama!" Rachel cried. "Jamie says we're going away. Are we? Are we, Mama?"

"We're not going with Fire Talon to the Menominee," Jamie said.

Elizabeth stooped, caught her daughter in her arms and lifted her high. "Yes, darling. Tomorrow. We're going a long way to a big English settlement called Charles Town. It's where I lived with my mama and my papa when I was a little girl."

"I want to go with Falcon and my friend Lynx," Jamie protested. "I don't want to go to the white town."

"How do you know?" Elizabeth soothed. "You've never seen a white settlement. Charles Town is a wonderful place with wide streets and ships. You'll see the ocean, Jamie."

"I don't want to see the ocean, Mama," her son argued. "I want to hunt rabbits with my friends. Falcon said he'd take me—"

"You'll make new friends," Elizabeth said. "And you'll meet your grandfather and your uncle and lots of cousins. You'll both love Charles Town."

"Will I truly, Mama?" Rachel demanded.

"Yes, bug, yes, you will," Elizabeth said.

"Oh. It's nice there?" her daughter persisted.

Elizabeth kissed the tip of Rachel's nose. "Yes."

Jamie folded his arms stubbornly across his small chest. "If Charles Town is so good, Mama—then why are you crying?"

Three days later, Hunt nudged the bow of the canoe against a rocky bank and jumped out to steady the boat while Elizabeth and the children disembarked. Fire Talon had sent canoes downriver with them; now they would continue east on foot with four men as escort. Badger remained in the village with Falcon. Hunt had left the big dog with Fire Talon's family as his promise that he'd return with the rifles and trade goods to pay for Jamie's ransom.

John Black Hat, a Delaware trader, was traveling to the settlements to buy supplies. With him was his son, a young brave named Strings His Bow. Their other companions were two unmarried Shawnee warriors whom Elizabeth knew from the camp. Cedar Bark and Red Shirt had agreed to go to Charles Town and help Hunt transport the guns they hoped to purchase for the new Shawnee village.

Leaving the river was hard for Elizabeth. The last sight of the canoes and their friends brought a lump to her throat. *I should be excited about going home, she thought. I'm going to see my father and my brother and sisters again.* But she knew that each step toward the sea would bring her closer to a final parting from Hunt.

Jamie trod close on Hunt's heels. Rachel had walked a long way before she'd asked to be carried, but Hunt hadn't let Elizabeth pick her up. Instead, he'd wound a red wool sash into a sling and tied her to his back.

"I can take her," Elizabeth had argued.

"You'll get your chance," Hunt promised. "It's a long way to the coast."

"I'm not going to be toted like a papoose," Jamie proclaimed. "I'm going to walk, and I'm going to shoot a rabbit for the evening meal." He pulled an arrow from his quiver and notched it on the bowstring. "Maybe a deer instead," he said. "A big buck with a hundred points."

"Yearlings make better eating," Hunt said to the boy.

"I could hit a deer," Jamie boasted.

"You have a good eye," Hunt agreed. "You'll make a fine hunter, but we don't need meat now. A real hunter never kills anything unless he's in need."

Jamie trudged in thoughtful silence for a while. "If we're attacked by wolves, I'll shoot them," he said.

Hunt nodded. "Good idea. You watch for wolves." He rubbed his jaw in the way he did when he was amused but didn't want to let on.

Elizabeth turned her head away to hide her smile when she saw Jamie imitate his motion perfectly. *I wish,* she thought. *I wish—*

Her reverie was shattered by the boom of a musket.

"Get down!" Hunt shouted.

Jamie spun around and Elizabeth grabbed his arm and dragged him toward the shelter of a large beech tree. Another shot rang out and Red Shirt groaned. The warrior staggered to his knees, but managed to raise his musket and fire toward the tree line where the ambushers lay in wait.

Hunt dragged Rachel off his back and thrust her into Elizabeth's arms. Neither child made a sound, but Rachel's face was ashen with terror. "Down," Hunt repeated.

A volley of shots peppered around them. Cedar Bark and Strings His Bow returned fire. Hunt waited and watched, his dark eyes grim as he surveyed the ridge above them.

"Who is it?" Elizabeth whispered to him. "You said we were in friendly territory." Jamie tried to put his head up to look, and she shoved it down.

Hunt silenced her with a motion. He glanced at John Black Hat. The Delaware held up one hand, then opened and closed his fingers twice.

Red Shirt pushed himself up on his hands and knees and began to crawl toward a fallen log. Elizabeth clutched Rachel against her chest and held her breath as the wounded warrior managed to cover a yard, then two. He had nearly reached cover when another rifle sounded from the high ground. Red Shirt sprawled forward and lay still.

"Half-breed!"

Elizabeth inhaled sharply. It was Yellow Drum's voice.

"Give me my son!"

"Shh," Hunt warned Elizabeth. "Stay where you are." He crouched down and signaled to John. John stood and fired. Immediately, several flintlocks boomed from the trees. Hunt sprang forward, leaped across the open space and grabbed Red Shirt. With a heave, he threw the wounded brave over his shoulder and dashed for cover amid a hailstorm of lead.

Elizabeth went icy cold.

"Is it my father?" Jamie demanded. "Is he shooting at Hunter?"

"Shh," she admonished him. "Keep still."

"I want to see," the boy insisted.

Elizabeth shoved him down into the leaves and pinned him with her knee. Rachel wormed closer; Elizabeth could feel her trembling.

"You are brave!" Yellow Drum yelled. "I have come for my slave and my children. You have no part of this. I give you your life, Hunter of the Far Mountains!"

"There's none here belongs to you," Hunt shouted back. "You were paid in rifles for the little ones!"

"My son is not for sale!"

"If this Shawnee dies, you've bought yourself a war, Yellow Drum," Hunter called out. "You gave your word. You smoked the pipe."

"Look behind you, half-breed!" the Seneca shouted.

Elizabeth's hopes sank as she looked toward the bottom of the slope. At least a dozen Iroquois warriors in full war paint moved from the underbrush.

"Surrender your weapons!" Yellow Drum ordered.

Cedar Bark swore a foul oath in French.

"You have four guns," Yellow Drum called. "We have twenty and three! Surrender and we will let you walk out of here."

"To a torture fire!" Cedar Bark shouted back. He began to sing loudly in what Elizabeth could only imagine was a Shawnee death chant.

Elizabeth stood up. "No!" she cried. "I want no deaths on my soul."

"Return to my longhouse," Yellow Drum called to her. "You may stay with my children and serve my wives as before."

"Father," Jamie said. "Father, I am here!"

"Come to me, son," Yellow Drum commanded.

Jamie looked at Elizabeth. She shut her eyes for a second and steeled herself for what must come. "He is your father," she whispered.

"You sold me to the Shawnee for rifles!" Jamie said. His small voice rang clear in the still forest. He notched an arrow in his bowstring. "You're a bad man. I don't like you anymore. Go away! Leave my mother alone!"

Yellow Drum laughed. "Your cub has teeth!"

"Put that bow down!" Elizabeth ordered. "He is your father. You will not shoot him."

"She has taught the boy honor," Hunt shouted. "What do you teach him, Yellow Drum?"

"This is none of your affair!" Yellow Drum roared. Clad in only a loincloth, weapons' belt, and moccasins, he stepped from the trees and strode downhill toward them. One half of his face was painted black, the other half yellow. A war club hung over one shoulder and a pistol was thrust into his belt. His shaved head was oiled, his scalplock twisted into a knot on his crown. "Throw down your rife and walk away," he yelled to Hunter. "I make a gift to you of your life."

Hunt shook his head. "I can't do that." He held his rifle sight dead-on Yellow Drum's heart.

"Please!" Elizabeth called.

"This woman is nothing to you!" Yellow Drum said.

"Will you let them walk?" Hunt asked, motioning toward John and his son.

"You may all go," Yellow Drum agreed. "All but the woman and my children."

"Go," Elizabeth pleaded with Hunt. "Please, go. You tried. No one could ask more of you. Save yourself."

Yellow Drum lowered his rifle until the barrel pointed directly at Hunt's belly. Elizabeth's mouth went dry as she saw the cruelty on Yellow Drum's face.

Hunt didn't flinch, and he kept his weapon aimed at the Seneca leader.

"You have proven yourself to be a man of dishonor," Hunt said with a lazy grin. "Why should I trust you now?"

"I don't want you—I want them," Yellow Drum answered.

"Shoot him," Cedar Bark urged. "Shoot the faithless Seneca."

"Yes," Yellow Drum agreed. "Shoot, and taste Iroquois revenge. My warriors will take you apart inch by inch. Shoot me, half-breed, and you and your friends will beg for death."

"Just go," Elizabeth begged. "He won't hurt Rachel and Jamie. Save yourselves while you can."

Jamie threw down his bow and ran to his father, his small fists flying. "Go away!" he cried. "Go away! I don't love you anymore!"

Yellow Drum ignored him. His finger tightened on the trigger of his rifle. "Decide, half-breed. Life or death?"

"Show yourselves!" Hunt shouted to the remaining Seneca. "Come out and show us who follows a leader whose words cannot be trusted."

Hard-faced Iroquois braves moved from the forest. Cedar Bark took a few steps back until he stood near John Black Hat. Both Shawnee and Delaware held their guns ready to fire, as did the Seneca.

"You follow Yellow Drum?" Hunt called in bad Iroquoian. "You are honorable men, yet you follow Yellow Drum?" He spat into the leaves in a gesture of utter disdain. "I spit on his honor."

"Hunt, no!" Elizabeth said. Black despair tore at her vitals. Hunt was going to die, and there was nothing she could do to stop it.

"Fight me," Hunt challenged Yellow Drum. "Fight me, hand to hand. If you can kill me, take the woman and her children. But if you take her, you must make her your wife."

Yellow Drum laughed. "If I kill you, I will do as it pleases me."

"If you kill me, my friends go free," Hunt added.

"Why should I agree to such an offer?" Yellow Drum demanded. "Why should I risk my life when I hold you in the might of my fist?"

Hunt made a show of glancing around at the Seneca warriors, those in front of him, and those at his back. "So that men will continue to follow you," he answered quietly. "So that the Seneca will not turn away at the name of Yellow Drum . . . and . . ."

"This amuses me," Yellow Drum said. "And what?"

"That your son will not despise you," Hunt replied. "If a man cannot teach his son to honor him, can he call himself a man?"

"And if you kill me?" Yellow Drum asked.

Hunt's gaze met the Seneca's. "We all go free."

"Are we to believe more of this liar's tales?" John Black Hat shouted. "Who speaks for Yellow Drum?"

"I will!" called a young Seneca brave. "Green Corn gives his word."

"Rattlesnake!" shouted an Iroquois in an azure hunting coat.

A grizzled Seneca raised his musket skyward. "Two Bulls."

"Prove your courage," Hunt said to Yellow Drum. "Prove it or deny your manhood."

Yellow Drum threw his rifle onto the ground. "Come!" he shouted angrily. "Kill me if you can, half-breed!"

"No!" Elizabeth cried. "Don't do it, Hunt. I'm not worth it."

Hunt shook his head. "You're worth it." He tossed his gun to her and she caught it. "Hold that for me," he said lightly. "It belongs to the boy if Yellow Drum lifts my hair."

Jamie kicked his father in the ankle. "No!" he protested. Tears streamed down his face.

"Woman, control this child," Yellow Drum ordered.

"Jamie," she called to him. Her hands were damp with perspiration. The barrel of Hunt's gun felt icy and she shivered. How could her hands be sweating, when she was so cold?

Jamie came to her, and she held both children against her as the Seneca formed a circle around Hunt and Yellow Drum. Most of the warriors she knew and more than one other looked away rather than meet her accusing eyes.

"Let my friends go now," Hunt said. "They have no part of this fight."

Yellow Drum nodded. "Let them pass," he ordered his men.

John looked from his son to Cedar Bark. The young Shawnee brave knelt by his friend Red Shirt and attempted to stop the bleeding of his wounds. Cedar Bark said something that Elizabeth couldn't understand. "We stay," John declared. "If we move Red Shirt, he will die."

"No man will fault you if you save your own skin," Hunt replied as he stripped away his shirt and belt.

John shrugged, and Elizabeth saw the pride gleaming in the Delaware's seamed face. "If I take the coward's way, my son will know," he said. "Fight well, Hunter."

Elizabeth stood absolutely still. She knew that she should go to Red Shirt and try to help tend his injuries, but she couldn't tear her gaze from Hunt. *I love you, Sundancer,* she wanted to tell him, but she didn't. She'd been long enough with the Seneca to know a woman's role. She'd not weep or shame him by begging for his life. She'd not reveal his secret name. No matter how much it hurt her, she'd hold herself erect and keep her face from showing what she felt for him.

Hunt flashed her a grin, then drew his knife.

"Knives and clubs," Yellow Drum said. He motioned to a Seneca warrior, and the man threw Hunt his stone-headed war club. Yellow Drum's eyes narrowed. "To the death."

Hunt dropped into a crouch. "To the death."

# Chapter 26

E lizabeth barely stifled a scream as Yellow Drum swung his war club at Hunt. Hunt sidestepped the blow and circled, looking for a weakness in the Seneca's defense. Rachel struggled to see what was happening, but Elizabeth kept the child's face turned away. If there would be blood spilled—either Hunt's or Rachel's father's—there was no need for her to witness it. When Elizabeth glanced down at her son, she saw that Jamie's features were taut. No matter how much she wanted to, she couldn't prevent him from witnessing this dreadful contest. He might be half Iroquois, but he was still only six, and her heart wept for him.

Yellow Drum charged Hunt, feinted with his club, and slashed up with his knife. Hunt blocked the blade with the shaft of his club, twisting away to avoid a powerful backstroke.

Elizabeth's lips moved in silent prayer. *Please God, don't let Hunt die.* How could anyone meet death on such a bright afternoon? Rays of afternoon sun filtered through the green canopy to frost the glen with sparkling diamonds of iridescent light; the air was sweet with the scents of spring grass and budding wildflowers. But the birds had fled before the warriors' cries, and the scents of moss and wild strawberries were nearly hidden by the musty smell of bloodlust.

Yellow Drum's face contorted in rage as he lunged again and again. His muscled chest and back streamed sweat; his knuckles gleamed white as they gripped his scalping knife in his left hand and his stone club in his right. In contrast, Hunt seemed calm, almost as though this was a game of skill that he was impervious to winning. Yellow Drum attacked; he reacted.

"Coward!" screamed a Seneca brave at Hunt when he dodged another blow and moved almost lazily to one side. "Fight, half-breed. Fight!"

"Use your knife!" another shrieked. "Gut him, brother!"

Abruptly, Hunt dropped his war club and tossed his knife to his right hand. Yellow Drum uttered a triumphant war cry and smashed down with his heavy club. This time, instead of dancing away, Hunt waited until the Seneca's massive weapon sliced through the air before springing into action. He twisted his body to avoid being struck, seized the wooden shaft in a powerful grip, and wrenched the club and Yellow Drum's arm backward. At the same instant, he thrust a foot behind Yellow Drum's ankle, deflected the Seneca's knife slash with his own blade, and threw weight against Yellow Drum's chest.

Yellow Drum fell heavily to the ground with his right arm pinned under him; Hunt moved with a speed that Elizabeth hadn't thought possible for a man. He threw his knife back to his left hand, and his knee struck Yellow Drum in the loins as he came down on top. Elizabeth heard the crack of bone, and Yellow Drum's face paled to the color of tallow. Before she could draw a breath, Hunt captured Yellow

Drum's knife hand, and pressed the steel of his own scalping knife against the Seneca's throat.

"No!" Jamie screamed. "Don't kill him! Don't kill my father!"

"Do it!" Yellow Drum spat.

Silence gripped the watching warriors. There was no sound in the clearing but the rasp of the combatants' breathing.

"Who does a child belong to? Mother or father?" Hunt demanded.

"My children belong to Raven," Yellow Drum gasped. "Kill me now, or I will hunt you for the rest of your life."

"Think, Yellow Drum. Do children belong to the mother or father?" Hunt repeated.

"To the mother."

"Yes," Elizabeth cried. "They are mine, Yellow Drum. They were never yours. They belong to me by Iroquois law."

"A slave has no rights," he countered stubbornly.

Hunt held the blade so tightly against Yellow Drum's flesh that a thin red line appeared along his tattooed skin.

"I am English, born free, and free as I stand here." Elizabeth picked up her daughter and walked closer to Yellow Drum and Hunt. Jamie kept pace with her steps. He looked as though he wanted to cry, but his frightened brown eyes were dry. "They are my children, not yours—and never Raven's."

"What say you, Seneca men?" Hunt asked Yellow Drum's followers. "What is the Iroquois law? Who does a child belong to—mother or father?"

"I will let my son choose," Yellow Drum relented.

"If they pick Elizabeth?" Hunt asked.

A muscle twitched along Yellow Drum's clenched jaw. "Then it is over between us," he said harshly.

Hunt inclined his head. "So be it," he said, and withdrew the knife. Yellow Drum stood up and cradled his broken arm; already the elbow was swelling.

"What shall it be?" the Seneca demanded of his son. "You are Iroquois. Do you return to our people, or will you remain with your pale-skinned mother?"

"I want my mother," Rachel declared. "I love her." She clung tightly to Elizabeth's neck. "I don't like that old Raven. She's nasty."

Hunt looked at Jamie. "Son? It's your decision."

Elizabeth put out her hand to him, but Hunt shook his head. "Jamie," she whispered.

Jamie took a step toward his father.

"He is Seneca," Yellow Drum said.

Elizabeth moaned softly as Jamie threw his arms around his father's waist and hugged him. Tears welled up in her eyes, and she turned away, too devastated for words. *I've lost him*, she thought. *I've lost my Jamie.*

"Good-bye, Father," the boy said in formal Iroquoian. "My heart has pride for you, but my mother needs me. I belong with her."

Elizabeth clamped a hand over her mouth and twisted around to make certain that her ears weren't lying to her. Yellow Drum's face looked like a slab of white granite. He laid a hand on the boy's head, and for the space of a heartbeat, his stone countenance cracked and Elizabeth saw raw pain etched on Yellow Drum's face.

"*I-ye-a-ha*," he said. *My son.* Then he spun on his heel and walked away without a backward glance at either of his children. The Seneca warriors followed him, treading soundlessly on the thick moss.

"Wait," Hunt called after them.

Elizabeth's eyes widened in surprise. What was Hunt thinking of? "Let them go," she began. "I—"

"You made a bargain with the Shawnee," Hunt reminded the Iroquois. "Yellow Drum sold his children for rifles, then he broke the bargain."

"Hunt, don't," Elizabeth whispered.

"You owe us some rifles," Hunt said. "Two dozen guns, forty beaver pelts, and ten strings of wampum."

"Your arrogance will see you in an early grave," Yellow Drum warned. "Have you not taken enough from me?"

"And then there's the matter of Red Shirt," Hunt replied, indicating the wounded Shawnee. "A blood-price must be paid for him, unless you want to risk a war of dishonor."

"Are you a fool or the bravest man I've ever faced?" Yellow Drum demanded.

Hunt shrugged. "The rifles are a debt of honor."

Yellow Drum murmured something to his men. Two threw down their weapons, then another. As Elizabeth stared dumbfounded, the Seneca continued to discard their flintlocks until seventeen lay on the leaves.

"Good," Hunt said. "And the rest of what you owe?"

"Pray to whatever Gods you worship that we never meet again," Yellow Drum said. "The only thing else you'll get of me will be the blade of my tomahawk."

"I count on you sending the rest of the goods to the Shawnee beyond the Great English Lake," Hunt answered. "If you do not, the Huron will learn of your perfidy, and soon, the Iroquois Confederacy will laugh behind your backs."

Yellow Drum raised his left fist and cursed him. "May *O-nish-uh-lo-nuh*, the evil one, devour your soul."

"I'll keep a watch out for him," Hunt replied, "but

if he tries to eat it whole, he might bite off more than he can swallow."

"Mother?" Jamie looked up at Elizabeth and held out his hand. "Did I choose right?"

"Yes, darling," she said, "you chose right. I do need you more than your father does." His small fingers tightened on hers as they watched the Seneca war party until they vanished through the trees.

"He didn't want me," Jamie said.

Elizabeth set Rachel's feet on the ground, and dropped to her knees. "No, darlings, you must never think that." She looked into her son's eyes. "Yellow Drum does want you. He wants you terribly."

"He didn't take me with him."

"He left you out of love. I know your father; I've lived with him for longer than you've been alive. Leaving you behind is the most difficult thing he's ever done in his life. He loves you deeply, Jamie. Never believe he left you for any reason other than love."

Jamie scowled. "He sold me for rifles."

"Yes, he did, but he couldn't live with that. He came after you both." Elizabeth touched his cheek. "Your father is a brave man and an honorable one. But he is human. You have to forgive him his mistakes and remember his love. Can you do that?"

"No," Rachel said.

Jamie nodded. "I think so," he said softly.

"There's no time for talking, woman," Hunt called. "Get over here and see if you can do anything for this man."

"I'm coming," Elizabeth answered. "Tend to your sister," she ordered Jamie.

Elizabeth didn't want to be calm, and she didn't want to attend to Red Shirt. She wanted to run weeping to Hunt, to let him hold her safe and close. She

was tired of having to be strong when she wanted
someone to take care of her—to protect her.

With a sigh, she straightened her back. This was not
the time to weaken; a good man's life might be at
stake. "Let me see his wounds," she said as she went
to Red Shirt's side. "Did the bullet pass through
him?" And then she stopped thinking of Hunt and
gave her full attention to the injured Shawnee warrior.

For two weeks they camped near the site of the Seneca ambush while Red Shirt hovered between life and
death. Hunt bathed his wounds daily, and Elizabeth
used the leaves and ground roots of the red blos-
somed painted trillium both as a poultice and as a tea
to stop the loss of blood and prevent infection. While
the patient was too weak to eat, she prepared a hearty
broth of wild turkey, cattail root, and wild onion, and
added bark of arrowroot to strengthen his heart.

Hunt carved a wooden spoon for her, and she used
that to dribble soup, medicine, and water between
Red Shirt's lips. She washed his injuries several times
a day with a tea made from the bark of choke-berry
and packed the holes with spiderwebs as the Iroquois
women had taught her.

Red Shirt lived, and when he recovered enough to
be carried on a litter, the two Delawares and Cedar
Bark started back toward the Shawnee hunting
grounds with him.

Hunt had scouted the area and found a shallow
cave. There, he hid the rifles until Cedar Bark could
guide a Shawnee party back to fetch them. "It doesn't
pay off my whole debt," he grumbled to Elizabeth,
"but it's a start."

"The debt is mine," she reminded him. "My father
will pay whatever is needed."

"You're my responsibility," Hunt argued. "Whatever is owed the Shawnee, it's up to me to take care of it."

"Do you forget that you just told Yellow Drum that I am a free woman?"

"I'm not sure about that. So far, you've cost me dearly," he said wryly.

"That may be true," she agreed, "but I'm still the best thing that ever happened to you."

"That sounds like a woman."

But the answering gleam in his eye told her that her words had struck home. Hunt Campbell might not be ready to admit it, but he loved her—she knew it in her heart. The problem was how to keep him from slipping away once they reached Charles Town, and ruining both their lives by trying to follow his own peculiar code of honor. It was a subject she needed to give much thought.

The weather grew warmer with each mile they walked to the southeast, and soon the children began to shed their outer garments and pick handfuls of wild strawberries. Elizabeth was pleased to see Jamie acting more like a six-year-old again. For the first week after the Seneca ambush and Yellow Drum's fight with Hunt, Jamie had hardly spoken a word and hadn't laughed at all. But as time passed, he seemed to put the incident with his father behind him. His normal high spirits returned, and he began to tease his sister and shadow Hunt's every step.

Another fifteen days of walking brought them to the fringes of white settlement. They saw the smoke of lonely cabins, heard an occasional cow bellow, and once, Hunt pointed out a horse's hoofprints to Jamie.

"How do you know the rider's not Indian?" the boy asked.

"The animal is shod." Hunt bent to touch the damp

ground. "See the mark of the iron nails? Most Indians ride horses without shoes."

But Jamie's curiosity wouldn't be satisfied so easily. "How do you know the Indian didn't steal a shod horse from a white man?"

"Hunt knows what he's telling you," Elizabeth said. "You should—"

"Let the boy ask," Hunt told her gently. His slow grin told them he was genuinely pleased with the question. "A man must use his own head, not just accept another man's judgment."

Placing a hand on her son's shoulder, he explained the differences in the depth of the hoofprints at the spot when the horse had rounded a bend in the trail. "A white man tends to lean back in the saddle, so." He arched his back to illustrate the lesson. "The Cheyenne of the plains are the best riders in the world. They taught me to move with the pony, to become part of the animal so that you don't tire him unnecessarily."

"Will you teach me to ride like that?" Jamie asked, his brown eyes wide with admiration.

"I don't imagine I'll have the time, boy, but your mama will see that you have a good instructor. Just remember, once you throw your leg over a pony, you can't be separate from him. You've got to think like he thinks, anticipate his actions, not lay back like a farmer on the seat of a hay wagon."

"I'll remember," Jamie promised.

"You'll each have your own pony," Elizabeth said. "I promise."

"I don't want a pony," Rachel complained. "I want a cow. Will you teach me to ride a cow, *No-tha*?"

Elizabeth stiffened. Had Hunt noticed that the child had used the Shawnee word for *my father* in addressing him?

"He's not our father," Jamie corrected. "He's Hunter of the Far Mountains. Our father is Yellow Drum."

"I like this father," Rachel retorted, throwing her arms around Hunt's leg and clinging tightly.

Jamie's face darkened like a thundercloud. "He's not our father!"

"Is too!" Rachel shouted. "Mine!"

"Stop it, both of you," Hunt chided.

"You're not," Jamie insisted. "Yellow Drum is—"

"He is your father, and you must respect him." Hunt glanced at Elizabeth in a silent plea for help.

She smiled smugly, abandoning him to his own resources.

Hunt sighed, pried Rachel off his knee, and set her beside her scowling brother. "You must be patient with your sister, Jamie," he said. "She is younger than you."

Rachel flashed her most innocent expression, the look that Elizabeth knew meant her daughter hadn't changed her mind one iota, and that she was actively planning a new attack.

"But she said—" Jamie began.

"She called me *No-tha*." Hunt fixed Jamie with a shrewd gaze. "Haven't I heard you speak to Fire Talon in the same way?"

Jamie gnawed his bottom lip in silence.

"*No-tha* can mean a person's sire or it can simply be a term of respect," Hunt explained patiently. "Rachel didn't mean *kne-hah*, which is *my father* in Iroquoian, did you, Rachel?"

Rachel beamed and nodded. "Hunt is my *kne-hah*."

"See!" Jamie sputtered. "I told you so!" He spun around and kicked at his sister. She dodged behind Hunt.

"No kicking," Hunt admonished sharply. "No hitting, and no kicking. A brave does not attack women."

"She's no woman. She's a papoose!" Jamie proclaimed.

"Am not."

Jamie tried to get around Hunt's legs and Rachel ran behind her mother. "She's stupid," Jamie cried. "She's dumb."

"Elizabeth?" Hunt looked at her.

This time she took pity on him. "Jamie is right," she said smoothly. "Rachel, you may not call Hunt *Father* in Seneca. Yellow Drum is your *kne-hah*. But Hunt can be *No-tha*."

"Fair enough," Hunt agreed. "Jamie?"

"It's not fair," he grumbled, but Elizabeth knew by her son's grimace that it was only a token protest and not a real expression of anger at injustice.

"My *No-tha*," Rachel murmured. "Mine."

"Now that that's settled, can we move on?" Hunt asked. "I want to make the river crossing before dark."

"Of course," Elizabeth replied. "Whatever you say." She glanced at Rachel and winked, and the little girl giggled. Hand in hand, they started off with the two males mumbling behind them.

Over the next rise, they found a road with wheel ruts cut into it, and beyond that the ground ran down to the river. Hunt led them downriver for another half mile to a ferry. There, they met two astonished white men who were all too glad to pole them across the water to an ordinary on the far side. The inn was large, consisting of a main two-story log building, several outbuildings, and a stable, all surrounded by a log palisade.

"I know this place," Hunt said. "It's run by a family

of Quakers, very respectable. You'll be safe here while we send word to your father."

Jamie and Rachel were so excited that they couldn't stand still. Elizabeth stood at the ferry railing, clinging tightly to their hands, certain that given the chance one or both would tumble to their deaths in the river. Her own pulse was racing, and her face flushed. She could feel the force of the ferrymen's gaze boring into her back, and she imagined what they must think of her—a white woman—with her Indian clothing and two dark-skinned children.

Once on the other side, she had no time to think. Jane Goodson, the proprietor's wife, swooped down on her and whisked her away to her private chambers. There, she and the children were fed and fussed over and dressed in sober English garments.

"Poor things," Jane exclaimed. "So long prisoners of the naturals. God be thanked for thy return to the bosom of thine own people."

Elizabeth caught no sight of Hunt for hours, and when she did, there was no time for them to speak privately. John Goodson, his three grown sons, their wives, servants, and two families who were staying overnight at the ordinary all plied her and Hunt with questions and tried to tell them the news of recent happenings in the Carolinas.

"A rider was sent to your father in Charles Town," Hunt managed to tell her between bursts of loud conversation.

Elizabeth nodded. The more questions these people asked her, the more she wished to be silent. She wanted to be alone with Hunt and her children. These whites talked too loud, and they smelled of sour sweat and dirty clothing. Her head ached, and her feet pinched in the hard leather shoes. She could hardly draw a breath in the whalebone stays and layers of scratchy wool that enveloped her. Worse, her hair had been pinned and tucked under a linen cap that had seen better days and worse owners; and she was certain something alive was crawling over the crown of her head.

No one had accused her of being an Indian's whore; no one had called her children *half-breeds*, but she still felt heartsick and miserable. She missed the friendly faces of the Shawnee women; she missed her comfortable Indian dress and moccasins. She missed Hunt's teasing and the companionship of the trail.

So when Jane Goodson announced that it was time that Elizabeth and the little ones were in bed, Elizabeth was all too happy to abandon the public room and retreat to a quiet room under the eaves. To her great relief, Jane assured her that she and the children would have privacy. No one else would share the chamber.

Murmuring thanks to the Quaker woman, Elizabeth soothed Jamie's and Rachel's fears, hugged and kissed them, and watched over them until they were asleep. Then she stripped to her linen shift, let down her hair, and brushed it out. Later, a need for fresh air drew her to the single window, and she pushed open the wooden shutter and stared out pensively into the moonlit night.

She sat there for a long time. For hours, the noise and smells of the ordinary—the clanking tankards, dishes, and voices, the odors of mutton and pork and ale—floated up from the rooms below. Hounds barked and chased a cat across the inn yard. Horses neighed and stomped in their stalls, and an evening breeze brought the dubious fragrances of pickling sauerkraut and a fresh manure pile.

A lantern bobbed as a maidservant went to the well for water. Elizabeth heard the splash of an empty pail striking the water, then seconds later came the creak of the windlass as the wench drew up the brimming bucket. A door slammed, and Elizabeth listened as footsteps thumped on the stairs.

Hunt didn't come to her room, and gradually, the inn grew still. The only sounds she could hear were the faint breathing of her children and the reverberating snores and coughs coming from an adjoining chamber.

"Please, Hunt," she whispered. "Please don't leave me alone tonight. I need you so." Eventually, her hopes deserted her. Dry-eyed, with a lump in her throat, she closed the shutter and crawled between the sheets of the ancient poster bed. Still, sleep would not come. She tossed and turned, thumping the lumpy feather pillow with both fists, trying to settle her mind enough to drift off.

Then a small *click* caught her attention. She held her breath and listened. Yes, she had heard it. A shower of hard objects rattled her shutter. Rising from the bed, she went to the window, unlatched the covering, and swung it back. She peered out into the night and smiled.

Hunt stood directly below in the inn yard. He looked a proper Irish yeoman in his boots and shirt and breeches with his hair tied into a queue at the back of his neck, but he was still the man she loved.

Her heart began to flutter dangerously as she leaned out. "What are you doing?"

"Throwing stones at your window."

The sound of his voice made her all giddy inside. "How did you know it was my window?" she replied.

"I'd be a poor scout if I couldn't track a single woman inside this palisade."

"Have you come to rescue me? To carry me away

from all this?" she teased, only half in fun.

"I miss you, cat eyes."

"Where's your flute?"

He grinned. "Even Quakers would notice an Indian courting flute."

She twisted a lock of hair around her thumb. "Will you come up?"

"Will you come down?"

"Hunt Campbell, you are a contrary man."

"Shh, you'll wake the children," he warned.

"And how am I to come down?" she asked.

He held out his arms. "Jump?"

"You'll drop me."

He laughed. "I'll not drop you, sweetheart, not yet, anyway."

"And if I do jump, how will I get back?"

"I haven't thought of that part yet."

"You want me to jump out this window in my shift and take the chance of getting caught and causing a scandal?"

"Trust me."

She gathered her courage and jumped.

# Chapter 27

*Charles Town, South Carolina*
*July 1765*

**E**lizabeth clung to the memory of that night of abandon she and Hunter had shared in the hayloft at the Quaker inn. It carried her through the awkward meeting with her father's new wife, Lady Gwendolen, the day-long thanksgiving services for her return that were conducted at their parish church, and the constant parade of visitors who wanted to stare at her. Thoughts of Hunt's passionate lovemaking even helped to ease her heartache in the long, restless nights she spent lying awake in her father's house.

Rays of sunlight filtered through the louvered shutters of the floor-to-ceiling windows of her elegant bedchamber. Elizabeth groaned and rubbed her eyes; she felt as though her head were stuffed with uncarded wool. *This must be what a hangover feels like,* she decided. But she hadn't overindulged in brandy-wine; she simply hadn't had enough sleep. She'd still been pacing the floor when the tall case clock on the stair landing had struck four.

"Mornin', Miz 'Lizabet Anne." Polly entered the

room with a breakfast tray. "You 'wake?" The whey-faced serving girl shuffled across the room in worn green slippers with the heel ends cut out.

Elizabeth sat up and pushed the hair off her perspiring face. Had Charles Town in July always been such a cauldron? She longed for the cool forests and clear mountain streams of the Ohio Country; the sticky heat and flies here were enough to drive her mad. But then, as Polly reminded her—at least twice a day—the family had always retreated to the country in summer.

"Gonna be a hot one," Polly said, dropping the tray onto a bedside table. "Sensible folks don't stay in Charles Town in hot time. They's 'fraid of the fever."

Lady Gwendolen had pleaded to move the household to Magnolia—the largest of the Fleming family plantations—miles inland from the coast. Elizabeth's brother Avery's wife and children were there already, along with Elizabeth's two younger sisters, and a bevy of house servants. But Sir John was determined to remain in town until the matter of Elizabeth's future was settled, preferably with a hasty betrothal and marriage.

"Choc'late, Miz 'Lizabet Anne?" Polly poured the steaming drink into a thin china cup. "Cook sent up fried eggs, her good sausage, and sweet-potato rolls."

Elizabeth caught a whiff of the greasy sausage and eggs, and the smell turned her stomach. "Take it away," she ordered. "Bring me some fruit, please, if you can find any in the kitchen. Hot tea, not luke-warm, no sugar or milk, and a piece of corn bread. No butter or jam." She'd lost her childhood taste for sweets and fatty pork. How she longed for some of Shell Bead Girl's tangy sassafras tea and the tiny corn cakes she baked on a hot stone.

Polly scowled. "What do I do with this breakfast?"

"I don't care. Eat it yourself."

The girl's blue eyes widened, a major demonstration of unfavorable emotion for Polly. As far as Elizabeth could determine, the indentured girl had two expressions, sour and suffering.

"If you say so, Miz 'Lizabet Anne, but . . ."

"But what?"

"I already ate this morning."

"Then give the tray to someone else. I don't care what you do with it. Just get it out of my sight and bring me something I can eat."

"I 'spose I'll eat it." Polly grimaced like a tortured martyr. "Cook gives me grits and porridge to break my fast, hardly enough to feed a blackbird."

Elizabeth rubbed her eyes again and tried to summon patience. The wench couldn't help it if she had the brains of an onion. Elizabeth forced a smile. "What time is it, Polly? I haven't heard the children this morning." She pushed back the mosquito netting and ran a hand through her tangled hair.

"Early yet. Master John not out of bed." She eyed the untouched cup of chocolate. "Isaac took them wild things to the market. Master Av'ry says Jamie should be learnin' somethin' useful stead'a getting into mischief. Rachel just tagged along, I s'pose."

"You should have asked me. I would have taken them if they wanted to see the market. They're too much with the servants." She rose and walked to a window. "Why is this closed? No wonder there's no breeze in this chamber. How many times have I told you that I want my windows open? If it isn't raining, leave them open."

Polly sniffed loudly. "My gran said night air will kill a body, and she lived to seventy and two. Cornwall woman, she were," she added as if that was the end to the argument. Shuffling to the window, she draped a silk wrapper around Elizabeth's shoulders.

Below, on the cobbled street, a shrimp seller plied her wares. "Shrimp! Hot shrimp! Spicy shrimp, hot as sin!"

Behind her came a slave girl, barely into her teens, with skin as black and shiny as polished ebony. "Oysters! Oysters! Fresh oysters!"

Polly was right, Elizabeth decided. It was early; there were no bankers or planters on the street yet. What society remained in Charles Town was shut tight within their houses; no one was abroad but slaves and the working poor.

"Master says you to stay home today, Miz 'Lizabet Anne. Master Peter coming to talk with Sir John 'bout your betrothal."

"Pieter, Polly; his name is Pieter Van Meer."

"No, m', he calls hisself Peter here in Charles Town, Peter Vaughn. Miz Gwendolen says he's a upstart Dutch pretending English gentry. That's what she says."

"He can call himself whatever he likes, but there'll be no betrothal with me." Her father had presented her with three proposed husbands already, and she'd only been home a few weeks. The Honorable George Welby was sixty and had just buried his third wife; the second was a prosperous sea captain who smelled of fish and referred to Jamie and Rachel as "the unfortunates." Pieter Van Meer—Sophie Van Meer's cousin, whom Elizabeth had met at her brother's first wedding—was a surprise, pleasant at first, and then not so delightful.

Pieter hadn't died in the Indian attack as Elizabeth had supposed. He'd been scalped, but he had survived the ordeal and covered his bald spot with a curled and powdered wig. Now a rather stuffy gentleman, Pieter had managed to ingratiate himself into the fringes of Charles Town society. Avery had explained to her that Pieter had tried his hand at banking—unsuccessfully. After that, there had been a string of unlucky business ventures. Now, she supposed Pieter felt that marrying Sir John Fleming's soiled daughter would save him from poverty.

"Fetch my tea, if you please, Polly," she ordered.

"If I please? Don't matter if Polly please or not, do it? Polly, carry this upstairs. Polly, dust this. Polly, mend that. No matter if Polly's got a cold in her head or her joints is achin'."

Elizabeth threw her a warning look.

"I'm going, Miz 'Lizabet Anne, I'm goin'."

Elizabeth resisted the urge to feel sorry for herself. She'd known that her homecoming would be like this. From the moment they'd arrived in her father's carriage from the Quaker inn, her own worst fears had begun to take solid form.

"Come in with me," she'd whispered to Hunt as he opened the front gate for her. Her father's house stood as solid and elegant as it ever had. She'd walked in the front door a thousand times as a child; now the thought of entering made her almost physically ill.

"It's not my place. Best you see your family alone," he replied.

"I'm afraid," she said.

"You? You're not afraid of anything. Pretend they're Iroquois," he teased.

"Hunt, don't leave me," she begged him.

Jamie moved closer to Hunt and took hold of his hand. Hunt glanced down at him and nodded. "If you're certain, Elizabeth."

"I'm certain," she said, gathering Rachel in her arms.

"Miss 'Lizabet, it's Ruth," a gray-haired woman called. "Thank God you be home again."

"Ruth." Elizabeth forced a smile for the cook.

A row of fresh-faced country girls in white aprons and mobcaps curtsied. "Miss," one murmured.

"This is a funny-looking longhouse," Jamie said in Iroquois.

"Speak English," Elizabeth reminded him.

Two footmen looked down their long noses at her. Hunt threw one an icy stare, and he jumped back as though he'd been burned.

"Miss Elizabeth." Joseph, her father's butler, bowed slightly as he opened the front door. "Welcome home."

Elizabeth nodded. "Thank you."

Jamie scowled at him.

Someone had chosen to send Elizabeth one of her mother's riding habits to travel in. The coat and waistcoat were of purple camlet, trimmed and embroidered with black satin. Elizabeth was fair roasting in the heavy material, and she could hardly draw breath in the tight stays and linen stock. It had been so long since she'd worn leather boots that her feet protested every step. Her riding outfit was topped with an oversized wool cocked hat edged with black and adorned with a single white plume.

The children wore sober brown clothing loaned to them by Jane Goodson; both had rejected the English shoes and walked easily in their own moccasins. Elizabeth wished that she could have shown so much common sense. After wearing simple Indian garb for so many years, she longed for something light and comfortable.

Her father was waiting for them in the west parlor.

"Courage, woman," Hunt whispered.

Elizabeth drew in a deep breath and tried to keep from trembling. "Father!" she cried.

He looked exactly as she remembered him the last

time she'd seen him here, nine and a half years ago. His rather old-fashioned full gray satin coat, embroidered waistcoat with silver buttons, and breeches were spotless; his black, silver-buckled shoes shone, and his pocket watch dangled from a silver chain. His Irish lace cravat was wrapped as snugly around his plump throat as ever, and he wore two large rings on his right hand, one a family crest, the second a ruby.

"Elizabeth." He held out his arms, and she ran to him. He embraced her stiffly and offered a cool cheek for her to kiss.

"Let me look at you," he said, stepping back. "You seem sound enough, freckled as a field hand, but I suppose that's to be expected, what with being with the savages so long." He lifted her fingers to his lips and kissed the back of her hand. "Damn me, but you're a sight for these old eyes, girl. Some gave you up for dead, but I never was one of them. Your mother's gone, you've heard that, I suppose?"

Elizabeth nodded. "But she died at home."

"Buried in our family plot. I've a spot beside her." He sighed. "You know I've remarried. Gwendolen Chambers, fine family, old stock. No titles in the lot, but landed gentry. Gwendolen brought a fine dowry, she did. You two will get on famously."

Elizabeth turned to her children and motioned for them to come forward. "James, Rachel, this is your grandfather, Sir John. Father, your grandchildren."

He cleared his throat and reddened before unbending enough to pat Jamie on the head. "Darker skinned than I'd imagined they'd be," he said.

Elizabeth stiffened. "They do favor their father," she agreed.

"Couldn't you have left them with the savages?" A tall, rail-thin woman with small gold spectacles and a black beauty patch on her left cheek swept into the room from the adjoining chamber. "Surely, the little things would be better off among their own kind."

"I am their own kind," Elizabeth replied hotly. "Where I go, they go."

"Daughter," her father said, "this is your new mother, Gwendolen. Gwendolen, my eldest daughter, Elizabeth."

"I know who she is, John," the lady replied tersely. "We've all heard enough about her coming."

"Your mother and I are so happy to have you home," her father said.

"Naturally, that goes without saying." Gwendolen gazed sternly at the children, and Rachel stuck out her tongue. "I can see I shall have the devil's own time teaching them manners!"

"Do not trouble yourself, madam," Elizabeth answered. "My children are my affair and mine alone."

"Yes, yes," her father soothed. "Your motherly instincts do you credit, my child. But it's too soon to make decisions that you may regret."

"You are fortunate to have such a dutiful father," Gwendolen said piously.

"I've moved heaven and earth to get you back, and I'll not abandon you on account of them," he said, glancing at Rachel and Jamie. "It won't be as easy to find you a husband, I'll grant you that, but it's not impossible. You are my oldest daughter. There's money from your mother's family, a substantial amount. That will do for a dowry."

"You can't expect your father to do more," his wife observed. "He has your two sisters to provide for, and then there are those we can expect God to grace us with."

Elizabeth suspected it would take a miracle for Gwendolen to quicken with child; the haughty matron was fifty if she was a day. "Where is Avery?"

she asked when the silence in the room became awkward. "I'd hoped he might be—"

"He's upcountry," her father explained. "Avery will be here as soon as he can. He is as overjoyed as the rest of us by your return." He looked at Hunt. "For that, we have you to thank, Campbell."

From the expression on Hunt's face, Elizabeth feared he cared for her father no more than she cared for her new stepmother. "I'll take my leave now," Hunt said. "Elizabeth and the children are worn out. They need rest and—"

"Of course they do," her father answered. "Come into my library, Campbell. We'll settle our affairs and you can be on your way."

"No," Elizabeth said. "I don't want—"

"I'll not leave Charles Town without seeing you again," Hunt said.

"Please stay. I'm not tired," Elizabeth protested.

But her father was already leading Hunt from the room.

"Brash woodsman," Gwendolen observed.

It was impossible for Elizabeth not to hear her father say, "You'll want the rest of your reward money."

Hunt's reply stunned her.

"No, I don't," he said. "I'm planning on returning what you already advanced me as soon as I can."

"That's not necessary. You brought my daughter; you couldn't have anticipated that there would be complications," her father answered. "You've earned your reward."

Hunt stopped in the hallway at the foot of the broad staircase. Elizabeth couldn't help thinking how small her father looked beside him.

"By complications, do you mean your grandchildren?" Hunt asked sharply.

"I wouldn't expect a man of your station to comprehend—"

"Father, please," Elizabeth said. "Don't—"

"Stay out of this, daughter," her father warned. "This is my affair."

"I comprehend well enough, Sir John, that it's the color of your grandchildren that gives you such a sour expression. I'd advise you to take a second look. Those two young'ns are prime. You'd do well to value them for what they are."

Her father's voice rose. "Our business is over, Mr. Campbell. If you have nothing more to say, I will ask you to leave my house."

"No." Elizabeth tried to follow them into the hall, but Gwendolen stepped in front of her.

"Best forgotten, that rough creature," her stepmother advised.

Elizabeth pushed past her, but Hunt was already at the door. "Hunt!" she cried.

"I'll be back," he said.

"You will not!" her father bellowed. "If you change your mind about the money, you are free to see my solicitor, Edmond Graham. But do not set foot in this house again."

Rachel started to whimper.

"Airs above his station," Gwendolen sniffed.

Her father's "Hmmpt!" assured anyone within earshot that he agreed completely with his wife.

Avery's arrival the next day had saved Elizabeth from fleeing the house within hours of arriving. Her older brother had been the only one Elizabeth had expected to love and be loved by. He hadn't disappointed her; Avery was as good-natured and as caring a brother as he'd been as a child, even if he'd turned into a younger version of their father in appearance. He'd greeted her with a welcome hug and kiss, sweeping her feet off the floor in his enthusiasm. Avery's green eyes had sparkled with good humor as he'd asked dozens of questions about her life among the Seneca.

Sir John had forbidden the subject to be discussed in his home. "No need to remind Elizabeth of her tragedy," Father had declared. "Less said, the better."

Yes, seeing Avery had been wonderful, but even Avery had his own family, his own wife and children. And Avery's wife, Nancy, had been cool toward Elizabeth. She'd forbidden her sons to play with Jamie, and she'd treated Elizabeth's children as though they were slaves. Avery tried to mediate, but Nancy had a sharp tongue and the willingness to use it. It was clear to Elizabeth that relations with her sister-in-law would always be strained.

Elizabeth thrust her foot into a blue satin slipper, then changed her mind and kicked the dainty thing away. The bare wooden floor felt cool on her feet. Soon, she would have to submit to layers of petticoats, shift, stays, buttons, ties, stockings, shoes, and gown. She sighed heavily, remembering the comfort of wearing only a short skirt in the heat of summer days.

"I wonder if Gwendolen would be shocked if I came down to breakfast bare-breasted?" she murmured aloud. Her father would have apoplexy; at the least, he'd order her confined to the St. John's hospital for the insane.

She was a wealthy woman in her own right. Avery had taken her aside and shown her the sums deposited for her in a prestigious banking house. The money left to her by her mother was to be administered by her father, Avery, or her husband, if she had one. If she married Pieter or any of the men her father proposed, that man would control her estates and her children's futures.

She should be free to do as she pleased; instead, she was as much a prisoner in her father's house as she had been among the Seneca. Perhaps more so . . . If her father decided to send Jamie away to school in Paris, as he had suggested, she'd be helpless to stop him.

She could run away. She'd threatened that much a week after she'd returned to Charles Town. It was as close to an argument as she'd had with her father. "I won't be separated from my children," she'd insisted, "and I won't marry to protect my reputation."

"Don't talk nonsense," her father had chided. "Where would you run? A red-haired woman with dusky children can hardly hide in the settlements. I would be remiss as a father if I didn't find you and bring you home to my care."

"You'll not shame us with your loose behavior," Gwendolen murmured. "The Fleming family name is a good one, without scandal. Be grateful your father puts your welfare before his own."

"Jamie and Rachel are not a disgrace," Elizabeth insisted. "They're bright, beautiful—"

"Illegitimate," Gwendolen said. She pursed her lips. "Pretty, yes, but very dark of skin. And those heathen eyes! They can never pass as white, not here, not even in the Caribbean Islands."

"We'll give them decent schooling, teach them a trade," her father suggested. "Needlework for the girl. The lad seems sturdy; he may have the physique to be a smithy or a wheelright."

"The girl child must certainly learn something useful," Gwendolen put in. "She'll never make a decent marriage with an Englishman."

"The French are not so particular," Avery said. "If we send Rachel to a convent in Paris, we might—"

"My children will stay with me!" Elizabeth

shouted. "With me, do you understand? I will make the decisions about their educations, and when they're old enough, they'll choose who and if they want to marry."

"She's impossible," Gwendolen said to her husband as Elizabeth swept out of the room with as much dignity as possible. "Where did she ever get such radical ideas? Choose their own marriage partners? I'm shocked, John, truly shocked. I expected better from your daughter."

That discussion had taken place two days ago. Since then, her father and stepmother had barely spoken two words to her, other than the normal civilities one performed for the servants' benefit. Father hadn't changed his mind; Elizabeth knew him well enough for that. Once he came to a decision, nothing would sway him from action, least of all the pleas of a wayward daughter. He loved her; she knew he loved her, but in his opinion no woman was mentally equipped to manage her own affairs.

"Women and spaniels," he'd been fond of saying when she was a child. "High-strung, both of them. Damned pleasant creatures, but not very intelligent. Need a strong hand."

Polly returned with the breakfast tray. Still sulking, she served tea, corn bread, and sliced melon, then left the room. Elizabeth took her cup of tea and stared thoughtfully at the bits of leaf in the bottom.

"Where in hell are you, Hunt?" she whispered. "Why aren't you here throwing stones at my window? Playing a flute to lure me away from all this luxury? Begging me on bended knee to become your wife and go with you to the far mountains to chew buffalo hides?"

She missed him. Rachel and Jamie missed him.

Even the promise of ponies and other children to play with hadn't stilled their questions.

"Where is *No-tha*?"

"Why isn't Hunter of the Far Mountains here?"

"Did the Seneca scalp him, Mama?" Rachel asked.

"Did he go away like our father?"

"No, he didn't go away," she answered as best she could. "He's in Charles Town. He promised he'd not leave without seeing us again, and Hunt never breaks his word."

Her words soothed the children but not her own uneasiness. Her father's house had become a prison with walls that grew closer every day. If Hunt didn't come to her soon, she'd find a way to escape and find him . . . before it was too late.

"Oh, my beautiful Sundancer," she murmured. "You've never failed me yet. Where are you when I need you most?"

# Chapter 28

**B**y afternoon, the South Carolina sun had become a ball of fire, scorching the town and making Sir John's dinner guests sweat like field hands, despite the reed fans the slaves kept in constant motion.

Elizabeth couldn't eat more than a few sips of the spicy crab soup in front of her. The long table, set with silver and crystal over sparkling-white Irish linen, groaned under the weight of food and drink. Two hams graced the board, along with a rack of lamb, fried chicken, roast beef, crab cakes, shrimp, and an endless array of breads and vegetables.

Her father sat at one end of the table, her stepmother at the other. Avery was to Elizabeth's left, and across from her sat Pieter Van Meer, his maiden aunt, Doortje Van Meer, and his solicitor, Jacob Greenwood. Her father's solicitor, Edmond Graham, was also present, along with some of Gwendolen's relatives, the minister, his wife, and another lady whom Elizabeth knew only as the vicar's spinster sister.

Rachel and Jamie were eating in the kitchen. Elizabeth wished she were with them—anywhere but here. Pieter's aunt was eyeing her as though she might abruptly sprout horns, and Pieter had twice brushed Elizabeth's ankle with his shoe.

The conversation at the table was general: the weather, crops, the capture of a pirate ship off the barrier islands. But Elizabeth knew that this assembly had been gathered to announce an alliance between the families, and she knew she was the sacrificial lamb.

Pieter, she had decided after their first reunion a few days ago, was a lecherous fool. He had visited the house twice. They had walked together in the formal boxwood garden and had sat in the east parlor under Gwendolen's watchful eye. Pieter had spent most of the time trying to look down the front of her gown and talking about her dowry. He'd patted a kitchen maid's bottom, and whispered something to Gwendolen's personal maid that had caused the girl to flush angrily.

Today, he stared pointedly at Elizabeth's bosom when not distracted by those of the serving girls. He'd even leered at the minister's plump, aging sister, who seemed about to burst the seams of her pink satin dress. Pieter talked overloudly and made no secret of his love for himself or his complete lack of understanding of any subject requiring the least amount of common sense.

Her father couldn't force her to marry Pieter; he just didn't realize that yet. Elizabeth wondered if she'd ever marry. Certainly no man could match up to Hunt Campbell, and if she couldn't have him, perhaps she'd remain single. She'd not given up hope yet, but each hour that she waited without word from him made her dreams fade a little more.

Polly had just removed Elizabeth's soup bowl when the front door knocker sounded, and Elizabeth heard voices in the entrance hall. Sir John looked up expectantly as his butler entered the room and came to his side. Joseph whispered in her father's ear, and Sir John shook his head.

"Tell him this is not a convenient time. Send him away."

"Who is it, dear?" Gwendolen asked.

"No one of importance."

Elizabeth listened to see if she could recognize the caller. At first, she heard only a murmur of exchanged words, then Hunt's voice rang out in the hall.

"I'll see Mistress Elizabeth. Now!"

Joseph hurried back, his face red and blotchy. The guests had noticed the disturbance and began to whisper among themselves.

"What is it, Joseph?" Sir John demanded.

Elizabeth dropped her napkin, pushed back her chair, and stood up.

"Remain where you are," her father commanded.

Hunt appeared in the doorway. "Elizabeth, I need to talk to you," he said.

He was wearing a single silver earring, a fringed broadcloth hunting shirt, doeskin breeches that clung to his muscular thighs like a second skin, a beaded hunting bag, and a carved powder horn slung over one shoulder. Hunt's head was bare; his black hair was drawn back into a queue at his nape and two eagle feathers dangled from the leather tie. A sheathed scalping knife with an elk antler handle hung from one lean hip. In his hands, he carried a Lancaster County rifle with a maple stock and silver inlay; he leaned it against the door molding and strode into the room as though he owned it.

"Sweet God in heaven!" Gwendolen shrieked.

The minister's wife gave a little gurgle of fright and plopped her limp hand into her soup bowl, splashing her sister-in-law's yellow silk bodice with red crab bisque.

"An Indian!" Doortje Van Meer squealed.

Elizabeth heard Pieter's gasp of outrage, but she had no time to spare for him. She stared at Hunt, beginning at the toes of his high Delaware moccasins and moving up his muscled body to the cocky grin on his face. "It's about time," she admonished. Her heart fluttered in her chest. *Sweet Jesus*, she thought, *he looks like a hunting hawk in a cage full of pigeons.*

His gaze met hers and he nodded. "I'm going back to the wilderness, Elizabeth," he said, ignoring the chorus of angry shouts from Avery, her father, and the solicitors.

Hunt pulled a small leather sack from his waist and dropped it onto an Irish hunt table along the wall. The heavy bag made a solid clink as it fell. "The rest of the money, Mr. Fleming." Hunt's eyes narrowed as they fixed on Elizabeth. "I could have sent the silver. I came to—"

*Say good-bye?* she wondered. *Damn him!* Hunt was as blind as her own father—as much a fool as Pieter Van Meer. If he walked out this door alone, he'd regret it to his dying day. She'd not let him make that mistake. "No!" she screamed. "You can't abandon me!"

"What's wrong with you?" Hunt demanded.

He reached for her, and she stepped back and pointed at him. "Daddy!" she wailed. "Stop him! Don't let him get away!"

"Seize that intruder!" Sir John yelled. "I'll not have such a common rogue invade my house."

Joseph lunged at Hunt, and he brushed him off as carelessly as a horsefly. "Elizabeth?" Hunt grabbed her arm. "What in heaven—"

She looked to her father. "He's made free with me, sir," she cried. "He took advantage of my innocence."

"Elizabeth!" Sir John thundered. "What are you saying?"

"I'm with child." She covered her face with her hands to hide her laughter. "He promised to wed me. Now, he means to flee and leave me to face the shame alone!"

Avery swung a fist at Hunt. He ducked the blow, seized her brother by the shirtfront and lifted him off the floor, holding him at arm's length. "What did you say?" Hunt shouted at Elizabeth.

"I'm four months gone with your child!" It was a lie. She'd had a showing of blood only a few days ago. But it was the only thing she could think of to stop him from getting away. Hunt would probably be angry with her, but difficult situations required strong solutions.

"Elizabeth!" Gwendolen gasped. "How could you? One bastard is forgivable, but three?"

Someone began to pray aloud, and a maid leaned out the window and shrieked for the law. "Sheriff! Sheriff! For God's sake, fetch the sheriff!"

A footman dove for Hunt's legs while a second one snatched up his rifle. Joseph came running with a broom, and Graham removed his coat and rolled up his sleeves to join the fray.

"No!" Elizabeth screamed, flinging herself against Hunt and clinging to his neck. "Don't hurt him. He has to marry me!"

Hunt dropped Avery and threw his arm around her as they crashed to the floor under the weight of the servants. One man caught the edge of the linen table-cloth and a ham and a cascade of crystal crashed onto the floor.

Hunt glared at Elizabeth. "Is this so, woman? Are you pregnant with my child?"

She crossed her fingers behind his neck and hung

her head. "Yes, Hunter," she whispered.

Hunt twisted around and sent a footman spinning with the back of his hand. "Get the hell off me," he roared. "I'll marry her."

"You will?" Elizabeth murmured.

"You'll do no such thing," her father snapped. "We'll have him arrested. Hung! We don't allow such—"

"Stop this shameful bickering at once!" the vicar proclaimed. "Sir John, remember your position."

Hunt got to his feet, pulling Elizabeth up with him. She pressed close, trying to appear repentant and firm at the same time.

"It would be best if you let him wed me, Father," she said.

"And do what? Live in the woods like an animal?" Sir John demanded. "He doesn't even have a job."

"I'm an agent for Ross Campbell and Sons," Hunt answered stiffly. "I've been licensed to open a trading post west of Lake Michigan. William Bennett of this town will vouch for me. He is the agent for Ross Campbell and—"

"I know who William Bennett is," her father said. "What will you expect in dowry, if I give you my daughter's hand in marriage?"

"Nothing," Hunt said. "I told you that—"

"Nothing but my mother's inheritance to me," Elizabeth put in. "And Mr. Campbell will take responsibility for my Indian children, won't you?" She smiled up at Hunt.

"You'll pay for this later," he whispered in her ear. To her father, he said, "I may not be what you'd want for Elizabeth. I know I'm not of her social class. I didn't think it would be honorable to take her from this." He motioned to indicate the house and all it stood for. "But I love her, and I came here to ask your permission to marry her. Her condition is as much a surprise to me as it is to you, but I assure you, I will do right by my children, all three of them."

"They're all yours?" Gwendolen fanned at her face and sank into a chair. "All?"

"The shameless jade!" Pieter exclaimed. "I wouldn't marry the baggage if she had twice the dowry. And neither will any other respectable gentleman in Carolina."

"Good for you that I'm no gentleman," Hunt said wryly. He glanced at the vicar. "I take it you're a man of God?"

"I am, but—"

"I said I am ready to leave Charles Town. If you want me to wed this woman, let's do it here and now."

"What?" Elizabeth's head spun. "Right now?"

"Now or never," Hunt said.

Elizabeth looked helplessly at her father. "Father?"

"Give her to him, John," Gwendolen urged. "They deserve each other."

"Highly irregular," the minister grumbled. "Banns to be cried, procedures to—"

"Now or never," Hunt repeated.

"Do it," her father said. "The sooner done, the better."

*"No-tha!"* Rachel and Jamie burst from the hall with squeals of excitement. "My *No-tha!*" Rachel repeated, squirming between her grandfather's legs.

"I don't believe you came here to marry me," Elizabeth whispered to Hunt. "You told me you were going west to the mountains."

"Hunter!" Jamie dodged around a footman and threw himself at Hunt. "Take me with you. I don't like Charles Town." Rachel escaped her grandfather's grasp and grabbed Hunt's other leg.

Gwendolen motioned to the maids. "Get those children out of here! At once!"

Hunt grabbed Rachel and swung her up on his shoulder. With his other hand, he pulled Jamie tight against his side. "They stay right where they are," he told Gwendolen. Then he turned his fierce black eyes on Elizabeth. "I was planning on crossing the plains to Cheyenne country, but a man's got a right to change his mind, doesn't he?"

She nodded. He was angry with her, but he wouldn't stay angry for long. His ire was as easy to see through as Jamie's. Once they were wed and far away from here, it would be time to tell him that she'd stretched the truth a little. "A man has that right," she agreed, "but a woman has a right to make certain that man does what will make him happiest."

"Sir John," Polly called. "The high sheriff is at the door. Shall I let him in?"

"Yes! Let him in," Elizabeth's father replied. "Let in the whole town. If my daughter's going to make me a laughingstock, why shouldn't everyone be in on the joke?"

"Shall we at least adjourn to the parlor?" Gwendolen asked. "A dining chamber is hardly the proper place for a wedding—"

"Say the words, preacher," Hunt said.

Nervously, the little man thumbed through the pages of his Bible. "Let us begin with a reading from the Gospel according to Saint Matthew, chapter three, verse two. 'The voice of one crying in the wilderness. Prepare ye the way of the Lord, make his paths straight.' "

Hunt reached out and yanked his rifle from the footman's hand. "Faster, Your Reverence. Get on to the part about 'Do you take this woman.' "

Sir John mumbled something about a ring, and

Hunt reached up and pulled the silver circle from his own right ear and slipped it on Elizabeth's finger.

The minister hurried through the ceremony, but Elizabeth paid little heed, hearing only snatches of what the man of God was saying. She stared into Hunt's eyes as she imagined what it would be like to wake up every morning and see him smiling back at her.

"He asked you a question, Elizabeth," Hunt said. "Do you or don't you?"

She blinked. "What?"

"Is this the sex part?" Jamie asked loudly. "Polly says sex be the best part of marriage."

"Do you or don't you take me as your lawful, wedded husband?" Hunt's husky voice was deep with emotion.

"And me, too," Rachel chimed in. "Don't forget me!"

"Yes, yes, I do," Elizabeth said. "I take you all forever and ever and ever."

Hunt grinned and squeezed her hand. "You'll not mind my taking you from your home?" he murmured.

"Wherever you are is my home," she answered.

He kissed her tenderly. "Elizabeth Campbell, you are the most beautiful sight I've ever laid eyes on," he murmured.

She clung tightly to his hand, welcoming his strength, feeling waves of golden happiness ripple through her. "Truly?" she whispered.

His devil black eyes narrowed. "I thought so the first time I saw you, and I've never had reason to change my opinion since."

"I love you with all my heart," she said. He grinned, and the twinkle in her eyes told her that she'd said what he'd been waiting to hear.

# Epilogue

*Wolf River, Wisconsin Wilderness*
*Summer 1769*

**F**our years later, Elizabeth paused by the window and looked out at the throng of children and ponies gathered in the meadow. Jamie was leading a little gray, barely taller at the withers than the watchful dog pacing close beside them. Red-haired Gordon clung to the pony's flowing mane and drummed his heels into the round, shaggy sides, but the patient animal never broke out of a walk.

Closer to the river, Rachel reined her pinto close to Star Girl's bright bay. The two ponies nibbled grass as the girls waved to friends coming from the direction of the Shawnee village. Nearby, Elizabeth recognized Fox's youngest son kicking a leather ball to another boy. The temptation was too much for Badger; barking excitedly, he abandoned Gordon's riding lesson and ran to snatch the ball in his teeth and run with it. Rachel and Star Girl laughed and cheered the dog on as the two boys ran after him trying to recover the stolen ball. Three more youths joined the chase to the obvious delight of the girls.

"Elizabeth?" Hunt said. "Are we having a conversation or not?"

"Oh, yes." She turned from the window and smiled at him. "I was watching the children. Gordon's proud as he can be on that pony. I just hope he doesn't take a tumble."

Hunt drained his mug of cider and rubbed his jaw thoughtfully. "Jamie's leading him, isn't he? I only said he could ride if Jamie was with him. Rachel's a good rider, but she's only seven. She's not old enough to teach Gordon."

"You know Jamie. He adores his little brother. He won't trust Gordon to anyone else. But I think it's Badger that's giving the riding lessons."

"Between the two of them, even Gordon ought to be safe." Hunt sighed and set his cup on the table. "We were discussing something important, Elizabeth."

"I told you what I had to say. You just don't believe me."

His eyes narrowed. "I didn't say I didn't believe you. You know how pleased I'd be if it were true, but after the way you lied to me over Gordon—"

She untied her apron and draped it over the back of a chair as she went to him. "I didn't lie to you about Gordon, honey. I said I was pregnant, and I was."

"You told your father and half of Carolina that you were four months gone with my child. You nearly got me hung."

She caught his hand and brought it to her lips. Strange how a husband's hand could be so familiar and still give her butterflies in her stomach every time she touched him. She smiled at him. "I wasn't lying to you, and I'm not lying now," she said softly. "Gordon is the proof of it, isn't he?"

"If you were four months gone, he'd have been born just after the New Year, not in May. You tricked me, woman. You forced me into a shotgun wedding."

He was right, of course. But the trick had been on her. She'd thought she was lying to him, but she *had* been pregnant—with Gordon, their auburn-topped bundle of mischief. "An error in calculation, nothing more." She nibbled at his knuckles. "Are you sorry?"

"Sorry I wasn't hanged? Hell, no."

"Hunter Campbell!"

He grinned and stood up, pulling her into his arms. "How many times do I have to tell you, Elizabeth? I stayed away until I could figure out how to offer for you. I came to your father's house that day to ask you to be my wife, not to say good-bye."

"How was I to know that?"

"I sent you a note, telling you how stupid I'd been and asking you to wait for me."

"I didn't get any note, Hunt."

"I gave it to a serving wench wearing slippers. Pansy, I believe her name was."

"A serving girl in slippers? I suppose they were satin slippers."

"They were, but they had the heels cut out."

"Polly was her name. I never got a note."

"I sent one."

"Now who's covering his tracks?" she teased.

He bent his head and kissed her tenderly on the lips. "No matter who made the bargain, it was the best one of my life. You're trouble, Elizabeth Campbell, always were, always will be, but I wouldn't trade you."

"Or I you." She stared into his eyes. "Are you sorry I kept you from your far mountains?"

He shook his head. "They aren't going anywhere. And who knows, we may get there yet—when the children are grown and settled with families of their own."

She looked around the spacious room and sighed contentedly. Hunt had built her a two-story log home with four rooms down and four up, the first year they'd come to the Lake Country. Since then, he'd moved the store to a separate building, built a barn and sheds, and added three more rooms to the house and planted an orchard. A French family had come to work for them at the trading post, and the older Dechenaux girls did most of the housework and helped with Elizabeth's children.

But it wasn't the solid house or the green forests and meadows that had brought her the most joy in her marriage. She had been welcomed by her old friends the Shawnee, and by the Indian people new to her, the Menominee, whose bountiful land they'd come to live on. All those things brought her happiness and peace of mind, but always it was Hunt who was the flame of her life. Hunt had proved to be a loving husband and a good father to Rachel, Jamie, and little Gordon. Each day, it seemed to her, they grew closer, and each time they made love, it seemed like a new and wondrous thing.

"Thank you," she whispered to him.

"For what?"

"For loving me."

"You're an easy woman to love." He kissed the tip of her nose. "But what is this about another baby?"

"I'm not going to tell you, now. You said I lied to you about our Gordon."

"Did I say that?"

"You did," she accused.

"And when was Gordon born?"

"May sixteenth, 1766."

"The prosecution rests." He kissed her on the

mouth again. "Admit your fault, woman. You lied to trap me into marriage."

Warm tingles ran the length of her spine. She caught his hand and placed it on her belly. "I've a daughter growing here, under my heart," she murmured. "Your daughter."

"A strange place for your heart," he replied. "I think this bears closer investigation." He cupped a hand under her breast. "I need to see if these are any bigger."

"Hunter! Not in the kitchen! What if the children should come in for—"

"You're right," he said. "You're always right, even if you can't add worth a damn. Come along, wench. We're for the marriage bed."

"In the middle of the afternoon? Your sister and Talon are coming for dinner and I've a goose to—"

"Let the goose see to its own fate." He kissed her under the ear and ran a hand suggestively over her bottom. "Talon of all men would understand."

Elizabeth laughed as he picked her up in his arms and spun around. "Don't," she protested. "You'll make me dizzy."

"Is there really another baby, darling?" he asked.

"I've missed three moon times."

"Like I said," he teased, "this needs careful investigation." He put one moccasined foot on the stairs. "I'd fill this house with our children, if it was up to me," he whispered to her.

She laughed and lifted her head for his kiss. "I suppose you lied to me when you said you couldn't father children," she said.

"It's what I believed," he replied, "but I thank the Creator that I was wrong." He took the stairs, two at a time.

"What shall we call her? It will be a girl this time. I know it will."

"Wrestle you," he dared her. "Two out of three falls. Winner picks the babe's name."

"And what would you choose? Something awful, I'm sure."

He pushed open the bedroom door, paused and kissed her with such tenderness and passion that tears came to her eyes. "Cheyenne Elizabeth Campbell," he whispered.

"I think that's a fine choice," she replied as he laid her down on the heaped quilts of their high poster bed. Hunt stripped his shirt off over his head, and she wiggled out of her loose Indian dress and held out her arms to him. "I like the name Cheyenne," she murmured. "We don't have to wrestle. I'll yield the match."

He grinned, the lazy smile that always made her heartbeat quicken and her breathing come hard. "I'd rather wrestle," he said.

"Have I ever told you that I love you, my precious Sundancer," she replied softly.

"Not enough, green eyes," he answered. "Never enough. But then, we've got a lifetime for you to try."